Derek reached to cup her chin, forcing her to meet his commanding gaze.

"The truth is, you don't love Reuben Walker, and you don't want to marry him, do you?" She tried to turn her head, but he held her steadfast. "The *truth,* Jessica."

Tears stung her eyes as she whispered in miserable admission, "No. No, I don't. Poppa made a pact with him, and I don't have any choice."

"Oh, yes, you do. You don't have to marry a man you don't love. You're a grown woman. No one can force you to do anything you don't want to do."

"You don't know how it is," she cried, staring up at him with wild, beseeching eyes. "When a girl's father promises her in marriage, it's a pact, and she has to honor it, and—"

No longer able to deny his longing, he silenced her with a kiss.

Dear Reader,

The July books from Harlequin Historicals range in setting from the coal mines of Pennsylvania to the French countryside as we, once again, bring you four historical romances.

Readers of our contemporary romances will easily recognize the author of *Torchlight,* Doreen Owens Malek. With this story of a miner and a mine owner's daughter, Ms. Malek tells of a love strong enough to survive social injustice and prejudice.

Lovers of Westerns won't want to miss Elaine Rome's *Stark Lightning*. Valentine Stark is caught unawares when her father's new ranch manager starts probing beneath her rough exterior.

In *The Daring, New York Times* bestselling author Patricia Hagan brings to life a North Carolina farming community in the throes of the Civil War. *Autumn Rose,* by Louisa Rawlings, takes place in France during the seventeenth century.

We hope you will enjoy the greater variety of settings and time periods as well as the many new authors that our expansion to four titles a month has enabled us to offer you.

Yours,

Tracy Farrell
Senior Editor

The Daring

Patricia Hagan

Harlequin Books

TORONTO • NEW YORK • LONDON
AMSTERDAM • PARIS • SYDNEY • HAMBURG
STOCKHOLM • ATHENS • TOKYO • MILAN

Harlequin Historicals first edition July 1991

ISBN 0-373-28684-8

THE DARING

PATRICIA HAGAN,

New York Times bestselling author, had written and published over 2,500 short stories before selling her first book in 1971. With a background in English and Journalism from the University of Alabama, Pat has won awards for radio, television, newspaper and magazine writing. Her hobbies include reading, painting and cooking. The author and her Norwegian husband, Erik, divide their time between their mountain retreat in North Carolina and their home in Bergen, Norway.

Prologue

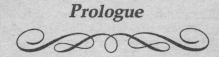

Blue Ridge Mountains
February 1847

Zeb Coulter, the image of sorrow, stood on the front porch of his farmhouse. With head bowed and shoulders slumped, his hands jammed into the pockets of faded, worn overalls, he was oblivious to the icy assault of the relentless wind.

Gray clouds loomed above the distant ridge; the bottom-land was already blanketed in white, with the upper mountain slopes crusted in frozen waves.

But Zeb did not notice, could not see through the mist of tears that veiled his eyes . . . his very soul.

He did not feel the gentle hand upon his shoulder, was not aware anyone had joined him on the porch until Preacher Dan softly urged, "You'd best come on in now, Zeb. You're gonna catch your death of cold out here. No coat. No hat. And it'll be time soon. Come on in now."

Zeb did not move. He had no sense of time, and only vaguely recalled there had been others urging him inside. He had ignored them as he ignored Preacher Dan. Zeb did not want to be in *there*. The odor of cigar and pipe smoke was suffocating, and the smell of food was unbearable—meat stews, bean soups, roasted chickens, fried chickens, fatback and collards—all prepared by the womenfolk to feed those who came to pay their respects.

News of a death always spread quickly, and people had arrived in droves, like ants to a picnic. Though Zeb's family had died out long ago, he had many in-laws, who had moved right in, taking over the house, setting up cots and pallets on the floor when the bedrooms were full. Others had been offered shelter at neighboring farms. But now they congregated in the house. Someone was playing a dulcimer, and the music was plaintive, mournful, straining to be heard above the constant buzz of voices.

Zeb did not want to go into that stifling, oppressive parlor and see again the narrow pine box that dominated the room as it rested on two chairs shoved together. Nor did he wish to subject himself to breathing the rich sweetness of the burning beeswax candles positioned at each end of the coffin.

Most of all, he could not bear the thought of having to look at her again—his beloved Melissa. Her older sisters had dressed her in a shroud of gray muslin, then wrapped her stillborn baby girl in a blanket and laid her in her arms. Even in death, Melissa looked so weary and exhausted from the long, anguished hours of childbirth that had ultimately taken her life. No, Zeb didn't want to look at her again. He wanted to remember her as she had been, so young and vibrant, filled with life . . . and love for him, which he had returned so eagerly.

Preacher Dan, himself shivering against the February cold, was gently insistent. Laying a hand on Zeb's slumped shoulder, he urged, "Let's get on with it. If we don't, it'll be dark by the time we get done up at the cemetery, and a lot of folks traveled a long way. They'd like to get started for home before nightfall."

When Zeb still made no move to turn from his trancelike vigil into nothingness, Preacher Dan tried another ploy to bring him out of it. Making his voice stern, he said, "You've got to get hold of yourself. Pull yourself together, my son.

We've got to bury the dead and get on with the living, and you've got to think of Jessica and Belinda, too, you know. Those little girls need you, and God expects you to look after them.''

God!

It was as though the dam had burst and all of his senses suddenly awakened to scream out in protest at the cruel injustice that fate, and God, had inflicted upon his life. Striking the air with his fists, Zeb exploded, ''Don't you dare talk to me about God, Preacher!'' His heated breath created large puffs of frost before his angrily twitching lips as he cried, ''Today, of all days, don't you dare lecture me about God and what *He* expects. What about *me?* Don't I have a right to expect somethin' in return for havin' tried to live by the Good Book all my life? I've been a God-fearin' man. I've obeyed the Golden Rule, or tried to anyway, as best I could, but I can't see where it's brought me nothin' but sorrow and misery! So why should I care what God expects? The way I see it, He owes *me* a few blessings!''

The two men's eyes locked, there in the frigid gray mist that swirled about them as snow began falling once more.

Hands appeared at the foggy windows to wipe furiously and create peepholes for curious faces to peer through, alerted by Zeb's rage.

Preacher Dan's hand dropped from his caress of comfort, and, in a low voice, he admonished, ''That's soul-searing blasphemy, Brother Coulter. Do not question God's will. And when the funeral is over and everyone is gone, we're going to get down on our knees together and pray to Him to forgive you for your sin.''

Zeb glared menacingly at the man who had been a dear and treasured friend for so many years; now none of that seemed to matter. ''Blasphemy, you say?'' he echoed with a bitter laugh. ''Well, let me tell you somethin', Preacher. I got every right to question God's will. I got every right to ask Him why I'm a-fixin' to lead the way up that ridge to the Coulter family cemetery and put my third wife in her grave alongside the other two. . . ." His voice broke, as his lips began to quiver and his shoulders to tremble.

Preacher Dan, struck with pity for Zeb's tormented soul, reached to console him.

Furiously, Zeb jerked away. Blinking back the tears, he hoarsely demanded, "You tell me, Preacher, since God won't. You're supposed to be his envoy here on earth, ain't you? So why don't you tell me how come a God that's supposed to be so merciful, and just, and loving, and kind, would take three wives, one after the other, from one man?" He paused to glare at him in challenge, then said with a contemptuous sneer on his lips, "You tell me all that, Preacher, and until you do, don't speak to me of blasphemy!"

"Oh, my son, my son. Have you never heard a sermon I delivered? Weren't you listening when I spoke of God's mysterious ways?" It wasn't much of a response, Preacher Dan knew, but for the moment it was the best he could offer. Then and there he made a silent vow to prepare a good sermon on the testing of faith before he made the circuit again next month.

Zeb had turned his gaze downward once more, dimly aware of how cold he was. He wished he could go inside to the warmth of the fire, only instead of seeing sweet Melissa, lying like a cold marble statue in the pine box, he would find her sitting by the hearth with her sewing. The baby would be sleeping in the cradle he had carved by hand, with little seven-year-old Jessica and three-year-old Belinda playing quietly nearby.

Preacher Dan prodded once more. "Come on now. Like I said, we'll pray together later. I'll stay as long as you need me to. I know you're troubled, just like God knows it, too, and we'll get down on our knees and talk to Him, and we'll ask for Him to give you strength, and—"

Suddenly, Zeb tersely declared, "It's over!"

Preacher Dan, at once bewildered and alarmed to see the almost crazed expression on Zeb's face, asked, "What— what do you mean?"

"Don't you see, Preacher? I'm cursed. That's why God took all three of my wives. He put a curse on me, for some reason I don't know about yet, and He don't want me to have a wife. And this time, to make me understand how it is, He took my baby, too."

Preacher Dan shook his head in genuine pity, fearing tragedy had truly teched Zeb Coulter in the head. "That's absurd," he offered placatingly. "There's no such thing as a curse, and—"

Zeb gave a mocking laugh. "Why, Preacher, don't you read your Bible? It's just full of curses in the Old Testament. Now I got one on me and, like I said, I might not know why it's there, but one thing I do know— I'm not gonna try to fight it anymore. I've got my lot in life, two little girls to raise all by myself, and that's the way it's gonna be. I won't never marry again unless God sends me a sign He wants me to, that He's taken away His curse."

Preacher Dan was not about to say so, but he had heard the talk—that Zeb Coulter was jinxed and that was why so much misfortune had befallen him. Preacher Dan knew, too, that mountain folk were infamous for their superstitions. So, unsure of what to say or do at that particular moment, he chose to remain silent and allow Zeb to wage his own personal battle with the demons within.

At last Zeb took a deep, ragged breath, pulled himself out of his depressive slump and, with head held high in resignation, turned and went back into the house.

All eyes were upon Zeb as he entered the parlor. People crowded back, making a path for him as he walked purposefully toward the coffin. Reaching it at last, he gripped the wooden side, forced himself to take one last look at Melissa. He leaned to kiss her stone-cold cheek, then touched his fingertips lovingly to the white rosebud lips of the baby cradled in her rigid arms.

Finally, he turned, swept the expectantly staring faces with a grave look and hoarsely cried, "I want everyone to know that I accept the curse God has laid on me."

A ripple of gasps and murmurs of astonishment went through the room, for no one had expected such a profound revelation. Those who looked to Preacher Dan for some kind of explanation saw only the top of his head, as he stared down at his shoes, unwilling to be a part of the pathetic scene.

Zeb raised his voice to gain their attention once more. "You heard right," he gruffly assured them. "I'm accursed. And I got no idea as to why, 'cause you all know me as a God-fearin' man. But it seems He's angry with me, and that's why all this grief has befallen. Maybe one day, He'll bless me again, but till He does, I won't be takin' another wife."

Once more, a wave of shock went through the crowd.

Zeb looked at little Jessica and Belinda. They were watching him with round, fearful eyes, not understanding what he was saying but sure it must be something terrible from the way all the grown-ups were acting.

Walking over to place a trembling hand on each little head, he whispered, "You little ones won't have a mommy, but I reckon that's your destiny."

Zeb Coulter then bowed his head and wept for the final time over that which fate had decreed.

Chapter One

Blue Ridge Mountains
November, 1860

Jessica stepped out on the back porch and took a deep breath, drinking in the sweetness of the crisp fall air. The azure sky was cloudless, an endless sea of sweeping blue.

Last night's relentless winds had finished stripping the remaining leaves from the trees, and she knew if she were standing on top of the ridge beyond the barn, the view for miles around would be breathtaking. Wistfully, she thought, if only there were time to go there, to meditate and contemplate and just be alone with her thoughts, how truly splendid the day would be. But it was Saturday, and there was so much to be done. Not only was tomorrow the annual Harvest Picnic at the church, but it was also her family's turn to host Preacher Dan, the circuit rider.

Even with lots to do, she was looking forward to both events. The picnic on the grounds was a happy gathering of the community, with plenty of fun, fellowship and, of course, delicious food. As for Preacher Dan's visit, she loved having him. After all, she'd known him her whole life, and he was getting on in years, claimed to be in his late sixties, though the older folk around swore he was nearing seventy-five. Always, Jessica was delighted to have the opportunity once more to sit on the front porch in the evenings after supper and listen to his tales of travel throughout the Blue Ridge, his accounts of people he'd met along the way. This visit was going to be an exceptional treat, because he'd be staying through the various harvest celebrations until Saturday, when Rose Letchworth and Early Whaley were getting married. She'd have his pleasant company almost a whole week.

With a sigh of resolution to get busy and finish her chores, Jessica made her way down the worn plank steps, gathering her knit cape around her as she hurried across the yard toward the barn. Fall was the busiest time of the year, when there was so much to be done in preparation for the winter. What with teaching school in the little red one-room schoolhouse in the valley, and the days getting shorter, it seemed she worked unceasingly from dawn to dusk. By the time she went to bed, she was exhausted. The previous week she had canned the last of the apples. She had also labored over the final harvest from the garden—butter beans, tomatoes, onions and cabbage. The jars of preserves were placed in neat rows on shelves in the basement, next to the jellies and canned fruits she'd prepared in the summer. In the little cave in the dirt bank behind the barn, she had carefully buried the harvest of sweet potatoes between layers of soil. Any time that was left in the evenings was spent grading papers and preparing lessons for the next day.

Jessica's immediate task now was to gather pecans to be cracked, shelled and made into pies for the church picnic. After taking a bucket and a rake from the barn, she walked across the pasture to the pecan grove on the other side of a rushing stream. Once across the rickety plank bridge, she raked through the crisp blanket of brown leaves in search of the thick hulls that contained the rough brown-and-black-striped nuts.

It didn't take long to fill the bucket, and she was almost finished when she heard Belinda calling to her as she came across the bridge. "Why didn't you wake me and tell me you were going to gather the pecans? I'd have helped you."

Jessica glanced up to smile at her sister, noting that Belinda's face was aglow. She had been visiting a girlfriend in Asheville, and while there, had met a young man who had captured her heart. He was all she'd talked about since she got home the night before. Jessica found that quite unusual, because usually Belinda regarded all her beaux nonchalantly. Marriage was not foremost in her mind. Instead, she had dreams and aspirations of becoming a singer, another Jenny Lind, a course their father adamantly opposed. "I thought you were still tired from your trip," she replied.

"Well, we didn't get much sleep, especially after I met Harmon. After that, I think I kept Nolia awake every night till dawn talking about him." She paused to take a deep breath, her eyes bright as she sighed dramatically before continuing. "Oh, Jess, he's so wonderful...and so sweet. I can't wait for you to meet him. And he's so handsome, too—tall, with hair as black as crow feathers, and he's got eyes as blue as the sky. I still can't believe he's going to court me. Why, he could have his pick of all the debutantes in Raleigh, and I'm just a simple little mountain girl."

"You may be a mountain girl, but no one can call you *simple,* and besides, I don't imagine there's a girl in Raleigh as pretty as you, and you know it."

Belinda leaned back against a tree, pursed her lips and nodded thoughtfully. She supposed what her sister said was true, and she didn't feel conceited to think so. All her life people had told her she was beautiful, but she didn't let it go to her head, she just accepted it. Now, for the first time, it really mattered, because Harmon was unlike any boy she'd ever known before. No longer was she dreaming of the day when she could leave home and go in search of Mr. P. T. Barnum to try to convince him she could sing every bit as well as his "Swedish Nightingale"! Instead, she was thinking how wonderful it would be to be the wife of Harmon

Willingham. "His father is a doctor, you know," she reminded Jessica.

"You told me. You said he was quite prominent."

"Oh, he's probably got one of the largest practices in Raleigh. At least, that's what Nolia's aunt told me, and she should know, because she and Harmon's mother are second cousins. That's why he came by to see her when he was in Asheville."

"You also said he's studying at the Citadel. What does he plan to do when he graduates?"

Belinda shrugged, the happy glow fading. "Dr. Willingham owns a lot of land that he leases out to tenants for growing tobacco and cotton. Harmon would like to just oversee the farms, invest in some of his own. But I guess we all have to wait and see what happens now that Mr. Lincoln got elected. With all the talk of secession, who can make plans for anything these days? Harmon says there's sure to be a war, though dear Lord, I pray not."

Jessica shared Belinda's fears, for she had heard the talk, too, knew the South was terribly upset over Abraham Lincoln, a Republican, being elected President. The state of South Carolina had sworn it would secede from the Union. If other Southern states followed suit, there could well be eventual conflict between North and South.

"So, where's Poppa?" Belinda suddenly wanted to know, frowning to think there were only two things he *could* be doing—drinking or stirring folks up with his views against secession.

Jessica sighed, shook her head. "Who knows? I didn't hear him come in last night, so he must've passed out somewhere. All he does these days is drink."

"That's all he's ever done."

"Not as much as the past few weeks. It's as if he's got something on his mind he's trying not to think about, and he gets drunk so he won't have to."

"He's pretty riled up about all the war talk," Belinda pointed out. "He says North Carolina hasn't got any business getting involved, since it's not known as a cotton-growing state, and there aren't that many slaves to be concerned about. Set them all free, he says, and stay out of the fighting if it comes."

"How well I know that speech," Jessica said with a rueful smile. "The slave population is only fifteen percent of Buncombe County. I've also heard him theorize that since the county's vote in the presidential election was so close to the statewide tally, it was an indication Buncombe is opposed to secession. But I don't think that's entirely what's troubling him. I mean, Poppa has been spouting his anti-slavery views for years. I was only a small child when he bought Mammy Sara from old Lukey Purvis, but I remember kinfolk talking in later years about what a disgrace it was, the way he bought her only to set her free, and then paid her a dollar a month to work as our housekeeper. He raised a lot of eyebrows then, and I'm afraid he also made some enemies, too."

"Oh, I loved Mammy Sara," Belinda said wistfully. "I was only ten when she died, but I cried so hard I got sick to my stomach. She was like the mother neither of us ever had, and her being a Negro never mattered to us."

"Not at all," Jessica agreed, stooping to pick up a large cache of nuts hidden beneath a pile of leaves. "It broke my heart. Poppa's drinking drove away the ladies from the church who tried to help out after Melissa died, and Mammy Sara was a godsend."

"I don't recall any of the church folks coming around after *she* died," Belinda pointed out reproachfully. "There was just you and me, and we had to do everything. Cooking, cleaning, the chores when Poppa was passed out drunk. It wasn't easy."

"Life never is. We do the best we can. I'm just glad Poppa scraped up the money to send me to the Teachers Academy in Asheville."

Belinda nodded, then bluntly declared, "And you should've kept on going while you had the chance, not come back here to bury yourself in this place."

Jessica raised an eyebrow, glanced up at the sister from where she was kneeling on the ground and murmured, "This is my home, remember?"

"That might be true, but what's here for you really, Jess? Think about it. You could've gone to Raleigh or Charlotte. You didn't have to come back here to this godforsaken place."

"God hasn't forsaken this place, Belinda."

"That's not the way Poppa tells it."

Jessica shook her head in dismay. She knew only too well that her father believed he was cursed. That was his only explanation for having lost three wives and a baby. God had it in for him, he said, but one day God would take away the curse and he'd be able to live a normal life, maybe even take another wife to share his golden years. People sneered behind his back, whispered among themselves how sinful he was. It was hypocrisy they said, for him to lie around drunk all week, then show up in church on Sunday looking for a sign from God that he'd been forgiven, the curse gone forever. Oh, yes, she knew all about her father and what he believed, as well as how their neighbors regarded him.

"So why did you want to teach here?" Belinda persisted. It was beyond her how anyone could want to stay in the little rural community when there were so many exciting places to live, even Asheville. She'd had a wonderful time all week, had dreaded coming home but knew her father would've come after her if she didn't.

Jessica smiled. "Because I like teaching children I've known since they were born. It's like they're my very own, in a way."

"They've got nicer schools in Asheville. All you've got is that dumpy little one-room shack in the valley."

"That 'dumpy little one-room shack,' as you call it, is wonderful. Small, but adequate and cozy. It was my idea to paint it red last summer before my first year teaching, and everyone says it's so pretty. Even Miss Satterfield said so, and I thought she'd be very picky of anything I did after she retired and I took over. And I was able to talk the district committee into buying that beautiful bell. You can hear it all over the ridges and maybe even beyond.''

Belinda bit down on her lip thoughtfully. The last thing she wanted to do was hurt her older sister. Even though there was only a difference of four years in their ages, Jessica had, in so many ways, been like a mother to her. Yet, she felt compelled to make her see her life for what it was becoming—stagnant. Boldly she asked, ''Have you ever taken a good look at Miss Satterfield and thought how maybe you'll one day be just like her?''

Jessica tensed, knowing exactly what her sister meant. Miss Satterfield was the epitome of austerity. She always wore plain dresses of gray or black with absolutely no adornment. Her hair was skinned back in a bun so tight it made her face look pinched and hard, even when she wasn't nagging, whining or complaining. The children called her ''onion face'' behind her back. She knew because she'd said the same thing when she was Miss Satterfield's pupil. Everyone said the woman was the way she was because she'd never married.

Finally, Jessica responded by turning Belinda's question back on her. ''I wish someone would tell me why it's such a stigma for a woman to be unwed. That *is* what you're referring to, isn't it? That the fact I'm not married will make me just like Miss Satterfield?''

Belinda was leaning against a pecan tree, arms folded across her chest. Framing her answer carefully, she said, ''Maybe. You don't have any beaux, Jess. Maybe it's because people just expect a schoolteacher to be an old maid. And don't ask me why. I don't know. I just hate to think of you winding up like Miss Satterfield.''

Pensively, Jessica contemplated the reality that the young, eligible men about didn't court her. *Too severe*, she once overhead someone say about her at a community dance. She always had her nose stuck in a book, they said, with no time for fun. And that was such a shame, they also lamented, because Jessica Coulter could be pretty—if she tried. So the men obviously preferred, and pursued, the giggly, bouncy, fun-loving girls like Belinda.

Perhaps she was, after all, destined to be like Miss Satterfield, never marrying or having children of her own, but, by God, she'd do her best to keep a bright outlook on life. None of her students would ever call *her* "onion face."

"I didn't mean to hurt your feelings," Belinda anxiously offered as Jessica got to her feet.

Jessica had enough pecans for three pies—two for the picnic and one for supper later. Let the squirrels and chipmunks have their own feast till she got around to gathering the rest. "I really don't want to talk about me. I've got a lot of work to do between now and tomorrow, with no time for nonsense like worrying about my future."

"But are you happy, Jess?" Belinda felt compelled to ask.

She flashed her a wry, mirthless smile. "I'm not *unhappy,* Belinda, and I don't ask for more than that out of life."

Belinda shook her head, not surprised that Jessica was putting her off. The subject was a sore one and always had been. She'd have liked for the two of them to just run away together for a life of adventure, but oh, no, Jessica had to be so sensible. Still, as they made their way back to the house, she could not resist teasing, "Well, there's always Reuben Walker, and he comes with a ready-made family."

At that, Jessica stopped walking to glare at Belinda and say sternly, "Jamie Walker might be a dear six-year-old, sorely in need of a mother's care and love, but Reuben Walker is a stodgy old man, and I'd rather die than marry him."

"He's not so very old. He's just past thirty, I hear."

"He acts like he's a hundred. He made his poor late wife Elizabeth old, too. He kept her there at that farm and worked her harder than a field hand. He never let her have any fun. She wasn't allowed to go to church socials, or quilting bees, and I never knew her to go anywhere beyond the valley store, and that was probably once a month, if that often. I used to make an effort to stop by every so often with a pan of cookies for Jamie, and I'd want to cry, because she was so starved for company. When she took fever last year and died, she *looked* like she was a hundred. And I swear, when I saw her lying in her coffin, she was smiling. She looked so peaceful, as if she were actually glad of dying to escape the hell Reuben made of her life.'' She shook her head slowly from side to side and firmly avowed, ''No, dear sister, don't even tease about that. I'd rather be thought of like Miss Satterfield than be the next Mrs. Reuben Walker.''

Belinda agreed but hesitantly pointed out, ''Poppa may be getting ideas, though. He's sure been hinting a lot lately about how nice it'd be if you two did get married.''

''Hinting?'' Jessica hooted. ''He's never hinted, Belinda. He started the day Elizabeth was buried, pointing out how perfect Reuben and I were for each other, how our getting married would join the two farms. And now that the year of mourning is almost over, he's making it very clear he wants Reuben to court me.''

''I know, I know,'' Belinda drearily agreed. ''I was just teasing, really, but I've seen it, too. All Poppa takes into account is that Reuben is a hard worker, and if he took over this place, he'd make it prosper. He's already got one son, and Poppa probably figures the two of you would have lots more—and *that* would certainly make his dream come true.''

How well Jessica knew her father's dream. The Coulter land had been handed down from generation to generation for more than one hundred years. He believed, as his ancestors did, that land was the only thing worth having. Do without, make any sacrifice, but never, ever, lose your land. By other standards, the farm was not a large place. Seventy acres, more or less. But most of it was bottomland, good for

tobacco and corn. And there were cold streams running
down from the ridges above to provide plenty of water for
cows, hogs, goats, turkeys, chickens and geese. In addition
to the pecan grove, there was a large apple orchard, a few
pear trees, lots of blueberry and plum bushes. Her father
knew, as Jessica did, that Belinda would not marry anyone
local and settle down close by, and his only hope for keeping the farm in the family was if his elder daughter would
marry someone local, preferably Reuben, and carry on the
Coulter tradition.

They walked on, and suddenly, sharply, Belinda confided, "I want you to know that even if Harmon doesn't
propose to me, I'm not going to stay around here much
longer. I have no future here."

Jessica was not surprised. "But where would you go?
How would you live? You know I'll help if I can, but my
teacher's pay doesn't stretch very far, especially since Poppa
is drinking more and does less and less around here."

"I don't know yet. Maybe all the way to Richmond. I do
have a good voice, and with training, I think I could join
one of those traveling shows, and—"

"Don't let Poppa hear you talking like that," Jessica was
quick to warn. "He'll tie you up and lock you in the
smokehouse." She was not altogether teasing.

Belinda kicked absently at a stone, made a face, then fervently stated, "Well, I'm going to do it, even if I have to run
away. I'm just not staying here to mildew."

Jessica gave her a nudge with her elbow and laughed.
"Don't be so gloomy. You know darn well that if you've set
your sights on Harmon Willingham, you'll have no trouble
at all charming him the way you've charmed every other boy
you've ever met. And if you don't get tired of him, like you
did of all the rest, you'll marry him and live happily ever
after. Now come on and help get these nuts shelled so I can
start baking."

The Coulter house was constructed of logs. At the front
a porch ran from one side to the other, and a balcony ex-

tended across the front of the second floor. Downstairs, there was a center hall, with kitchen and dining room to one side, parlor and two bedrooms on the other. The kitchen was large, with ample room for a table, so Jessica had turned the dining room into her bedroom long ago. Belinda and their father used the bedrooms on the other side. Upstairs were four rooms, only two of which were furnished, but they were used only on the rare occasions when there was company. Jessica's mother had had few relatives, and while Belinda's had come from a large family, her kin seldom visited because they did not get on well with Zeb.

Everything smelled pleasantly of lemon oil, as Jessica had spent the evening before polishing every piece of furniture. She had opened the windows upstairs to freshen the air. No one had stayed up there since the last time the Coulters had been hosts to Preacher Dan.

Jessica got the hammer from the pantry and, with Belinda's help, cracked all the nuts on a large flat rock in the backyard. Then they went in the house and sat down at the wood table in the kitchen to pick out the meats from the shells. Once they were settled at their task, Belinda began to talk about Harmon once more.

Jessica listened with loving tolerance, then, when Belinda finally stopped talking long enough for her to get a word in, she asked, "Well, when am I going to meet this marvelous beau of yours?"

Belinda shivered with anticipation. "Thursday. His family is having a special birthday dinner for his aunt in Asheville, and he said he'd come out here early in the morning to get me and take me back to meet them."

"That certainly sounds as though he's serious, already wanting you to meet his family. Maybe you should invite him to stay a while for coffee and dessert when he brings you home. Preacher Dan will still be here, and I'll have plenty of leftovers from our Harvest Eve dinner."

Belinda pursed her lips thoughtfully, then remarked gloomily, "Poppa isn't exactly at his best when Preacher Dan is around, you know."

Jessica nodded. Preacher Dan didn't approve of their father's drinking and let him know it in no uncertain terms. He also refused to talk about the so-called *curse* and told Zeb he should try to get his life back together on his own, instead of waiting for a sign from God before doing it. "Well, maybe he'll be on his best behavior if we've got a special guest," she optimistically offered.

"Well, if he finds out Harmon is going to the Citadel, then he's going to get on the subject of secession. That could lead to a tense conversation."

The sound of a rider coming into the yard made them look at each other in uncomfortable apprehension, and a few moments later Zeb walked into the kitchen. They smelled the whiskey at once, but felt some relief to note he wasn't reeling or staggering, which meant he hadn't had much to drink—yet. It was, after all, early in the day.

Jessica asked if he wanted his lunch, reminding him there was leftover fish stew from the night before. He shook his head. She stared after him as he crossed the room. One of her mother's relatives had once told her he was quite a handsome man when he was young. He would, she mused, be far from unattractive today if he took better care of himself. He still had plenty of hair, thick and black, and the streaks of gray were not unbecoming. And when he was not drinking, an occasion that was becoming more and more rare, his blue eyes were clear and alert, not bloodshot and lackluster. But through the years of bitterness and sadness, he'd stopped standing straight and tall, and was now a bent and broken man in both body and spirit.

He was almost to the hallway when he paused and matter-of-factly said, "Reuben and his boy will be here for supper tomorrow."

Jessica stiffened, then dared to remind him, "Preacher Dan is going to be here. I really wasn't wanting extra guests to fix for."

He was in the doorway to the hall, and he stopped dead still for an instant. Then he stretched out his arms to grasp the door on each side of him, as though bracing himself. He took a deep breath, held it, let it out in a rush and said, without turning around, "Well, it's just fine, Jessica, that Preacher Dan is gonna be here, too. Makes it real convenient, 'cause it'll be a perfect time for Reuben to talk to him about comin' back for your wedding."

Belinda looked wildly at Jessica, who stared back at her in horror. Then they both looked at Zeb, who finally, slowly, turned to face them. His eyes were narrowed, and he raised his stubbled chin ever so slightly in a gesture of defiance. "You heard me right, girl," he said to Jessica, an arrogant rasp in his voice. He lifted a finger to point at her almost accusingly. "You're gonna marry Reuben Walker. I just got done makin' the covenant with him, and it's all set."

A great roaring had begun in Jessica's head, making it difficult for her to speak, especially around the knot of fear in her throat. "You—you don't mean it," she whispered, shaking her head slowly from side to side in disbelief. Beside her, Belinda reached to clutch her hand tightly, as though to give evidence of her sympathy for her plight. "Poppa, you can't be serious."

With a sneer and a firm nod, he assured her, "Oh, yes, I'm very serious. Smartest thing I've ever done. He's a hard worker, but his place is small. He can't do what he wants with his land 'cause of the way it lays. If he joins up with my land, he can have some good crops. He's already got one son. Healthy and big-boned as you are, you two can have a dozen more. Twenty years from now, this farm can be the biggest and best in Buncombe County. And Reuben thinks like I do, too, when it comes to slavery. He's agreed he'll pay for labor."

Zeb crossed the room to stand on the other side of the table from where Jessica sat with Belinda, both of them staring up at him in fear and disbelief. "But aside from all the gravy I'll get out of this marriage," he continued, "the fact of the matter is that Reuben needs a wife. He needs a mother for the boy he's already got. So it works good for everybody. We made us a deal, and it's all set and agreed on."

The sound had to fight its way up from the very pit of her horrified soul, and it came out like the hoarse cry of a desperate, trapped animal fighting with everything within for survival. "No!" Jessica was on her feet, clutching the edge of the table. "No, I won't marry him! You can't make me, and—"

Zeb's hand moved so fast she didn't see the blow coming, only felt the sharp sting of the slap across her face. Belinda leaped to her feet to gather her in her arms and glare at him in condemnation, ready to try to ward off his next blow, should there be one.

"There ain't no need of this!" he roared, shoulders trembling with his wrath. He opened his hand and stared down at it, as though stunned that he had lost control, allowed those now-stinging fingers to become a weapon against his own flesh and blood. "Ain't no need at all." He looked at them again, this time making a fist and shaking it menacingly. "Ain't no need, 'cause it's done and done! I made a covenant with Reuben Walker for you to be his wife. And when Preacher Dan gets here, you all can set the date. Reuben figures Christmas, and that sets well with me. The sooner the better!"

He turned and strode angrily from the kitchen, muttering to himself.

Jessica could only stare after him, washed with absolute hopelessness and despair.

Chapter Two

Life had not been easy for Jessica. She'd never truly known a mother's love, and her father's heart seemed as dead as his broken dreams. The care of her younger sister had fallen on her shoulders when she was but a child herself. Yet she had accepted her lot in life—till now.

Outside her bedroom window, the rooster crowed loudly, lustily. Jessica did not want to get out of bed, even though she'd been looking forward to this day for weeks—the Harvest Picnic, Preacher Dan's arrival. But after last night, she wished she could hide in her room all day long, maybe even forever, because she just didn't care about anything, anymore.

She supposed she should not have been surprised by her father's ultimatum. In the mountains it wasn't unusual for a girl's marriage to be arranged by her family. Sometimes it was even done at the time a daughter was born. But she'd just never thought such a covenant would be made for *her*.

She thought back to how Reuben, in the past few months, had come around more and more. It was unheard of that he should officially court her, or anyone else, till his wife had been dead a year, but he'd certainly managed to convey his intentions by doing subtle little things like making sure he and his son, Jamie, sat next to her in church. Sunday evenings, if the weather was nice, he'd drop by to sit on the porch for a spell. If it was raining, he'd come into the parlor, where she had no choice but to politely serve him hot mulled cider; then she'd busy herself elsewhere in the house if her father was there to keep him company. There were the times he'd just happen to drop around the schoolhouse when the big bell rang, ending lessons for the day. He'd offer her a ride home in his buckboard wagon, nice and neighborly. No one could censure his behavior, and people smiled and whispered how the widower and the school-marm were so right for each other.

Through it all, Jessica had remained polite but aloof, cordial but reserved, hoping he would lose interest. Now she knew that had been just wishful thinking. He wasn't fooling her, either. Even though he pretended he wanted a mother for his son, she knew better. His real motive was the Coulter land. His father was poor by any standards in the Blue Ridge. And her father didn't care as long as he got what he wanted: perpetuation of Coulter blood on the land, as well as someone to look after him in his old age.

Tears stung her eyes, and she furiously wiped at them with the backs of her hands. The thought of marrying Reuben Walker, or any other man she didn't, *couldn't* love, was repugnant. She'd just have to talk to her father again and show him that he'd made a terrible mistake. She'd try to convince him that even if Belinda did marry and leave home, Jessica would never forsake him.

Yet, even as the desperate thoughts assailed her, Jessica sadly knew her situation was hopeless. His mind was made up.

Finally, she forced herself to get out of bed. After bathing at the washbowl on the dresser, she put on her favorite Sunday dress, a soft peach gingham with a high ruffled collar and long, puffed sleeves. The skirt was long and full, and she didn't need many petticoats, which she didn't own, anyway. While young girls like Belinda might wear frills and flounces, Jessica dressed conservatively, as was expected of a teacher.

Looking in the mirror above the dresser, she carefully scrutinized her face and saw only a slight reddening from her father's angry slap. There was no ugly bruise, thank goodness. Still, her cheek hurt—*and* her feelings.

After setting a pot of coffee on the stove to boil, she went out on the back porch to get the big wicker basket she had woven years ago. The weather, she noted, was almost perfect for a picnic on the church grounds. Though a bit chilly, which wasn't unusual that time of year, the air was as crisp as fresh-picked green apples.

She packed the basket with fried chicken, potato salad and pickles she had made and packed in glass jars early in the summer. She added three jars of string beans, a sack of corn pone and, finally, two of the pecan pies she'd managed to bake late last night, after the distressing scene with her father. She'd been so upset, she wouldn't be surprised if it turned out she'd accidentally substituted salt for sugar!

When that was done, she paused for a cup of coffee. Ordinarily, she savored the quiet time before anyone else was up and about, for she could ponder her thoughts in peace. This morning, however, there was nothing happy to contemplate, only the miserable turn of events. She gulped down the coffee, nearly burning her throat, then began frying large slices of smoked ham and stirring a bowl of fresh eggs to scramble in the tasty gravy.

As she stood at the stove, sadness was a tight lump in her throat. Now it was over. The dreams. The wonderful daydreams she had about one day meeting a very special man and falling deeply, happily in love. So many hours she'd spent in sweet thoughts, high on the ridge in her favorite spot. She would close her eyes and think how it would be with the special man she would love.

They would hold hands as they walked through the beauty of the hills, where cicadas chirped by day and katydids fiddled by night. They would hear summer sighs in the trees, as crimson fronds of sumac shouted a prophecy as old as time. They would nibble on fox grapes, blue-black and heavy, fallen from the vine, and delight in the splendor of papaws and maypops yellowing in the sun. Their hearts would burst with love amid the other blossoms dotting the landscape—haunting purple asters and brilliant red cardinal flowers, standing like flambeaux in the meadow.

And they would run like children, laughing at life and reveling in the glory of each other... her faceless lover and she.

Jessica sighed, pensively shook away the warm thoughts. Dishing up the food, she set it on the table, then turned to call Belinda at the same moment the girl appeared in the kitchen doorway. Sympathy was mirrored in her cornflower-blue eyes.

"I think I was awake half the night worrying about you," she offered. "Are you okay?"

"I'll be all right," Jessica said tonelessly, not wanting to talk about it. It was bad enough to *feel* the misery.

Zeb walked in just then and heartily assured her, "Of course you will." He flashed both of them a big smile as he took his place at the head of the table. Gone were the cobwebs of drink, and as usual on Sunday, he was cheerful. Sunday meant church and the hope that perhaps this would be the day he'd waited for so long, the fateful day when he would at last receive God's sign the curse was lifted from his troubled soul. Then, afterward, if nothing happened, he'd feel meaner than a stepped-on snake and start all over trying to drink away the misery till the next Sunday.

"Yep," he said confidently as he reached to stab a piece of ham from the platter. "I'd say, for the first time in your life, Jessica, everything is gonna be all right. Now you'll have somebody to look after you when I'm gone."

Jessica could not resist gently pointing out, "I don't need anybody to look after me, Poppa. I've got a job, remember? I'm a schoolteacher. And schoolteachers can get by just fine on their own."

He snorted, reached to scoop up a big helping of eggs. "That's not the way it's supposed to be. Woman needs a husband. Man needs a wife. The good Lord knows how *I* tried to have it that way, but for reasons known only to Him, it just didn't work out. But it will for you. Reuben is a good man. He'll make you a good husband.''

She exchanged a woeful look with Belinda, took a deep breath and dared to say, ''But Poppa, I don't love Reuben. I will *never* love him, and—''

He cut her off by slamming his fist on the table and, with a flash of rage, cried, ''Now you just hush up, girl! I'm not gonna sit here and listen to foolish talk.'' He glared at her with blazing eyes, cords in his neck bulging from his anger. Pointing his fork at her, shaking it, he said, ''I knew you was gonna give me some sass about this, 'cause I'm not blind, and I seen the way you been puttin' Reuben off. Whenever he comes over here to call, you say as little as possible to him and then run off first chance you get. I knew that was what you were doin', and I knew you'd keep on doin' it, 'cause you're stubborn, and you're selfish. You don't give a fig about this land. It don't make no difference to you if you don't give me grandsons to carry on the farm, and—''

''Poppa,'' Belinda interrupted then, voice sharp with indignation. No matter the consequences, she felt compelled to defend her sister. ''You aren't being fair. Jessica hasn't got a selfish bone in her body. She's worked so hard all these years taking care of both of us, and—''

''You ain't got no say in this, girl,'' he cut her off, regarding her through eyes narrowed with contempt. ''Especially when you're just like her. You don't care anything about me or this place. All you think about is yourself. You'd run off tomorrow if you had any place to go. Reuben knows that, and that's why he wasn't interested in marryin' you. Says you're too flighty. So keep your mouth out of this.''

He turned to Jessica once more, saw that she'd shrunk away to stand on the other side of the kitchen. She was, no doubt, afraid he'd lose his temper and slap her again. He was sorry about that, but he wouldn't say so. She had to re-alize he meant what he said, that she was going to marry Reuben Walker whether she liked it or not. "Like I told you last night, it's all settled, and there's no need in arguin' about it. When you get off your high horse and really think about it, you'll see it's the best for everybody."

Jessica turned away to hide the tears she could no longer hold back.

Satisfied that the discussion was finally closed, Zeb wolfed down his breakfast, then said he'd see them in church. "I'm gonna ride my mule, so's I can come on back when I get ready. I don't like all that lollygaggin' around after eatin'."

When he'd gone, Belinda tried to put her sympathy into words, but Jessica held up a hand for silence. "Please, I just don't want to talk about it anymore."

Belinda nodded, and her heart ached for her sister.

They loaded the wagon, hitched up the remaining mule, then began to make their way on the bumpy dirt road. Attempting to get Jessica's mind off her misery, Belinda began to talk about her favorite subject at the moment—the virtues of handsome Harmon Willingham.

Jessica settled back on the rough plank seat. Though she wasn't going to say so, she couldn't help wondering how Harmon, with his social and financial background, would react to the way Belinda lived. While the Coulter family was not impoverished, they were far below the Willinghams' station in life.

They lived about two miles, as the crow flies, from the little white church with the tall steeple. Jessica gave the mule the reins, letting him pick his own way along the rocks and ruts of the rough and uneven road. As Belinda's voice droned on and on, Jessica turned her attention to the countryside and the sweet beauty of fall. She liked this season the best, with berries ripening on the scarlet stems of the poke-berry, and the deep red of woodbine. She could see squirrels busy among the hickories, and whippoorwills still sang a mournful requiem to summer amid the bare limbs of the sourwoods. Corn was hardening on the stalks of the fields they passed, and she saw sliced apples drying in the sun on the porch steps of the few cabins along the way.

At last they reached the church in the vale, an almost hallowed spot in its tranquil surroundings. A gentle waterfall trickled down the rock wall of the hill just beyond. In the hemlock grove, long wooden tables had been built by some of the menfolk, and already the ladies were busy making ready for the picnic by spreading gingham cloths and laying out tableware.

Jessica groaned silently as she saw Reuben hurrying toward them. He limped slightly from the injury he'd received when a horse threw him, then fell on him, many years before. She felt herself tensing as he helped them both alight. He was wearing a corduroy coat over his overalls and a felt hat. His skin, Jessica noted, was still leathery brown from long hours toiling in the summer sun. He was not unattractive, and she supposed some girls might find him appealing, but it was his eyes she did not like—black and beady. And when he touched her, his flesh was always cold, as if he'd just stepped out of an icy mountain pond.

Belinda wasted no time in hurrying away from the unhappy situation, while Jessica waited in silence as Reuben tied the mule's reins to the trunk of a nearby oak; then he went to get her food basket from the back of the wagon. Returning, he looked at her with a smug expression and said, "I understand your pa told you I've asked for your hand in marriage and that he's agreed."

She nodded curtly. "He told me you two had made a covenant." She couldn't resist bitterly adding, "But no one asked me how I feel about it."

He seemed taken aback, but only momentarily, as he coolly responded, "No one figured you'd object, Jessica."

She looked him straight in the eye and said, "Well, I most certainly do object, because the fact is, I don't love you."

He offered a wry, mirthless smile. "It's not important that you do love me. All that matters is that you'll be an obedient wife and a proper and loving mother to Jamie...as well as all the children you will bear me. And I do intend," he pointed out, "for you to have as many as the good Lord sees fit to bless us with. That's all I expect of you. Now come along. It's almost time for service."

Jessica fought back the impulse to cringe as he placed a possessive hand on her arm and began to walk toward the picnic area.

He continued, "Your pa thinks its best if we live with him, and I agree. My house is really too small for all of us. I'd planned to build one when me and Elizabeth had more children, but that didn't happen. Your house is just right with all those rooms upstairs."

Jessica was getting madder by the minute. He and Poppa had made their plans. No one cared about what she wanted.

"Of course," he went on as they drew nearer to the women at the tables, "we don't say anything to anyone for a while. My year of mourning isn't up, and we don't want to raise eyebrows. But I will talk to Preacher Dan while he's here and set the wedding date. Christmas Eve will be a perfect time."

"Yes, that's about a year and a day since Elizabeth died, isn't it?" Jessica could not resist the sarcasm. "You just can't get much closer than that, can you? Besides, I'm sure you're anxious to get *Poppa's land* ready for spring planting."

He set the basket down on the table. Then, making sure he kept his voice low so no one else could hear, he warned her, "You'd better learn right away that I don't tolerate insolence in a wife, Jessica. You'll hold your tongue or feel a buggy whip on your back!" With that, he abruptly turned on his heel and walked away.

Instantly Jessica was awash in cold fear. He wasn't making an idle threat, she knew, for she'd seen with her own eyes the evidence of his cruel ways. Jessica stood there watching after him, inwardly cringing to think how in just a few weeks she would have to submit to him in *every way*. She could not bear the thought of him touching her. Though she knew nothing about marital relations, she'd seen animals mating on the farm, and certainly knew how babies were made. Bile rose in her throat at the idea of Reuben doing *that* to her.

"Jessica!"

She roused herself from her anguished thoughts to see that Naomi Billingsley was waving to her.

"Over here, dear! There's a nice breeze, and you can put your things here that need to be cooled."

Jessica forced a pleasant expression and hurried over.

"I hope you brought more than one of your famous pecan pies. They don't last long," Naomi complimented her.

"I brought two." Jessica was surprised at how dull and dead her voice sounded, an echo from her heart, no doubt.

With eyes twinkling, Naomi teased, "I saw how Reuben Walker nearly broke his neck rushing to meet you and your sister. Everybody is saying he's just waiting till his year of mourning is over, and then you will be the next Mrs. Walker."

It was all Jessica could do to keep from groaning out loud. Naomi was known as a busybody, always sticking her nose in other people's business, and she was also a terrible gossip. Jessica had learned long ago to watch what she said around her and didn't dare give even the remotest hint that the rumors were, sadly, true. Instead, she maintained her composure and smoothly changed the subject by asking how Naomi's daughter was. Everyone knew Leona Billingsley was the apple of Naomi's eye and her favorite subject.

Naomi was only too glad to oblige with the information, "Oh, she's doing just fine, thank you. She just got back from Atlanta, visiting my brother and his family." She paused to giggle with pride, then rushed to confide, "My sister-in-law wrote that she couldn't sweep her front porch for all the young men calling on Leona. I'm surprised she didn't come home with a ring on her finger."

Jessica would have been surprised if she *had*. While Leona Billingsley was admittedly a very pretty girl, she unfortunately lacked the personality to go with her looks. She was spoiled and willful, and everyone knew she couldn't keep a beau for long. Sooner or later, though, with her mother's help, she'd find herself a husband. Oh, how Jessica wished Leona could take *her* place and marry Reuben.

They began to secure the tablecloths with small rocks, lest the breeze blow them away during the church hour. Naomi remarked that Preacher Dan had not arrived. "He's usually here an hour or more before service. I hope he hasn't had any problems." A few of the other women echoed their concern.

Jessica, too, hoped he was all right; when she'd seen him last, about a month ago, she'd noted how tired he looked, pale and drawn.

At quarter to eleven, Herbert Billingsley came over to say that he and the other deacons had decided to start the service on time even though Preacher Dan hadn't arrived. "No doubt something has happened," he said fearfully. "First thing, we'll pray for his safe deliverance."

The bell began to clang, and Jessica turned to go inside with the others. Just as she started up the stairs toward the brightly red-painted doors, little Polly Sue Packer came scurrying down, ribboned pigtails bouncing as she held her long gingham skirts in her fingertips to keep from tripping on her petticoats. Seeing Jessica, she pleaded, "Oh, M-M-M-Miss J-J-J-Jessica, w-w-will y-y-you..." She began to blink as tears of frustration gathered in her round blue eyes.

Filled with compassion, Jessica knelt beside her. "Now remember what I told you," she said sternly, clutching the child's shoulders gently. "Take a deep breath and speak very slowly. There's no need to rush. Now try again."

Polly Sue drew in her breath and began once more, hands clenched at her sides as she desperately attempted to control her voice. "P-please..." she said, easier this time, "go with me...to...the outhouse."

Jessica could hear the sounds from inside the church, old Bert Toliver strumming his guitar for the chords of the opening hymn. She and Polly Sue would be late, but it was much more important to go with her than to be on time, especially as Jessica had a special affinity for the child. She took her hand. "Of course, I'll go with you."

The winding path was terribly overgrown, since it was only used on Wednesday evenings and Sundays, when people came to services. The two picked their way along to the wooden shack, with its half-moon carved in the splintery door. When Polly Sue was done, they started back.

They were coming up the last rise, just stepping into sight of the church, when Jessica, ever alert in the woods, saw the snake. It was lying at the edge of the path, apparently having slithered out from the dense undergrowth. Instinctively, she pushed Polly Sue to one side. It was a moccasin . . . and very deadly.

Polly Sue saw it and began to cry and stutter all at once, but in her most authoritative teacher voice, Jessica commanded, "Hush. You'll scare him into striking. Stand very still and don't make a move." Miraculously, the child obediently froze.

Jessica's eyes fell on a big rock, just a few inches away. Moving very, very slowly, her eyes riveted to the snake all the while, she knelt and closed her fingers about it. She straightened, took aim and brought the rock crashing down on the snake's head. It was pinned down but still thrashing. She quickly lifted the rock to hit it again. It continued to wriggle, but she'd heard that a dead snake could wiggle till sundown, could even deliver a deadly bite. She wasn't anxious to find out if that bit of mountain folklore were true.

She took Polly Sue's hand to pull her along. "We're late. We have to hurry."

She stepped out of the brush and into the clearing, and that was when she became aware of the stranger standing there—a very handsome stranger, she saw at once. He was tall, with broad shoulders, looked fit and well in a neat black suit, white shirt and black string tie. When he politely re-moved his wide-brimmed hat, she noted his thick, black hair, the way it brushed his collar. But his eyes impressed her most. The color of warm coffee, they were. Though he'd not spoken a word, she felt strangely drawn to him for a reason she could not understand.

He offered a friendly smile of compliment and ex-plained, "I arrived just in time to see you finish off that snake, and I must admit I'm quite impressed. Most women would've screamed and run."

Polly Sue pulled free of Jessica's hold and excitedly be-gan running toward the church to let everyone know a stranger was about.

Demurely, Jessica explained, "When you've been raised in the mountains, you have to learn not to scream and run." She looked at him quizzically. "I don't think I've seen you around these parts."

"Well, you'll be seeing a lot of me for a while, I'm afraid."

"Afraid?" she echoed, not understanding, then caught the grimness in his voice. The pieces began to come to-gether—the way he was dressed, the Bible he was carrying in one hand. With an icy prickle of fear running up her spine, she asked, "Where's Preacher Dan?"

He explained that Preacher Dan was his uncle, and was very sick.

"How serious is it?" she wanted to know.

"It's his heart. His doctor isn't very optimistic that he'll ever be able to ride the circuit again, so I'm taking his place for now. I'd just finished at the seminary the week before he got so bad off, and—" He gave a short laugh of chagrin. "I'm sorry...I didn't introduce myself. Derek Stanton." He shifted the Bible beneath his arm and held out his hand to her.

She shook it, then introduced herself.

"Uncle Dan told me I'd be staying with your family. I'm grateful for your hospitality."

"We're pleased to have you." And she meant it. Even though she'd looked forward to seeing Preacher Dan again and was now worried over his condition, it was going to be nice to have someone new as a guest. It would be interesting to hear someone else's views, tales of his experiences in life.

Just then the church doors opened, and the congregation began to spill outside, curious and alarmed all at once. Several of the deacons headed quickly in the direction of Jessica and the newcomer. "Well, it seems you're about to meet your flock. Welcome, Preacher Stanton. I hope you'll like it here, and that we can make you comfortable in our home," Jessica told him sincerely.

He smiled again, and his voice was like a caress against her face as he murmured, "I'm sure I will, Miss Coulter. I sure like it fine so far."

He turned to meet the deacons, and Jessica stood back to watch. Despite the misery that had wrapped her like a shroud since her father's decree of the night before, she suddenly felt good inside, warm and pleasant and dreamy as a summer breeze.

In only a few seconds, Preacher Stanton had touched her life, and she knew, somehow, they would become good friends.

Yet, in the same instant, she felt a wave of sadness that reminded her they could never be anything more.

Chapter Three

Derek focused on the girl with the flaming red hair and emerald eyes as she stood before the congregation singing a hymn. But his mind was racing as he gathered courage to deliver his sermon. He hoped the fact it was his first would not be obvious. During his brief time at the theological seminary he had been required to write a lecture and preach it to other students in practice. That experience however, had not prepared him for the crowd that now regarded him expectantly.

His uncle had told him that the folk of the Blue Ridge were set in their ways, didn't take easily to outsiders. He'd told of how they'd been so leery of him on his first few visits that he'd had no choice but to camp out in the woods, because no one invited him to stay in their home. It had taken nearly a year to fill the pews of the church.

Even though he was plagued with self-doubts, Derek Stanton intended to try his best to be a good minister. No matter, he told himself over and over, that he'd not been spiritually called like his uncle. He was morally committed by the deathbed promise he'd made to his mother.

He could still remember being racked with emotion that night he'd sat beside her bed and held her cold, almost translucent hand. She had drifted in and out of consciousness for a time. Suddenly, she rallied to lucidity and focused lackluster eyes upon his face as she begged him, in a feeble voice, to promise to forsake his sinful ways and take up the Lord's work. She wanted him to follow in her brother's footsteps as a preacher of God's word.

Derek and his uncle had exchanged bewildered and uncomfortable glances, and then he'd spoken the words she desperately pleaded to hear in the closing seconds of her life. She took one last breath, and her head rolled gently to the side. She had died with a smile on her lips, and Derek knew he had to do his best to make her last wish come true.

The pretty redhead began another verse of the hymn, and Derek let his mind drift back to those earlier years of his life, when it seemed trouble was his constant companion. His father had died when he was just a boy, and the man his mother married not long after had turned out to be a drunkard, surly and mean. When Derek turned fifteen, he'd left his native New Orleans despite his mother's tearful protests. He drifted from place to place, never putting down roots. He took one day at a time and let the future take care of itself—till he lost his heart to a dark-eyed, fiery beauty in El Paso.

A muscle tightened in his jaw as Consuela's face flashed in his mind. She had bewitched him, and he'd believed her when she swore to return his love.

What a fool he'd been!

He'd realized too late she was using him to take him for what money he had, while hoping that when her jealous *bandido* finally came home, Derek would rid her of the problem by killing him. But because Derek was a good shot, when the ultimate showdown came he'd been able to settle things by wounding the man.

He'd left town then, vowing never again to be so quick to trust a woman, much less give his heart.

The next years had been spent drifting in and out of jobs, and towns...and more women's beds than he could remember.

Finally, he'd gone home to visit his mother. By then a widow, she was overjoyed to see him, begged him to stay in

New Orleans and settle down. Tired of the rambling life, he'd been actually thinking about doing that, but bliss and optimism were short-lived; his mother became ill and died soon after.

He'd then gone to a seminary for a year in his quest to honor his vow, and now, as the red-haired girl finished her song, the day of reckoning was upon him.

He waited till she returned to her place on the choir bench before getting up to walk to the pulpit. He gripped the edges of the podium in front of him nervously as he scanned the sea of faces. For the most part, they looked wary and suspicious—except for one. Jessica Coulter, she'd said her name was, the young woman he'd spoken with outside. She was gazing up at him from the third pew, a reassuring smile on her lips as though she could sense his anxiety. Did he imagine it, or did she even give an ever-so-slight nod of encouragement? He glanced at the stern-faced man seated to her left, the small boy next to him. Her husband and son? He hadn't seen a wedding ring on her finger. There was an old man on her right. Her father, perhaps. Derek took note of the strange look in his eyes—haunted, yet hopeful; he also seemed nervous, maybe even a little frightened.

The congregation began to stir a bit impatiently. Derek cleared his throat, looked down at his notes and then began his sermon on the topic of giving thanks; harvest time was a wonderful opportunity to reflect on all God's wonderful blessings. His delivery was, he feared, a bit stilted, for he kept referring to his notes to quote the appropriate Bible verses, but he told himself that one day he'd be able to call them from his memory, as Uncle Dan so easily did.

At last he finished, and after a benediction he glanced around, relieved to see that the air of the congregation was a bit more relaxed. People were murmuring among themselves, nodding now and then. Maybe, he dared optimistically hope, he'd make a good preacher yet—despite his self-doubts.

He stepped down from the pulpit and immediately the church deacons descended to welcome him wholeheartedly.

Zeb sullenly watched, then shook his head in blighted hope. It was just another Sunday without a sign God was removing His curse. Shoulders slumped, he got up and stepped out into the aisle. He felt a wave of annoyance as Widow Haislip appeared, as she did every week after service, to offer a flirting smile and a silent reminder that she was there when he wanted her. He gave a polite nod but no encouragement. Oh, she wasn't an ugly woman by any means, but he had no intention of taking up with her or any other woman till the Lord gave His sign.

Persistent, Widow Haislip fell into step beside him and attempted conversation. "Your younger daughter has the voice of an angel, Zeb. You must be mighty proud." When he didn't respond, she rushed on. "And I hear the new preacher is staying at your house this week. He's not wearing a wedding ring. Wouldn't she make a fine preacher's wife?"

Zeb grunted. He had not really thought about it. The truth was, marrying off Belinda was the least of his worries. As pretty as her sainted mother, she'd never be an old maid.

"I made extra chicken, just for you," she went on to inform him, tucking her hand possessively in the crook of his arm, "and a sweet potato pie. I thought maybe we could fix our plates and find a nice shady spot and eat together."

He continued on his way, pretending not to hear, and she stared after him and gave a sigh of disappointment. All that talk about him being cursed was a lot of nonsense, as far as she was concerned. He had the makings of a good husband, and all he needed was a Christian wife to help him walk that narrow path of righteousness. She wasn't going to give up on making him realize that fact.

Outside, in the hemlock grove, Jessica stood behind one of the picnic tables and dished up potato salad. All around, everyone was talking about the new preacher. She'd noticed his nervousness; when he'd stared at her so forlornly, she'd felt compelled—she didn't know why—to try to communicate that he had one friend anyway. While his delivery had been a little awkward, she'd sensed that beneath his anxiety he might have a pleasing personality and wit.

As word spread that Derek Stanton was, indeed, an unmarried man, Jessica watched as eager mothers proceeded to maneuver their eligible daughters for introduction to him. She knew they were all thinking what a fine catch the handsome minister would make.

Naomi Billingsley came to Jessica's table, eyes shining as she boldly asked, "Dear, wouldn't you rather me take Preacher Stanton into my home this week? After all, I know you always have Belinda's kin for dinner at Harvest time, and she was telling us how her new beau from Raleigh is going to be calling, too. I thought it might be easier for you if you didn't have another houseguest."

Jessica was taken by surprise, didn't quite know what to say. She didn't dare admit she was looking forward to having the new preacher around for a week.

"Well?" Naomi asked impatiently. "I'll go speak to your father, if you prefer, but everyone knows you run that house, dear," she brusquely added.

Belinda breezed up just then, holding out her plate for a dollop of salad. Glancing from Naomi Billingsley's anxious face to Jessica's slightly perplexed expression, she asked if anything was wrong. When Naomi quickly explained, Belinda promptly shook her head and said, "Oh, no, we've been looking forward to this, and Jessica has gone to a lot of trouble getting ready. We'll enjoy his visit."

Jessica knew that Belinda understood what she was feeling, that having Preacher Stanton around would ease the tension in the household, if only for a little while. She was probably also thinking that his presence might encourage their father to be on his good behavior when Harmon Willingham arrived. Jessica also noted the way Naomi's eyes narrowed almost angrily, how she suddenly stiffened before icily responding, "I thought you had a new beau, dear!"

Belinda blinked in exaggerated innocence. "What does that have to do with anything, Mrs. Billingsley?"

Jessica turned away lest her amusement show, as Naomi, momentarily taken aback, stammered, "Well—well, I only meant.... If you've made plans, I understand." She turned and hurried away.

Jessica and Belinda looked at each other and burst into giggles as Belinda declared, "He'd never get out of the web she'd spin, for sure. She and Leona would both be like preying spiders, and—" She fell into embarrassed silence as Derek Stanton walked up.

He held out his plate. "What a pleasure," he remarked amiably, "to find myself in the company of two charming ladies—one with a lovely voice...and one who's not afraid of snakes," he added with a twinkle in his eye.

Belinda, puzzled by the latter remark, looked at Jessica, who explained with a shrug, "I was walking Polly Sue back from the outhouse, and I killed a moccasin."

At that, Belinda proudly affirmed, "There's not much my sister is afraid of."

"Your sister?" He glanced from one to the other.

Jessica knew he was thinking how they looked nothing alike—she with her brown hair and brown eyes, and Belinda with her red hair and green eyes. "Yes, but we had different mothers."

"Well, you're both pretty," he said in a way that was not flirtatious but merely honest. "Uncle Dan said Coulter hospitality was wonderful, but he failed to tell me I'd have so many lovely hostesses." He paused, suddenly curious, then, with his usual candor, remarked, "I don't recall being introduced to a Mrs. Coulter. Which one of your mothers—"

"Neither," Jessica cut him off and hastened to add, "they're both dead."

"I'm sorry."

"No need to be," she gently pointed out. "It was a long time ago." Wanting to change the subject, she remarked that she planned to help the school children write a letter to Preacher Dan to wish him a speedy recovery. "He was always so good with them. Whenever he came through, he'd make a point of staying over Sunday night, if possible, just to come to the school on Monday and speak to them, have a little Bible study before he left."

He raised an eyebrow. "You're the schoolteacher here?"

She nodded. "I'm in my second year."

"Well, you don't look like a schoolteacher," he quickly assured her.

At that, Jessica felt her cheeks grow warm, and she realized, with extreme embarrassment, that she was actually blushing for the first time in her life. She was relieved when, just then, Naomi Billingsley appeared once more.

"Preacher, would you honor us with your company for supper tomorrow night?" she asked, grasping his arm.

Derek had already met Mrs. Billingsley's daughter and knew the motive for her invitation, just as he knew the reason for the many requests for his company by other mothers with unmarried daughters on their hands. "Well, I understand Miss Jessica has something special planned for tomorrow night," he hedged, the play of a smile on his lips as he turned mischievous eyes on her in a plea to substantiate his fib.

"That—that's right," she said, catching on. "I was just saying how I'd planned my special chicken and dumplings."

Naomi's mouth became a thin line of vexation. "Perhaps another evening then," she said tightly. "You let me know when you're free."

Pleasantly, Derek explained he would be meeting with the deacons in a little while to go over the list of shut-ins and those needing special counseling, as was the custom. "Everyone is being so kind," he said with a helpless shrug. "So many invitations. I really don't think I'll have time to accept them all, but perhaps I will be able to drop by for tea."

"That would be nice," she conceded, "but do try to fit in an evening for supper."

When Mrs. Billingsley walked away, Jessica gave a mock gasp, touching her fingers to her lips as she cried, "Preacher, I can't believe you actually told a lie and even asked me to back you up!"

"It wasn't a lie," he defended with a grin. "You *are* having a special supper tomorrow night. I've got a feeling all your suppers are special, Miss Jessica."

The three of them were swept with the laughter of camaraderie, as Derek proceeded to confide how being the target of desperate mothers seeking a son-in-law could be annoying at times.

Enchanted by Derek's tall tales, Jessica and Belinda didn't notice Reuben when he came to stand behind them. Derek saw his disapproving glare and fell silent, noticing how a shadow seemed to descend upon Jessica when she turned and saw him. He was also puzzled by the way Belinda at once excused herself, her face also mirroring disappointment over the intrusion.

Reuben glanced from Jessica to Derek and coolly announced, "Well, I didn't mean to interrupt your good time."

Jessica, attempting to be polite, began, "Reuben, have you met—"

Curtly, he interrupted her to say icily, "I'm a deacon in the church, Jessica, or have you forgotten? Of course, we've met." With a detached demeanor, he addressed himself to Derek. "I believe I overheard someone say Preacher Dan might not be well for quite some time. Is that so?"

"I'm afraid it is."

"Then you will be his *permanent* replacement?"

"Probably not. I'd like a church of my own so I can settle down, have my own flock to shepherd," he added blithely, not willing to admit he'd had his fill of traveling.

Reuben ignored the attempt at geniality, and instead crisply remarked, "Someone said you're from New Orleans. Why would you want to settle down in the mountains?"

"You have to ask?" Derek responded with mock incredulity, gesturing with a sweeping wave to indicate the beauty of the Blue Ridge all around them.

Reuben cared neither for his flippancy nor for the almost conspiratorial smile the minister exchanged with Jessica. Not that Reuben was jealous. Jessica was as good as his, and she'd never go against her father's wishes, anyway. He was, however, concerned about the conversation he'd overheard among some of the ladies. Mrs. Billingsley had implied it wasn't altogether proper for Preacher Stanton, a young and unmarried man, to be lodged at the Coulter house where Zeb was dead drunk so much of the time. It was, she'd decreed with a sniff of disdain, almost the same as Jessica and Belinda being with a man unchaperoned, heaven forbid. When someone else suggested Zeb might not imbibe with a man of God around, the gossipy woman had pointed out with a sneer that such scruples certainly had never stopped him when Preacher Dan was his houseguest. The others had agreed.

Reuben decided to let the stranger know exactly where he stood if he had any notions about Jessica. With a smug glance in her direction, Reuben asked, "Can we assume you will be returning at Christmas?"

"I suppose so . . ." Derek began, observing the sudden look of dismay that had come over Jessica as she turned back to her serving table. "I believe the circuit will bring me back around then."

"Good. You see—" Reuben paused for effect, enjoying the moment "—I'm a widower, and since my respectful time of mourning will be over near the holidays, I thought it'd be a nice and sentimental time for me to take a new wife, as well as a mother to my son, Jamie. We haven't announced it yet, of course, because I think it'd be proper to wait till closer to the end of mourning time, but—'' he gave a happy sigh ''—I wanted to make arrangements with you while you're here this trip, so all that will be taken care of.''

Derek guessed that Reuben Walker was telling him it was Jessica Coulter he planned to marry. Yet for some reason he couldn't understand, Derek hoped he might be jumping to conclusions. ''Well, congratulations, Mr. Walker,'' he said with a flourish. ''And who is your bride-to-be?''

Reuben feigned surprise, gave a soft laugh as he reached to catch Jessica's hand and pull her back around to stand beside him. He felt a slight flash of annoyance at her reluctance to do so. ''Why, didn't she tell you? Jessica, here, is going to be the new Mrs. Reuben Walker. Like I said, t'wouldn't be proper to make a formal announcement for a few more weeks, but I don't imagine it will come as a surprise to many, will it, honey?''

Jessica couldn't help but flinch at the endearment, neither could she resist the tide of misery that swept her from head to toe. Grateful for the interruption as someone stepped up to hold out a plate for salad, she jerked from Reuben's grasping hand without responding to his request for confirmation.

But Derek had seen her reaction, felt her abject desolation. He knew his concern for her happiness and welfare went beyond a pastor's concern for the emotions and well-being of his flock. He felt something more, and he wasn't sure it was a good thing.

Reuben stared after Jessica with a frown. She needed a few lessons in obedience, for sure. Turning back to Derek, he confirmed, ''Then we can count on you to officiate at the wedding Christmas Eve. I've decided on that date.''

Derek was still looking at Jessica.

''Preacher?'' Reuben curtly prodded.

Derek forced his attention back to the conversation, chiding himself. ''Christmas Eve, did you say? Yes, I'm sure I can arrange to be here then, if,'' he suddenly, impulsively, felt the need to add, ''it's agreeable to *both* of you.''

Reuben snapped, "Of course it is." What was wrong with this man, he wondered angrily, that he should need affirmation from a woman before accepting the word of a man? Turning to Jessica, he tersely asked, "Are you about done serving? I want you to eat with Jamie and me. I've saved a place at one of the tables."

"No!" Jessica surprised even herself with her own burst of assertion. "No," she repeated. "You go on and eat, Reuben. There's still plenty who haven't been served."

"Very well." He had no choice but to allow her to have her way this time. "I'll see you for supper at your house tonight. We'll have us a talk then."

She ignored him, biting back tears as she wondered for the hundredth time how she'd ever be able to bear having him touch her. God forgive her, but in that moment, she knew she'd rather die than marry him—but to refuse to do so would mean going against the way she'd been raised. *Honor thy father and thy mother,* she'd had instilled in her all her life.

When Reuben had finally left them, Derek suddenly felt awkward, assailed by a maelstrom of strange emotions. He started to take his leave, then hesitated to say, "Miss Jessica, I'll be needing directions to your house. My uncle didn't tell me how to get there."

She told him she'd be glad for him to follow along when she and Belinda left. Her father, she'd noticed, had disappeared, no doubt anxious to begin drinking away his latest disappointing Sunday.

As Derek walked away, carrying his plate of food to join the others, Jessica couldn't help staring after him and dizzily wondering what it was that seemed to draw her to him. She felt comforted by his presence, as though they'd known each other before, were somehow old friends. True, he was a minister, and she supposed that had something to do with the way he made her feel. Yet Preacher Dan had certainly never affected her in that manner. She'd never blushed, for heaven's sake, nor felt an inner fluttering at just his nearness.

There was something about Derek Stanton that was unnerving and upsetting.

Whatever it was, and however sinful it might be to admit it to herself, Jessica knew she liked the feeling.

Chapter Four

Monday morning Derek awoke to the delicious smell of freshly boiled coffee. He rolled out of bed, reveling in the shivery fall air as he stood before the open window, gazing out at the Coulter farm. It was a beautiful place, all right, nestled in the framing arms of the ridges rising to the mountains. Yet he knew it was not a happy home he was visiting.

Last night at supper, tension had been so thick he could have cut it with a butter knife. Zeb Coulter hadn't appeared at all, and Derek didn't believe the flimsy excuse offered by Jessica that her father wasn't feeling well. He'd smelled the whiskey on the man's breath late in the afternoon, and figured he was somewhere in his cups, too drunk to make it to the table. Jessica had looked as if she were going to burst into tears any second. Reuben Walker seemed mad about something, stony faced and pouting. Belinda had excused herself after taking only a few bites, and if it hadn't been for Derek's running conversation with the boy, Jamie, he doubted a word would have been spoken during the meal. He, also, took his leave as soon as politely possible. He'd heard Reuben's wagon going down the road shortly afterward and knew there'd been no socializing.

He turned now from the window and went to the dresser and the waiting pitcher and bowl to wash and shave. As he did so, he thought of Jessica and the hidden spark in her

cinnamon eyes just waiting to ignite in humor and mirth—
except when Reuben Walker was around. Then the shadow
descended, like an invisible cloud of doom. He knew, without a doubt, she didn't want to marry him. Derek wondered how that unhappy betrothal had come about.
Prearranged, no doubt, but why? If Zeb Coulter was going
to pledge either of his daughters, Belinda would seem the
logical choice. Jessica was already established as the community schoolteacher, and it wasn't uncommon for women
in her profession to be spinsters. So why would she be forced
into a marriage she obviously didn't want? It wasn't any of
his business; he'd admit to that. But he'd liked her from the
beginning, when he'd watched the way she defended that
child and herself in a situation that would have made lesser
women swoon. He also found her to be extremely pretty, in
a soft, elegant kind of way. Women he'd known, unfortunately, had too often been like Consuela—lovely, but too
bright, too brazen.

He gave himself a mental shake. Jessica Coulter would
make a good friend, nothing more, and he made a solemn
vow, then and there, not to get involved in her relationships
unless asked to do so in his capacity as preacher. He'd keep
his feelings and opinions to himself.

When he went down to the kitchen, Jessica was bustling
about making ready a huge platter of sausage and scrambled eggs. "Good morning," she greeted him brightly, filling a huge mug with the aromatic coffee. "Did you sleep
well?"

"Wonderful. In case you hadn't guessed, this is my first
preaching assignment, and if all the places I visit are this
nice, I might be tempted not to settle down in my own
church . . . just stay on the circuit for all the side benefits."

She laughed at that. "Well, Preacher Dan never talked
much about the other homes where he stayed, but he always seemed to enjoy himself here. He never left his plate
empty, and that was a compliment." She set a platter of hot
biscuits and a crock of fresh-churned butter on the table.

He noted his was the only place set and asked, "Aren't you having breakfast? And what about Belinda and your father?"

She told him Belinda had already left. "Luther Gaither came by to take her in to the settlement to help in his store. She works there sometimes, and today they've got a wagon load of supplies coming in from Asheville. They need her to help get the shelves stocked."

"And your father?"

She frowned. "Preacher Stanton," she solemnly began, "you might as well know my father drinks. A lot." She then proceeded to tell him about how Zeb believed he'd been cursed, because he had lost three wives and a baby.

Derek shook his head in protest. "It isn't always easy to accept God's will when trials are thrust on us, but He's not a cruel God, and . . ." His voice trailed off in pity for an instant before he went on to lament, "I suppose I should try and talk to him, but if my uncle couldn't do anything all these years, I doubt I'd be of much help."

"You wouldn't," she flatly told him. "He hasn't got any more use for preachers than he has for God."

"Well, that's a shame, because he's not going to find any peace in that bottle."

Jessica glanced at the clock. It was nearly seven. She had to be at the school to ring the bell by eight and said so, adding, "I'm sorry to leave like this. Do you know your way around these parts? Do you need directions anywhere?"

"Let me see. . . ." He reached in his pocket for the list of names he'd been given the afternoon before when he met with the deacons. He couldn't resist saying, "I had intended to go over this with Reuben last night, get all the directions from him, but he didn't seem in a very talkative mood."

"That's just his way," she said, attempting to smooth things over, all too aware that Reuben had indeed been rude and pouting. Though he hadn't come right out and said so, she knew he didn't like Derek Stanton staying there, because he was young and unmarried—and handsome.

Scanning the list Derek held out, she was able to advise that he shouldn't have any trouble finding the people he was to visit. "Old Frank Barnes lives about a half mile down the road, on the left, and he can direct you to the Murphys. They're not too far from him." One name leaped out at her. "Sudie Temple. I didn't know she was sick, but I'm not surprised. She's nearly seventy, but since her only daughter died last summer, it seems as if she's just given up. She's been going downhill ever since.

"You might have some trouble finding her place," she continued. "It's situated on the other side of Hanging Dog Creek, but there's no bridge there anymore. It washed out during a bad storm we had at the end of summer. Sudie's sons want her to move out of there, anyway, since she's been so depressed and poorly. They want to take turns having her live with them and their families, so they haven't bothered to fix it, figuring sooner or later she'll give in. But—" she paused to smile fondly "—Sudie is a stubborn old bird and swears the only way she'll leave her home place is in a pine box. Anyway, the creek isn't terribly deep, but if you don't know where to ford it, your horse might step in a hole and break a leg. You'll need someone to help you cross."

She was standing close to him, and Derek thought how good she smelled—like fresh air after a spring rain. She was wearing a pale green dress that complemented her ginger-colored hair, and he wondered how she'd look if she unfastened the severe bun at the nape of her neck, allowing the silken tresses to flow freely. He gave himself another mental shake for allowing his mind to wander, yet yielded to impulse and asked, "Well, would you have time later today to show me the way? We could take your wagon and mule, if your father wouldn't mind."

Jessica admonished her heart for leaping so foolishly at the idea of riding with him, drew a breath and let it out slowly as she commanded herself to stop behaving like a silly young girl. He was a preacher, a man of God, and she was merely being a good hostess. "Of course," she said when she was finally able to speak in a calm tone of voice. "I'm usually home from school by three, but it will be dark by five-thirty or so. We'd save time if you'd meet me at the school."

"Wonderful," he was quick to agree. "In fact, I'll come around two, if that's all right, and then I can have Bible study with the children. How many do you have?" he wanted to know.

"Seventeen. Ages six to fifteen. They're all good children. I guess the only worry I have is with Polly Sue Packer, the little girl you saw me with yesterday. She's a precious child, and I love her dearly, but when she stutters the other children make fun of her, and it breaks my heart."

Brow creasing with his sudden interest, he asked, "How old is she? Ten? Eleven?"

"Ten."

"Was she born that way?"

"No, and it'd be easier to accept, I think, if she had been, but actually it's a mystery to everybody. It started last summer, when her mother died. She was Sudie's daughter, by the way." She paused for him to grasp that, then continued, "Anyway, I've tried to work with Polly Sue as best I can, and I find that if I can get her to calm down, relax and take deep breaths, she can almost get the words out without stuttering."

Derek nodded, more to himself than to her, then said he'd try to spend a little extra time with her.

"She's a lovely child. You'd enjoy her, I'm sure. Now I've really got to go. You eat all you want, and I'll look for you around two."

She took her wool cape from a hook next to the kitchen door and wrapped it around her shoulders before going out.

Derek watched her and thought how, despite the general gloomy atmosphere that seemed to hang over the household, Jessica brightened the room with her celestial charm. He also found her quite beautiful and appealing.

It would, he wistfully acknowledged, be a constant battle within not to yearn for anything beyond friendship.

Jessica groaned at the sight of Reuben's wagon at the hitching post outside the school. He was waiting just inside, out of the wind. Jamie, she noticed, had already taken his seat at one of the L-shaped wooden desks.

In his usual brusque way, Reuben got right to the point. "I've been doing some thinking, Jessica, and I've decided it'd be best if the preacher moved his things over to the Billingsleys. It doesn't look right, him staying there in the house with you and Belinda, with your pa never around. It's the same as not having a chaperon, and he ought to see it that way himself, but since he doesn't, you'll have to be the one to tell him to move on."

For an instant, she couldn't believe her ears. Then it came to her that he was quite serious, and with a laugh of incredulity she informed him, "Why, I'll do no such thing, Reuben, and I should think you'd be embarrassed even to suggest it."

"Embarrassed?" he echoed. "That's absurd. After all, I *am* your fiancé, even though it hasn't been officially announced, and that does give me certain rights."

She didn't like being reminded of her fate, and his doing so only served to increase her irritation. Bitingly, she reminded him, "Mr. Stanton is, after all, a preacher, and I should think—"

"He's a man!" he interrupted. "An unmarried man with no woman to satisfy his natural needs. Being alone in a house with two young women is a temptation few men could resist."

Indignant rage was starting to boil through her veins as she looked up at him with blazing eyes, her fists clenched. "How dare you say such a thing? And I resent your implication that my sister and I would likewise be tempted! I'll thank you, Reuben, to mind your own business."

Silently, he raged within, thought how she'd pay for her insolence with a buggy whip across her back as soon as the vows of obedience were spoken on their wedding day. "I'll speak to your pa."

"Well, you just do that!" She brushed by him, heading up the center aisle for her desk at the front of the room.

Shaking his fist at her retreating back, he hoarsely cried, "Even the Bible preaches to avoid the appearance of evil, Jessica Coulter!"

Without turning about, she frostily countered, "I seem to recall something in there about casting the first stone...."

"I have no sin," he roared. "I can throw all the stones I want to!" He struck at the air with his fist.

She reached her desk, stood behind it to stare at him in frosty condemnation for a few seconds before offering a mocking smile and responding, "Seems you can throw tantrums, too, Reuben, but please do so away from the school. It's a bad influence on my students."

At that, he furiously turned on his heel and stormed out of the room. Jamie, who'd been pretending to read his primer, raised the book so Miss Jessica wouldn't see his silent giggles.

Jessica had a difficult time focusing her attention on the lessons that morning. Several times she had to blink back tears of frustration and despair as she thought of the gloomy future, her miserable existence as Reuben's wife. It wasn't fair, any of it. She'd studied hard to be able to teach; she wanted her life to continue as it was. She didn't need a husband, and she wasn't at all concerned about one day being truly alone, when Belinda left home as she was sure to do, and her father died. She'd be quite happy in the little log cabin that Miss Satterfield now lived in. It had been built in just one day by the menfolk in the valley and was meant to house the schoolteacher. Actually, Miss Satterfield should have vacated it when she retired, but no one had said anything, because it wasn't needed— Jessica had a home for the moment. And, while she would never admit it to her father, she didn't care about hanging on to the Coulter land any more than Belinda did. That *damn* land, she thought, allowing herself a silent curse, was behind all the misery, anyway. If not for the land, her father wouldn't care if she never married. But she was trapped, and she knew it. And the desolation she felt wasn't helped by having Preacher Stanton around, she privately admitted, because he was so nice, so comfortable to be with; it made her wonder what it would be like to have a husband just like him. Still she would not ask him to leave as Reuben had decreed. And she was certainly not going to say or do anything to let the man know he was arousing in her some terribly confusing feelings. She'd just enjoy his company while he was there and try not to think about anything else. There would, sadly, be time later for rueful thoughts.

As the hour of two o'clock grew closer, Jessica found herself glancing frequently at the clock on the wall. She admonished herself for looking forward to Derek's arrival, yet couldn't help the sudden rush she experienced when the door finally opened and he walked in.

She'd been allowing the children to take turns reading from Charles Dickens's *Nicholas Nickleby*. It was, she knew, a bit difficult in places, but when Polly Sue Packer actually volunteered, Jessica wasn't going to deny her the chance. As a few snickers rippled through the room, she sharply rapped her desk with a ruler in warning. Silence fell, but as it happened, just as Derek walked in, Polly Sue was having a very difficult time saying "Nicholas." In an effort to end the stuttering, the girl changed the pitch of her voice, which resulted in a wave of giggles across the room.

Jessica saw Polly Sue's lower lip quiver and her hands begin to tremble as she held on to the book. Rapping on her desk once more, Jessica used Derek's arrival as a means for the child to escape the nightmare. "We have a guest!" she announced, louder than necessary. To Polly Sue, she softly said, "We'll get back to our reading later. You may take your seat."

Derek proceeded to walk around the room and greet each student individually. Some he had already met in church the day before. He then went to the front and began to tell a story from the Bible. Jessica watched the reaction of the class as they listened. He was not, she privately acknowledged, as good a speaker as his uncle, though she was sure time and experience would remedy that flaw. What did impress her the most, however, was the air of uneasiness in his every word and gesture. It was as though Derek Stanton were trying to convince himself of what he was saying; then she felt guilty over that deduction and told herself her reaction was due solely to being used to the mannerisms of Preacher Dan. Yet Derek had instant rapport with the students, she quickly noted, and when he'd finished his story, they began to raise their hands to make comments and ask questions. The lesson quickly turned into a discussion period, and she stood to one side, leaned back against the wall with arms folded across her chest to watch in pleasure. Seldom had she seen so much interest and participation by her students.

Three o'clock—the hour to ring the bell and end the school day—slipped by, so engrossed was Jessica, along with the others. Derek had launched into yet another tale from the Old Testament, and the children were fascinated by his dramatic storytelling ability. He leaned on the edge of her desk, gestured as he talked, melodramatically changing his voice as he spoke for different characters. Now and then he would walk about the room, waving his arms to make an exciting point.

Jessica later wondered just how long he would have continued had it not been for Josie Barrow's mother coming to see why her daughter hadn't got home yet. Everyone laughed to realize how absorbed they'd become, and several of the students in their teens asked Derek if he'd promise to come back the next day to continue the story. Looking to Jessica for her nod of agreement, he said he would try to fit another visit into his schedule.

When everyone had gone, she praised him effusively. "You really do have a way with them. You're to be commended, Preacher Stanton."

"Please!" he said then, holding up a hand of protest as he laughed. "Call me Derek. I know there are those who wouldn't consider first names between us exactly proper, but I just feel ridiculous having you call me *Preacher* Stanton, or *Preacher* Derek, and I sure don't like thinking of you as *Miss* Jessica. How about it?"

"All right, Derek," she said, liking the sound, liking the feeling that they were more than minister and schoolteacher. To quell the warm stirrings at his nearness, the way he was smiling down at her so intimately, she cleared her throat self-consciously and changed the subject. "So! Do you think you can fit in another visit this week?"

He pursed his lips thoughtfully, reached into his pocket to draw out his list once more. "Let's see. Most of what I've got to do is in the evening. I don't see any reason I can't come back tomorrow, if you'd like for me to."

"I'd love it. So would my students. It's all settled." She went to her desk and began to gather papers for grading that evening. "We'd better be going if I'm to show you the way to Miss Sudie's. Besides," she added with a nervous glance toward the window at the rumble of thunder, "I don't like the sound of that."

Just as they stepped out the door, rain began to fall in torrents. "We'll have to wait it out," Derek said matter-of-factly. "We'd be drenched."

"We'll probably have to wait till tomorrow anyway," she quickly explained. "We shouldn't try to ford that creek after a rain. Maybe we'd just better get some of Miss Sudie's kin to show you the way in the morning."

"If it comes to that..." He let his voice trail off, not wanting to reveal he'd been looking forward to her company more than anything else.

For an instant she wondered about his wistful tone but didn't dwell on it, for suddenly she became aware of how alone they were. They were wrapped in their own cocoon against the elements, as wind and rain slashed at the closed windows and door. The only other sound in the room was their breathing, which seemed to intensify with each new roll of thunder across the sky. Jessica tore herself from his almost hypnotic gaze upon her, went to her desk and began nervously to straighten and rearrange. "Thank goodness, it's not December yet," she began to chatter. "There's a saying if it thunders in December, we'll have a heavy snow within ten days, and goodness knows, we don't need snow this early in the season."

"No, we don't," he said quietly, almost morosely. He felt the need to distance himself from her, for a personal storm was raging within to rival the fury of the one outside. He went to stand across the room and stared through the window at the driving rain.

She rattled on, saying there'd no doubt be times he'd find himself snowed in somewhere on the circuit between the end of December and the end of March, the period when the Blue Ridge experienced the worst winter had to offer. Derek listened, gaze riveted to the world outside, felt a wave of guilt to think how he hoped he'd be snowed in right here, in the valley, near her, and... *Stop it!* he commanded himself, clenching his teeth so hard his jaw ached.

She saw the rigid way he was standing, the set look to his face. He seemed almost angry about something, she mused worriedly, and she was just about to ask if anything was wrong when he all but shouted, "The rain is letting up! We can go now."

She watched as he hurried to the door and flung it open to step outside on the little porch. Gathering her papers once more, she went to join him, and saw that although it had almost completely stopped raining, the road was now a river of mud. "We can't go to Miss Sudie's. The creek will be way up."

"I'll just go tomorrow," he said quietly.

Jessica nodded, murmured, "Yes I think that would be best." Then, somewhat awkwardly, she added, "I guess we'd better get back to the farm now."

"Yes, I guess so."

Neither made a move to walk down the steps, and in that strange, prolonged moment of silence, Jessica felt a sudden wave of fear. But why? What was she afraid of? Never in her entire life had she experienced anything like the feelings coursing between them in that frozen moment of awareness. At last he politely held out his arm to her, and they began to move toward the hitching post, where Jessica had left the mule and wagon tied that morning. Derek's horse waited there too. "I guess," he said slowly, "I'll ride along beside you."

She nodded, didn't trust herself to speak just then.

He helped her up into the wagon, untied the mule and handed up the reins, then mounted his horse. Looking toward the western mountains reaching heavenward, he remarked, "Maybe the storm isn't over yet. I can still hear thunder."

She popped the leather strips over the mule's rump, then she wondered whether what he heard was in fact thunder— or the beating of her heart.

Chapter Five

Zeb hadn't made an appearance by the time Jessica was ready to serve supper, so she and Belinda were able to enjoy Derek's company without tension. They listened, enraptured, as he responded to their questions about his travels and about what it was like living out west and in New Orleans.

It was so easy, Jessica thought as he spoke, to forget he was a preacher. He'd changed from his austere black suit to trousers and a plaid flannel shirt, and he looked comfortable and relaxed. He ate two big helpings of chicken and teased Jessica that she'd made her special dish so she couldn't be accused of having fibbed to get him out of Naomi Billingsley's invitation.

It was a pleasant time, marred only when Belinda, during a rare lull in the conversation, blurted, "I'm going to miss evenings like this after Jessica gets married—" Then, seeing the look that flashed on Jessica's face, she rushed to smooth over her blunder. "What I mean is, nothing is really the same after someone gets married, right?"

"I guess not." Jessica managed a tight smile as she got up to serve the baked apples and fresh cream she'd prepared for dessert. "I've got to get used to the idea myself."

Derek looked from one to the other, well aware of the sudden tension. Belinda moved to refill his coffee mug, as he wondered whether he should make any comment on the subject, but he was spared the decision when the door opened and Zeb walked, or rather, staggered in.

"Pa, you're late," Jessica lightly scolded. "Wash up, and I'll get your plate."

"Don't want nothin'...." He shuffled across the room, heading for the door that led to the hallway. "Ain't hungry." He went on out.

"Sad," Derek murmured with a pitying shake of his head. "I'll try to catch him tomorrow before he hits the bottle again, say a prayer with him."

Belinda was quick to warn, "Well, it won't do any good. He'll probably turn your ears blue with his cussing if you even try."

"I doubt that." A faint smile teased the corners of his lips. "I wasn't always a minister, Belinda."

They finished dessert, talked awhile longer, then Derek said he'd best get to bed.

The moment he was gone, Belinda cried, "Oh, Jessica, I'm sorry I said what I did. We haven't had a chance to really talk about it since that awful scene with Poppa, but you know how I feel. I think it's terrible."

"I know." Jessica was grateful for her concern, as well as her love, but pointed out there wasn't any need in either of them worrying about it. "What's done is done. I tried to explain to Reuben this morning that I don't want to marry him, but it doesn't matter. And he's not fooling me. He may say he wants a wife and a mother for Jamie, but he really wants to get his hands on this land, and we both know it. He doesn't care about anything except having his way.

"The saddest part," she continued after a thoughtful pause, "is that I never thought Poppa would go this far. He's dropped hints since the day Elizabeth Walker died that Reuben and I would make a good match, and every time he said anything, I made it clear I wasn't interested. But his mind is made up that he's going to keep this land in the Coulter family, and how I feel doesn't matter."

"You could run away," Belinda said matter-of-factly, "like I plan to do if Harmon doesn't ask me to marry him."

Jessica laughed softly, but not in ridicule. "We've talked about this before, little sister."

"And like I told you before, I'd go to Richmond. I even know how I'd get there. I'd make my way to Morganton, and from there, I'd go by train, by way of Salisbury and Danville.

"And I don't think I'd have any problem finding a job," she said, rushing on to share her dreams. "There are lots of singing halls there—"

"Is that what they call them?" Jessica interrupted to inquire with the cynical raising of an eyebrow.

Belinda didn't respond to that, instead confiding how she would also change her name. "To something pretty, like Belva. That's French for Belinda. Poppa wouldn't think about that if he came looking for me."

"Well, it sounds like you've got your plans made, but what do you propose for me? I can't carry a tune." Jessica turned away lest her sister see the amusement on her face and think she was mocking.

"Get a job teaching there. You wouldn't have any problem."

Jessica shook her head adamantly. "This is my home. I can't run away."

"Then stay here and be miserable the rest of your life!" Belinda snapped. "Have a baby every nine months for that—that *tyrant*. He'll beat you as he did Elizabeth, may she rest in peace. You said it yourself—she was probably glad to die.

"And you can make fun of me if you want to, Jessica," she hurried on, losing patience, "but I'm not going to stay here and be miserable along with you. There's nothing for me here, not the way Poppa is. Besides, Harmon will ask me to marry him. I pretend otherwise, but a girl knows when a man is serious, and believe me, it's just a matter of time till he proposes, and I'm sure going to say yes."

Jessica faced her, somber once more. "I'm sure he will. You've always had your pick of beaux and could've found yourself a husband long before now, if you'd wanted to." She felt a sudden need to challenge. "But do you love him? Or are you just wanting to escape? And does the fact that he comes from a wealthy family have anything to do with it?"

Belinda gave her long hair a haughty toss, lifted her chin in defiance and crisply replied, "If I'm not totally in love with him, I soon will be. And what difference does it make if I am using him to escape? I'll make him a good wife, and he'll never be sorry he married me. As for his family having money, that's just an added bonus. But you don't have any hopes you can ever love Reuben, and you'll live the rest of your life struggling to eke out a living between this farm and his. Is that all you want out of life?"

Jessica shook her head, blinking back the tears.

Belinda sighed once more, gave her sister a hug and suggested it was best if they just didn't talk about it right then.

Jessica agreed, grateful to end the depressing conversation. Nothing was to be gained by lamenting over her fate. It was sealed.

Jessica extinguished all the candles and lanterns burning in the rest of the house, then sat before her dresser to begin her nightly ritual of unpinning her hair from the austere bun and brushing the waist-length tresses. She felt so terribly melancholy, thinking about Belinda's gloomy philosophy. Maybe she could never love Reuben, and maybe he would be cruel at times. She'd just learn to keep her mouth shut and fill her life with the joy of her students, as well as the babies of her own she would no doubt have. Long ago, during her growing-up years when so much responsibility had fallen on her young shoulders, she'd learned to compensate for disconsolation by telling herself it didn't matter if she wasn't happy—she only asked not to be *unhappy,* and if she didn't think about her lot in life, accepted things as they were, then she could cope.

She was about to go to bed when she heard the sound of horse's hooves; whoever was riding into the yard was riding hard. Gathering her robe around her, she took up the lantern from her dressing table, padded out into the hall and hurried to the front door. Stepping out onto the porch, she held up the light to see the anxious face of Caleb Temple.

"The preacher," he tersely cried, "he's stayin' here with you all, ain't he, Miss Jessica?" She quickly nodded, and he rushed on. "Well, would you wake him up and tell him to get over to my aunt's as quick as he can? I'm goin' after Doc Jasper, but I think she's failin' fast. Tell the preacher he needs to get there and be with her at the last." Then, without waiting for a response, he reined his horse around and dug in his heels to go thundering back toward the road.

Jessica rushed upstairs, knocked on Derek's door and, when she heard him sleepily answer, called, "It's Miss Sudie. You have to get over there at once."

There was the sound of stirring about, and then he was yanking the door open, already in his black trousers and in the process of buttoning a white shirt. By the lantern's glow she could see the intense concern etched on his face as he quickly said, "I'll never be able to find my way there in the dark. Do you think your father would be sober enough by now if you woke him up and asked him to ride with me?"

Regretfully, she shook her head. "It takes more than a few hours' sleep to bring him out of one of his states. I'm afraid he won't be fit for anything till nearly noon." She hesitated, but just for an instant, as it seemed only natural to offer. "I can ride with you. I'll get dressed and meet you downstairs."

"Thanks," he said, relieved. "We'll take my horse. It'll be faster than the wagon."

She hurried to change into a warm woolen dress, not taking time to wind her hair into the usual bun. Instead, she wrapped a knit scarf around her head, then went into the kitchen to find Derek already there. He held the door open for her, and they plunged out into the cold, dark night.

With Derek holding the lantern to guide their way, they crossed the yard to the barn. He quickly saddled and bridled his horse, mounted and pulled her up to sit sideways in front of him. She felt a strange rush as his arms went about her to take the reins, thought how it was the first time in her whole life she'd ever been so close to a man. He was warm against her, and she liked the feel of his broad chest, the strength of his arms as he reached around her to take the reins in his hands.

They rode through the night, guided by the light of a quarter-moon above. A mile down the road, Jessica pointed to the gnarled oak that marked the narrow path that would take them down to the creek and the Temple farm. She wondered all the while whether it was concern for Miss Sudie that made Derek seem so tense—or the fact their bodies were so close together as they rode. Was he experiencing the same, strange feelings that were coursing through her in an almost frightening way? She chided herself for liking the needling ripples of pleasure, but then a little voice within assured her that she had no reason to feel guilty, for her reaction was perfectly normal. She was a woman, he was a man. It was only if she ceased to keep her feelings secret and under control that it could be wrong.

Derek told his burning conscience that he should feel no guilt for the way he felt with Jessica so close. Temptation of the flesh was nothing to be ashamed of, he knew. The problem came in mustering strength to deny and resist such temptation, which was something he'd been having trouble with since beginning his new life. Maybe he should find himself a wife, if for no other reason than to satisfy his natural urges. A pity, he bemoaned, that Jessica was promised to someone else. Otherwise, he knew he'd be thinking about courting her, for never in his life had he known a woman who affected him so—and not just for pleasures of the flesh. He enjoyed her company, found her charming, witty and intelligent, and, yes, he'd been touched by witnessing the special way she had with children. What a perfect couple they would make—he, a minister, she, a schoolteacher. An idyllic marriage, for sure. And maybe, with such a life mate, he'd overcome his feelings of inadequacy as a minister of God. Perhaps his prayers would be answered and he'd feel that his mother's dying wish had actually been God calling him to His service. Derek didn't like the nagging within that filled him with self-doubt. Yet, there was nothing he could do about either of his problems for the moment, so, hoping to ease the tension, he attempted conversation. "How many sons does Miss Sudie have?" he asked.

"Five." She didn't recognize the voice as her own, so shaken was she with the nearness of Derek.

"And Polly Sue lives with one of them?"

She took a deep breath and let it out slowly, hoping her nervousness would not show. "Bert. She lives with her Uncle Bert and Aunt Violet. Her father was so grief-stricken, he didn't even attempt to keep the family to-gether. He just wandered off. Nobody knows where he is. It's a pity.... I wish one of the others would've taken her in, but she was the oldest of five, and it seems nobody ever wants an older child. They were all eager to take the little ones, though, especially the baby."

"And what's wrong with Bert and Violet?" Derek asked.

"Violet is a bit too strict, to my way of thinking. So's Bert. Their other children, Betsy and Willy, aren't old enough to go to school yet, but I see them in church, and they're like little shadows—they never smile, never laugh or giggle, they're just ramrod straight like their parents. It's sad, and it's not a good situation for Polly Sue, when she's already developed this speech problem."

He was thoughtful for a moment, then said, "I'll make it a point to go by and see them one evening, give them a chance to talk about any problems they might be having."

"Can't hurt," she murmured, unable to deny yet an-other delicious wave as he reined the horse into a sharp curve, and his right arm brushed harder against her. She was relieved to see the light through the trees ahead, could hear the gurgling waters of the creek. "It isn't much farther," she said.

They reached the bank, and in the dim moonlight she could see that the waters had receded since the downpour earlier in the day. Jessica knew exactly where to ford, and guided him among the rocks. "I'm sure the Temple boys will be busy at first light repairing the bridge," she pointed out, "especially if Miss Sudie passes away. There'll be so many people calling."

"Well, it seems that might be the case," he agreed quietly, as the horse stepped out of the water and onto the bank.

The cabin was situated on a slight knoll, and several oil lanterns had been prominently positioned along the porch railings. Saffron light eerily illuminated the faces of the few people gathered there in the chill of night, watching as Derek and Jessica approached.

As Derek dismounted, then moved to help Jessica down, she saw Nate Temple walking toward them, a grim look on his face. "Nate . . ." she said hesitantly, holding out her hand, "you remember Preacher Stanton."

Nate nodded, shook Derek's hand, then somberly informed him, "Seems you're too late, Preacher. Momma couldn't wait for you. She's gone."

"I'm very sorry." Derek held onto Nate's hand, then suggested, "Would you like to gather the family for a prayer?"

"Ain't too many here yet, Preacher, but I reckon it'd be nice for those what are."

Gently, Jessica offered, "I don't think anyone realized just how sick your mother was, Nate. It happened fast, didn't it?"

He nodded dully. In an unwavering voice he explained, "She's been up and down since my sister died. It weren't no surprise."

Derek felt the need to explain why he hadn't got by sooner, how they'd felt the creek would be difficult to ford.

"It was," Nate assured him. "That's why Lulie, Caleb's wife, didn't go after nobody when she saw Ma seemed feebler than usual. She was afraid of the high water, herself. My brother, he'd been to Asheville, and when he got home and his younguns told him their ma wasn't back, he took off over here and then went after us and the doctor. Ma passed on, Lulie said, just a few minutes after he left. She was gone when I got here." He turned to Jessica. "I reckon since ain't many of the womenfolk got here yet, Lulie would appreciate your helpin' with Ma."

Jessica did not hesitate to oblige. She had helped prepare a few bodies for the grave in the past and knew what had to be done.

The dwelling, which Jessica had visited many times through the years was known as a "dog trot," two rooms on each side of a narrow hallway that ran from front door to back door. The parlor was to the left, connected to a small dining room, with a porch kitchen to the rear. Two bedrooms were to the right.

Lulie Temple was grateful when Jessica offered to take care of laying out Miss Sudie. She hurried off to the porch kitchen to make coffee and start preparing food for the horde that would gather as word of the death spread through the valley and the ridges.

Jessica busied herself, bathing Miss Sudie by candlelight and dressing her in the shroud set aside years ago for this time, as was the custom of the elderly.

Finally, it was done. Jessica laid coins on Miss Sudie's eyelids to close them forever, then covered the body with a sheet to await the arrival of Ben Daughtry, the local undertaker, who would be bringing the coffin.

She was exhausted. Light had begun to streak the sky in the east. Gratefully, she took the mug of steaming coffee Lulie had ready for her. She gulped it down quickly, knew she had to be getting home. While the Temple family would be in mourning and busy preparing for the funeral, her own life had to go on, which meant ringing the school bell in only a few hours.

Retrieving her cape from where she'd left it in Miss Sudie's room, she moved quietly about to speak with the family members who had arrived during the past few hours. She promised the women she'd return after school to help with whatever needed doing.

She found Derek on the porch, where lanterns still burned, but already the first light of dawn was chasing away the night shadows. "I'll take you home," he said, without being asked. "Then I'll come back."

Neither spoke the entire way to the farm. It was only when they'd dismounted inside the barn, that the tension and emotion both had been struggling to suppress, managed to surface. He had helped her alight by placing his hands about her waist and setting her on her feet. But when her toes touched the ground, he found he could not, at once, let her go. Time seemed to stand still as he continued to hold her, so close she could feel the warmth of his breath upon her face. Their eyes met and held in sudden, silent awareness, both overcome with the emotion that had isolated them from reality.

Jessica felt a quickening, wondered what it would feel like to have his lips on hers, dared to actually want his kiss.

Derek felt a great roaring within his body, as well as his heart, as he held her so dangerously, so tantalizingly close. She was gazing up at him with frightened eyes, but he could see, within the spicy cinnamon depths, that she was experiencing the same emotions of desire that were boiling through his veins. *No!* his brain screamed. *Don't do it! Don't get involved.* Yet his heart was crying out for him to fervently claim her mouth in a kiss.

Derek was weakening. Every nerve within him was on fire. One kiss. For all time. He couldn't deny himself.

In that tumultuous instant Jessica told herself to pull away, yet she was mesmerized by his caressing eyes, magically frozen in his grasp and delighting in the sensation.

They moved to kiss, each yielding, but at that precise moment, the sound of footsteps outside caused Derek to release her abruptly.

He turned back to the horse and began to loosen the cinch and unsaddle.

Jessica nervously cleared her throat, smoothed her skirt as she unconsciously moved to distance herself from him.

"Jessica? You in here?"

She drew in her breath, stifling a moan as she recognized Reuben's irate voice. "Yes," she had no choice but to reply.

He stepped into the barn, cold, suspicious eyes darting from her to Derek, who was continuing to work with his horse and did not turn around. "I thought that was you I saw ridin' with the preacher up the road, so I came over to find out what in thunderation is goin' on at the crack of dawn."

"Sudie Temple died last night. I showed Preacher Stanton where to ford the creek. Pa was passed out drunk." She clenched her fists at her sides, hating herself for explaining, justifying, for she was assailed by a rebellious flash. It wasn't any of his business—yet—what she did! Their betrothal hadn't been announced. His expected year of mourning wasn't even over yet, so what right did he have to barge in and ask questions? Yet she knew part of her anger was frustration, for she was sure Derek had been about to kiss her, and she wondered with a warm glow what it would've been like.

"Next time," he said tersely, "when there's an emergency in this family, you send the preacher to fetch your future husband."

Infuriated and humiliated, Jessica gathered her skirts to brush by him, head high. She didn't like being chastised like a child in front of someone, especially Derek.

Reuben watched her walk away, then looked at Derek Stanton once more. He was rubbing down his horse, obviously ignoring Reuben's presence. So be it. That showed he knew his place. Jessica would damn well know hers, too, once he had that ring on her finger—the ring he'd yanked off Elizabeth's swollen finger before they nailed down the lid on her coffin. He turned on his heel and left.

Derek sighed and shook his head wistfully.

One kiss.

For all time.

That was all he had wanted from her. He would gladly have done penance for the pleasure.

Chapter Six

Jessica was exhausted after her sleepless night. The school day seemed endless, and she gave the students many assignments to read, so she wouldn't have to work quite so hard.

As they studied, she allowed her mind to drift back to the annoying scene with Reuben in the barn that morning. Thank goodness, propriety demanded he keep the wedding plans secret till the anniversary of his wife's death. Otherwise, she knew it would be next to impossible for her to have any time at all with Derek. No matter, that their relationship could never go beyond friendship, she was enjoying herself for the first time in her life. It meant so much to share intelligent conversation with a man, to talk of worldly things beyond the Blue Ridge. Jessica read everything she could get her hands on, always had. Books were her solace in those years when she'd been denied childhood due to the responsibilities thrust upon her. Now, it was a treat to be around someone with whom she felt she could discuss any topic. At least, that was what she was telling herself. In reality, she had to admit she just enjoyed being with Derek for himself. Charming, witty, handsome, he was like a rainbow after a summer storm. And there was no denying, either, the way he set her pulse to racing, her heart to pounding. And was it so wrong, she asked her nagging conscience, to feel that way about him? Soon, she'd be married to a man she could never love, would probably secretly loathe. So why shouldn't she seize the opportunity to enjoy a man's company for the only time in her life? No harm could come of that, and whether Reuben liked it was of no consequence. She was still free to live her life as she chose... if only for a little while longer.

When she took the class outside for recess, she noted the thick, gray bank of clouds looming above the ridges to the west. The air was bone-chilling cold, and there was a definite smell of impending snow. She knew if she wanted one more harvest of ginseng before the snows came, she needed to make her trek today to the secluded spot where it grew so abundantly. She had managed, so far, to keep that spot secret, for seng, as it was called by the mountaineers, was in high demand. But first, she'd have to go back to the Temple cottage and once more pay her respects and deliver the two fried chickens she'd found time to prepare before leaving for school that morning.

At five to two, she dismissed the class, citing threatening skies as the reason. Actually, she knew from her years in the Blue Ridge that snow probably wouldn't start falling till late in the day, but she needed an excuse to leave early herself.

Hurrying home, she packed the crispy chicken in a basket, then headed straight for the cabin.

She wasn't at all surprised to see the bridge had been repaired and the yard filled with wagons, carts, horses and mules. She spotted Derek's palomino at the same instant she felt a thrill to know she was about to see him again. That morning, after Reuben's sudden and unpleasant appearance in the barn, she'd not had a chance to speak with Derek. When he came into the house, he'd gone straight up to his room, declining breakfast, saying he'd like to take a nap before going back to be with the Temple family.

She nodded to those gathered on the front porch, and thought how awful it would be if there were a heavy snow. Folks couldn't be outside, and the grave diggers would have a terrible time working in the frozen earth. Inside, the hall was also crowded, and she moved to the parlor, knowing before she entered what she would see. The coffin, set between burning candles, dominated the room. A few chairs had been positioned next to it, where family members could take turns receiving condolences.

Jessica passed through to the porch kitchen, which was crowded with women. There was food everywhere. Huge tin washtubs were filled with fried chicken, and she added hers. The table was laden with bowls of potato salad, sweet potatoes, deviled eggs, ham and sausage biscuits. There were platters of sandwiches too numerous to count, and cakes and pies and cookies and fried apple and pear turnovers. The atmosphere was the same as that in other households she'd visited after the death of someone old: the death was expected, accepted, and provided the occasion for a family reunion, a picnic, as it were.

Lulie Temple saw Jessica and hurried over to give her a grateful hug. "Thank you for what you did. I'm afraid I just wasn't able. Things just sort of got to me, and—"

"No need to apologize, Lulie. You'd been through enough. I didn't mind. It had to be done." She glanced around. "I knew the Temples were a large family, but even so, I thought I'd met them all. I'm seeing some unfamiliar faces."

"I don't think you ever met the kin from Hendersonville. They were Pa Temple's clan." She proceeded to walk Jessica around and make introductions.

All the while, Jessica was thinking that she had to leave soon if she were to get to the ridge before the snow began. She began to work her way back toward the parlor, intending to slip away, when the sound of a child sobbing out on the back porch caused her to turn curiously in that direction.

Through the screen door, she saw it was Polly Sue Packer crying. She was sitting cross-legged on the ground, and her Aunt Violet was kneeling in front of her, the woman's face contorted with rage. She was gripping the girl's shoulders and shaking her so hard her head was bobbing to and fro as her aunt ordered, "Shut that up, do you hear? Shut it up, I say! You're a big girl, and you're being ridiculous, and I won't have it, do you hear me?"

Polly Sue began to cry harder.

Violet Temple stood up, grabbed one of Polly Sue's pigtails and gave it a vicious yank as she ordered, "Get up! Do you hear me? I said for you to get up! We're going out back of the shed, and I'll teach you to mind me!"

Jessica could stand by no longer. She pushed open the screen door and stepped onto the porch. Struggling to keep down her temper, she managed to ask in an even tone, "Is something wrong, Violet?"

"Nothing I can't handle!" Violet snapped back. Polly Sue had got to her feet, and was leaning toward her aunt to ease the painful tugging on her braid.

Jessica moved closer. "But what's the problem? I've never known Polly Sue to be any trouble. What on earth is wrong?"

Embarrassed to have an outsider witnessing a family problem, Violet released her grip on Polly Sue's hair and turned to face Jessica in her fury. "She acted the same way when her momma died. She didn't want to kiss her goodbye. Granny had to make her, she did, had to hold her by the nape of her neck and shove her face down into that coffin, with her screamin' all the time. Well, now it's her turn to kiss Granny goodbye, and she's going to do it—"

"No, she isn't!"

Both Violet and Jessica turned at the sound of Derek's commanding voice. He had been standing inside the door listening, and like Jessica, he couldn't resist attempting to help the child. Stepping onto the porch, he walked over to take Polly Sue's hand and draw her away from her aunt. Then he knelt beside her, brushed away her tears and softly told her, "It's all right, now. You don't have to be afraid."

Suddenly, Violet exploded. "Preacher, I'll thank you to stay out of my family business. Now I told her to kiss her granny goodbye, and she's goin' to. The other children obeyed.''

For the moment, he ignored her outburst as he continued to minister to Polly Sue. She was still trembling, fighting to hold back fresh tears. "You go find your cousins, and you play for a little while. Then we'll talk, all right?''

She nodded, looked fearfully at her aunt, then turned and ran from the porch, disappearing around the side of the cabin. Only then did Derek stand and face the wrath of Violet Temple. "Now let me tell you something," he said sternly. "You're wrong, very wrong, to force her to kiss her dead grandmother. Children are confused by death, puzzled and afraid. When you force something like that on them, it can have terrible effects later. And what's the purpose?" he challenged, steely eyes upon her.

Violet looked from him to Jessica, who'd joined him in looking at her so condemningly. "Why—why—" She groped for an explanation. "It—it's paying respect." Her chin jutted up defiantly. "I kissed all my kin when they died.''

"Well, that was your choice, but you've no right to force anyone else to do the same, especially a child.''

Violet gave an exaggerated sigh. She didn't want to argue with the preacher, but neither did she like his interference. "You know, you're making it very difficult for me. Granny told Polly Sue that God would punish her for the way she didn't want to kiss her own mother, and if you, a man of God—" she paused for emphasis "—let her get away with being disobedient, it's going to make her believe God doesn't punish folks.''

Derek glanced at Jessica. He could see by the look in her eyes that she shared his indignation over such a concept. He was thinking of something else, too—that Polly Sue's stutter might be the result of the bewildered child's believing God was punishing her. He took a deep breath, offered a quick silent prayer for guidance in choosing the right words, then said to Violet, "I don't go along with your theory, Mrs.

Temple. Our God is a merciful God, and I feel He would be very sympathetic to the fright and bewilderment of a young child. I'm asking you to let it go. Just don't say anything else to Polly Sue about kissing her grandmother goodbye. If she sees her cousins, or her brothers and sisters doing it, and wants to do likewise, fine. Otherwise, leave her alone. Please.''

Violet pursed her lips and looked at him with narrowed, reproachful eyes. She thought he was wrong but didn't want to say so. It was easier, she figured, to just do as he asked and let it go. "Very well," she said tightly, "if you think it's best.''

"I do." He offered a patronizing smile, reached to clasp her hand in both of his. "This is a trying time for you, I know, but belive me, it's best for Polly Sue.''

After Violet hurried back into the house, Jessica couldn't resist saying, "Thank you for standing up to her that way.''

"Somebody had to," he said matter-of-factly.

Jessica was quick to point out, "Well, she never would've listened to me, or anybody else.''

"I was thinking," he said, more to himself than to her. "What Violet said about Granny having told Polly Sue that God would punish her for not wanting to kiss her dead mother goodbye..." He looked at her sharply and asked, "Didn't you tell me it was right around the time her mother died that she started stuttering?''

"Yes, but—''

"That might be it." He snapped his fingers. "It's worth a try.''

Puzzled, Jessica followed him as he rushed down the steps into the yard and rounded the cabin in search of Polly Sue.

They found her way down by the creek, where she'd gone to sit on the bank despite the chilling wind. As they approached, she looked up in fright, then a look of relief came over her face. Jessica stood back while Derek sat down beside her. For a few moments he didn't speak, just let her become used to his presence, then slowly, and in a calm friendly voice, he began to talk. "Your aunt isn't going to make you kiss your grandmother goodbye, Polly Sue."

Polly Sue looked relieved, and there was a trace of a grateful smile on her lips, but she remained silent.

Derek picked up a dried pine needle, chewed it thoughtfully for a few seconds, then quietly remarked, as though merely thinking out loud, "You know, Polly Sue, I disagree with what your granny said about how God would punish you for not wanting to kiss your mother goodbye. He's not like that."

Sharply, she turned to gaze up at him, and there was no mistaking the hope in her eyes. "Are you sure?"

"I'm sure." He nodded, still chewing on the pine needle as he stared across the creek into the woods beyond. "And I'm also sure He understood that you were scared, and that it was your grandmother who asked you to do it, anyway. Not Him. It wasn't as if you were breaking one of His commandments, so He had no reason to punish you."

"He—He didn't?" she ventured to ask, hungrily searching his face for confirmation that it was really so.

He shook his head again. "No. As I said, He had no reason. You weren't being disobedient, or sassy. It was just something you didn't want to do, for reasons of your own, and frankly, I don't think your granny had a right to ask you to do it, if you were against it."

She swallowed hard, took a deep breath. "You don't?"

"No, and I think your aunt is wrong, too, and I told her so, and she's not going to bother you about it anymore." He turned to flash an assuring grin, reached to give her braid a playful tug. "So. You've got nothing to worry about. Why don't you go play with your kin and forget about it? Sneak yourself a drumstick out of the kitchen and go have fun."

"I will. And thank you, Preacher Stanton." She jumped up and ran skipping toward the cottage, happier than she could remember ever being.

Jessica stared after her in wonder and murmured, "She didn't stutter. Not once."

"No, she didn't." Derek got to his feet, and brushed pine straw off his trousers.

Awed and impressed, she declared, "You were so perceptive, realizing that was the root of her problem."

With humility, he explained, "It was just a guess, but when the pieces fit together, I decided it was worth a try. All she needed was for someone to tell her that her speech problem wasn't a punishment from God, but that wasn't going to happen till someone was able to figure out her way of thinking. I'm glad I did."

"But you have an extraordinary way with children, anyway. I saw that in class yesterday. They were hanging on to your every word. Preacher Dan never had that effect. They were even asking today when you'd be back."

He was pleased to have been received so well but regretted having to admit it wouldn't be possible for him to make a return visit this time on the circuit. "The family has set the funeral for Thursday afternoon, which means I've only got tomorrow and Friday for my regular visits."

"I'm sure the children will understand."

"Well, maybe next time."

In that prolonged moment of silence, their eyes met and held. Jessica wondered about his perplexing, almost troubled expression, as he debated over the confusion in hers. At last, he was the first to bring them out of their musings. "Well, I guess we'd better get back inside. If you can stay a while longer, I'll hitch my horse to the back of your wagon and go back with you."

"I wish I could," she declared so adamantly that for an instant, she was embarrassed and rushed to cover herself. "I mean, I'd like to, but I've got to be going." She told him about the need to harvest the ginseng because of the ominous snow clouds.

He listened as he walked with her to where she'd left the mule and the buckboard wagon. "Sounds interesting," he said finally. "I've heard of ginseng but never seen any. Maybe one day you'll take me with you."

He had touched her arm, as he was about to help her up into the wagon, and she felt as though she'd been burned. Not really meaning to, she jerked away, reached out and hoisted herself quickly up into the seat.

Taking the reins, she didn't dare look at him, for she was thinking she'd never be able to share the secret of the ginseng with him, or anything else, for that matter, because once he left this time, they'd never know another moment of quiet communication. On his next visit he would perform the marriage ceremony of her and Reuben. Thoughts of that event provoked a feeling of dread and nausea from deep within.

No, never again, would they know such warm friendship, and that made her very sad.

She was able to whisper only a faint word of parting, then, almost roughly, she snatched the reins to turn the mule toward the creek.

Derek stared after her, bewildered by her sudden change of mood, from friendliness to despondency. He was almost positive it had something to do with her pending betrothal to Reuben Walker. And it wasn't fair. Not for a wonderful girl like Jessica. Maybe, in some cases, when a girl was homely, or dependent, unable to care for herself, then it was justified for a parent to step in to ensure that she have a husband. But not Jessica. She was well educated, mature, quite able to fend for herself. She was also pretty enough that he doubted she'd have any trouble finding a husband on her own, if she chose to do so. He had an idea, however, that she'd been denied her youth by the responsibilities thrust upon her by her father. Now, at the thought that she was going to be coerced into marrying someone she didn't love, Derek's heart went out to her. And not just for charitable reasons. He'd realized in the short while they'd known each other that he cared for her. Really and truly cared for her. And though he'd vowed not to become involved with a woman ever again, the past days of enjoying Jessica's company had gnawed away at all those resolutions.

If, he pondered almost angrily as he turned toward the cabin, Jessica truly didn't want to marry Reuben Walker, then he, as her minister, had a right to intervene on her behalf, did he not? That was part of his job as shepherd to his flock.

He went to speak once more with the Temple sons, in turn, explaining he had another call to make but would return in the evening. All the funeral arrangements had been made, so there was nothing else to discuss there, anyway. He knew he just needed to be around should anyone wish to talk to him about their grief.

He rode quickly back to the Coulter farm. Belinda was in the kitchen, making a pot of tea, and when he asked about Jessica's whereabouts, she said she didn't know. She'd only got home a few moments ago, and Jessica had already been gone. "Ginseng," he said then, hoping not to sound desperate or anxious. "Where would she go to pick ginseng?"

She motioned him to follow her to the back porch, and then she pointed toward the barn, and the sweeping ridge stretching skyward just beyond it. "There's a path among the rocks. She'd have gone that way." Giving him a quizzical look, she couldn't resist asking, "But what's wrong? Why do you need to see her right now?"

"Oh, no reason, really." He tried to sound nonchalant. "She just said she'd like to show me her ginseng sometime."

"Funny," Belinda softly remarked. "She's never even shown *me*. That's a closely guarded secret."

But Derek hadn't heard. He was already on his way.

The climb was arduous, and he soon understood why it wouldn't be wise to take such a hike in the snow. He wound his way up, easily able to follow her trail. At last, he spotted her, near the top. He called out to her, lest he take her by surprise and frighten her.

Recognition was a wide grin of welcome on her face. "How on earth did you find me?" she called.

He scrambled to catch up, explaining when he reached her that Belinda had pointed him in the right direction but had admitted the location of the ginseng was a longtime secret.

It was a long trek up to the peak of the ridge, and they were so busy picking their way among the rocks and keeping surefooted along the trail that there was no time for conversation. But by the time they reached the top, Derek was ready to explode with the wonder of it all. "My dear God!" he cried in reverence, slowly turning all the way around in a sweep of the mountainous landscape and the majestic peaks on the horizon. "I've never seen a view like this. In all my travels, I've never seen anything like it."

Proudly, Jessica pointed out Mount Mitchell, considered the highest point of the Blue Ridge Mountains and so named for Elisha Mitchell who had died exploring it. Then she told him of the natural bounty of the land. Like the Cherokee Indians, she knew how to gather native plants for their medicinal value—bloodroot, snakeroot, sassafras, dogwood, balsam, mayapple and raspberries.

Shivering against the biting wind that swept across the ridge, she gestured to the ominous black-gray clouds rolling above them. "We really need to hurry. If the snow comes, I don't want to be up here."

Kneeling, she searched among the fallen leaves and underbrush, then found what she was looking for. Derek knelt beside her as she pointed to a golden plant, different from any other around it. Deftly, she dug down with her hand and produced its odd-shaped root. She explained, "This is what we're after. The root. It's called 'green gold' and it's one of the world's rarest and most valuable plants. Mountain people have been gathering it to make extra money since the 1700s. It takes a lot of plants to produce much dried root, though. Two ounces of fresh ginseng dries up to only about a quarter of an ounce, and it's bought by the pound."

"What do you do with it?" he asked.

"I sell it to Luther Gaither at the settlement store, and then he sells it to a Chinaman in Asheville. The Chinese, by the way, are the ones who gave it its name. Ginseng means 'man-shaped,' because the root resembles the shape of a man. They use it as some sort of rejuvenating tonic. I don't make a great deal of money, but what I do make I set aside for the time when Belinda gets married. I want her to be able to have a nice wedding gown, a hope chest filled with linens and things for her new home."

Derek could not resist the impulse to ask, "What about your own?"

She blinked, not understanding at first what he meant, for she tried with every fiber of her being to push back all thoughts of her sealed fate. Then, realizing what he was asking, she was caught off guard and clumsily countered, "Oh, that doesn't matter...." Her voice trailed off, and she flushed to realize her own innuendo.

They were kneeling, side by side, as he helped her to gather the ginseng. He looked at her then in quiet contemplation as the confirmation of his suspicion washed over him. "It doesn't?" he asked quietly, as he slowly got to his feet.

Jessica also rose, brushing self-consciously at her skirt. "I mean..." she floundered, desperate to cover for the slip of her tongue, "that I'm older, and, well, it's just more important for Belinda to have a nice wedding."

He stood so close, they were almost touching, and Derek searched her face for reaction as he dared to press deeper. "Could it be that your own wedding doesn't matter because you don't want to marry Reuben Walker?"

She shook her head ever so slightly, and hedged. "I—I don't know what you mean."

Suddenly he reached to cup her chin in his hand, forcing her to meet his commanding gaze. "I think you do. The truth is, you don't love Reuben Walker, and you don't want to marry him, do you?" She tried to turn her head, but he held her steadfast. "The truth, Jessica."

Tears stung her eyes as she whispered in miserable admission, "No. No, I don't. But Poppa made a pact with him, and I don't have any choice."

Incredulous, he admonished, "Oh, yes you do. You don't have to marry a man you don't love. You're a grown woman. No one can force you to do anything you don't want to do."

"You don't know how it is," she cried, staring up at him with wild, beseeching eyes. "When a girl's father promises her in marriage, it's a pact, and she has to honor it, and—"

He silenced her with a kiss, no longer able to deny the longing. His lips touched hers, as gently as a butterfly whispering to a rose. Then, with the quickening of his desire, his tongue began to trace a warm line between her lips, urging, coaxing them apart. Jessica froze in utter terror at first, for she'd never been kissed before. But slowly pleasure replaced fear. She shuddered with surrender, and his tongue plunged into her mouth, caressing and stroking. His arms moved to wrap her in an embrace, holding her tightly against him. And Jessica's hands, suddenly with a will of their own, slowly moved to clutch his shoulders in near desperation.

An eternity later, when he finally, reluctantly pulled his mouth from hers, their breathing was coming in frosty gasps. The first gentle snowflakes had begun to fall, touching their faces in cold awareness of newborn emotions. For long moments, they could only look at each other in reverent wonder.

Derek was waging a private battle, telling himself it could only mean trouble if he didn't keep a tight rein on his heart. She was promised to another by a rigid code of the mountains, and if he dared try to oppose it, word would spread, and he'd be finished as a circuit rider. Everyone would condemn him. Yet he knew within himself that what he was feeling for Jessica went deeper than attraction between a man and a woman. He feared, God help him, that he was falling in true love for the first time in his life.

Jessica had never known such confusion. Did his kiss speak of love? she wondered. Or merely desire? And was it wrong for her to feel as she did about him? So many questions to be answered, and how could she think above the roaring of her heart? "I think," she said finally, in a voice so nervous it was alien to her own ears, "that we'd better go back."

He nodded slowly, unnerved by the thought dancing in his mind that, where his feelings for her were concerned, there would be no going back.

Chapter Seven

At breakfast the next morning, Jessica didn't fail to notice that Derek ate quickly and left when Belinda did. He was as polite and charming as always, but it was obvious he did not want to be alone with her. In the wake of their new and stirring awareness of each other, she could understand the need to avoid temptation. Nothing in her world, she knew, would ever be the same again. She had tasted the sweetness of her first kiss and felt the embracing arms of a man who could send shivers down her spine with just a warm glance, or an accidental touch in passing.

Despite her inexperience with men, Jessica instinctively knew that Derek cared for her. The kiss on the ridge had affirmed that. And when, at last, she had gone to bed the previous night, she had lain awake for long hours to stare into the darkness and relive each second of the time they were together. Never would she forget the way he'd caressed her with his eyes as he'd gazed at her before their embrace. Something shining within the coffee-colored depths told her the light came all the way from his heart. She knew, beyond a doubt, she returned that intensity of emotion.

She dared to think of what it would be like to marry Derek and share his life, his ministry. The night she and Belinda had enjoyed his company so much during supper, he'd wistfully confided that he would like to have a small church of his own one day, so he could leave the circuit and settle down, have roots somewhere, take a wife and have a family. It seemed like a wonderful life. Derek would make a loving husband and doting father. How much fun it might be, ministering together to the congregation. Maybe she could even teach somewhere.

But Jessica sadly was forced to remind herself that it was a waste of time to dream such dreams. Her future was set.

Meanwhile, Derek supposed it was an ironic blessing in disguise that he was unexpectedly experiencing his first funeral as a minister, for no one would wonder why he wore an expression of gloom or suspect he was suffering personal grief and turmoil.

He tormented himself by thinking how much he would have enjoyed being with Jessica and her pupils again. Telling exciting stories from the Scriptures to children was much more fun than preaching of fire and brimstone. He'd even thought a few times during his studies at the seminary of maybe one day teaching a Bible class. He liked working with young people, and he had been delighted to find Jessica shared his interests.

She was, beyond a doubt, the most wonderful woman he had ever met, possessing everything a man could want in a life mate. But the confirmation of his suspicions that she didn't love Reuben, much less want to marry him, only complicated matters. He knew, despite everything, he should give up, cast all thoughts of her from his mind, but he was helpless against the callings of his heart. When he'd kissed her, she had momentarily resisted. He'd felt her indecision and fright. But when she yielded, he'd felt more than rising passion, and had thought of little since as he pondered whether she might truly be falling in love with him. And he had to be sure, absolutely sure, before he approached her father and asked for her hand.

He was fairly confident that Zeb Coulter had his mind set on her marrying Reuben, but maybe, he dared hope, Zeb just wanted her married, and didn't care to whom. It was understood in the mountains that a father liked to see his daughter married as early as possible to ensure her future security. Zeb might be just as willing to have Jessica married to Derek as to Reuben. He didn't know, but he intended to find out, as soon as he could be sure in his own mind what Jessica was really feeling for him. Till that happened, however, he was going to make sure he avoided any chance of another intimate encounter like the one on the ridge. His bitter experience with Consuela had painfully taught him to go very, very slowly in affairs of the heart, lest he wind up once more feeling like a fool. After all, he told himself, he hadn't known Jessica very long. Although his first impression was one of beauty and intelligence and quiet refinement, he still intended to make sure he didn't get burned again. Besides, he was well aware that as a preacher he was held up for scrutiny more than most men; the last thing he wanted was to be criticized and condemned for attempting to court a woman already betrothed.

He waited till the last possible moment to show up for Wednesday supper and only appeared out of politeness, because he was expected. After he'd said grace, he announced to no one in particular that Sudie Temple's funeral would take place at four o'clock the next day.

Belinda remarked, "That's a bit soon, isn't it? I mean, most folks are buried on Sundays."

He told her that the family wanted to have the burial while relatives were around for the Harvest festivities. "They're also concerned about the weather. I understand from some of the old-timers that last evening's dusting of snow was just a forerunner of what's sure to come...something about wooly worms." He smiled. Glancing at Jessica to share his mirth, he wished he hadn't. He saw the melancholy on her face, and wondered if its cause was the same as his.

Jessica assumed he'd looked at her for explanation and lightly obliged. "The old folks say that when the wooly worms have exceptionally heavy fur, it means we're in for a colder winter than usual, and an early, deep snow. The same is true of squirrels gathering nuts early, and extra thick bark on the trees.''

Zeb, who'd surprised everyone by showing up at the table, spoke up. ''Diggin' a grave in the snow ain't easy. I should know,'' he added with a bitter snort.

Wanting to change the grim subject, Belinda suddenly announced, ''Well, I'm afraid I won't be back in time, and frankly, I'm glad. I don't like funerals. I did go by the house to pay my respects, though.''

Zeb looked up then to demand irately, ''And just where do you think you're going? You know dang well your mother's vulturous kin always come to stuff their greedy faces at our Harvest dinner, and it ain't me they come to see, anyhow. They ain't got no more use for me than I've got for them, and I sure as hell don't plan to entertain them.''

''Poppa, stop it!'' Jessica scolded him for using profanity in front of Derek. She darted an anxious glance in his direction but saw he was concentrating on his dinner, pretending not to notice.

Zeb snorted. ''If he ain't heard the words before, he won't know what I'm sayin', anyhow.''

Derek did not look up, having no intention of getting involved in a family dispute. ''Don't mind me,'' he murmured.

''I don't!'' Zeb irritably snapped. He'd had a stiff drink from the bottle he kept hidden beneath a loose board in his room, and it was just enough to make him cantankerous. ''But what I *do* mind,'' he went on, still glaring at Belinda, ''is you thinkin' you can just sashay off any time you want to without askin' my permission. You think 'cause you done finished school that you can just priss around all you want to. I say it's time you settled down and got married.''

Belinda quickly defended herself. ''Poppa, I told you several days ago that Harmon Willingham was coming to get me on Thursday morning to spend the day in Asheville with his family. He's a wonderful young man, and I think he's wanting to court me and ask me to be his wife, and that's why I'm not going to be here."

Zeb grunted. "Well, I reckon that's different then." He apologized to Derek. "Sorry about bein' so irritable, but frankly it ain't easy raisin' daughters alone and tryin' to find decent husbands that'll take care of 'em after I'm gone. But I finally got Jessica spoken for. Now all I got left to worry about is Belinda."

Belinda saw the pain that flashed on Jessica's face, and she rushed to take the attention from her sister by saying, "Poppa, I'd really like for you to meet Harmon. Do you think you'll be up early enough to have breakfast with us before we go?"

He flashed an indignant glare. "I'm a farmer, remember? I always get up early."

Belinda and Jessica exchanged knowing looks, both well aware that their father seldom got out of bed before noon, because he had usually drunk himself into a stupor the night before. Jessica had had to milk the cows before daylight in order to get to school by first bell, and she hadn't been the least saddened when they all finally died—no matter there was seldom money to buy milk and they had to do without.

"Of course, I'll be here to meet him." Zeb reached across the table to stab another biscuit angrily with his fork. "If he's got notions about marryin' you, I sure intend to look him over."

Jessica groaned softly when she heard Belinda press on to request, "Will you promise not to get into a discussion about the possibility of war?"

"Possibility?" He laughed around mouthfuls of bread, then shook his knife for emphasis. "That just shows how much you don't know, girl. Possibility, indeed!" He snickered. "War is a certainty now that Mr. Lincoln got himself elected. He's a fine man, and he don't hold to slavery any more'n I do, so the South will pull out of the Union and secede and plummet straight into war—and *hell!*

"And I got a right to say so," he continued. Then he paused to look at her suspiciously before asking, "Say, how come you're so concerned about me tellin' the truth in front of this Mr. Harmon Willingham? Is there somethin' about him you ain't tellin' me? As I recall, you haven't said anythin' about him or his family. Let's hear it. Maybe I won't want him courtin' you."

Belinda looked beseechingly at Jessica, but Jessica could only give a helpless shrug. There was nothing she could say or do to alleviate the tension. Finally, Belinda spoke, the words tumbling out almost frantically. "He comes from a wealthy and prominent family in Raleigh, and his father is a very respected doctor. He's a gentleman, and I'm sure you'll like him. It's just that I don't think the table is a place to debate, that's all."

Zeb grunted. "Well, I ain't goin' out of my way for him or anybody else. If I got something to say, I'll say it. It's my house, and if he don't like it, he can get the hell out."

Jessica had leaned to get the platter of fried chicken to pass to Derek and caught a whiff of the whiskey on her father's breath as she did so. She knew then it was best to steer the conversation to a less volatile subject—and quickly. Offering the chicken to Derek, she pleasantly remarked, "I hope you're going to enjoy my roast turkey on Thursday."

"Actually," he said, not meeting her gaze and offering a perfunctory smile, "I won't be here. When I was over at the Temples' this morning, Mrs. Billingsley reminded me I hadn't been by to visit. She invited me for dinner with her family, and I accepted."

Jessica struggled to mask her disappointment. "Well, I had expected you'd be here, but if you'd rather go over there...." Her voice trailed.

"I've imposed on you all enough as it is, and you do expect other guests. It'd be best if I weren't in the way, too." Dear God, he heatedly wondered, didn't she know why he was trying to avoid being around her? Didn't she know how agonizing it was to pretend he didn't care? He found himself wishing then and there he could address Zeb Coulter and ask for permission to court her properly, but everything within him demanded he go slowly.

Jessica was deeply disappointed. She'd looked forward to the day only because Derek would be there. Belinda's relatives' visit was always a miserable time. They couldn't stand Zeb and used every holiday as an excuse to stop by and be obnoxious. This year, however, she had hoped having an outsider as a guest would make them less aggressive. Also, she couldn't deny feeling a bit jealous that Leona would have his company instead!

"We have a special church service in the morning, too, don't forget," Derek went on. "So I won't have much time for dinner, anyway. I'll have to eat there and run, because I'll need to get back to the Temples and make ready for the funeral."

"Well, whatever is convenient for you. If you change your mind, though, there'll be plenty of food here for everybody."

Zeb pushed himself back from the table and grinned with satisfaction to think he might be getting both his daughters married off before long. "Maybe you should rush this beau of yours along a bit," he said to Belinda. "Then when the preacher, here, comes back at Christmas to marry Jessica and Reuben, we could just make it a double wedding."

Jessica drew in her breath sharply, and Derek noticed and looked at her in suppressed sympathy.

"Yep, that would be good timing," Zeb went on, pleased with himself. "It might get kind of crowded around here, what with Reuben and his boy moving in, especially when my grandsons start arriving, so if you can rush things along, all the better."

Tension had descended like an invisible net. Derek, unable to bear the thought of Jessica's pending marriage, much less the ordeal of having to officiate, pushed his chair back and stood. "Thank you for a nice meal," he stiffly addressed Jessica. "I've got to get to the church now for prayer meeting. Will you excuse me?"

"Of—of course." Jessica was flustered, suspecting his real reason for such an abrupt departure.

Derek glanced around. "Is anyone else going?"

"Not me." Zeb also got up, shuffled toward the door and said he was going to the store for a while.

As soon as the door closed behind him, Belinda shook her head worriedly and cried, "Sooner or later he's going to get in trouble over there. All those men do is stand around the fire and drink whiskey and run their mouths. Poppa is making everybody in the valley angry with his talk against war."

"I know, I know." Jessica hated to agree, aware that Derek was standing by the back door listening uneasily. But she talked on so she wouldn't have to dwell on the aching and confusion boiling inside her. "Some of the parents have approached me wanting to know how *I* felt, asking if I share his views. I have no intention of taking a stand either way, but it shows their concern, how Poppa is stirring everyone up. They consider him a traitor to his people."

Belinda looked at Derek and suddenly felt the need to ask, "What about you, Preacher Stanton? How do you feel about the South seceding?"

He was thoughtful for a moment, not really wanting to get involved but unable to think of a polite way out for the moment. "Well, for a start, I don't think slavery is the whole issue. I think it's a question of the North declaring war to try and preserve the Union."

Belinda persisted. "But how do *you* feel?"

"As a minister, I naturally stand for peace, but... I'm afraid I couldn't defend the right to hold a man in bondage if there's a war."

Belinda gasped. "You mean you'd fight for the North?"

Jessica joined her in staring at him in fearful anticipation.

He repeated, "I stand for peace." He looked at Jessica fondly. "Like you I don't want to take a side either way."

"But I only meant in the classroom," she explained. "Personally, I stand with the South, of course—"

"Don't *you* Preacher?" Belinda asked, still wanting confirmation of his loyalty. "I mean, you are from Louisiana, and that's part of the South...."

"Lovely ladies," he said as he reached to open the door, "let's not trouble ourselves with the subject for now. Let's just leave everything in the hands of our Lord." With that parting statement, he stepped outside and closed the door behind him.

Belinda stared after him, hands on her hips, head cocked to one side in thoughtful musing. "I do believe that man would stand with the North. What do you think?"

Jessica just wanted to get her mind off Derek Stanton altogether, at least for a little while. "I think we'd best get ready to go to prayer meeting and do as he suggested—*leave it to the Lord.*"

Chapter Eight

It was torment for Jessica to sit in the congregation and listen to Derek preach. She didn't hear a word he said as she stared up at him and thought how compellingly handsome he was. She felt a delicious tremor then to think about how he'd actually held her and kissed her with melting tenderness. Never, not even if she lived to be a hundred, would she forget how she'd felt in that instant. Over and over she had relived that radiant moment in her mind.

Yet now, as he included her in his general sweep of the audience, it was as though it had never happened. He was, she realized with a jolt of pain, like a stranger as he stood there, separated from her by his ecclesiastical status. And, because of that weak instant the day before, gone was the camaraderie they'd enjoyed in those first days. In its place was uneasiness, which saddened her greatly. It would have been far better, she reluctantly admitted, never to have known that sweetness than to have had it destroy their warm and growing friendship.

Reuben had taken his usual seat beside her, which only served to antagonize her in her already miserable state. As soon as service ended, she attempted to bolt from her place, but his hand snaked out to wrap tightly around her wrist and hold her where she was. Though his lips were curved into a smile, his eyes were blazing with his arrogance. "I think," he said quietly, tightly, between clenched teeth, "that you should invite me to dinner at your house tomorrow. It's only proper."

"What is proper," she defiantly whispered, so as not to be embarrassed by anyone overhearing, "is for you to do the decent, expected thing and wait till your wife has been in her grave for a year before you start courting me."

His brows shot up, and he stiffened with quiet rage. "That's nonsense. No one would fault me for looking for a mother to my boy. As long as it's a year till we're married, nobody will say anything. They all know you're my choice, anyway, so it's only natural you'd invite me to have a meal with your family."

She tried to jerk from his grasp, but he continued to grip her so hard she was struggling not to wince with pain. "We have other guests coming. Family. There's no room."

"I'll speak to your pa," he warned.

"Do it then!" She raised her voice enough that Widow Haislip, moving along the row just behind them, sharply glanced their way.

Reuben saw her and released his hold on Jessica at once. He forced a pleasant expression as he said, "Well, that's a shame you've got so many guests for dinner, Miss Jessica, but I'll be glad to come for supper instead." He turned then to make his way across the row to the center aisle where some of the deacons had gathered to talk.

Jessica rushed on out, well aware that when the day came that she belonged to him, he'd take revenge for her defiance. No matter. She was desperate to avoid his company for as long as possible, despite any price she might have to pay later.

She saw that Belinda was standing with some of her friends to share her excitement over Harmon's expected arrival in the morning. She'd be in no hurry to leave for home, so Jessica wearily sighed and began to walk toward the doors. Then she hesitated when she saw Naomi and Leona Billingsley. Able to hear only snatches of conversation, she could still discern that they were expressing to the women near them their excitement over the handsome new preacher accepting their invitation for dinner at their home. Jessica didn't want to hear.

Turning around, she headed in the other direction. A side door opened to a hallway beside the small utility room, whose door led to the small cemetery outside. Most families had their own graveyards on their land, but a few preferred their loved ones to rest in peace near the church.

She stepped out into darkness, momentarily taken aback by the eeriness of the graveyard. In the moonlight, the tombstones appeared as ghostly sentries of the night. She shivered from natural uneasiness as well as the chill breeze. Gathering her wool cape around her, she took a deep breath of resignation and prepared to make her way around to the front of the church, and the waiting, welcome light of the lanterns there.

She had taken only a few steps when a masculine voice softly calling her name caused her to freeze where she stood.

"Don't be afraid, Jessica. It's me."

She turned slowly, heart pounding, relief washing in welcome waves as she recognized Derek stepping out of the shadows. "You!" She gasped, laughing at herself for the momentary fright. "What are you doing lurking around out here?" She laughed again, warmed by his nearness.

Even in the moon glow she could see the twinkle lighting his eyes as he gazed down at her in open adoration. "Actually," he said slowly, huskily, "I was hiding."

"Hiding?" She blinked, bewildered. "From whom? And how did you manage to slip outside? You're supposed to be at the door shaking hands with everybody."

Mischievously, he confided, "When everybody had their eyes closed during the benediction song, I darted out the side door. They'll think I left early to go to the Temple wake."

"Then who are you hiding from?" She persisted.

"Son-in-law-hungry mothers. Husband-hunting women. Sinners who think a magic word from me will rid them of all guilt." He shrugged, then, eyes locked with hers to convey a message of longing, he whispered, "And I guess, most of all, I'm hiding from you."

She shook her head in wonder, then swallowed a completely unexpected bubble of hysterical laughter as she echoed, "From me? But why?"

He moaned, deep in his throat. Then, torn with emotion, he yielded to the confession of his torment.

"Because," he whispered huskily, miserably, "the truth is, I'm falling in love with you, Jessica Coulter."

She drew a steadying breath and nervously rubbed her hands together beneath her cape as she struggled to gather her thoughts. *Dear God, could it be true?* Was he actually speaking the words she'd never dared believe she would hear? All at once, she realized she wanted to confide the same to him, to let him know that what she was feeling for him was wonderful and spellbinding. Together, they would search for a way to be together, in the right sort of way. *Dear Lord, was it possible her fate was not sealed, after all?*

She parted her lips, but no sound came as she struggled to speak. Finally, she was able to whisper, "Oh, Derek, I— I love you, too."

He moved to gather her in his arms, to seal their newly declared devotion with a fervent kiss, but out of the corner of his eye he saw the movement of someone stepping out the side door. In a flash, he leaped silently back into the shadows, grabbing Jessica's arm and pulling her with him as he whispered for her to be quiet. "I think it's Reuben. If he finds us out here, he'll make a scene."

They watched and waited for what seemed like forever as Reuben glanced about at the shadows with narrowed eyes. Evidently, he'd seen Jessica go out that way. They held their breath in hopes he wouldn't follow, for there was a likely chance he'd notice them when he passed by. Finally, they were able to sigh with relief as he turned and went back inside.

"He's going to be looking for me," Jessica said fearfully. "And you're right. He will make a scene. He thinks I belong to him," she said, almost fiercely.

"We're going to change all that, Jessica. Now that I know you feel the same, I'm going to talk to your father and tell him I want to court you, and we'll talk to him together, if you want to, so I can be there when you tell him you don't want to marry Reuben, and—"

"Has anybody seen Jessica?"

They could hear Reuben's irate voice from the front porch of the church. It wouldn't do, they knew, for him to find out about them before they'd had a chance to tell her father. "I have to go," she softly cried, turning back to the rear of the church. "I'll go around, come up on the other side. My wagon is tied there, and he'll think he just missed me, and—"

He clutched her shoulders in the desperation of the moment. "Meet me tonight in the barn. At midnight. Everyone will be asleep. You can sneak out of the house. I'll wait till then to return from the Temples. They'll be having an all-night wake, anyway. We've got to talk, make our plans. Oh, Jessica..." He searched her face in the moonlight and found the mirrored love he sought. "We'll work everything out. We have to." His lips claimed hers in an almost bruising kiss, then, releasing her, he turned away quickly to disappear into the shadows.

She stared after him, shaken, and yes, even a bit frightened, but inside, Jessica Coulter had never known such happiness and joy.

It would work out. She knew it would. Now that she realized she did love him, and, wonder of wonders, he loved her, too, they couldn't let anything stand in their way.

Chapter Nine

The hour crept toward midnight. Jessica lay across her bed fully dressed. Quite still and thoughtful, she stared into the darkness, listening for any sound of her father returning, but all she could hear was the occasional scrambling of mice within the walls, settling noises in the creaky old house and the wind rattling the windowpanes. By this time, she figured, he had passed out drunk at the store. He did that sometimes, as did so many of the menfolk who drank themselves into a stupor. Rather than let them attempt to make it home, Bud Creech just let them sleep it off on a pile of feed sacks in his storage room.

She'd had difficulty getting Belinda to go to bed, because she was so keyed up and excited over Harmon coming for her the next morning. Jessica didn't want to appear anxious to get rid of her, but, as time passed, she started getting nervous. There had been times in the past when they'd sat up till two or three in the morning, bundled beneath blankets in Jessica's room, sharing secrets and giggling as only sisters who are close will do. But finally Jessica had pointed out that if Belinda didn't quit talking and go and get some sleep, she'd have bags under her eyes and not look so pretty. It had worked. Belinda had hurried off at once, and Jessica had been able to settle down and count hours, then minutes, till the time for her fateful rendezvous.

She felt as though fireflies were dancing inside her stomach, lighting every nerve in her body with anticipation mingled with fear. He'd said he loved her. That thought flashed over and over. He'd said he loved her, and she'd said the same to him, and now there wasn't any turning back. But, the question was, no turning back from what? Where was it all going to lead? If they loved each other, then they'd want to be married, and she knew, beyond all doubt, her father would never agree. If she became Derek's wife, she'd leave home and, sooner or later, Belinda would also go. Coulter land would not be passed down to Coulter blood; never would her father stand for that—though he'd be helpless to prevent it. If it weren't for Jessica's teacher's pay, they wouldn't have been able to pay the taxes the past two years, anyway. It seemed the older Zeb got, the more he drank.

Jessica hoped, however, that Derek, being a minister, would by a miracle be able to reason with her father, make him see how wrong it was, how sinful, to expect her to marry a man she didn't love just to fulfill his dream.

This night she and Derek would make plans for the future, but she could not deny she was also looking forward to being in his arms for yet another deliciously dazzling kiss. He was, she felt confident, the man destiny had meant just for her. No matter it had all happened so fast; this was the way it was meant to be.

At midnight, when the long-case clock in the hall began to strike the hour, Jessica could wait no longer. She prayed she was right in thinking her father had passed out at the store, and it was now safe to leave the house.

All was still and quiet as she carefully opened the back door. Stepping out into the yard, she found a half-moon lighted the way. Jessica was so happy she felt as though her feet never even touched the ground as she floated on her cloud of bliss to the barn.

Inside, she was engulfed by the darkness. She lit a lantern and turned the wick down low.

As she glanced around, neither Derek nor his palomino could be seen, so she went to a bale of hay and sat down to wait. As she did so, she bumped the edge of the bale, felt something hard and investigated to see what had been hidden there. A jar of moonshine! Shaking her head in pity and dismay, she put it back as it was, lest her father accuse her of snooping.

Time seemed to stand still. It must be quarter past twelve, she fretted. What if Derek had been delayed at the Temples'? She could recall how, on occasion, Preacher Dan had sat up with a family for the all-night wake before the funeral. Perhaps Derek had felt obligated to do the same.

She began to shiver. The night air was cold and, in her excitement, she'd taken her light wool shawl from the hook by the kitchen door, instead of the heavy one. She wished she'd waited till she saw Derek ride up before she went out to the barn. But that would have been taking a chance on her father coming in to sit down at the kitchen table to brood. He did that sometimes, till the wee hours of dawn. She'd have been trapped then, with no way out of the house, because the front door squeaked when it opened, and he would have heard her had she tried to sneak out that way.

Deciding to hurry back for the warmer shawl, because the cold was becoming unbearable, she moved to leave her hiding place but froze at the sound of a horse approaching at a very slow gait. It had to be Derek, and she felt a thrill—which quickly changed to a flash of terror at the sound of her father's slurred voice in the night.

"Damn you, mule, be still!"

She knew right away he was drunk. Frantically, she glanced around in search of a better place to hide. No doubt, he'd head straight for where he'd hidden his whiskey. She darted for the ladder to the hayloft, and scrambled up. There was just enough time to climb to the top and throw herself into the pile of loose hay there before she heard the barn door screech open, and the sound of her father staggering in.

Slowly, careful not to make a sound, she maneuvered around to lie on her stomach so she could peer down and see what he was doing. As she'd anticipated, he headed straight for the bale where she'd been sitting to retrieve his hidden jar of corn liquor.

Suddenly, Jessica's heart leaped to her throat in even more overwhelming terror, as she realized he was taking the jar with him and settling down at the foot of the ladder to the hayloft. Unscrewing the lid, he lifted the jar to his lips to take a long, greedy swallow. Then he closed his eyes and promptly passed out!

She knew she was trapped, with no way out as long as he was down there. Slumped back against the ladder as he was, she couldn't crawl over him, and if she tried to go part of the way and then jump the last few feet to the floor, the sound might wake him. What would she say when he wanted to know what she was doing up in the hayloft in the middle of the night? Tears of frustration stung her eyes, but Jessica refused to cry. Long ago, before she had accepted her life as it was, she'd learned that crying did nothing except make her feel ashamed afterward for being so weak. She was proud to have achieved, through the years, a certain degree of self-control. But in light of the hopeless situation confronting her now, she felt washed with self-pity. Poppa could stay where he was all night long and into the morning, depending on how much he'd had to drink. She'd known him sometimes to sleep the clock around. *Dear Lord,* she prayed, *don't let this be one of those times!*

Her imagination began to run wild, and she became tormented with all sorts of consequences if she were trapped all night. Never would she be able to get the family feast cooked in time for dinner. And what about Harmon Willingham? Belinda would panic if she weren't around by the time he arrived. How was she going to explain any of it?

She clenched her fists in fury, ground her teeth together and with fierce determination told herself there had to be a way out of this nightmare!

Suddenly, there was the noise of the barn door slowly scraping open. She instinctively covered her mouth with her hands to stifle a gasp she couldn't hold back as she saw that Derek had arrived. He was moving slowly, cautiously, as he stepped into the circle of the lantern's mellow light. She ached to call out to him but dared not make a sound.

Derek froze at the sight of Zeb, and he quickly glanced around before starting to retreat. Just as she was about to try and signal to him, her father woke up with a start.

"Huh? What?" He stared at Derek, looked about wildly, remembered where he was, then, over the roaring pain in his head, harshly demanded, "The preacher! What do you want?"

Derek mustered composure and, almost apologetically, explained that he'd just arrived from the Temple family wake and was putting his horse away.

"Well, get on with it, dang it." Zeb settled back against the ladder, closing his eyes once more. "I'll be along in a little while...." And then he drifted away, returning to drunken slumber.

Jessica raised herself cautiously to see Derek unsaddling his horse. How she ached to do something to let him know she was there; but she dared not take the chance, and could only watch in silent anguish as he finished his task and left. She knew he'd probably think she'd seen her father in the barn and turned back to the house. He'd go on to bed, assuming she'd done the same.

She scooted back against the wall, gathering hay and some old feed sacks around her to ward off the chill. Again she felt like giving in to tears but gritted her teeth and did not succumb. She didn't know what she was going to do, but for the moment she had to keep warm.

She laid her head on her knees and tried to sleep, but she was too tense, too worried over what the consequences of this night's plight were going to be. If only her father would wake up and go in the house. Maybe if she found some-

thing, dropped it nearby to make a noise, startle him, then—
She froze.

There was a soft, scraping sound, and her flesh prickled with fear. Rats! Of course, there were rats in the barn. She had seen them, lots of times, big and ugly, and if one ran across her foot, or worse, her face, then she'd not be able to hold back the screams! She was desperate to grope around for a weapon but dared not move in the darkness for fear of touching one of the scurrying creatures. All she could do was sit there, helpless, and pray the noise had only been her imagination running away with her. But then she heard it again, only this time she could tell where it was coming from—the other side of the loft doors, which were directly behind her. It was a drop of maybe twenty feet to the ground, too far to jump without breaking an ankle, or worse, her neck. Already she had contemplated that desperate way out and decided not to chance it.

She scrambled to her feet and began to back away from the doors. Terror was a constricting knot in her throat. Oh, dear Lord in heaven, what kind of monster was out there trying to get to her?

Then came a blessed wave of relief as she heard Derek's voice, barely audible as he called, "Jessica, can you hear me in there?"

With a hushed sob of relief, she scrambled on her hands and knees to the hay door, fumbling for the latch, and whispered, "Yes, yes, I hear you...." Her fingertips touched the latch, but she didn't dare push the doors open, unsure of his location. "Where are you?"

"Up here."

He maneuvered to lean down from the gable to pull the doors open himself.

The cold night air rushed in, and she craned her neck upward, straining to see in the waning moonlight. Weak with relief, she remembered to keep her voice low as she called, "Oh, thank God! But how did you know I was here?"

He quickly told her that when he was late leaving the Temples', he figured she'd already be waiting for him in the barn. When he saw her father passed out, he had suspected she might be trapped inside. Checking her room and finding her not there, he knew for sure. The loft, he figured, would be the likely place she would have hidden.

He had used a rope he found hanging on the outside of the barn to lasso the top cross beam, then scaled the wall on the far side. "Now the trick is to get us both down from here without breaking our necks. I didn't dare go inside for a ladder. I was afraid I'd wake him up."

He swung down to where she waited, then instructed, "Now, hold on tight, and I'll lower us to the ground."

She did as he said, squeezing her eyes shut. Then there was the exuberant sensation of flying through the cold air, and she clung to him tenaciously, even wrapping her legs about his as they made the rapid descent to the ground. When they hit, they did not hit hard, but they did lose their balance and fell together in a heap.

"Are you all right?" he asked at once, scrambling to his feet, bending over her, searching her face in the dim light.

"I—I think so," she said hesitantly, rubbing her bottom, which had taken the blow. She would be sore, for sure.

"Can you get up?"

He held out his hand, and she took it, and when he'd pulled her to her feet, she stumbled, fell into his arms. For an instant, they could only gaze at each other in silent wonder and unspoken longing, but then Derek could resist no longer. He gathered her near, closing his mouth over hers.

Jessica's senses reeled at his taste and touch. Gentle were his lips, yet persuasive. And while she felt his hunger, she knew he was struggling for control. As she swayed against him, her arms went about his waist, and he held her even tighter. The kiss deepened. As his skilled lips aroused her to even greater heights, she couldn't help pressing even closer to him, and not once did she resist, or want to deny either of them such ecstasy.

Derek knew, beyond all doubts, that Jessica was innocent, didn't, and couldn't, realize the dangerous flames she'd caused to ignite inside him. They were both tempting terrible trouble, and it was that clear thought rising above the fire within that gave him the strength to end the kiss, and take a step back, pushing her from him as he did so. "No!" he cried wretchedly. "No! It can't be like this, Jessica!"

Suddenly frightened by his strange and unexpected behavior, she looked up at him wildly and demanded, "What's wrong? What have I done?"

"You haven't done anything. I shouldn't have asked you to meet me out here like this. It looks as if we're ashamed for anyone to know how we feel about each other, and that's not right."

She shook her head. "No, it's just that we wanted to talk about...things." She was stabbed with the anxious thought that perhaps she'd misunderstood his intentions. "I—I thought it was because of the pact my father made with Reuben, and—"

"Yes, that's the reason, all right," he agreed, almost angrily. "But it's still wrong, don't you see? What if you had got caught out there? What if we'd both got caught? It would've looked bad. Real bad. The unmarried schoolteacher, promised by her father to another man, sneaking out of her house in the middle of the night to meet the unmarried circuit rider. That would've given the folks around here fodder for gossip for the next several winters by the fire! We can't risk that, Jessica. We both have our reputations to think about."

Stiffly, misinterpreting his meaning to suggest their relationship had no future, she stammered, "Maybe I'd better just go on inside now, and—"

"No!" he cried furiously, reaching for her once more and beseeching her in the moonlight with desperate eyes to grasp what he was trying to say. "Don't you see? I do love you, Jessica, but I don't want any blemishes on that love. And it's you I'm thinking about. I don't want anyone saying bad things about you, questioning your virtue. That's why I shouldn't have asked you to meet me out here. I should've waited and talked to you inside the house, in broad daylight, so I wouldn't be so tempted to take you in my arms and make love to you, and there wouldn't be a chance someone would find out, and—'' He shook his head in frustration. "What I'm trying to tell you is that I think it's best I go ahead and speak to your father as soon as he sobers up, and tell him I'd like to court you. I think it's best to be open and honest.''

Jessica's heart leaped with joy. Not only did she have no doubts that she loved this gentle and wonderful man, but truly she felt he was a miracle given to her by God Himself, in answer to her prayers for reprieve from a loveless marriage, as well as a heavenly reward for all her years of loneliness and sacrifice. Still, she knew the path to ultimate happiness for them was not going to be easy. "He's not going to like it,'' she warned. "He has a strong motive for wanting me married off to Reuben.''

He raised an eyebrow and warily urged, "Then tell me. I need to know everything.''

As she spoke, Derek's eyes narrowed, and his expression of worry and concern deepened. "You're right,'' he said worriedly when she'd finished. "He isn't going to like it, but I promise I'll do everything I can to get him to change his mind, to make him see it's wrong to expect you to marry someone you don't love in order for him to satisfy his own selfishness. This is only land, for God's sake, and he's playing around with someone's life, because of his own crazy way of thinking, and that's wrong. Terribly wrong. I've got to convince him of that.''

"We'll both convince him,'' she assured him, reaching to grasp his hands. "I promise I'll stand by you the whole time, and—''

"Shh!'' He held a finger to his lips. Looking beyond her, he could see that the barn door was slowly opening. They were standing at the corner, unfortunately in the opposite direction from the house. She couldn't go around the barn and escape that way, because of the fenced pasture. "It's your pa coming out," he whispered. "Stand real still, and maybe he won't see us."

The door opened wider, and they both saw her father, holding high above his head the lantern she'd lit earlier. When he stepped out and into the night, they were caught in the spreading halo.

Jessica had already dropped Derek's hands, but they were still standing so close they were touching.

Despite his drunken state, Zeb registered surprise—and anger. "What the hell are you two doin' out here?" he cried, hurrying toward them.

Derek never realized he could be so adept at lying, for the words just tumbled out. "Jessica mistook me for a prowler when she heard me coming in, and when she went to get you, she realized you hadn't come in yet, so she came out here to see what was going on. I guess I startled her."

Suspiciously, he raked them with his eyes, then gave Jessica a quick nod and thundered, "You get in the house, girl. Now."

She retreated with a last desperate glance at Derek. Now was not the time to argue about anything. They'd been caught in a difficult situation, and her father was not sober.

At once, Zeb pointed out, voice still slurred from drink, "You know, I don't think this looks too good, even if you are a preacher. Folks might get the wrong idea."

"Sir," Derek began, wishing the man were sober so he could go ahead and attempt reason, state his intentions. "We weren't doing anything wrong, and—"

"Don't matter!" Zeb interrupted sharply, incredulously. "Like Reuben Walker said, 'avoid the appearance of evil'! Says it's in the Good Book. He said he reminded Jessica of that, and you, of all people, sure oughta know it for a fact. You see, him and Jessica are gonna be married soon, and he wouldn't like it, her bein' out here with you like this, and I don't want it to happen again. Understand? I don't want my daughter's reputation ruined by folks gettin' the wrong idea, and I sure don't have no intentions of anybody messin' up the pact I made with Reuben."

Derek knew, without a doubt, he should just turn and walk away, but his heart overrode the warning of his brain. "I don't suppose it would make any difference to you that your daughter doesn't happen to be in love with the man you want her to marry, would it?" he dared to ask.

"Nope!" Zeb was quick to confirm. "'Cause she don't know her own mind, don't know what's best for her. I do."

Derek started to respond but was finally able to convince himself it was best to wait. "Well, Mr. Coulter, I guess we'd both better get some sleep now."

Zeb nodded. He wished his head weren't about to burst open with a headache, because Preacher Stanton had never done anything to him, and he didn't want to be rude. Still, Reuben had cornered him at the store earlier and told him how folks were going to start talking if he didn't quit passing out in the barn and leaving the preacher to sleep in the house, unchaperoned, with the girls there. Reuben had made it clear he didn't want any gossip about the woman he intended to marry. That had shaken Zeb up, plenty, but at the time Reuben had confronted him, he'd already had too much to drink and so hadn't been able to make it inside the house at first.

"Listen, Preacher," he said finally. "I've known more misery in my life than most men, and I figure the Lord owes me the blessin' of seein' her married off to somebody that'll take good care of her.

"As for you sayin' she don't love him . . ." He paused to laugh at such a ridiculous notion, because he figured if Stanton thought otherwise, he might not be willing to perform the ceremony, and Zeb sure didn't want any snags or delays. "Why, Jessica worships the ground that man walks on. She might tell you different, because she's still worried about his year of mournin' not being over yet, but the fact is, she's loved him for a long, long time. Folks have been sayin' since the day Elizabeth Walker was laid to rest, that it'd be only natural and fittin' for him and my Jessica to one day get together."

Derek shook his head, bewildered and confused. Surely, Jessica hadn't lied to him. She wasn't the sort to trifle with a man, not like Consuela.

Or was she?

Foolishly, he'd thought the same about Consuela.

Maybe Jessica was merely having second thoughts about Reuben because a new man had suddenly come into her life. Perhaps, for the first time, she saw an option for her future that hadn't existed before.

"Yeah, we'll talk tomorrow," Zeb was wearily saying as he turned toward the house. "I just want to keep things nice and smooth and avoid the appearance of evil, like the Good Book says, and everybody will be happy...." He shuffled on his way, not waiting for Derek.

Derek stared after him. Assailed with thoughts too complex to sort out in a hurry, he was sure of only one thing for the moment.

It would be best for everyone if he left the Coulter house.

Chapter Ten

When Jessica awoke just before five o'clock, she felt as though she hadn't even been to sleep. Physically and mentally exhausted, she had no idea when she'd finally drifted off into restless, troubled slumber. The instant she opened her eyes, the memory of last night washed over her, and she was consumed with urgency to learn what had taken place after she left Derek and her father together outside. She'd heard Derek come in not long after and immediately go upstairs, but hadn't dared follow him to ask questions for fear her father might be close behind.

She got up and quickly dressed, then hurried to get the stove going and start preparing food for the Harvest feast. All the while she listened for sounds from upstairs to indicate Derek was awake. If he came downstairs before anyone else got up, they'd have time for a private talk. Yet she hesitated to go and awaken him and felt so frustrated not to know what to do about the situation. All she was sure of, as butterflies danced inside her stomach, was that she loved him and wanted to be with him forever and always.

By eight o'clock the turkey had started to turn golden, and the smell from the oven was tantalizing. Sweet potatoes were ready for roasting, and jars of turnip greens and collards were on the table, to be heated later, as well as butter beans, crowder peas and a fresh slab of fatback for seasoning. A batch of corn bread was already in a skillet, and dough for yeast rolls was rising near the warmth of the stove.

Just as Jessica was about to yield to her feeling of desperation and go upstairs to awaken Derek, Belinda breezed into the kitchen, sparkling with excitement. Lovely in a pale green velvet dress, she whirled around and asked, "Do you think I can compete with all those rich belles in Raleigh that Harmon is used to?"

Despite her preoccupation with her worries, Jessica couldn't help but laugh that her sister could even ask such a ridiculous question. Belinda's face glowed as brightly as candles on a Christmas tree, her emerald eyes outshining the jewel from which they'd taken their color. "You're stunning and ravishing and beautiful and you know it!" Jessica was quick to assure her. "Like Cinderella waiting for Prince Charming."

"He is my Prince Charming!" she exulted, hugging herself dreamily. "And we're going to get married and move to Raleigh and live happily ever after."

"I hope so," Jessica murmured, trying to keep her apprehension from showing. Families like the Willinghams married money—not poor farmers' daughters. But maybe she was worrying for nothing. Maybe Harmon's family was not like that. After all, Belinda was a beauty, with a pleasing personality, and any man should be proud to have her for his wife, rich or poor.

"Did Poppa come in last night?" Belinda asked soberly.

Jessica didn't want to confide what had happened, and instead told Belinda that she'd heard their father ride in some time after midnight but hadn't seen him that morning.

"I'll go find out." Belinda left, only to return almost immediately. "He's asleep, and I'm not going to wake him up," she reported. "He's always cranky when he's been on a binge, and I don't want him to meet Harmon when he's like that. Just remind him to be on his good behavior tomorrow night, please?"

Jessica nodded absently, more concerned over why Derek wasn't up and moving about. Every morning he'd risen as soon as he heard her in the kitchen, and today, of all days, he needed to get started on his busy schedule. Finally, she couldn't stand it any longer. "I need to wake up Preacher Stanton," she said to Belinda, who was keeping vigil at the window, awaiting Harmon's arrival. "I'll be right back."

She tiptoed up the stairs, not wanting to wake up her father. Belinda was right. Let him sleep. He was always at his worst when he woke up after heavy drinking the night before.

She knocked softly on Derek's door, and when there was no response, knocked harder. Finally, reluctantly, she turned the knob, pushing the door open and at the same time apologetically calling, "I'm sorry to intrude, but it's getting late, and—"

She blinked, bewildered. He wasn't there!

Stepping inside, she saw the bed was neatly made; but what truly puzzled her was that none of his things were there. Gone were his clothes, and the satchel in which he carried his Bible and sermon notes. She knew then he wouldn't be coming back—but why? What could have been said to cause him to leave without a word?

She heard Belinda, downstairs, forget all about wanting their father to keep on sleeping as she excitedly called, "He's here, Jessica! Harmon is here!"

Resignedly, she turned to the kitchen, tried to focus on the moment at hand. Belinda was now the image of composure, with the same nonchalant air she acquired when any of her beaux came to call. She gave no hint that her heart was about to leap out of her chest as Harmon Willingham's step was heard on the porch. Jessica hoped she could be equally collected when she went to church and confronted Derek later that morning; she intended to find out what was going on, no matter what.

Belinda introduced Harmon, and Jessica thought he was as handsome as her sister had said—maybe too handsome.

He was nattily dressed in a red silk shirt and cream-colored velvet suit, accented by a black silk cravat. His boots were spit-polished black leather. His hair, dark and wavy, just touched his shoulders, and he had a nice smile beneath a pencil-thin mustache. Then Jessica took note of his eyes. Oh, they were a nice shade of blue, but there was no warmth, no depth of feeling there. He seemed to exude an aura of self-importance. And while Belinda's manner was insouciant, Jessica could see that Harmon, himself, suffered no lack of confidence.

A little earlier than the usual time, Jessica hitched up the mule to the wagon and left for church, hoping to see Derek before the service began. But already the church was filled, and he was nowhere in sight. She didn't dare go in search of him, lest eyebrows be raised.

She didn't take her usual place, but instead wedged herself between Widow Haislip and Lula Creech so she wouldn't have to endure Reuben next to her. He gave her a furious look when he saw what she had done and sat down directly behind her.

When Derek finally appeared to stand behind the pulpit and lead the opening prayer, it was all Jessica could do to keep from trembling from head to toe. To sit there and look at his dear and handsome face, to relive in her mind the ecstasy of his wonderful lips on hers, was almost more than she could bear—especially in the wake of all that had happened since.

The hymns were a blur and, when he at last began to deliver his sermon, Jessica knew it wasn't her imagination that he looked everywhere but at her. She wondered if anyone else noticed how tense he seemed, the way his hands trembled ever so slightly when he touched the pages of his Bible or his notes.

He concluded the service by suggesting everyone offer their own personal prayer of thanks for their blessings.

Jessica asked God to grant the only true happiness she had ever known in her life. She prayed that she and Derek would be together always—as man and wife.

Derek took his place at the door for goodbyes. Jessica hung back, wanting to be last in line to speak to him. Even if she had to ask him to step outside for privacy, she intended to find out why he'd moved from their house.

"Are you expecting lots of company, dear?" Widow Haislip asked as she pushed along in the aisle next to Jessica.

"Oh, the usual. Mostly Belinda's kin. They always come by."

Window Haislip clucked sympathetically. "Yes, I know, and much to your poor father's dismay." She leaned to conspiratorially whisper, "He visits me sometimes, you know, and we talk. He's told me how they're always picking on him—Lucille and Charlie and Cora and Luther, that crowd from Hendersonville. It's terrible. The poor man has enough misery as it is, without having to endure their nagging. I told him not to put up with it this time, to just walk out and come on over to my house. I'm preparing extra food, in case he does. You try to get him to, if they start in on him again, all right, dear?"

Jessica nodded absently. The last thing on her mind right then was her father's displeasure over his in-laws' visit. She was relieved to see that Reuben had got caught in the crowd at the center of the aisle, while she'd succeeded in moving to the side. She frowned at the sight of Naomi Billingsley pushing Leona forward, whispering frantically in her ear. With irritation Jessica guessed that Naomi was, no doubt, urging her daughter to be her most charming when she took the preacher's hand.

Jessica hung back as much as she could without looking obvious, but there was a large attendance, and Derek was being surrounded by those wanting to meet him for the first time, as well as those who wanted to express their pleasure with his first visit. Glancing in Reuben's direction, she realized they were going to meet at the door at about the same time. She'd never be able to ask Derek anything then; in fact it was doubtful she'd get to say a word, anyway, with so many people gathered around him.

"I forgot something," she said suddenly, turning around and making her way through those surging from behind. She kept on going, making sure Reuben wasn't watching as she stepped out through the same door as the night before. Derek's palomino was tied to a tree at the rear of the church, and fortunately a thick cluster of rhododendron offered seclusion from the rest of the grounds, as well as from the road beyond.

Nearly a half hour passed before Derek came around the corner, and he stopped short at the sight of her. "What— what are you doing here?" He glanced about to ensure they couldn't be observed by anyone else.

She wasn't concerned with being coy or demure or applying any of the methods Belinda said a woman should use when dealing with a man. The long hours of worry and anxiety made her get straight to the point, and she cried, "What happened out there last night, Derek? Why did you leave me without a word? I thought you said you loved me, and—" She couldn't go on, felt like a fool, shook her head and started to rush by him in retreat, but his arms snaked out to catch her. He grasped her shoulders and, with a gentle shake, forced her to meet his anguished gaze.

"I do love you, but I don't know what to do about it, Jessica. Things have moved too fast, too soon, and I feel like if the world doesn't slow down, we're both going to fall off—right into more trouble than we can deal with."

Wretchedly, she shook her head. "I don't know what you're talking about," she whispered.

"Too much, too soon," he repeated, continuing to hold her, devouring her with his eyes. "I'm confused, Jessica. I don't know which way to go with this. You're promised by your father to another man. He let me know last night that he intends for you to keep that promise."

"But I don't love Reuben Walker!" she vehemently reminded him.

Derek drew a ragged breath. "But before I came along, you were resigned to marry him, weren't you?" he asked solemnly.

She couldn't deny it; it had never occurred to her to go against her father's wishes before.

"You see," he went on, when she didn't respond. "As I said, Jessica, things are happening too fast."

She faced him, unflinching. "Do you love me?"

His nod was firm, his tone confident. "Oh, yes," he said. "I love you, above and beyond everything, but I don't want to make a mistake. I don't want you to make a mistake. We've got to be sure. That's why I moved out of your house this morning, so I'd have time to think all this through, and give you time, too. Don't you know it's torture now for me to lie in bed upstairs, thinking, dreaming, of you downstairs in yours? I may be a preacher, Jessica, but I'm also a man, with natural needs and desires, and it's torture, and—" He shook his head in desolation. "We can't afford to make a mistake. It could ruin both our lives. Don't you see that? If we got caught sneaking around and meeting in the shadows, everyone would think the worst. I want to court you out in the open. I want to ask you to be my wife, and..."

No more could they deny the avowal of their love, and they fell into a torrid embrace. He kissed her till they were breathless and, when at last they drew apart, Jessica begged, "Come back, Derek. To the house. Today. You say you worry about what people will say, but how do you think it will look if you move out now, in the middle of your visit?"

He gave a helpless, defeated shrug. "I guess you're right. But what happens next? This is Thursday. I'm leaving Sunday afternoon. I'm not due back till Christmas—to perform your wedding ceremony, for heaven's sake!" He ran his fingers through his hair, turned away in desperation. "This is a mess. A big mess."

"It doesn't have to be." Jessica couldn't remember in her whole life ever being so sure of herself as she was now. "Today is going to be especially busy, I know, but tomorrow we can both face Poppa and tell him how we feel about each other. We'll have to find a way to make him understand that it's wrong of him to expect me to marry a man I can't love—a man I actually loathe—just for him to make sure his precious land will live on with Coulter blood. Who's to say I'll have sons? Who's to say I'll even have any children? We can tell him all that."

"And if he won't listen, what then? If he insists that you marry Reuben despite anything either one of us has to say, what do we do then?"

Jessica bit down on her lip thoughtfully. She hadn't had time to think of that tragic possibility, but she knew if it came to that, she'd be desperate enough to do anything. And she was about to confide as much to Derek, when he nervously pointed out, "Look, we can't keep standing here. Everyone hasn't left the grounds yet, and if we're seen back here like this, it'll only make matters worse. And I'm expected at the Billingsleys. We'll talk later, all right?"

"Will you come back to the house?" she asked anxiously.

He nodded, a faint smile teasing his lips. "I guess I'll really have to practice what I preach, won't I? Like avoiding temptation, because I do love you, Jessica," he fervently added as he reached to trail a gentle finger down her cheek. Finally touching her lips, he then mounted his horse and left.

The Harvest dinner was as unpleasant as always, once Belinda's aunts arrived with their families. They were disgruntled to learn she had a new beau and they hadn't arrived in time to look him over, so subsequently they took out their frustration when Zeb appeared at the table. Eyes bloodshot, a five-day stubble of beard on his face—because he only shaved on Saturday when he took a bath—he looked as awful as he felt. And he was in no mood for their usual sarcasm and contempt. Still, he managed to hold his tongue—for a while, anyway.

"Well, I'm glad for a change that you did waste most of the day in bed," Lucille cracked when Zeb shuffled into the kitchen where her husband, Charlie, was carving the turkey in Zeb's absence. "It wouldn't have done for Belinda's beau to see you like this. And it's obvious you've been drinking. I can smell it."

Cora haughtily chimed in, "So can I. Disgraceful."

Jessica tensed but was grateful to see that her father was trying to hold his temper. In an attempt to change the subject, she began to talk about how the new circuit preacher had cured Polly Sue's stuttering, but no one really paid any attention, and, during a lull, Luther suddenly deliberately goaded Zeb when he declared, "Well, I don't think it's gonna be much longer before we teach them Yankees to stay out of our business."

Jessica moaned, knowing all hopes of a peaceful meal were gone, as Charlie quickly joined in to expound his own views, agreeing, "That's right. Lincoln bein' elected don't give us no choice but to fight. I hope he drops dead before he takes office, and—"

"Enough!" Zeb had been sitting with head bowed over his plate, ignoring them all, but he jerked up to pound both fists at once on the table, setting dishes to rattling. "I won't have such talk at my table!" he exploded. "Not about a fine man like Abraham Lincoln. You all don't know beans, anyway! Lincoln wants freedom—for *all* men. But what do you idiots care about the slavery issue, anyway? You're all poor as church mice and never owned a slave, so why are you so anxious to see blood spilled?"

"Poppa, I don't think—" Jessica tried to intervene, but it was too late.

"Stay out of this!" he roared. "Nobody comes in my house defending slavery *or* war!"

Charlie puffed up at once to snarl, "Well, if you don't feel any loyalty to the South, why don't you just move up North and live with the Yankees?"

"And why don't you get the hell out of my house?"

At that, Cora screeched in echo, "*Your* house, Zeb Coulter? Your house, did you say? This was my sister's home, too, and if she were still alive, she'd not tolerate you ordering her kin to get out."

"That's right!" Lucille chimed in. "We came to visit and have dinner on Harvest day in our sister's home, and that's what we're going to do."

Zeb pushed his chair back so fast it fell to the floor in a loud clatter as he leaped to his feet. Sweeping his in-laws with a furious glare, he announced, "Well, you go right ahead and have yourself a nice time eatin' my food, but, by God, no law says I've got to break bread with you vultures!"

With that, he stormed out of the house.

The angry muttering continued, but Jessica refused to be drawn into the conversation. Finally, she managed to get the table cleared and the dishes washed, all the while ignoring them.

As they were leaving, at last, Charlie paused to bitterly advise, "You better try and talk some sense into that stubborn pa of yours, Jessica, 'cause when war comes, as it surely will, he's going to get himself in a whole heap of trouble with that traitorous mouth of his."

Jessica bit her tongue to keep from telling him that if he and the others hadn't been so argumentative, the nasty scene would not have happened. The last thing she needed was for her father to be in a bad mood for the next few days, and, no doubt, he would be, thanks to them. She stifled her anger, however, and bade them a polite goodbye. They were planning to attend Miss Sudie's funeral but would be going home from there, thank goodness. She hated the times when they invited themselves to stay the night.

By the time Jessica arrived for the Temple funeral, the crowd had overflowed from the cabin and people were gathered outside. She stood at the very edge of the group, almost down to the creek bank, shivering in the brisk, cold wind blowing down from the ridge beyond. A glance at the ominous sky told her that the thick, gray clouds billowing in would deliver more than the light dusting of snow they'd received earlier in the week. It looked as though a full-fledged winter storm were about to descend.

Derek, also noticing the darkening skies, cut the service short so that the pallbearers could take the casket up to the hill behind the house and get the burial completed as soon as possible. At his suggestion, the immediate family opted to go back inside, rather than continue with prayers at the graveside.

Glancing up, he saw Jessica standing to one side and felt a warm tremor in his heart. He had no doubt that he loved her. He only hoped he could convince her father of that fact, as well as make him see that his daughter's happiness should come before his own. A frown creased his forehead as he saw Leona Billingsley moving toward her.

As Derek watched from afar, Leona greeted Jessica with a glowing account of the most enjoyable dinner of her life.

"Preacher Stanton is so charming. We had such a wonderful time. He said if you didn't have any special plans, he'd try and visit us for supper again before he leaves." She craftily watched Jessica for any negative reaction, for the thought had occurred to her that the spinster schoolteacher just might have designs on the man. No matter that there was talk that the widower Reuben Walker intended to declare for her on the anniversary of his wife's death. Leona figured any woman in her right mind would prefer the handsome Derek Stanton, and Jessica was no half-wit, for sure.

Jessica knew what Leona was up to but didn't intend to fall into her trap. Pasting on her most obliging smile, she said, "Whatever Preacher Stanton wants to do is fine with me, Leona. I've got no special plans. He's welcome to stay or go. Whatever suits him best.''

Leona smothered a giggle of relief. ''I knew you'd understand.'' She hurried on her way.

Jessica figured Derek could get himself out of that one. She didn't dare appear to care one way or the other.

As she urged the mule toward home, it occurred to Jessica that she would be alone with Derek that night if her father stayed out drinking again. That was very likely, in view of how angry he'd been when he stomped away from the table and out of the house. He'd express his frustration by drinking too much whiskey. But no matter. No one need know she and Derek were alone, and they would have all the time they needed to decide how best to break the news to her father, when they finally succeeded in catching him in a sober moment.

She sighed with relief as she rounded the last curve in the road, for the snow was really coming down now. Already the ground was covered, and there was no sign the storm would let up. She hoped Derek would follow shortly and not be caught in the storm.

Reaching the barn, she quickly got down from the cart and rushed to open the doors, but just as she reached them, they swung open in her face. She stifled a groan as Charlie beckoned her to hurry.

''Come on, come on inside. We got here just in time ourselves.''

Luther spoke from where he was rubbing down one of the horses. ''The womenfolk are already inside getting supper on the table. It's sure good you cooked so much food, Jessica. Ain't no telling how long we'll be snowed in here.''

She quickly turned away, lest the bitter frustration be mirrored in her face.

Chapter Eleven

Never had Jessica known such desperation. If the storm continued through the night, roads would be impassable by morning, and they'd all be snowed in together. That thought was unappealing enough, but she was also concerned that Derek hadn't showed up yet.

After the family had gone upstairs to bed, Jessica kept a vigil at the back door. From there, due to the whiteness all around, she had a clear view of the path to the barn, and would see Derek when, and if, he did arrive.

She'd stood there perhaps an hour when his golden palomino finally came into view. Snatching her wool cape from the hook by the door, she hurried out and moved through the snow as fast as possible. Ahead, she could see the glow of the lantern appear through the window of the barn. By the time she got there, he had already started to unsaddle his horse.

"Jessica!" he cried, at once seeing the anxiety on her face. "What's wrong?" It seemed so natural that he take her in his arms.

"I knew that once you came inside, we wouldn't be able to talk." She told him how Belinda's kin had returned, deciding not to attempt the trip home because of the bad weather.

He smiled, and with a tender gesture brushed her hair back from her face. "Then we'll talk here."

"And what if Poppa comes in?" she worried. "It'll be worse than last night if he finds us together again."

With a frown, he told her of having stopped by Creech's store, because he'd seen Zeb's mule tied up outside. "I don't think we have to worry about him coming home tonight at all. There was a big crowd of men gathered there, as it seemed they'd rather be snowed in with their drinking friends than with their wives." He laughed, remembering the scene when he'd walked in. "They nearly broke their necks trying to hide their whiskey. The last person they wanted around was a preacher.

"As for your pa," he went on, becoming serious once more, "he was well on his way to getting drunk. I heard one of the men say he'd been hitting the bottle since early afternoon."

"I'm not surprised." She told him of the scene at the dinner table. "He's never got along with them. I hate that it happened now, because it's only going to make him harder to reason with when we tell him about us."

"Yes," he murmured softly, as he continued to hold her. "Us. That has a nice sound, doesn't it?"

"If it comes true," she pondered out loud, assailed by fears. "Poppa has his mind made up, Derek. And it's all because of this land, and—"

"It will work out," he sharply interrupted. "We'll make him understand how much we love each other. He'll have to listen to reason. We'll make him."

"But we have to do it soon. Before you leave. Don't forget Reuben thinks it's settled that I'll marry him in a month, and the sooner he realizes that's not going to happen, the better it will be for everyone."

Outside, the wind had picked up in intensity, and snow had changed to sleet and now assaulted the barn windows with a rain of ice. The barn was drafty and cold, and despite the warmth of his nearness, Jessica shivered in Derek's arms. He, too, was chilled, and took her hand. "Come on. It will be warmer up there in the hayloft, out of the draft, and if your pa does stagger in,'' he added with a wink before turning down the lantern, ''we'll just stay there and let the whole world search for us.''

She laughed at the possibility of such a predicament and quickly crawled up the ladder. He was right behind her, and they tumbled together on the hay, as delighted as children playing hide-and-seek with their friends. But then the moment became serious, and they lay back, side by side, searching each other's face in the scant light, endeavoring to find confirmation of devotion.

Derek was the first to put thoughts into words. ''Are you sure, Jessica? Your father led me to believe you intended to marry Reuben all along,'' he added quickly.

''Oh, for goodness' sake!'' She gasped in horror at such a notion. ''That's not true, Derek. Not true at all. He's nothing more to me than a neighbor, and I have to say I've found it hard at times even to be civil to him, because of the way he treated his wife before she died.'' She told him of bruises she'd seen on Elizabeth Walker, how she'd aged before her time due to her life of misery. ''Why would I even think of marrying such a despicable man?''

''Your father seemed to think you understood how it is with the land, that you love it as much as he does and want to see it stay in the Coulter family. What he said got me to thinking that maybe I was just the first opportunity you'd ever had for any other kind of future.''

''That's not true, Derek, not at all.''

''It just happened so fast.''

Her hand touched his as she tremulously whispered, ''I know, but it's as if I've always loved you but never thought you existed, except in my dreams. Since I was a little girl, I've wondered what it would be like to have a husband to love me and take care of me. I've always been the one to do the caring for other people, and I saw how lonely my father's been without anyone to share his life with him. I didn't want that. I'd accepted my lot in life, tried to fill the emptiness in my heart with devotion to my pupils, but the longing was always there, the longing to feel like this...with someone. And now that I've found you, I don't want to lose you. Oh, Derek . . .'' Her fingers gently stroked his, needing to touch, to feel their warmth. She brought his palm to her cheek, pressing it in a gesture of infinite devotion and tenderness of heart. At the same instant, she could feel the sudden and unfamiliar heated rush in her loins as she avowed, ''If I can't have you, then I wish we'd never met. I'll be tortured forever thinking how wonderful it would've been to be your wife.''

The sweetness of her touch filled him with longing that was almost painful in its intensity. Never had he known such desire, kindled by love he'd never believed could exist. There was no will left to resist as she took his hand and pressed it against her mouth, softly licking his fingertips. He felt himself grow rigid with want, and yet his entire body was tense as he struggled to abstain from rising hunger.

Finally, he moved his hand to caress the nape of her neck as he pulled her face close for a smoldering kiss. Her arms went about his strong back as she pressed yet closer.

Neither was aware of the sounds of ice pelting the sides of the barn; they were oblivious to everything except the love that blazed between them into one constant, overwhelming fire.

Their lips were teasing and caressing, exploring the wonder of a heaven they'd never known existed except in their dreams. As he delighted in the touch and feel of her, Derek realized he'd never known such tenderness in lovemaking before. It had always been bold and wanton, even with Consuela. With Jessica, he felt the need to move her along gently, wanting to savor each and every joy their bodies could bring. Never had he touched or been touched in such delighted intensity, never had he taken time to savor all the pangs of longing that could torture so deliciously. Derek honestly tried once more to pull away, for beneath the swirling vortex of emotion, he knew what they were doing was wrong, that they should deny their passion till they had the right. Mustering every ounce of strength and willpower he possessed, he pulled back to hoarsely whisper, "Jessica, we mustn't...."

But Jessica had already done battles with her own conscience, and a lifetime of misery and longing had made her too weak to do anything but reach out and grasp even a fleeting moment of happiness to call her own. Her hands upon his back tightened, and her lips moved to rain tiny kisses upon his cheeks, his eyes, along the powerful line of his jaw and on to his neck. Greedily, she wanted to savor every part of him, in case this should be all she were ever to have.

And Derek was also overwhelmed, powerless to fight any longer. Primal need took over and, with one graceful movement, he rolled her onto her back. He fell on top of her, his body straining to feel her closer against him.

Her cape had fallen away, and his fingers nimbly, quickly unbuttoned her dress. Jessica did not resist, for she had surrendered to the calling of both body and soul. His mouth continued to devour hers softly, hungrily. With her bodice open, he moved to caress her naked flesh, fingertips dancing to leave a trail of fiery desire in the wake of his touch. She felt as though she were floating on a gentle cloud of bliss, rocked every now and then by a soft breeze of ecstasy. His touch was the sun, warming, bringing life and hope; his lips were the moonlight, cool, yet illumining even the darkest recesses of her heart. Rivulets of unfamiliar pleasure moved through her in tantalizing promise of yet greater joy to come. There was no fear, no apprehension, no wondering as to right or wrong or why or wherefore, only the here and now and the all-consuming passion that was lapping over her body like breakers on the shore.

He maneuvered to lift her skirt, then cast aside her undergarments. His knee slipped between hers to part her thighs for the sweet assault of his caress. Arching up against him, she gasped, "Love me, Derek. Please, please love me...."

"I do." He nibbled gently at her throat as he reached to unfasten and release himself. "And I always will. I swear it, Jessica. You're all I ever want in this life...."

He moved on top of her and entered with a gentle thrust. Jessica felt a sharp pain, and he hesitated, not wanting her to be hurt in any way. But she let him know she was ready to continue, ready to endure any momentary discomfort to fulfill their love, and the rhythm of joy began to spread through her loins, like molten lava within her veins, reaching all the way to the depths of her heart.

Crescendo quickly built to an explosion of ecstasy unequaled by anything she had ever imagined, and he soared with her to the pinnacle of consummation.

They lay together, spent, exhausted...and struck with the wonder of what they had discovered in each other.

Derek was finally able to find his voice. "It's just beginning." He cradled her tightly in his arms. "We'll make a future together, Jessica. I promise you that."

His voice broke the spell, and she was struck by a cool tremor of guilt. Feeling her shiver, he quickly asked, "Did I hurt you?" He raised himself on his elbow to peer down at her anxiously.

She shook her head and bit on her lip before pleading for reassurance. "Tell me it wasn't wrong, Derek. Tell me we couldn't help it...."

His soft laugh was adoring, not mocking, as he rained tiny kisses across her face and huskily whispered, "No, we couldn't help it, my darling, and it wasn't wrong. I feel as if in God's eyes we're already married, because you had to be His special gift."

"But it's a sin—"

He silenced her with a kiss, then shook his head adamantly and said, "No, not when we love each other as much as we do, Jessica. It was good and natural, and it just proves how much we do care for each other."

He rolled over on his back then, releasing her to fold his arms behind his head as he stared up at the rafters, shadowed and mysterious in the mellow light coming from below. Quietly, somberly, he began, "I've got to tell you something, Jessica, now that we've sworn to love each other and know we want to spend the rest of our lives together."

"Go on," she urged. "I want to hear anything you have to tell me. I want to know everything about the man with whom I want to spend all my days."

He told her about the deathbed promise to his mother, then dared confide his doubts about his decision to be a preacher. "I try my best," he said, "but I sometimes wonder if it's enough."

"I haven't heard any criticism. Everyone seems to like you. Why do you feel this way?"

"Because I didn't have a divine calling, like the other students I met in seminary. They could all recount some vision, or dream, or a feeling they'd had all their life that they were *called* to preach. All I did was make a promise to my dying mother. Maybe..." He sat up then to face her with sudden awareness. "Maybe I'm thinking about all this right now, because I'm looking to you to help me, Jessica." He searched her face in the dim light for some sign that she understood, somehow. "All along, I wanted my own church, but that was so I wouldn't have to constantly be meeting new people as a circuit rider. Now it's for a different reason—so we can put down roots together, build a house, make a life, have children."

"I want that, too, Derek," she tenderly assured him, "and that's the way it'll be. I know it will."

"Unless the church has other ideas," he grimly remarked. Then he went on to explain his personal concerns over the ever-increasing clouds of war. "There's going to be a division in the church, I'm afraid—a split over slavery. It's not unexpected. There have been splits in other denominations in the past few years. The Methodist Episcopal Church, for instance, split in 1844 into Northern and Southern divisions. It's just a matter of time till we do, too."

"And if that happens, which side would you take?" she asked warily.

"I really don't like to think of it as taking sides. The fact is, unlike a lot of my peers, I don't feel it's all a slavery issue. Especially for North Carolina. From what I've been able to gather from folks I've talked to, the 'fire-eaters' in South Carolina and other states of the deeper South might be talking secession, but North Carolinians, for the most part, favor the national Union. What we've got is people from the mountains who are not slave holders, folks living in the swampy regions of the East where the soil isn't good for growing cotton, anyway, so they've no need of slaves, and then there are the Quakers in the central region. None of them see any reason to be concerned over preservation of a slave system when they don't have a part in it. So if North Carolina does ultimately secede when other states do, it won't be because of slavery, it'll be from a desire to unify the South and stand together against the North."

Jessica persisted. "And would you fight for the South?"

He was quietly thoughtful for a moment, then said, "Frankly, I hope I don't have to make that decision. That's one of the reasons I'm hoping for that little church of my own, to be all settled down so I might not be expected to march off to war. The other reason—" he rolled to his side to gaze at her tenderly "—is you, my sweet. Till now, I hadn't thought much about a wife, a family, but you make me want those things. And that's why I felt the need to tell you how I've come to be what I am, because the truth is, I've still got my doubts it's what I want to be. I need you by my side to help me figure all that out."

"And I need you, too, Derek. For the first time in my life, I know what it is to have a real reason for living."

"I've got to go ahead and talk to your father. My schedule was changed by the funeral, and I'm going to have to work very hard to fit in everything before I leave Saturday."

Fearfully, she asked, "And what if you can't catch Poppa sober enough before then? What do we do?"

"I've got to be in Waynesville for Sunday service. I'll come back after that. I'll have to, because we've got to get everything settled and out in the open." He gathered her close as he whispered, "Because I love you, Jessica, and I want you for always...."

Passion ignited quickly, and they climbed once more to the stars. And when, at last, they reached the highest pinnacle in unison, it was as though a whirling comet exploded, to shatter the sphere of their existence.

They lay together, unwilling to part and end the enchantment of the moment. Jessica wanted to stay in his arms till the first light of dawn, to feel the warmth of his body against hers, to revel in the wonder of their love. She started to speak, to tell him these things that were in her heart, but at her first sound, he tensed and at once covered her mouth gently with his hand. She realized he had been lying there listening for something—but what?

In answer to her unspoken question, he whispered, "Someone's coming."

"Oh, no! It's Poppa!" She gasped in terror. "We're trapped!"

Carefully, quietly, Derek moved to the edge of the loft to peer down into the huge chamber below. Equally cautious, Jessica joined him. They could see the barn door was opening, ever so slowly.

Hunched over, arms about his stomach as though attempting to hold back the pain, Zeb took but a few faltering steps before collapsing, unconscious, to the floor.

Derek was already scrambling down the ladder, as Jessica's hands flew to her mouth to stifle a gasp of horror.

She saw that her father had been brutally beaten.

Chapter Twelve

Deciding Zeb wasn't seriously injured, just bruised and suffering a bloody nose, Jessica and Derek judged it best to cover him with blankets and leave him in the barn, rather than risk moving him to the house where his in-laws might find out what had happened. Zeb, they knew, would want to keep the incident as quiet as possible. When they had attended to him, they bade each other good-night and retired to their rooms.

Jessica got up at first light to make breakfast for Belinda's kin, who were relieved their fears of a major winter storm had proved groundless. Derek, on pretense of just being obliging, had their wagon and horses ready so they could be on their way as soon as they'd finished eating.

As soon as they left, he and Jessica quickly moved Zeb, who was still sleeping off his whiskey binge, into the house.

As they stood together at the foot of his bed staring down at his swollen face, Derek shook his head and regretfully said, "He might not be in any shape to reason with by tomorrow, Jessica. We'll have to wait and see."

He left to make his rounds of visitation, and to meet at the church with the couple getting married. Jessica, anticipating Belinda's return from Asheville with Harmon Willingham, began her chores.

It was early afternoon when Zeb finally opened his swollen eyelids. The world looked dim and fuzzy; he tried to raise his head but gave up when it felt as if an anvil was pressing down on it. With a rumble and a roll, his stomach heaved, and he hoped he wouldn't throw up. He ached miserably, from head to toe. Even drawing a breath was anguish, for the rise and fall of his chest hurt his bruised insides. What had happened to put him in such a fix? he wondered. He'd been at Bud Creech's store, that much he remembered. He must have passed out, because he could remember waking up in the back room, with its offensive odors of sour mash and slop bucket. Wanting to get out of there, he had returned to the front of the store, and then his memory peeled open like an orange, and it all came tumbling back.

Culver Hardin had been there, and he was spouting off about how he couldn't wait till war finally came, so's he could shoot some Yankees and teach them never to mess with the South again. At first, Zeb hadn't said anything, because his mouth was dry as sawdust, and he needed a drink real bad. It was later that Culver had singled him out to challenge. "You ain't sayin' nothin', Coulter. Are you for us, or agin us?"

Zeb was just peppery enough to bellow back, "It'll be a cold day in hell 'fore I go to war for slaves, when I ain't never even owned one and ain't plannin' to."

At that Culver's eyes had narrowed, and his lips had curled back in a snarl of contempt as he hollered, "Then you ain't nothin' but a goddamn traitor, you son of a bitch!"

The room had exploded into raucous laughter, which, combined with Culver's cursing, turned Zeb into a raging bull. He ducked and charged, driving his head straight into Culver's big stomach. Culver, however, was a huge man, and hardly felt the blow. No stranger to brawling, Culver proceeded to beat Zeb till the other men watching got worried he would kill him and finally stopped the fight.

Zeb couldn't remember much after that first punch, only pain. Lots of pain. Somebody else was shouting "traitor," and then the world just started spinning faster and faster, and he supposed he fell off eventually, because everything else was a blur. He had no idea how he'd got home or into his bed.

In the distance now, he could hear voices coming from the kitchen. He recognized Jessica and Belinda, but there was a man's voice, unfamiliar. Though the anguished effort made his eyes water, Zeb slowly got up and went to the door, opened it to listen. He still couldn't identify the man talking, but he sure didn't like what he was saying. Over the clatter of forks against plates and sounds of eating, he could hear him describing how plans were already under way by the young men of the state to form regiments in preparation for war. Suddenly bristling with curiosity over who this was in his house, obviously in favor of war, Zeb quietly crossed the hall but remained to one side, out of sight.

"Of course, when war comes," Zeb heard the stranger exuberantly continue, "I'll want to be among the first to go. I've already written to Professor Daniel Hill. He's the manager and commandant of the Military Institute at Charlotte. I've heard he's organizing a regiment to be called the First North Carolina, and I want to be a proud part of it."

In a flash, Zeb was through the door to bellow, "You're a damn fool like the rest of those fire-eatin' nitwits! And who the hell are you, anyway?"

All eyes were upon him; everyone was stunned. Jessica was aghast, and Belinda looked as though she were going to faint. But Harmon Willingham looked up from his bowl of turkey soup, noted Zeb's fierce expression, then coolly challenged, "I beg your pardon?"

"You heard me, boy. I said you were a damn fool. North Carolina should just stay out of it. The soil ain't never been well suited for growin' cotton, there aren't that many rich planters with large slave holdings, and—"

Jessica came to life then, and rushed to help him into a chair, for he looked as though he were about to collapse.

"Poppa, calm down," she sternly admonished. "This is Belinda's beau, Harmon Willingham, of Raleigh. He's our guest, and—"

"Don't want no fire-eaters in my house," Zeb railed.

Belinda cried, "Please Poppa. Don't do this!"

Zeb lashed out to demand of Harmon, "Boy, does your family own slaves? Is that why you're so danged anxious for war?"

Harmon cleared his throat, then boldly confirmed, "Yes, sir. We do own slaves, and we don't intend to free those slaves and lose what generations and generations of Willinghams have toiled to build, just because ignorant Northerners want to dictate to Southerners how they should live. If it takes a war to defend that, then yes, I'm anxious to go on and get it over with, so we can get back to living the way we choose."

"Holdin' a man in bondage to do your work for free is a cowardly way to choose to live, if you want my opinion!"

Zeb and Harmon locked fiery gazes, and Harmon was finally the first to break it by swiftly getting to his feet. He directed his words to Belinda. "I'd planned to stay the night, my dear, but I think it best I return to Asheville now. Will you walk with me to the carriage?"

"Maybe," Zeb said, also getting up, "she don't want to go."

Belinda stood so quickly, her chair tipped over and she rushed to follow Harmon.

The moment the door closed behind them, Jessica turned on him to say, "Poppa, how could you? How could you do such a thing? Belinda whispered to me Harmon planned to ask your permission to court her, and now you've probably ruined everything for her."

Anger faded to desolation, and Zeb wearily shook his head and mumbled, "Hell, I don't know, girl. Sometimes I wish the Lord would go ahead and take me, 'cause I sure don't get nothin' out of livin' no more."

She dropped to her knees beside him and took both his hands in hers as she attempted to comfort him. "It doesn't have to be that way, Poppa, if you'd stop drinking so much and stop saying things that get people riled up. I don't want war any more than you do, but if it's inevitable, then I'll stand with the South. That's all anyone wants you to say, too. Stop goading people."

He looked at her then, his defiance returning. "I'm no hypocrite, girl. I say what I think, especially under my own roof. And the way I see it, the only thing I've got to live for now is seein' you married to Reuben Walker and havin' sons to keep this land in Coulter blood."

Jessica turned her face, lest he see the truth there, that she had no intention of fulfilling his dream. He got up and shuffled back to bed, a man of broken faith, and she could only stare after him, still on her knees, sadly thinking how Derek was her one and only hope for a future worth living. If she lost Derek, then she, like her father, wouldn't feel there was any reason to exist.

When Belinda came inside, she was beside herself with rage. "How could he do that to me? And what's wrong with him, anyway? His face! All black and blue. And his eyes, swollen shut, almost. Who did that to him? And why did he do this to me?" she repeated shrilly.

Jessica told her what little she knew about Zeb's beating. "Preacher Stanton said he heard some men talking at the Temple wake about how Poppa was making everyone angry with his vehement stand against secession. No doubt he got into a fight at Creech's store.

"As for your situation," she continued with a sigh, "I'm sorry it happened, but you should've warned him about how Poppa is, Belinda. True, we had no way of knowing Poppa would overhear, but still, it wouldn't have come as such a shock to Harmon when he exploded."

"I know, but I hated to bring up the subject because Harmon stands so fiercely with the South."

"Is he very upset?"

"He'll get over it, I think," Belinda ventured optimistically. "He said he'd write to me, and he'll come back at Christmas." She sighed and threw up her hands in frustration. "I just don't know. I can only hope he cares enough about me to overlook Poppa's rudeness."

As the day passed, Jessica was too concerned with her own situation to dwell on Belinda's problems. Her father shuffled listlessly about the house, for although the snow had melted, the weather outside was chilling to the bone. Had Derek been there, she knew he'd have attempted to talk to Zeb, but she decided perhaps it was well the preacher wasn't around. Her father kept cursing and muttering beneath his breath, and she knew the reason for his frequent visits to the barn was to drink the liquor he had stashed away there.

She was just putting supper on the table when Reuben arrived. He regarded her coolly and then addressed Zeb, because he'd heard about the fight. "Zeb, you gotta watch that mouth of yours," he started right in. "Culver Hardin is big and he's mean, and after last night he's really got it in for you. If I were you, I'd just stay away from the store for a while, till things cool down."

Zeb gave a mocking snort. "Things ain't gonna cool down till the rabble-rousers get the war they want, and I'm not hidin' behind locked doors scared to speak my piece."

Belinda, sitting glumly, couldn't resist interjecting, "Even if he stays at home, he still makes enemies."

Zeb shot her a menacing glare. "You watch your tongue, girl. You ain't too big for me to take out behind the woodshed and tan your hide." He motioned Reuben to take the place that had been set for Derek, who hadn't yet arrived. "You might as well get used to sittin' at your own table," he said, managing a smile with swollen lips. "It's not long till Christmas."

Reuben glanced at Jessica, irritated by the way she ignored him. "Seems some folks around here don't share our enthusiasm," he muttered.

Zeb laughed and said it didn't matter, then proceeded to give his own account of the fight with Culver Hardin, embellishing the story in his own favor. Reuben obliged by expressing approval when expected as he proceeded to gorge himself on the turkey stew Jessica had made. He interrupted Zeb once to ask Jessica to fill a container with stew for him to take to Jamie.

Belinda, who was still angry and humiliated, couldn't bear her father's company, nor did she have any appetite. Without bothering to excuse herself, she got up and retired to her room.

Jessica, tense and nervous over Reuben's presence, listened for any sound of Derek returning. If Reuben would go on and leave, then she and Derek could seize the opportunity to inform her father of their desire to marry. But Reuben apparently had no intention of leaving. He and Zeb got into an enthusiastic discussion about their plans for spring planting.

Over Jessica's objections, Zeb brought out a jug of cider. It had obviously fermented, because after consuming only a few cups, both he and Reuben were tipsy.

"Have you two no respect or decency?" she railed indignantly. "We've got a preacher for a houseguest, who's going to be here any minute. How does it look for him to walk in and see the two of you drunk?"

Reuben snapped at her, saying she'd soon have to learn her place, and Zeb grunted in agreement, and after that they paid no attention to her. She didn't want to go to bed and have Derek walk in on their rowdiness, so she sat near the stove with her sewing basket to wait them out.

At last she heard the sound of the palomino coming in. Confident that they were too soused with cider and engrossed in conversation to notice her, she got up and moved quietly to the back door. Pulling her cape around her shoulders, she was about to leave, when Reuben suddenly looked up to ask sharply, "Where are you goin'?"

"We need more wood for the stove." She went on out before he could say anything else.

After hurrying to the barn, she rushed through the doors and exclaimed, "Thank goodness you're back. I wanted to tell you Reuben is here. He and Poppa are sitting at the table drinking, and I don't think he's going to be leaving any time soon."

He pulled her into his arms and kissed her tenderly. "Well, I'll talk to your father as soon as I can, Jessica, but try not to worry. We know we love each other, and that's all that matters," he reassured her.

"They're even talking about spring planting," she glumly told him, then dared to point out, "if you were a farmer and willing to stay here on the land, I think we'd have Poppa's blessings for sure."

Derek tensed. He feared this moment, for at the back of his mind all along had been the dread that Jessica might not be willing to leave home. She might truly love him, but blood, he knew, was thicker than water, and when it came to making the decision to settle elsewhere, she could very easily balk. "Is that what you want?" he asked, tension heavy in his tone.

Jessica dared to wonder if he might be persuaded to make her world his. In the mellow light from the lantern he'd fired up, she gave him her most beguiling smile and whispered, "You know, it's not a bad idea. I mean, you could settle in at our church here, and farm, too. I'm already established teaching, and we'd have a secure future, and—"

His arms dropped from about her as he brusquely told her, "I'm not even sure I'm meant to be a preacher, Jessica, but one thing I do know—I'm no farmer. Besides," he continued, turning to unsaddle his horse, "I've got dreams of my own. I don't intend to live out your father's."

Twisting her hands, she watched him anxiously. She hadn't really thought much about his taking Reuben's place in her father's dream, but it would solve a lot of problems. What difference did it make, anyway, where they settled as long as they were together? When she pointed this out to him, he kept his back turned, and she could see the stubbornness in his rigid stance.

Finally, he turned around to face her. His frustration was mirrored on his handsome face, he was slump-shouldered, and suddenly seemed defeated. Shaking his head ever so slightly, he confessed, "I can't do it, Jessica. I won't do it. We've got to make a future somewhere else, not here. I don't want to be a farmer."

"But you just said you aren't even sure you're meant to be a preacher," she countered. "What are you meant to be, Derek? What do you *want* to be?"

"I'm not sure."

"Then how can you be sure you love me?"

"I just know that I do. I know that you're the one thing in this life I want."

He stepped toward her, intending to take her in his arms again, but she held up her hands in rebuke. Too long she'd kept her fears inside her. "No. That's not enough. I've got to know you'd be willing to stay here if Poppa won't give us his blessings otherwise."

They stared at each other, pride keeping a distance between them.

"I think," Derek said, with the finality of the closing of a coffin lid, "that if you love me as you say you do, you'll make a life with me wherever fate takes us."

"And I think," she coolly told him with a defiant lift of her chin, "that if you love me, you'll do whatever it takes for us to be together."

In that prolonged moment of silence, they were searching their very souls for answers. At last, Derek dared break the spell. "Don't you think we love each other enough to work all this out in time?"

His words weren't a solution by any means, but they were enough to dispel the tension and cause the two to fall into each other's arms once more. He showered her face with kisses, and she clung to him with tears streaming down her face.

"It has to work out," she whispered tremulously. "It has to."

"And your father will see reason," he vowed passionately. "It just seems as if everything is working against us right now. I can't charge in there and tell your father I want to marry you, with him drunk. And he won't be sober enough by morning, either. There's nothing to be done except for me to come back Sunday. But it'll be night before I can get here. It's a long ride from Waynesville, especially if the weather is bad."

"I'm going to hide his whiskey," she said with fiery determination. "I don't care how mad he gets, there won't be a bottle anywhere around this place."

He held her away from him then, lovingly smoothing her hair back from her forehead as, filled with desire, he lustily suggested, "Why not let him have a few drinks, enough to make him sleep soundly? I can talk to him first thing Monday morning." Inch by inch, his hands on her arms were drawing her closer to him. His lips touched hers, inviting, warm, brushing slowly back and forth. "We could have time to be together, like this...."

His mouth opened on hers, and Jessica felt the quickening of her pulse. His tongue began to flick teasingly against her lips, inviting, and she yielded and slid her hands about his shoulders to return his kiss with fierce shyness. Though she still felt a bit guilty, she could push aside her nagging conscience with the rationalization that they would soon be married.

For the moment, however, they were both aware that propriety demanded control. They were playing with fire and knew it. But only with great determination was Derek able, at last, to end the kiss and step away from her. "They're liable to start wondering where you are, so you'd better go inside. It wouldn't do for them to find us here."

She nodded. "Wait a few minutes and then come in."

Impulsively, he reached out for her again. "Once more," he whispered, "to remember till Sunday...midnight...."

Outside the door, peering through a crack, Reuben was trembling not with cold, but with rage. His fists were clenched as tightly as his teeth, and pain throbbed through every taut nerve in his body. He was glad he'd decided to be chivalrous and help Jessica bring in the wood, for now he knew why she was so defiant and belligerent. And, somehow, he was able to muster the willpower to turn and walk away and leave them as they were—for the moment.

Reuben had heard Derek say he'd return at midnight Sunday.

He intended to see he got a proper greeting.

Chapter Thirteen

For a moment, Reuben feared Zeb Coulter was going to drop dead from his anger.

"Why didn't you tell me all this while the son of a bitch was still in these parts, so I could shoot him? How come you tell me now?"

"This is the reason, Zeb—'cause of the way you're acting right now." They were standing behind the church outhouse, which was where Reuben had chosen to break the news to Zeb about Jessica's tryst with Derek Stanton. It was Sunday morning, right before the church service, which was conducted by the deacons when the circuit rider wasn't present. Reuben had figured that at such a time and place, Zeb wouldn't act quite so crazy, yet now he was worried he wouldn't be able to keep the man from tearing out of there like an angry bull. "Now, you've got to get hold of yourself, and—"

"He ain't gonna take her away from here!" Zeb grabbed the front of Reuben's coat and gave him a vicious shake. "I done been kicked in the teeth too many times, and all I've got left to live for is knowing I've been able to do what my kin before me did—pass Coulter land to Coulter blood. That may not seem like much to some folks, but it's all I've got, and it's everything to me, you understand?"

Reuben was trembling in his boots. "Of course, I do. Isn't that why we made the pact in the first place? Because I understand how you feel. Think about me in this, too," he rushed to add. "How do you think I feel, knowin' the woman I want for the mother of my children is sneakin' around meetin' another man and huggin' and kissin' up to him? I saw them with my own eyes, Zeb, so help me."

Zeb released him to slam a fist into his palm. "I wish I'd seen it. Oh, Lord, how I wish I'd been there to see it." He began to pace about in agitation.

Reuben seized his chance to fuel the flames in preparation for his plan. "If they'd had any decency, they'd have gone to you, Zeb, and told you face-to-face what was going on, and they'd have courted out in the open. The very fact they were sneaking proves it's nothing but sin and lust. Shameful enough your daughter turned out to be a Jezebel, but with the preacher, it's even worse." He gave a mock shudder, pretending to be overcome with disgust. He wasn't going to confide he'd heard Derek and Jessica avowing their love, in case Zeb got the idea he could persuade Stanton to stay and take over the farm. What difference would it make to Zeb whom he had for a son-in-law, so long as he had one? But what if he liked the idea of Stanton better than Reuben? Oh, yes, Reuben had thought of that awful possibility, too—that Zeb might figure he was better off not to attach his land to Reuben's. Reuben had no intention of letting that seed of thought germinate in Zeb's brain.

"Where's he preachin' today?" Zeb suddenly, sharply asked. He wasn't going to sit back and do nothing. He intended to make sure Derek Stanton didn't return to Buncombe County.

"It doesn't matter. He'll be back tonight. I heard them talking."

Zeb stopped his pacing, glared down at him with nostrils flared, a muscle in his jaw twitching. "I'm listening. You tell me everything."

Reuben proceeded to recount the tense exchange between the two lovers over Derek's refusal to become a farmer. "So that's our ace in the hole. Don't you see?"

Zeb was too angry to rationally figure out anything. He shook his head.

"It's not enough to just break up their meeting tonight," Reuben explained. "Stanton is making a fool out of Jessica, telling her he loves her in order to get what he wants. Don't you see? And if you just run him off, she's going to pine away for him. She might even run after him."

Zeb said in a low, lethal tone, "Not if he's dead, she won't."

"You really want to hang for murdering a preacher? Think about it. There are other ways, better ways, that won't get either one of us in trouble, and, most of all, Jessica won't wind up hating us both."

Zeb calmed enough to grasp his logic. "Go on."

"We'll surprise them tonight, and after that leave everything to me, all right?"

Zeb thought about that a moment and decided he really had no choice. Reuben was right that Jessica might run away, and Zeb didn't want that. She was his only chance. Belinda sure didn't intend to stay around home. She was already pining away, thinking she'd lost that arrogant young whippersnapper, Harmon Willingham. "All right," he said finally. "We'll do it your way."

"Good!" Reuben slapped a hand on his shoulder. "Now let's get inside to the service and act like we don't know anything. We don't want to risk making her suspicious."

They started up the path, and Zeb laughed and said, "Wouldn't it be funny if today, of all days, I got the sign I've been waitin' for all these years that God was takin' away my curse?"

"Don't be surprised if you already haven't, Zeb," Reuben soberly told him. "Maybe God arranged for me to find them together as a sign—for both of us."

Zeb thought about that, then decided it wasn't what he had in mind. He'd know when the Lord lifted the curse. He wasn't sure exactly how—only that he'd know, for sure.

* * *

Jessica wondered why her father was acting so strangely. He hadn't started drinking the minute church was over, depressed by another Sunday without a sign from God. Instead, he'd roamed around the farm all afternoon, bundled up against the cold and seeming to be deep in thought about something. At supper he'd hardly said a word, had eaten very little. Afterward, he'd said he and Reuben were going coon hunting and got up and left. That filled her with relief, for she'd not have to worry about either of them seeing Derek. She wanted this night with him, in his arms, she thought with a warm flush that spread from head to toe. Tomorrow they'd let the world know they were in love and intended to make a life together.

She was also grateful that Belinda didn't want to sit up and talk, as she usually did. She was still very upset over Harmon and would probably remain so till she received some word that meant he still cared for her, despite the unpleasant scene with Zeb.

At eleven-thirty, Jessica decided she'd be better off waiting in the barn than walking aimlessly around the house. Above a thin fog, the sky held only scattered clouds, and a full moon's yellow-silver radiance penetrated the mist, providing enough light for her to move from house to barn without groping or stumbling in the mantling night. The air was cold, but not frigid, and with her wool cape wrapped tightly about her, she could stand just inside the barn door without shivering, to watch for Derek's approach. She had brought the tiny watch that had been her mother's, which she wore on a ribbon around her neck. Every so often, the moon would burst from behind the clouds to give full light, and she knew the magic hour of midnight was almost there.

She was stiff from standing, and not altogether comfortable with being in the barn with all the strange noises. Mice skittered unseen in the darkness. She could hear a screeching owl on the ridge above.

But there was something else, something she couldn't discern. It was a feeling that gnawed like invisible gnats upon her flesh. She told herself she was overreacting from anxiety and, yes, a touch of eagerness to have everything out in the open, once and for all, so she and Derek wouldn't have to sneak in the shadows as though ashamed of their love.

Finally, from her vigil at the door, she saw movement at the edge of the skeletal forest. Straining to see, she held her breath, then gasped aloud with joy, for the moon leaped from behind a cloud and out of the mist, and she could see Derek making his way toward her.

She could not wait. She bolted from the barn and ran to him, and he saw her coming toward him and laughed, the sound catching on the night wind. He held his arms wide open, and she fell into them, and he lifted her up and swung her around and around. Finally cradling her in his arms, he lowered his mouth to cover hers in a searing kiss of glory yet to come. Then he carried her quickly into the barn, kicking the door shut with his foot as he continued to hold her and kiss her.

The match striking against the wall exploded in a small blinding flash, and before Derek and Jessica could react, the wick of a lantern was fired, and the interior of the barn was flooded with sudden light.

It all happened so quickly.

There was Zeb, holding the lantern high, and in its glow his face was like that of a demon from hell.

Beside him, Reuben grinned maniacally, as he aimed the shotgun and harshly demanded, "Set her down and get away from her, and do it fast."

Derek had no choice but to obey, and as he lowered Jessica to her feet, he protectively pushed her behind him.

Reuben snarled, "I said, get away from her!"

Derek held up his hands. "Now wait. We need to talk about this. You don't understand, either of you."

Jessica came out of her stupor to leap between them and scream, "Have you gone crazy? Get out of here with that gun before you hurt somebody. This is none of your business—"

"Shut up, girl!" Zeb warned, stepping forward to give her a rough shove to one side. Caught unaware, she went sprawling to the floor and could only look up helplessly as he growled at Derek, "You ain't got nothin' to say that I want to hear after what you've done to my girl." He signaled Reuben with a nod. "Get him out of here, and see that he keeps on goin'."

Derek looked at Jessica. What could he do? A shotgun was inches from his face.

She scrambled to her feet to protest wildly, "You can't do this. I won't let you!"

Zeb held her back as he shook his fist and raged at Derek, "So help me, if I ever see your face in these parts again, I'll kill you!"

Derek started toward the door, with Reuben pointing the gun at his back. With wretched eyes, he looked at Jessica, then threw Zeb a menacing glare as he vowed, "They won't keep us apart, Jessica."

At that, Reuben jammed the gun muzzle into Derek's back, giving him a shove through the door, and threatening, "Don't push your luck, *preacher*."

When they were gone, Jessica whirled on her father, but froze in terror as she saw a stranger coming toward her, with mayhem in his wildly bulging eyes.

"I've got to punish you, girl." His voice was as chilling as a waiting grave. "I've got to beat the strumpet demon out of you."

She refused to cry as the leather belt slashed across her back. It tore her dress, leaving her flesh bare and vulnerable to deeper agony. Yet she would not succumb to tears. Instead she ground her teeth together and swallowed against the rising screams each time a blow fell. But Zeb Coulter was sobbing brokenly as he administered the punishment he felt was necessary to purge the evil demons from his daughter.

Belinda didn't know what brought her out of a sound sleep, but she awoke and sensed something was wrong. She got up to discover there was a light in the barn. Curious, she stepped out on the back porch. She could hear her father yelling, but couldn't make out what he was saying, and then she realized with a start that she could also hear the sounds of someone being whipped. She didn't take time to put on shoes or robe, but instead gathered her nightgown around her ankles and dashed across the frost-covered yard.

Bursting wildly into the barn, she screamed at the ghastly sight before her. Jessica lay sprawled on the floor, her back, exposed beneath the remnants of her dress, covered in bruises and bloody welts . . . and her father still continued mercilessly to rain blows upon her.

"Stop it! For God's sake, stop it! Have you lost your mind?" Belinda threw herself across Jessica, just as the belt came singing down once more. It struck the side of her head, and she screamed. The sound abruptly brought Zeb out of his frenzy of rage; woodenly, he looked at Belinda, trying to remember who she was.

Despite the excruciating pain, Belinda remained where she was to shield her sister from further blows. Tears streaming down her face, she looked up at him to plead, "Poppa, what's going on? Why are you doing this? You were killing her—"

"Had to . . . had to." He shook his head, tossed the belt to one side. With his shoulders slumped in regret of the castigation, he shuffled woodenly out of the barn to disappear into the night.

Belinda turned to Jessica and cried, "Oh, Jessica, are you hurt bad? Can you hear me?" She shook her gently. "We've got to get you to a doctor. Can you move? Can you get up?"

Jessica's eyes fluttered open, and, weakly, feebly, she moved her head from side to side in protest. "No doctor. I'll be all right. No one must know. Please. Just help me get in the house."

Straining, Belinda got Jessica to her feet, then laid one arm across her shoulder. With great effort she helped her hobble along to the house. "Don't faint on me," Belinda urged over and over as she felt her sister slumping. "We're almost there. Just a little farther."

Jessica shook her head, attempting to clear it to cast aside the temptation to just yield to the beckoning arms of oblivion. Remembering that Belinda had taken the final blow, she worriedly asked if she was hurt.

"The strap hit the side of my head. It hurts, but there won't be a bruise on my face, thank goodness." She helped Jessica to her room, then, after lowering her to the bed, stood over her with fear-widened eyes and demanded, "Now tell me what that was all about."

"Poppa found me there with Derek."

"Preacher Stanton?" Belinda echoed incredulously. "But why? I mean, what was he doing back here at such an hour, and..." Her voice faded to an astonished gasp as understanding dawned. "You and Preacher Stanton? Oh, Jessica, no! You should've known Poppa would never stand for that. Oh, dear Lord!"

"Reuben was behind it all. Derek came back to tell Poppa he wants to marry me. Somehow, Reuben found out I was meeting him, and this was his way of taking revenge."

"I'd say he did a good job, because Poppa sure went crazy." She looked down at her in wonder. She'd never have guessed her sister had the grit to defy her father, much less become embroiled in a romance with someone as handsome and different as Derek Stanton.

She used scissors to carefully cut away what was left of Jessica's dress. Rolling her sister on her stomach, she cleansed the bruised and torn flesh, then hurried to the pantry for the jar of chickweed-and-starch paste used to promote healing of cuts and burns. Applying it as gently as possible, eyes brimming with tears of sympathy, she asked, "Does it hurt terribly?"

Jessica could have told her that while the outer pain was truly excruciating, *nothing* could compare to the hurting inside. "It doesn't matter. I have to know what Reuben did to Derek. He took him out of the barn at gunpoint."

"He probably just made sure he left. Reuben is no killer. I hope and pray word doesn't get out about this. Harmon is already looking down on this family after the way Poppa acted, and it sure won't raise his opinion any if he hears about this."

Jessica quickly, curtly defended herself and Derek against this slight. "We love each other. We want to be married. There's nothing sordid or ugly about any of it."

"I'm not saying there is, but you can be sure Reuben will make out that there is. What about you? Your reputation? God, Jessica, you could lose your job. Schoolteachers have to be above reproach. You know that."

"People will believe what they want to, anyway. Besides, Derek will come back and straighten everything out. I know he will."

"For your sake, I hope you're right, Jessica, but I'm afraid I don't share your optimism. Regardless of how he feels about you, you've got to remember his first commitment is to the church, and Reuben will be sure Derek's superiors hear about all this. They'll probably order him to stay away from you."

Jessica had to agree that was likely, but didn't confide to Belinda what Derek had told her about his self-doubts over being a preacher. Perhaps the reaction of his superiors wouldn't matter all that much, and he'd be willing to give up his position for her. That would solve all their problems, because her father wouldn't have any reason to object. In fact, once he calmed down and thought about it, he'd welcome Derek marrying her to protect her virtue, which Reuben was sure to do his best to besmirch.

"Get some sleep," Belinda said, leaving her. "Things always look brighter in the morning."

Jessica hoped so, because gloom certainly prevailed at the moment.

Derek opened his eyes and wondered why the world was spinning. He closed them, trying to shut out the pain. Gingerly, he touched the lids, winced with pain at the same time he felt the swelling.

By the sun above, he figured it was probably midday. Where the hell was he? And why did he feel as if he'd been kicked by a horse? He was lying on the ground; with great effort, he pulled himself up to a sitting position, grateful that there was a tree behind him, so he could lean back and try to get himself together. Taking a deep breath, he felt alarm at the sudden stab of pain in his side. That could mean a cracked or broken rib. But why? The world was still going around and around, just like his head, or was it his head turning while the world was actually standing still?

He felt a wave of nausea, closed his eyes and ground his teeth together so tight he sent anguish singing through his jawbone. Heaving and gagging were the last things he needed right then.

A few moments passed, and slowly the memories came flooding back. Reuben had led him out of the barn, asked where he'd left his horse, then marched him there, across the frost-covered field with the gun pressed into his back. And the palomino was the last thing Derek saw; he remembered nothing after a sudden explosion of pain. He guessed Reuben must have thrown him across his horse after beating him with the gun butt, and that after a time he'd fallen off.

He tried to get up now but slumped back against the tree in fresh waves of anguish. He was desperate to get in touch with Jessica, but knew that for the time being, he had to get to the boardinghouse in Asheville where he sometimes stayed, to give his injuries time to heal.

Finally, holding his side against the excruciating pain in his ribs, he dragged himself to where his horse lazily grazed nearby. He managed to hoist himself into the saddle, then he slumped forward against the horse's neck. He could feel slumber calling him, offering respite, if only for a little while. He resisted, as his blurring mind struggled to word the letter he so much wanted to send to Jessica.

But sleep triumphed . . . and he drifted away.

Chapter Fourteen

Zeb Coulter was oblivious to the wind's bite as he sat on the creek bank. He had been there since midmorning. Now the sun had begun to drop behind the ridge, and long shadows crept about the rocky ledges. He was neither cold nor hungry, for the only emotion he had felt during the past hours of brooding was sorrow. It seemed to have plagued him most of his life—sorrow for the loss of his wives and baby, sorrow that he'd not been able to either pray away, or shake away, God's curse.

He sighed out loud, the only sound he had made in a long time, and a doe drinking from the creek, upwind on the other side, suddenly realized she was not alone, and bolted and ran.

But Zeb didn't notice the deer any more than he was aware of anything else in the world just then. He could only sit, shoulders hunched in desolation, head down in despair, as he stared at the crumpled letter he held in his wrinkled, weathered hands.

My dearest Jessica,
I can't begin to tell you how it hurt to leave you that night, but a man can't argue with a gun in his back. Only God knows how I've ached to return for you but feared the consequences for you should I fail in my attempt to take you away with me. I write to you now to

ask that you meet me on Christmas Eve at the old stage depot on the Asheville road. I don't know what the future will hold for us in these troubled times. I can only promise to love you with all my heart and try to do everything I can to make you happy. I pray you love me as I love you and that you will be there.

All my love,
Derek

At last, with the words Derek Stanton had written to Jessica burned into his tormented soul forever, Zeb crumpled the letter into a tight ball, and viciously tossed it in the bubbling current. It bobbed momentarily, as though struggling to survive, then was swept underwater and out of sight.

He was grateful Reuben had got that letter to him. Lost in his misery the past weeks, Zeb hadn't thought to keep an eye out for the mail. Reuben had. Zeb couldn't read too well, so Reuben had gone over it with him.

They had agreed it wasn't enough to destroy it. Jessica might figure her mail would be intercepted and take off to Asheville to look for Derek Stanton and find out why she hadn't heard anything from him. So Zeb hit on the idea of telling Widow Haislip the whole story and asking for her help.

She had been horrified. When he confided his desperate plan to stop things before they went any further, she had considered it her Christian duty to oblige him. He wasn't fooled, though; he knew she was jumping at the chance to make him beholden to her. But he didn't care about that. All he wanted was to get the mess over with.

He had dictated what she was to write to Stanton, signing Jessica's name. She'd even mailed the letter for him. Then she'd further obliged by writing what he wanted her to say in Derek's name to Jessica. She had posted that letter in Asheville. He wasn't worried about the widow telling what she'd done. She'd never want anybody to know she had been involved.

Thanks to her efforts, he'd felt secure everything was taken care of, and enjoyed a slice of fresh gooseberry pie and a cup of coffee afterward. He had patronizingly agreed with the widow that they should spend more time together, all the while feeling like an ant trapped in a doodlebug hole, anxious to escape.

He hoped that once Jessica received the fake letter, she would believe it. He hoped also she would realize she had to marry Reuben to protect her good name.

Zeb finally got to his feet, stiff from the hours of brooding. Making his way up the creek bank, he realized how cold he was, chilled to the bone, in fact. He took his parka from where it was rolled on the mule's rump, wrapped it around him and climbed up onto the animal's bare back.

He could almost taste the whiskey waiting for him at Creech's store.

Another lonely, miserable day was ending for Jessica. She gathered her papers from her desk, left the schoolhouse to make her way to the settlement store. Rain two days before had turned to sleet, then ice, and the world was still painted in crystal and diamonds, sparkling and dazzling in the last golden rays of light.

The week before Christmas, December 20, South Carolina had made good her threat to withdraw from the Union. North Carolina, conservative for the most part, had condemned the action but opposed using force to bring its neighboring state back in. Tension reigned and fiery tempers had erupted in the general assembly. It adjourned two days after South Carolina's secession, not to reconvene before January, and all over the state meetings were being held to debate the issue of North Carolina also seceding. Most citizens, it appeared, wanted to remain in the Union but they were willing to follow the lead of other Southern states.

Unlike Belinda and almost everyone else, Jessica was not preoccupied with the ever-beating drums of war. Other fears and worries overshadowed that threat. Since that terrible night in the barn tension hung about her like a shroud—unseen but felt. Zeb appeared only at mealtimes, and not always. He ignored her then and spoke only when absolutely necessary. A few times she had tried to talk to him, to tell him it was not as he thought, that she and Derek truly loved each other, but he had given her such a blistering look of scorn and condemnation that she had shrunk back in silence; she feared that if she went on she would trip him into a rage once again.

She was living for the day Derek either returned or sent word for her to meet him. She kept her one bag beneath the bed, packed with a few clothes and even fewer personal treasures—a hair ribbon and Bible that had belonged to her mother. She wanted to be ready should he come for her without word or warning.

Reuben had dropped by a few days after the tragedy to inform her piously that if she would stand up in church in front of everyone, confess her sins and ask forgiveness of God and her neighbors, he'd be willing to marry her despite her immoral behavior. "I've spoken to the deacons about all of this, of course, and they're sending a committee to Asheville to speak to the church authorities there. Stanton won't be coming back here, so you'll be spared that humiliation."

Jessica had turned her back on him in silence, telling herself he wasn't worth her rage.

He then warned if she didn't agree, she'd be asked to resign her teaching post. "Parents won't stand for a woman teaching their children who won't ask God to forgive her sins."

Still, Jessica said nothing.

"Very well." He gave a ragged sigh. "Have it your way, but I have my pride, Jessica, and I won't wait forever. I've had to do a lot of soul-searching, anyway, to convince myself to take you for my wife after what you've done, but I am a Christian, and part of being a Christian is being able to forgive. I'll give you till Christmas."

She turned then to look at him in contempt. "It was always the land, wasn't it, Reuben? That's all you were ever interested in."

He was taken aback by her question at such a time but then laughed. "Of course. What other reason would I have?" And, with that, he turned on his heel and left.

Since then, the deadline for the ultimatum he'd given her had moved ever closer. No doubt, when he realized she wasn't going to give in, he'd make sure everyone knew about what had happened. She'd worry about it then. For the present, she was concerned only with why she hadn't had word from Derek. There should have been a letter, and she was suspicious her father might have destroyed it, and now she intended to ask at the store if anyone had picked up her mail lately.

When she entered, Naomi Billingsley, who was looking over bolts of newly arrived fabrics, gave her a cool stare, barely acknowledging her nod of greeting. Naomi's husband was a deacon; she was bound to have heard something. But Jessica had no idea what Reuben was saying, and told herself not to worry, because soon she'd be leaving the settlement forever, anyway.

Luther Gaither saw her and cheerily called from behind the counter, "Hey, Miss Jessica, I don't know if it's the one you been looking for, but a letter came for you this morning." He took it from a shelf behind him, and it was all she could do to keep from snatching it from his hand in her eagerness. "That it?" he persisted curiously as she took it from him.

"Yes, I think so," she responded absently, trying to keep from breaking into a run as she hurried out of the store. No one was in the street, but she went around the corner of the building, not wanting to be seen—especially if her father, or worse, Reuben, were anywhere around.

The paper crackled in the winter wind as she began to read, but as her eyes scanned the paper, it was the shaking of her hands that made the letter tremble in her grasp.

Dear Jessica,
I don't know where to begin. I can't come back for you, because I have got to do my duty and marry a girl who is going to have my baby. I am leaving the ministry and won't be coming back. I wanted you to know that, so you won't be waiting for me. I'm sorry if I hurt you, and I hope you will find happiness.

Sincerely, Derek

Jessica pressed back against the wall, then slid downward to the ground. She began to rock to and fro, as she broke the vow she'd made to herself so long ago and began to cry.

Derek responded to the knock on his door with a curt, "It's open." He was propped in bed, his chest still tightly bound to aid his broken ribs in healing. Christmas Eve was only a day away, and, by God, no matter how much it hurt, he was going to be waiting for Jessica at the old stage depot.

He glanced up to see Nathan Robard and Seth Phillips. Nathan was the man he reported to in the ministry. Seth was his assistant. They were tight-lipped and grim, and he supposed he'd been expecting them before now. "Sit down." He motioned to the two wooden chairs by the window. He wasn't wearing a shirt and gestured to his bandages. "As you can see, I'm not up to being a very good host."

The two men exchanged frowning glances, then Nathan got right to the point. "You got that beating because you were trifling with the daughter of one of your flock, isn't that true, Mr. Stanton?"

Firmly, he denied, "That's not true!" He did not fail to notice the way they had avoided addressing him as Preacher, or Reverend.

"That's not what we heard from the deacons there," Nathan fired back. They report that Zeb Coulter justifiably beat you for molesting his daughter, a virtuous woman, and attempting to seduce her, and—"

"You wait a minute!" Derek leaped to his feet, ignoring the sharp stab of pain in his side. "That's all a pack of lies. I love Jessica Coulter, and she loves me, and we're going to be married. I went there to tell her father that, but it was a trap, and a bastard by the name of Reuben Walker is the one that beat me half to death with his gun butt, because he wants to marry her to get his hands on her daddy's land. That's the way it was, and I don't give a damn what they told you."

The two ministers exchanged yet another glance, then Nathan frostily declared, "We have every reason to believe the deacons, Stanton. Do we need to remind you that it was only after careful deliberation and out of respect for your uncle, that we allowed you to replace him on the circuit? And that we did so with reservations because of your...shall we say, questionable background?"

Warily, Derek challenged, "And what do you know about my background?"

Nathan gestured to Seth to take over, and he did so, after nervously clearing his throat. "We heard you shot a man in an argument over his wife."

Derek lowered himself gently into his bed before responding. "What difference does it make? It was a long time ago. It's over. History. I've been to seminary, I've dedicated myself to preaching. What more do you want? I thought forgiveness was one of the principles of Christianity," he couldn't resist adding.

At that, Nathan harshly cried, "You, as a minister, a representative of the church, must hold yourself up as an example. You can't risk even a breath of sin or scandal. We've no choice but to dismiss you."

Derek was raging inside but held his tongue. There was no need to lose control; he'd figured all along Reuben Walker would see to it this happened. And no matter. After tomorrow night, he and Jessica would be leaving this place, anyway. And if she didn't meet him, he'd know she'd hadn't got his letter. Then would be the time when he'd lose control, all right, because he planned to go after her, and God help anybody who got in his way.

"Very well," he said finally and gestured for them to leave. "You're going to believe what you want to believe, so I don't think we've got anything else to say to each other."

They turned to go, relieved the confrontation was over. Then Nathan remembered something, reached inside his coat to toss the letter on the bed. "This came for you at the office."

He didn't hear them close the door, wasn't even aware they were gone, because at once he tore the envelope open and quickly read the lines that subsequently broke his heart.

Derek,
It was a mistake for me to think I could ever leave my home and run away with you. Reuben has forgiven me, and we are now married. I hope you wish for my happiness as I wish for yours. I'm sorry if I hurt you.
                                        Jessica.

He tore the letter to shreds.

Through the haze of anguish, he heard jubilant cries coming from outside. Someone was shouting, spreading the news that troops in South Carolina were preparing to seize Fort Moultrie and Castle Pinckney. Florida, Alabama and Georgia were said to be preparing to follow South Carolina in seceding from the Union.

Derek no longer felt the pain of his broken and cracked ribs. That anguish was overshadowed by the desolation of his heart.

He got up and crammed what he could of his belongings into his haversack, abandoning the rest. Then he made his way downstairs, mutely settled his bill at the desk and walked out.

The nation was on the brink of war. He'd already toppled into the pit of futility. He had nothing left to lose. He was going to join up with the Federals. Not because of states' rights, or slavery, or any other issues the fire-eaters talked about. He only wanted to get as far away from the bad memories as he could.

As he headed out of Asheville, moving north, Derek wasn't concerned about what the future held for him.

All he knew at that moment was that he never wanted to forget Jessica Coulter.

Her memory would remind him of what a fool he was, if ever again he was tempted to love another.

Chapter Fifteen

As the year 1860 drew to a close, war seemed inevitable, but almost everyone believed that if it came, it would not last long. With a population of more than twenty-two million and having most of the country's factories, telegraph lines, ships, railroads, minerals and monetary wealth, the North felt confident at being opposed by only a small group of Southern states with a population of only nine million. One-third of the South's population was Negro slaves. The South couldn't believe it would be actually invaded but felt if that happened, the Federals would be easily beaten. The Southerners' advantage was in their morale; they felt they were defending their homes against an oppressor.

But despite all the war clouds, neither side was ready. The Confederacy had no standing army, no armed vessels. The majority of the sixteen thousand men of the United States Army was stationed in the West to guard frontier posts against Indian raids.

In support of South Carolina's secession, senators from Mississippi, Alabama, Florida, Georgia, Louisiana, Texas and Arkansas gathered at the Capitol of the United States on January 5, 1861, to pass a resolution urging their states to secede also. On January 7, the citizens of Wilmington, North Carolina seized Fort Caswell and Fort Johnston near the mouth of the Cape Fear River.

As the drums of war beat ever louder, Jessica sadly realized that when dreams end, nightmares begin. There seemed no hope for any happiness, and her only panacea was her teaching. Working with her students kept her mind off her misery, if only for a little while. At home, her father ignored her and everyone else, being almost constantly drunk. Belinda was optimistic that a proposal from Harmon was imminent, for he'd no doubt want to get married before marching off to war.

Then, when Mississippi, Florida, Alabama and Georgia pulled out of the Union within ten days of one another, Reuben appeared at the schoolhouse on a Friday afternoon to give Jessica a final ultimatum.

"I've tried to be patient about all this," he began. Only the two of them were there, for class had ended for the day. "I realize it's been a difficult time for you, knowing how you've shamed your family, but I'm a forgiving man, Jessica. I'm still willing to marry you and make a decent woman out of you, but my patience is growing thin. Any day now, North Carolina is going to secede, and already troops are forming and getting ready to go off to war. I'd like to do my duty and go with them, but because of my game leg, I'm not fit. So I want me and you to get married as soon as possible, settle down, get busy having younguns, and—"

"I'd rather die than marry you, Reuben," she interrupted brusquely.

For an instant, he could only stare at her in shock, then, eyes narrowing to angry slits, he cried, "You'd better think about what you're saying, woman. There's plenty of speculation as to why Stanton was relieved of his post, but out of respect for me, the deacons have kept silent, because I told them I was willing to marry you and guide you to a righteous life. But one word from me, and all the Blue Ridge will know what a harlot and jezebel you are."

"You do what you have to do, Reuben," she said with finality. She gathered her things and walked out to leave him staring after her, his mouth agape.

Monday morning, as Jessica was starting out for school, she was surprised when Belinda appeared, wanting to ride into the settlement with her. "I'm pretty sure the next letter from Harmon will be a proposal," she said excitedly, taking a seat beside Jessica in the wagon. "And I'm going to be at the store every day waiting for the mail cart to come in."

Jessica smiled. It was nice that someone was happy these days. "You should have lots of company. There's always a big crowd at the store waiting for the latest news."

They rode along in silence for a while, then Belinda asked the question that had been burning inside for so long and that she'd been afraid to ask. "What's going to happen to you when I leave, Jessica?"

Jessica blinked, momentarily taken by surprise, then replied in a dull monotone. "Nothing. Nothing at all. I'll keep on teaching. Poppa will die one day, and so will Miss Satterfield, and then I'll move into her house, and I will die one day. That is what is going to happen to me," she finished with a bitter smile.

Belinda could only murmur, "I'm sorry." Then she offered, "Maybe you can come to Raleigh and live with me and Harmon. His family has a huge house. He told me his brother and his wife and their two children are living there, too. There'll be room for all of us, I know."

Jessica reached to pat her knee in grateful affection. "Don't you worry about me. You live your life and be happy, Belinda."

"I'm sorry things turned out like they did. I really am. Till you told me about the letter from Preacher Stanton, I really thought he'd come back for you."

"So did I." She gave a ragged sigh. "But he had an obligation to fulfill. I guess it wasn't meant to be."

Belinda bit down on her lip thoughtfully, then dared ask, "Do you think he loved you when he said he did? I mean, do you have lots of nice memories before the bad things happened?''

Jessica mused over that for only an instant, then admitted, ''Yes, I guess I do. As for him loving me, well, I'll never know for sure if he did or didn't, but at the time, I believed he did. Maybe that's all that really counts, anyway.''

Belinda made no comment, for she just didn't know what to say.

When they reached the school, Belinda took off for the store at once, while Jessica tied the mule and went inside. She still had a few moments till it was time to ring the bell, but already there were children gathering in the yard. It was one of those rare January days when the weather was not so terribly cold, and she thought it'd be nice to have recess outdoors.

She was proud of her teaching position. North Carolina, she felt, had come a long way toward establishing a statewide educational system since it came into being in 1838.

The Mills River Academy near Waynesville, on the other side of Asheville, had been one of the first schools. Then, with the advent of the statewide system, each county had been divided into school districts six miles square with six committeemen each. Schools started up in every mountain county and education was well on its way in the state of North Carolina.

Jessica was lost in thought about her job, the only pleasure she knew, when she walked into the one-room schoolhouse that morning. However, she came to an abrupt stop in the doorway at the sight of the grim-faced men standing at her desk.

She recognized them at once as the six committeemen of her school district.

Malcolm Chalmers, the chairman, didn't bother to greet her but curtly nodded to the man on his right, James Franklin. He snapped, ''Close and lock the door. We don't want the pupils coming in to hear this.''

Jessica stood rooted where she was, and winced at the glance of contempt James Franklin shot her way as he moved to obey.

"Miss Coulter, would you come forward, please?" Malcolm stiffly said.

Jessica took only a few steps before sinking down to one of the benches. Her knees would support her no longer. She knew, without being told, why they were there, and her heart was breaking into tiny bits and pieces over the ugly situation.

With the others gathered behind him, as though in line to take aim, fire and execute a condemned prisoner, Malcolm cleared his throat and got straight to the point. "We have had a report of impropriety, Miss Coulter. We have been informed that your licentious and immoral behavior has led to the dismissal of a man of the cloth. Such behavior cannot be tolerated in a woman teaching our children. Therefore, we have come to inform you that you are, at once, dismissed from our school system.

"Further," he went on, "we will mark your record accordingly, so that you will never again hold a teaching position."

In the silence that followed, Jessica ground her teeth together so tightly her jaw ached as she fought to hold back her tears. She was determined not to give the pompous, holier-than-thou bastards the pleasure of seeing her cry. No matter that they knew only what Reuben had told them. No matter that she really had no defense. They didn't care that she had loved Derek Stanton, had dared to believe they'd marry one day. They wouldn't be moved if she told them she'd already been punished by her humiliation over it all. No, she wasn't going to offer any explanation for anything, nor would she give them satisfaction by begging for forgiveness, or another chance.

Forcing her trembling legs to support her, and mustering every ounce of dignity she had left, Jessica got up and walked to the front of the room. The committeemen shrank back, seeing the cold, steely look on her face. "I'd like to clear my desk," she curtly informed then, then proceeded to do so.

They glanced at each other nervously, then Malcolm Chalmers regained his bravado and gruffly goaded, "Well, do we take it then that you've nothing to say for yourself?"

She looked him straight in the eye. "Would it matter if I did?"

"No, no..." he blustered. "But we thought we'd give you a chance to explain yourself, and—"

"Explain myself?" she echoed with an incredulous laugh. "What do you expect me to tell you? You've listened to what Reuben Walker had to say about me, and you don't care about my side, at all. Frankly, I don't think it's any of your business, anyway."

They gasped in unison, for the committeemen were not used to such effrontery or disrespect. "I think—" Malcolm motioned to the others "—this meeting has ended."

"Before it even began," she cracked, dumping the contents of her drawer on the desk.

They hurried out, and furiously blinking back tears by then, Jessica frantically stuffed her personal belongings into her satchel, after emptying it of homework papers and lesson plans. She'd have no need of those anymore, she sadly realized.

She wasn't thinking beyond the moment at hand, not yet worrying what tomorrow might hold. All she wanted was to get out of there as fast as possible and take refuge at home, because now the gossip would spread like wildfire on a ridge in a summer drought. She might as well have been declared a witch and publicly burned at the stake, for she was surely an outcast from this day forward.

Hearing the door open hesitantly, she glanced up to see Polly Sue. "Miss Coulter," she said in the firm, self-assured tone she had possessed after Derek's miraculous "cure." "Those men, they said we were supposed to stay outside, that you were leaving and weren't going to be our teacher anymore."

Jessica managed to swallow past the constricting lump in her throat and regretfully confirm, "Yes, that's right."

"I just want you to do one thing for me...."

"Yes, go on, Polly Sue," Jessica urged. Dear Lord, she thought, what could the child possibly want from her? And what could she give her, anyway?

"If you see the preacher, would you thank him for showing me God isn't angry at me?"

At that, Jessica ran down to her and knelt to gather her in her arms, and the tears did flow as she hugged the girl tightly and whispered she should never again in her whole life feel that God could be angry at a little child. Then, fearing total collapse, she grabbed up her satchel and ran out of the school.

The settlement was nothing more than a crossroads. Besides Luther's store, there was a blacksmith, Bud Creech's store, a barber shop and a few houses. Jessica moaned when she saw that the tiny intersection was crowded with carts, wagons, horses, mules and more people than she could remember seeing gathered there at one time in her whole life. Most of them were clustered in front of the store, a small, squat building, with a large, sweeping porch across the front called a dock, where people backed up their wagons for the loading of huge bags of feed, hay and other staples. She could see Luther standing at the edge of the dock before an anxious sea of faces as he read from a newspaper just received from Asheville.

"A dispatch has been received in Wilmington stating that a United States Revenue cutter with fifty men and eight guns is on its way to Fort Caswell. Citizens of Wilmington have now seized these fortifications so vital to their city's welfare...."

Cheers went up from the multitude, for it was evident that North Carolina would not allow its forts to be garrisoned by

Federal troops. They applauded this positive step toward secession.

Belinda, her face flushed with her own personal excitement, spotted Jessica and waved to her as she began to push her way through the crowd in her direction. She was waving a letter, and Jessica could see she was crying with joy. It had to mean that Harmon Willingham had, indeed, written to propose marriage. How Jessica wished she could share in Belinda's joy, but with her own world now totally destroyed, she wanted only to retreat and hide in her misery.

Finally reaching her, Belinda confirmed, "He's asked me to marry him, Jessica. Right away. He says we're sure to be at war real soon, and he wants to make me his wife before he goes. He says we can be married in Asheville, at his aunt's house, and..." Suddenly, she saw the look in Jessica's eyes and anxiously cried, "What is it? What's happened? Tell me—"

"Later," Jessica said, grabbing her arm. "Let's just go home. I want to get out of here." She had seen Malcolm Chalmers talking to Luther Gaither's wife on the loading dock, and Elsa Gaither had shot a glare of contempt at her before rushing to speak to Eula Potts. She saw Eula gasp, then turn to Minerva Haverkamp.

Belinda allowed herself to be jerked along but protested, "I don't understand. Why aren't you in school? You don't care about the war news, so why should you declare a holiday, and—"

"Please, Belinda. Hurry. I'll tell you everything later. I just can't stand being here another second."

They reached the wagon. Jessica wasted no time in clambering up, but Belinda nearly lost her balance as Jessica shook the reins before she even had time to get settled.

Intending to skirt around the crossroads, she turned the mule down the path between the schoolyard and the store, only to be stopped by someone lunging out to grab the mule's harness. She recognized Culver Hardin just as he grinned up at her to taunt, "Yeah, I reckon you are in a hurry to get out of here, now that everyone knows about you and that preacher. Why don't you take your cowardly daddy and go on up north and join the Yankees? We don't want your kind around here!"

A hush had fallen over the crowd. Belinda gasped in awareness of what was going on, as Jessica was stabbed by the vicious, condemning looks. Dear God, she wildly thought, how could people she'd known and befriended her whole life turn against her so easily? "Mr. Culver, please," she begged. "I don't want trouble with you. Let us pass."

Belinda, terrified, clutched her arm and whispered, "What's going on? Why is everybody so angry with you?"

Jessica ignored her as she stared down into Culver Hardin's leering face. He was obviously enjoying himself, and the crowd was surging in their direction. Suddenly, Luther Gaither saw, and not having heard the rapidly spreading gossip because of being occupied with reading from the newspaper, leaped from the loading dock and shoved his way through. He didn't know what was going on, but he did know he'd never had any use for Culver. He'd heard about the fight at Creech's store between Culver and Jessica's pa and figured this scene was stemming from that. And he didn't intend to stand by like a coward while Culver bullied Miss Jessica as he was doing.

"I reckon that's enough of that!" he roared, jerking Culver back from the mule. "Aren't you ashamed of yourself? Devilin' a lady 'cause you got a beef with her pa?"

Culver Hardin guffawed, "Lady? Did you say lady?" Those around joined in to snicker as Culver went on, "Well, let me put a bee in your bonnet, Gaither, if you think she's any kind of lady...."

Jessica saw her chance to flee and did so, slapping leather across the mule's rump and sending him on his way. Those standing in front scattered, cursing as they did so, and Belinda, sobbing wildly, screamed for Jessica to tell her what was going on.

Zeb had distanced himself from the crowd gathered in front of the store. He wanted to hear the latest news, like everyone else, but didn't want to get into another debate. He wondered how many people in the Blue Ridge felt as he did but were wise enough to keep their feelings to themselves just to avoid trouble. He found himself wishing he had done that a long time ago, just kept his mouth shut, but knew, deep down, it was impossible. Unfortunately, that was just not his way. When he felt strongly about something, he had to speak his piece. And the truth was, he could not remember ever feeling so strongly about anything as he did about the inevitable, infernal war. Zeb also figured he'd had enough grief in his life without going into battle. And if God wasn't going to take away His curse, then Zeb would at least try to live out the rest of his days in peace.

But when he saw Culver Hardin yelling at his daughters about something, all hell broke loose inside him. But by the time he pushed his way through, Jessica had managed to get away, and Culver was screaming at Luther to mind his business.

Zeb lost all control and slammed his hand on Culver's shoulder, hoarsely demanding, "Who the hell you think you are messin' with my girls like that?"

Culver was already swinging his first punch as he turned, meaning to slam his fist into Zeb's face. But this time Zeb was sober, and he was mad, and he was ready. He ducked, and when he did, he butted Culver in his big stomach, knocking the breath from him as he slammed backward into the crowd.

Everyone began to back up, forming a wide ring around the two men. Zeb could hear, past the angry roaring in his ears, that they were actually cheering Culver on. He realized he'd made more enemies than he'd thought by his openly expressing his views against the war. His enemies didn't stop to think that he wasn't taking a stand *for* the Union. All those rednecks saw was that he wouldn't side with the Confederacy.

Zeb crouched, legs apart, fists doubled, ready as Culver quickly recovered and charged. His dodge was not fast enough. He took a glancing blow to his chin that dazed him just long enough for Culver to slam a beefy hand on the side of his head and knock him to his knees.

But Zeb was not going to be whipped again. He saw Culver draw back his leg to kick him in his face and finish him off, and he quickly grabbed his ankle, at the same time thrusting upward to knock his foe flat on his back.

Culver raised his head, shook it in bewilderment. He was a big man, who couldn't remember ever losing a fight. Now he was staring up at scrawny old Zeb Coulter and facing his first defeat. "You coward! You traitor!" he shrieked, struggling to get up.

"I ain't aimin' to hurt you, Hardin." Zeb backed away, but his fists were still clenched. "I just want you to apologize for smart-mouthin' my daughters and keep away from 'em. You got any beefs about my family, you come to me, damn you!"

"Yeah! I sure will!" Culver snarled and charged once more, head down.

Zeb sidestepped, not realizing he had been backed up against a wagon. Culver didn't see it in time and smashed his head straight into the wheel. It exploded beneath his charge, and his head crashed through the spokes. With a shriek of pain, he bounced back, clutching his face. The women looking on gasped in horror as blood ran from between his fingers. Some of the men lunged forward to offer aid.

Zeb stood there and watched, feeling no guilt over Culver being hurt, though he hoped the injury wasn't too bad—just enough to teach him a lesson so there'd be no more fighting in the future.

Culver had rolled to his back and was thrashing and moaning, and one of the men trying to help him managed to get a good look. He yelled frantically, "Get Doc Jasper. Get him quick! His eye's been gouged out by a spoke!"

Someone bolted from the crowd to obey the command as Zeb realized suddenly that all eyes were turning on him accusingly. He glanced around nervously, not liking the odds. He saw it was best to take his leave quickly but felt compelled to offer an apology of sorts. "Hey, I didn't mean for this to happen. It was an accident." He reached his mule and quickly mounted, urging him into a fast trot away from the angry mob, their shouts and jeers following after him.

He hid among some rocks for a half hour or so, to make sure no one was behind him, then headed for home as fast as he could coax the old mule. When he got there, he wasted no time in finding his hidden jar of moonshine and taking a big swallow that burned his stomach and made his eyes water. Then he just stood there, wondering what he should do next. The Hardin clan was a mean bunch, and Culver's sons weren't going to take their pa's injury lightly. Zeb supposed he should wait till things calmed down a bit, then go and see Deputy Dan Cowley and tell his side. The sheriff was all the way into Asheville, but Cowley lived in these parts and was regarded as the local law. He'd surely be fair and understand it was all an accident. Hell, everybody knew what a brawler Culver Hardin was, anyway, just as everybody knew that while Zeb might drink a lot, maybe too much at times, he was no scrapper. He kept to himself, and it was no shame to defend himself if somebody picked on him, asked for a fight. Cowley would understand, all right, and he would make sure the feud ended before it got started. He had to, Zeb thought desperately, tipping the jar up to his trembling lips once more, because he didn't want to have to fight the whole Hardin family.

Suddenly the barn door swung open, and Jessica was looking at him with wide, startled eyes. "Poppa, what on earth has happened now?"

The moonshine had hit hard and was already swimming through his veins to make him indignant and feisty. He stared at her momentarily, and all he could see was a wayward daughter who had brought shame on the good Coulter family name. He took another swig of the clear, but volatile, liquid, before sneering, "If it weren't for you, none of this would've happened."

Jessica blinked. "I don't understand."

"Culver Hardin!"

"Oh, Poppa!" She threw up her hands in disgust as she realized he must have witnessed the ugly scene. "Why didn't you just leave like I did? Why do you waste your time trying to talk to fools like that? Did you have an argument? Another fight?"

Disgruntled, but still indignant, he solemnly nodded. "I reckon a man has to defend his family's honor, even if the rest of his family don't care!"

"So tell me about it, and put that whiskey away," she pleaded. "That isn't going to help."

She reached for the jar, but he held it away from her. "You don't tell me what to do, girl—" His voice faded as they both heard the thundering sound of horses approaching. Together, they rushed to the window.

"It's Deputy Cowley," Jessica cried, whirling. "Oh, Poppa, that's the law out there. What have you done? You didn't shoot Mr. Hardin, did you?"

"No, but only 'cause I didn't have no gun!" He met her fiery glare with one of his own, even though, at the time, he hadn't been angry enough to kill Culver. But he knew he would have if necessary to save his own life.

There were two men riding with the deputy. Seeing Zeb and Jessica staring out the window, they reined their horses to a halt before the barn doors. Deputy Cowley shouted, "Come on outta there, Coulter. I want some words with you."

Zeb walked outside without hesitation, with Jessica closely following. He motioned her to stay behind, but she didn't, anxious to hear the details of whatever trouble there was. She saw Belinda running out of the house, didn't want her to hear, but it was too late to stop her.

Zeb coldly stared at the men in turn, then addressed Deputy Cowley. "I reckon I want some words with you, too. I didn't start that fight, and it weren't my fault Hardin bashed his head in that wagon wheel. All I did was step to the side, but he was mad as a chargin' bull and just rammed himself right in. So what I want you to do is talk to them hothead boys of his so's they won't come around tryin' to avenge their pa. Everybody in the Blue Ridge knows what a bully Culver Hardin is, anyway, but I don't want no more trouble, and you can tell them boys that if they come around here lookin' for some, they're gonna get more than they can handle."

Belinda reached them then, face pale in anticipation of more catastrophic news. She was still reeling from the blow of Jessica's humiliating dismissal. "What's happened now? What's Poppa done?"

Zeb's eyebrows shot up, and he looked at her incredulously, cheeks slightly coloring.

Deputy Cowley's reply to Zeb was terse. "Hardin'll be blind in that eye, and if I was you, I'd lay low for a while."

"Might help if you'd get yourself a gray uniform," one of the other men snickered. His comrade joined in, but Deputy Cowley maintained his severe expression.

"Hear me now, Dan Cowley!" Zeb shook his fist at the deputy. "You've known me all your life, and you know I'm a God-fearin' man, and I don't go around lookin' for trouble. What happened today weren't my fault, just like I told you. Now I'm sorry as I can be that Hardin's bullyin' cost him an eye, but there's no need of more trouble over this. You tell his boys that, you hear me?"

"Oh, I'll tell 'em," Cowley was quick to assure Zeb, "and I never said any of it was your fault. I talked to some other folks, and they agreed it was a fair fight, and even if you had put his eye out by your own hand, I wouldn't have no cause to lock you up. The reason I came out here was to tell you to just stay home for a while till things cool down. Don't go down to Creech's store and get liquored up, because if the

Hardin boys find you out somewhere, there's no tellin' what they might do. They don't care whether it was a fair fight or not. All they know is their daddy is missin' an eye.''

Belinda swayed and clutched Jessica's arm even tighter, and her whisper, ''Oh, my dear God,'' was barely audible.

Cowley was not through. ''I'm gonna tell you something else, Coulter, for your own good. Feelings are running high these days, and anybody that don't take sides with the South is asking for big trouble. If I were you, I'd jump on the right side, and I'd jump fast.'' Cowley had also heard the nasty gossip about Miss Jessica and the circuit rider; he knew the whole family was being looked down on but he was not going to say so.

Zeb's eyes narrowed. He clenched his fists for the second time that day in anticipation of having to defend himself. ''Nobody does my thinkin' for me, and I'm not ashamed of how I feel.''

''I'm just offering some friendly advice.''

''Well, go offer it to the Hardin boys. They step on my land, I'll blast 'em to hell.''

Deputy Cowley's mouth tightened in a grim line. He pointed a gloved finger at Zeb and warned, ''You don't blast nobody, you hear? I run this end of the county. I take care of upholding the law. If those boys come over here, you send for me, and I'll take care of it. You hear?''

Zeb smiled. ''I reckon there wouldn't be time to send for you, and the law can't touch me for defending myself, especially on my own property.''

Cowley motioned to his men. ''Let's go. I've spoke my piece.'' They reined their horses around and rode away at a fast pace.

Belinda wailed, ''What else is going to happen in this family to bring shame?''

Jessica turned, shoulders slumped, and headed back to the house. There was nothing she could say or do.

Zeb returned to the barn, needing a drink badly.

* * *

Belinda knew, in that moment, there was nothing left for her there. And she could not risk Harmon hearing about all the shameful things that had happened and maybe deciding he didn't want a wife from such a family. If she went to his aunt's home in Asheville, as a declaration of her stand against her father's and her sister's behavior, well, that would solve the problem.

By God, she would do it!

Chapter Sixteen

Before dark, Belinda had packed a small satchel, lamenting that she had so few things to take with her. Maybe the sheer desperation of her act, a bold declaration against her father's disloyalty, would detract from her appeal to Harmon's family. But then, she reminded herself, Harmon had seen her home and knew her family was not affluent like his and others of his station in life.

It had been hard, during supper, not to appear nervous. Her father hadn't come inside and no doubt was bundled up in a cave on the ridge, lying low with a stock of moonshine. She and Jessica had eaten in silence, then she had claimed a headache and retired to her room.

She wrote a note to leave on her pillow, explaining where she had gone. She didn't have to explain why. Jessica would know. She felt a bit sad, for she was deserting her sister in her darkest hour, but what could she do for her, anyway? To stay was to risk losing Harmon, for how much humiliation could he stand over her family?

Belinda knew the road to Asheville well and decided to take Rascal, the old mule that was easiest to handle. He was slow but sure, and she figured she could make the trip in around two hours or so. She had planned to time her departure just before daylight, not wanting to be on the road at night. She'd heard talk of how growing tension over the impending war caused the menfolk to drink more, and they were up and about at all hours. So she had lain down and tried to sleep. But she was too keyed up, and finally, after tossing and turning for hours, she got up and padded restlessly to the window. As she stood there drinking in the mystical beauty of the silver-tinted night, she decided she should just go ahead and leave right then, especially since she couldn't sleep. It was light enough to make her way in and out among the shadows, and dawn could not be so far away.

Rascal didn't like being taken from his stall, and when she crawled up on his back, he stubbornly refused to budge. She was forced to dismount and then lead him by his harness all the way to the main road. By then, he realized it was his task to give up the rest of his night's slumber and he reluctantly began to plod along. It was good, Belinda thought resignedly, that she had left earlier than planned. Otherwise, at Rascal's pace, it would have been noon before she got to Asheville.

The old mule trudged along at a steady pace, following the road as it wound down into the valley and became flat, level and smooth. Belinda was not unnerved by the night, harbored neither uneasiness nor fear. She was able to relax, leaning forward so that her head rested on the back of Rascal's neck. Before long, she was lulled to a dreamy state of oblivion to all that was around her.

She did not see the three men gathered on a slight knoll to her left. But they were watching her with keen interest.

Jake Hardin picked at his teeth with his knife. Earlier, he and his brother, Rufus, had eaten fresh possum stew at Creech's store, while hoping Zeb Coulter would show up, though they really didn't think he was that stupid. After hearing that Cowley and his boys had warned him to stay low, they'd all figured he'd take the advice. So they'd enjoyed the stew, but the whiskey gulped down with it had only fueled their anger. At one point, they'd been about to charge on over to Coulter's place and tar and feather him, but Tully Hodgkins showed up then and said they were wasting their time. They wouldn't find him there, and it was best they didn't get him at his house, anyway. Sooner or later, he'd come out of hiding and then they could jump him out on the road and nobody could prove who did it. Coulter would tell, of course, if he was still alive, but as mad as they were, that wasn't likely, not if they could ambush him with no witnesses. Beating a man, Jake acknowledged, was one thing. Everybody took their licks and got some back. But to maim and disfigure him by gouging out an eye, making him blind, well, there was only one way to deal with a mean-ass son of a bitch like that. It was the code of the hills, and Jake and his brother were hell-bent to honor that code. Zeb Coulter was as good as dead.

But Tully had made them realize they did need to cool off and wait till the time was right. He had his cousin with him, Ryan Tanner, who was heading up a Confederate regiment from farther west, near Franklin, and had come to get Tully to join up with him. Tully was willing, especially since most of his kin came from that part of the state, anyway. He reckoned he would rather go fight with them than the boys from Asheville, so he had told Ryan he would go with him, and the two were having a last night to celebrate with Tully's friends.

After much revelry, they had wound up on the ridge to drink till the sun came up, and then Tully and Ryan would be heading to Franklin. Jake had chosen the spot because it offered a sweeping view of the road that led to the Coulter place, and he was in hopes of maybe waylaying Zeb whenever he came in from his hiding place. It was a perfect place for an ambush.

Only it was not Zeb Coulter whom Jake spotted coming down the road. "I think that's one of his girls."

Rufus squinted, straining to see through a drunken haze. "Yep." He grinned. "That's Belinda. Zeb's youngest."

"How can you tell?"

"Look at her hair, stupid. Ain't no other girl in the Blue Ridge got hair that red. Looks like sunrise, right there in the moonlight."

Jake stared, then snickered. "Yeah, that's Belinda, all right. I'd know her anyway. I've had a yen for that little filly ever since she blossomed into a fine piece of woman flesh."

Tully got up from where he'd been sitting, moving easy to keep from being sick to his stomach. His head was pounding, but he wanted to know what was going on. He stumbled to where they stood staring, then agreed that, indeed, that was Belinda Coulter riding on the back of a slow-plodding mule.

Rufus mused aloud. "She must be takin' supplies to him. Why else would she be out this time of night?"

Jake guffawed. "Why, indeed? It must be somethin' important, 'cause it just ain't safe for a woman to be out alone at this time of night, especially with dastardly scoundrels like us lurkin' about, eh?"

Rufus joined him in a nasty, but soft laugh, careful lest the noise carry to her. "Yep, I'd say that's about right. Maybe we should go and tell her that, so she'll hightail it home . . . after she tells us where her daddy is hid out. Let's go get her!"

Ryan Tanner had settled a bit away from the others. He was no more fond of the Hardin boys than he was of his cousin. Tully was just another soldier recruited, that was all. He had never sought his company through the years for hunting trips or such, much less drinking binges. Ryan had not intended joining in a binge this night but had gone along with the revelry to ease the building tension within. Like so many Southerners Ryan had encountered in his recruiting duties, Tully didn't realize the seriousness of the impending confrontation. Blindly, stupidly, they thought the war would not last long, and that the South would quickly, and easily, win. Ryan knew better. He had talked with those who were to be high-ranking officers, as well as informed government officials, and he knew, as they did, that the war would be costly...and bloody. Unable to convince the hotheads of the reality, Ryan went about his job as best he could. So this night he had allowed himself some respite from stress, allowed the whiskey to take him away—and now found himself wishing he hadn't. His head was pounding, and he felt terrible. Tully could go to hell, as far as he was concerned at the moment, could stay with his rowdy friends till dawn. He was going on to Asheville, to check into a hotel room and sleep away the misery before going home.

Ryan heard the commotion in the distance and shook his head in an attempt to clear it. No more revelry this night. He'd had enough. He got up and staggered over to where he'd left his horse, forced himself up into the saddle. Unlike the others, he hadn't bedded down for the night, intending to stay only long enough to let some of the whiskey wear off before continuing on his way.

He started down the back side of the ridge to avoid the others, who sounded as though they were revving up for another rowdy session with a new bottle of "popskull."

Then he heard a woman screaming in terror.

He reined around and kicked his horse into a full gallop, all the way down the steep ridge, glad the stallion was surefooted amid the rocks and brush. In the moonlight he could see the three of them, gathered around her, and she was kicking and struggling on the ground as they fought to suppress her. But by the time he got there, she lay very still—unconscious. "What the hell is going on here?" he shouted as he slung them away from her, one by one.

Rufus guffawed. "Aw, she just fainted, that's all. Good thing, too. I was gettin' ready to knock her up aside of her head to stop that yellin'. She'll wake up in a minute. That there is Belinda Coulter, Zeb's youngest girl. No doubt but she was on her way to meet him somewheres, and we're gonna make her take us there."

"The hell, you are!"

Rufus's eyes narrowed. Nobody gave him orders. "What did you say, soldier boy?"

Ryan matched his threatening glare. Drinking and being rowdy were one thing. Ryan liked a good time as well as the next man. But when it came to roughing up women, he wouldn't stand for it. "You heard me. You aren't touching that girl again. Fight your battles with men, Hardin, not women."

Suddenly washed with shame for having been a part of Belinda's abduction, Tully dared defend his cousin's stand. "He's right. Leave her be."

Boldly, Ryan turned his back on Rufus and Jake to kneel beside Belinda to make sure she wasn't injured. Even in the faint light, he could see she was beautiful. Ryan wasn't aware of the way that Rufus was signaling behind him to his brother.

"Is she hurt?" Tully asked worriedly, dropping to kneel beside him.

"I don't think so. How far are we from her house?"

Tully scratched his chin thoughtfully. "Probably no more'n a ten-minute ride."

Ryan nodded to the mule, lazily standing nearby. "He know the way there?"

"I'm sure he does. What're you thinking?"

"I'm thinking that since she's not hurt, the thing for us to do is get her on that mule and head her for home, and let's get out of here. We don't need any trouble."

Rufus spoke up then, sharing a secret grin with Jake. "Yeah, you're right. That's the thing to do. Our fight is with her pa. We'll just bide out time and wait for our chance to get him. It'll come. No need in havin' the law come down on us because we roughed up his daughter."

Relieved the tension was over, Ryan moved to lift Belinda and gently place her on the mule's back. She stirred, moaned softly as she attempted to escape the velvet abyss of oblivion that had mercifully taken her away from the horror. Still dazed, she opened her eyes only long enough to look up into the face of the stranger, then she faded away once more.

But that one brief glimpse had been enough for her to see something that would haunt her forever. *Cat's eyes.* Green and gold and burnished orange, almost glowing in the dark.

The first pink ripples of a rising sun were visible on the eastern horizon. Soon it would be daylight. Ryan gave the mule a firm pat on his rump and sent him at a determined gait back down the road toward the Coulter farm. Then he mounted his horse again and waited for Tully to fetch his. To Rufus and Jake he said, "You boys go on home, sleep it off. Tomorrow, you'll be glad you did."

"Sure, sure," Rufus quickly assured him, giving Jake a nudge, and adding that they'd best be on their way.

Ryan watched them head west, disappearing over the ridge, then he and Tully set out for Asheville.

He wasn't aware that once Rufus and Jake had got over the ridge, they had turned east to follow the mule carrying Belinda Coulter home.

The man seated across from Derek in the dining room of Wormley's Hotel in Washington, D.C., had introduced himself as Major E. J. Allan. Derek knew his real identity. He was Allan Pinkerton, who'd emigrated from Scotland to America. In 1850 he became Chicago's first professional detective, and he was now working with the federal government. Pinkerton wanted to know why Derek had left the South to pledge his loyalty to the North. Derek was truthful, saying he was humiliated by having been dismissed by church authorities due to a misunderstood relationship with a young woman, and, wanting to make a new life, he'd volunteered his services as a chaplain in the Union army.

After politely responding to all the man's questions, however, Derek had one of his own. He looked him directly in the eye and curtly asked, "So what's all this about? Since when are volunteers interrogated by majors?"

Pinkerton took a sip of his brandy before saying, "You're very astute. I like that. I'm Allan Pinkerton, by the way."

"So what's this all about? I signed up to be a chaplain for the Union army. If need be, I'm willing to take up arms and fight, but I have to say that I'd prefer to continue with my life's work." He saw no reason to confide that work hadn't been his idea, but his dying mother's.

"Well, we have enough preachers. What we don't have enough of is men with intelligence and guts. I hear you've got both, so I'm taking you into the Secret Service."

Stunned, Derek said, "Wait a minute. I think you've got me mixed up with somebody else."

"No, you're the right man, all right. Does the name John Fremont mean anything to you?"

At once, Derek knew whom he was talking about. Fremont was the celebrated Western explorer who had openly encouraged Americans to provoke a war with Mexico, and fought to take land from Mexico once war broke out. Then a quarrel with General Stephen Kearny over authority had led to his being found guilty of mutiny and court-martialed. President Polk had remitted the penalty, but Fremont resigned from the army and went on with his expeditions, finding gold in California and becoming quite wealthy. He got involved in politics, becoming the new Republican Party's first nominee for the president. The Democrats however, launched an attack on his legitimacy, and, lacking the political skills necessary to overcome it, he lost out to Buchanan. Derek had known him for a brief spell during the war with Mexico but had thought little or nothing about him since.

He said as much to Pinkerton, who chuckled. "Well, he certainly holds you in high regard. He's in Europe now, raising money to buy English arms and weapons. Mr. Lincoln plans to make him a major general and put him in charge of the Department of the West. I spoke with him before he left for Europe, and I went over a list of preachers we had signed up—because I like to think they can be trusted," he added with a wry grin. "Anyway, he saw your name and said you fought beside him bravely, and he was impressed because of your youth.''

"Youth is right. I was still wet behind the ears in those days." Derek laughed, shook his head. Those days seemed so long ago.

"Well, if you're willing to serve your government in the Secret Service, we'll shake hands on it and get to work making sure no one assassinates our President-elect." He held out his hand, and Derek took it.

Pinkerton went on to explain that because of death threats, it would be necessary to smuggle Mr. Lincoln through Baltimore and into Washington for his inauguration on March 4. "After that," he went on, "I plan to send spies to infiltrate the Southern armies to learn their positions and strength. You need to start familiarizing yourself with daguerreotype equipment, as you'll be posing as a neutral war photographer."

"And just when do you think war will actually break out?"

"We just received word from New Orleans, that the United States Branch Mint and Customs House and the schooner *Washington* have been seized by the state of Louisiana, which, as you know, seceded a few days ago. Our government can't continue to tolerate the defiance of these secessionists. I'd say the war could start officially any day now. In fact, in my opinion, it's long overdue."

After Pinkerton left, Derek had another glass of whiskey and sat lost in thought—but not about his new and unexpected position. Instead, he thought once more about how it was said folks don't miss what they've never had. Well, he was sure missing something now—the kind of love he thought futures were built on.

Chapter Seventeen

Jessica lay in bed, dreading the day ahead. Her father had gone into hiding, and Belinda would probably stay in her room brooding. And what reason did she, herself, have for living, anyway? When the committeemon dismissed her, they'd taken away the only joy she had left. She got up and went into the kitchen, thinking that maybe if she made coffee, Belinda would share a cup. There was no need for her to be depressed. After all, Harmon had proposed, and there were wedding plans to be made. They'd just hope and pray if he did hear the gossip, it wouldn't make any difference in his feelings for Belinda.

Then, glancing out the kitchen window, she saw Rascal standing out in the road. With a sigh of resignation, she grabbed her cape from the hook by the back door and went outside. No doubt, she thought, her father had got so drunk he forgot he was to stay in hiding, and had staggered in during the night to take refuge in the barn and left the door open. Yet as she hurried toward the mule, icy stabs of apprehension began to prickle her spine as she realized he was wearing a harness. She distinctly remembered taking it off the night before. Then she realized the barn doors weren't open at all, were, in fact, tightly closed. Had her father dared ride to the store later last night, after all, only to run into the Hardin boys? If so, and if he'd been hurt, he might have fallen off the mule on the way home.

She turned and ran back to the house. She'd need to get some warm clothes on, and get Belinda up to help her search along the road.

"Belinda!" she yelled, opening her door. "We've got to go look for Poppa—" She stopped short. For a few seconds, she could only stand there, staring at the neatly made bed and the note propped on the pillow. Then, all at once, with soul-stabbing clarity, she knew. It wasn't her father who'd taken Rascal out last night. It was Belinda. But dear God, where was she?

Nearly hysterical with terror, Jessica ran out to where Rascal was waiting and scrambled up on his back. With a determined kick in his fat sides, she could only prod him into an unhurried gait. As they moved along the road, her head whipped methodically from side to side, eyes keen and searching for any sign.

They rounded the first bend in the road, and her blood ran cold as she saw Belinda lying in the dirt, her clothes in shreds. Leaping down from the mule and dropping to her knees, she cradled her in her arms, rocking her to and fro. Tears of shared pain streamed down her cheeks as she looked in horror at her sister's bruised and swollen face.

Belinda's eyes were blackened by the blows that had stilled her horrified screams in the night. She couldn't see Jessica through the hazy blur of pain, but she could hear her, take comfort in her presence. Yet she did not speak.

Jessica was frantic. "I've got to get you home...get Doc Jasper. Can you stand, Belinda? Can you help me help you?" She got up, reached for her hand, but Belinda just lay there. And when, finally, she did open her eyes wide enough to look up at her, Jessica shivered to realize they reminded her of Sudie Temple's just before she'd laid the coins on them to close her lids—unseeing, dead.

With great effort, she got Belinda home and into her bed. Crying softly, she tended her as best she could. The bruises were bad, but they would fade. There were some scratches. Those, too, would heal. But as she lay there, so quiet and still, Jessica knew that the real damage was inside. Those scars, those injuries, would never heal. And each time she spoke to her, it was like hearing the echo in a graveyard, as though Belinda weren't there at all but just a shell of what had been a beautiful and robust girl, in love with life and all that was in it.

Jessica left her long enough to hurry down the road to Frank Temple's house and ask him to go for Doc Jasper. All she told him was that there'd been an accident, not revealing what had really happened.

Hurrying back, she filled a basin with quickly heated water to bathe her sister in hopes of washing away some of the sordid memories. All the while, Belinda never made a sound, did not move.

Jessica desperately tried to bring her back from the netherworld where her tormented mind had taken her. "Belinda, you've got to get hold of yourself. The doctor will be here soon, and he'll help you, and you'll get over this. I promise you will. And those monsters responsible will pay. I swear it!"

Belinda continued to lie like a zombie, unseeing, unfeeling, reposing in some other realm of existence that offered, if only for the moment, peace from the demons.

When she heard the sound of Doc Jasper's carriage coming into the yard, Jessica hurried to meet him and explain what she thought had happened. With a grim nod, he brushed by her and went into Belinda's room to begin his examination.

Not knowing what to do with herself just then, Jessica decided to make a pot of coffee, but through the kitchen window she saw Deputy Dan Cowley riding in. This time he was alone and walked right into the kitchen without so much as a knock on the door.

At once, he said, "I saw Frank Temple in town. He said you sent him to fetch the doc. What's going on?"

It wasn't as Jessica would have liked it to be, but she supposed it was best to get it all over with. She had hoped Doc would be able to bring Belinda around, give her a chance to get over the shock before she had to start answering a lot of questions. So she told him what little she knew. He then wanted to know if she had any idea who was responsible. "I don't know," she replied. "I have my suspicions, but I don't want to say anything before Belinda has a chance to tell us herself."

"She might be ready to do just that," Doc Jasper said as he walked into the kitchen.

Grimly, the deputy asked, "Was she raped?"

"I'm afraid so."

Jessica's fist flew to her mouth to stifle a sob. Though she'd expected it, having it confirmed was still a blow. "But is she going to be all right?" she cried, when she could speak.

He explained that, physically, she would recover. Bruises, lacerations, scrapes were injuries that would heal in time. Mentally, he wasn't so sure. "She's in a state of shock right now, which is understandable. She'll probably slip in and out of consciousness for a spell. I can't say for sure how long it will be before she comes out of it entirely."

Cowley was quick to remind him, "But you just said she might be ready to tell us who did it."

"She's trying to say something. I can't tell what. Moves her lips. Makes some kind of sound." He motioned to Jessica. "You go on in there, and maybe you can understand her better'n I can."

Jessica started for the door, then hesitated, looking at each of the men in turn. Sternly, she decreed, "My father is to know nothing about this, understand?"

They exchanged puzzled looks, then Cowley pointed out, "That's going to be kind of difficult, wouldn't you say, Miss Jessica? I mean, he's got a right to know his daughter was raped."

"But not now!" she cried. "Can't you see if he finds out about this, finds out who did it, before you can arrest them and put them in jail where he can't get his hands on them, he'll kill them himself. I know he will. And so do you!''

Deputy Cowley conceded that made sense. He figured Zeb Coulter's endurance was pretty well exhausted, anyway. He sighed with resignation. ''All right, if you can make out what she's tryin' to tell you so I can get my men and go after whoever she says did it, we'll try to keep it quiet till we can get 'em locked up.''

Jessica went in to Belinda, with the deputy and the doctor right behind her. ''Can you hear me?'' she asked as she sat down beside her, trailed her fingertips lovingly, gently, down her bruised and swollen cheek. ''Can you hear me, Belinda? Please. We want to help you. We want to know who did this.''

For the first time, Belinda evidenced some spark of life. In a sudden flash, her eyes blazed and fastened upon Jessica's startled face. Her voice, no more than a ragged whisper, was barely audible, but the words burned like a searing torch. ''Rufus...Jake...and the man with the eyes of a cat.''

And then she was still once more, going back to wherever her mind found solace from the torment.

Doc Jasper spoke through gritted teeth. ''Those bastards! I didn't think even *they* were low enough to take out their anger on a helpless, innocent woman.''

''Well, neither did I, Doc,'' Cowley was quick to agree, ''but I had a feeling they were responsible, due to the trouble in town yesterday between their pa and hers.'' He looked at Jessica then. ''But what was she talking about—a man with the eyes of a cat?''

She could only shake her head in shared frustration.

''It's a shame,'' Cowley said, sounding as though he really did not think so, ''but with folks in these parts feeling like they do about Zeb, I guess something like this was bound to happen sooner or later.''

At that, Jessica exploded. ''How can you be so callous? You actually think my pa's stand against war should provoke something like this?''

He regarded her with cool, shaded eyes. "Don't blame *me,* Miss Jessica. These are tense, crazy times we're livin' in. Your pa would do well to keep his goddamn mouth shut. Now I'll just head on back to town and get me some men together to go get the Hardin boys and lock 'em up before Zeb hears about it and does something crazy, like take the law into his own hands, and—"

They all turned at the sound, like that of an animal gone mad, staggering in the last throes of its misery and anguish.

Zeb stood in the doorway, where he had been listening, unnoticed, for the past few moments. His face was like the face of a demon awakened—eyes bulging, cords in his neck threatening to burst, nostrils flaring with the rushed heat of his breath. His entire body trembled from head to toe with his rage.

And before any of them could speak or move, he ran from the house, his screams of rage echoing wildly, eerily, up and down the foothills and the ridges above.

Once he got over the shock, Dan Cowley followed Zeb, expecting he could catch up with him. After all, a man on a mule couldn't outrun a man on a horse. The truth, however, reversed his assumption, for Zeb had ridden away on Cowley's horse and had driven away Doc's horse, as well.

Jessica was right behind the deputy, just in time to see her father galloping down the road and disappearing around the bend. "He'll kill them!" she cried, running down the steps to grab Cowley's arm. "You've got to stop him," she desperately urged. "He'll kill them, for sure."

Cowley cursed. "Goddamn it, if he does, girl, he'll hang. Damned if I'll put up with anybody takin' the law in his own hands in my bailiwick!" He struck out running, yelling over his shoulder he was going to Frank Temple's place to borrow a horse.

With a lump in her throat, Jessica went back to Belinda's bedside, wanting to be there should she awaken. There was nothing anyone could do to stop her pa now, and suddenly she found herself wondering if she really cared. It was as

Deputy Cowley had said—folks were angry with him, and something bad was bound to happen. Now that it had, who would care? Jake and Rufus would probably not go to jail for what they had done to Belinda. A jury would declare that they had been temporarily insane over the maiming of their father, for which they blamed Zeb, and that it was unfortunate Belinda was the one to suffer for it. The Hardins would go free, while Belinda would never forget the horror. Such an outcome would be neither right nor just, and Jessica found herself thinking that if her pa killed those two savages, so be it. She only hoped he would keep on going, head straight North and never come back.

Doc Jasper stayed a little while longer, then said there was nothing more he could do for Belinda. "I'm leaving you a bottle of laudanum. When she wakes up, she's liable to get real upset. Give her a spoonful every few hours to keep her calm. Nothing is really going to help her but time."

Jessica told him to help himself to one of the mules to get back to town, but when they went outside, Frank Temple was waiting to give the doctor a ride.

While morning turned to afternoon and afternoon to evening, Belinda mercifully slept. But as the sun sank in the west, she awoke and began to cry softly. Jessica was there to try to comfort her. "It's going to be all right. Just don't think about it, honey. Try to forget...."

Belinda stared at her, haunted by the agonizing memories that would be with her always. "Forget?" she cried incredulously. "Oh, dear God, Jessica! You can't know...can't know...what it was like. Those...those savages...all of them...sick...sickening..."

She turned on her side, and Jessica patted her shoulder awkwardly, not knowing what to do or say. She decided the best thing was to let her cry it out, talk it out, whatever helped pull her up from the depths of her horror.

"I was running away...." Drained of tears and her voice devoid of emotion, Belinda knew the poison, the rage, had to come out or it would destroy her. And she wanted so desperately to be strong, to make sure those responsible paid for what they'd done. The words had to be spoken, the story told. "I was leaving, to show contempt for Poppa, and they must have been waiting for him and saw me instead. I know they did it to get even with him. They didn't care that it was me. It could've been you. I fainted, and I don't know how many there were, or how many times, or..." Her voice caught on a sob, and she burrowed her face in the pillow.

Jessica reached to smooth her hair back from her face and whispered, "Try to sleep, honey—"

"No!" Belinda all but screamed then, rising up. "Don't you see? When I sleep, I just have to wake up to this, and that's the way it'll be till I get it all figured out. That man, that stranger. He was in on it, too. And why? I never saw him before, don't know who he is. Why would he want to hurt me, too?"

"I don't know. Are you sure no one called him by name?"

Belinda shook her head, closed her eyes in painful reverie. "I probably wouldn't have remembered him at all, if it hadn't been for those eyes. Cat's eyes. Like a panther's, shining in the moonlight. I saw him just for a second, and then I must have fainted again, because all I remember after that is pain, and grunting, and ugly words."

Jessica reached to cradle her, hold her, rock her back and forth till sleep once more mercifully took her away from the misery, if only for a little while.

Night fell, wrapping the world in a cloak of purple velvet. Jessica stood on the porch and looked out into the tranquillity, and she knew somehow that the aura of peace was but a transient thing. Something else had happened. Something horrible. She could feel it in her bones.

Later she sat by Belinda's bed, about to retire, herself, and hoping the heavy dose of laudanum would allow her sister to sleep soundly the rest of the night. She heard the sound of a horse coming hard and fast down the lane. She felt no particular apprehension, for she had thought someone would come that night.

It was Frank Temple, and he burst through the back door before she could even get to the kitchen. She had only to take one look at his ashen face to know the news was as terrible as she had expected it to be.

He exploded with the horror. "He killed him, Jessica. Your pa shot Rufus Hardin, shot him dead. And he wounded Jake. Doc says he might not live through the night. I waited till they got him locked up before comin' to tell you, 'cause I was afraid I'd be bringin' news he'd been killed, too. He held the posse off for a while, but then he just gave up, like he don't even care anymore."

Jessica was surprised at her own calmness. "He probably doesn't, Frank. He probably doesn't."

He stood there, expecting her to become hysterical, and when she remained serene, he blinked, bewildered. "Well, aren't you upset, Jessica?" he cried. "I mean, your pa is in jail for murder, for God's sake, and—"

"Not for *God's* sake," she coolly interjected. "For Belinda's sake. He did this for her, you know."

"Yeah, yeah—" he waved his arms wildly "—but the thing is, he gunned them down in cold blood. He waylaid 'em at their own place. They never had a chance. He shot Rufus right between the eyes, and that's murder, no matter the reason he done it."

"He's in jail. He'll get a trial. We can only hope the jury and judge will understand he was out of his mind when he did it. Belinda will testify, and so will I, and everyone will sympathize, and—"

"It ain't gonna be like that."

Jessica regarded him sharply. There was something coldly ominous in his demeanor. "What are you talking about?"

He glanced away nervously, not wanting to tell her.

Jessica took a step toward him, knowing there was more. "Go on. What is it? What is it that you don't want to tell me?"

"It's like I said," he began slowly, "I waited till they had him locked up before I came to tell you about it."

"But there's something else, and I want to know what it is." Icy nails of apprehension raked up and down her spine.

"They got him locked up, all right. In that little jail in the back of Cowley's barn that he uses for a holding cell till he can transfer a prisoner to the big jail at Asheville. He plans to take him in the morning, but I don't think he'll last till then, 'cause a lynch mob was gathering when I left to come tell you. They're gonna drag him outta there and hang him before daylight, I just know they are. Cowley, he says he ain't gonna let it happen, but I could tell he's just putting on a show. He don't really care. He's pretty mad at the way your pa just took off like he did and shot them boys down in cold blood, even after what they did to Belinda. Oh, he'll pretend to hold 'em off, but I can promise you he ain't gonna try very hard.

"There's nothin' nobody can do," he went on, nervously twisting his straw hat in his hand as he gave her the rest of the bad news. He'd set out for Asheville to get the sheriff to come help out. "But one of the Hardin cousins is posted at the road to stop anybody from crossing the bridge. They don't want outsiders, and I don't think anybody can stop them now, anyway."

Woodenly, she thanked him for coming and murmured she'd better get back to Belinda.

"If I hear anything else," he assured her, backing out, "me or somebody else will come tell you. I'm headin' back to town now."

Jessica went to her father's room and rummaged in the old wooden chest till she found what she was looking for. It was an ancient pistol that had belonged to her grandfather. She wondered if it would even fire, decided just the threat that it might was ominous enough. She tied it to her leg beneath her skirt.

Despite everything that had happened, any past hurts he'd inflicted, he was still her father, and she loved him. And by God, she wasn't going to let them hang him.

All seemed strangely quiet when Jessica reached the Cowley place. There was a small bonfire in front of the barn, and from her vantage point on a hillock, she could see two men sitting near it, rifles lying across their laps. She could not see Deputy Cowley. The barn itself would have seemed deserted save for the glow coming from a small window at the rear. The slender bars gave evidence that it was the small holding cell, where her father would be.

Dismounting, she knelt beside the mule and tried to decide the best way to get to her father. If she crept along in the darkness and got caught, then it would be obvious she was up to something. She decided instead to just ride right on to the house. Dan's wife, Matilda, was a kind and compassionate woman who would understand a daughter's need to see her father at such a time. Everyone also knew that when it came to his wife, Dan Cowley was so softhearted he could not deny her anything. Therefore, she was the key. No matter that later, after it was all over, Matilda might be angry with Jessica. Jessica wasn't thinking of future consequences, only of the moment at hand and what she had to do.

She got back on the mule and rode straight for the house. She managed to get to the white picket fence surrounding it before yet another deputy came charging out of the night to ask what the hell she was doing. Then he recognized her and yelled, "Hey! It's Coulter's oldest girl."

Then other men appeared, as well as Dan Cowley himself. Indignantly he marched right up to her as she swung down off the mule. "Miss Jessica, have you lost your mind? You could've been shot. The hills are full of drunk rednecks, and all of them have got guns and are spoilin' for trouble. The Hardin family is probably out now roundin' up an army to charge any minute now, so you best get on back home. You got no business here.''

Furious, she demanded, ''Why don't you take my father to Asheville tonight? How do you think you and a handful of men can possibly hold off a lynch mob?''

''They've got the bridge blocked, I'm told, and it'd be more dangerous to try and ride out of here than to wait till dawn. Now you go on,'' he urged once more. ''I'm doing everything I can to protect your pa.''

''I want to see him.''

''No!'' He shook his head adamantly, ''I want you to get out of here now.''

Suddenly, Jessica bolted past him to run up the steps and start pounding loudly, frantically, on the front door. He came after her, tried to pull her away as it opened.

Matilda Cowley peered out fearfully, and Jessica cried, ''Tell him, Mrs. Cowley, please, that I've got a right to see my father before they take him away.''

At once, Matilda met her husband's defiant eyes. ''Of course, you do, dear,'' she declared, ''and if Dan doesn't take you out to the barn, I'll do it myself. Dan!'' She turned her fury upon him. ''Take this girl to see her pa right now.''

The deputy knew it was no use arguing with both of them. ''Oh, all right, but if shootin' starts, I'm not responsible if she gets hit. Come on.''

Doggedly, he headed across the yard toward the barn, with Jessica right behind him. ''I mean it,'' he growled. ''If they come, you best just hit the dirt, 'cause there's no telling what those fools are liable to do. Your pa was crazy to do what he did—ride right on the Hardin place like he did and bushwhack them two boys.''

''They asked for it. When they raped my sister, they deserved whatever they got.''

''That's for a court to decide,'' he snapped.

Jessica hotly retorted, ''Well, you see to that and get my pa out of here.''

He motioned to the man standing in front of the doors to step aside, then led her on in. The barn smelled of hay and manure, but also of the tension of the night—so thick it was almost smothering.

He took her all the way to the back, where she saw the small barred cubicle. Her father sat on a bench in a corner, shoulders slumped, head down. She called his name, and he looked up with eyes that were as dead as his hopes and dreams.

"What are you doin' here? You need to be home with Belinda."

She stepped closer to wrap her fingers around the cold steel bars. "She's asleep. And I had to come, Poppa, because I wanted to tell you..." She hesitated, swallowed, feeling awkward, for theirs had never been a relationship of demonstrative feelings of affection. And since the night he had beaten her, she had found it difficult to feel anything beyond pity for him. She forced herself to go on, voice thin, strained. "I wanted to tell you I'm sorry I couldn't do what you wanted and marry Reuben, and I'm sorry you mistook what happened with Preacher Stanton, and I love you, and I'm praying you'll be all right."

He looked at her then, strangely, a little furrow appearing on his brow, because he knew by the nervous way she was acting and the strange tone in her voice that wasn't the real reason she had come. He cleared his throat and gruffly said, "Well, that's good. That's real good. I needed to know that. Especially now."

Dan Cowley was shifting his weight from one foot to the other impatiently, and he walked over to the window in the end of the building to peer out, apprehensive of any sign that the Hardin clan and their friends were returning. Jessica seized the opportunity to move quickly. Deftly she leaned over, untied the gun from her leg and let it drop soundlessly to the hay-strewn floor. Then she quickly covered it with straw.

Zeb's eyes grew wide, and he shot a glance at Cowley to make sure he had not seen Jessica's action.

"Pa, you'll be okay," she said awkwardly. "No jury will sentence you to hang for what you did, not after what those monsters did to Belinda."

Zeb shook his head. "Just get on out of here. Go home and look after your sister and the farm. Don't fret about me."

Dan walked back to where she stood. "He's right. There's nothing you can do here. You had your visit. Now come along."

Jessica continued to cling to the bars. Finally, she whispered brokenly, "Goodbye, Poppa," and turned away, sadly wondering if she would ever see him again.

She was almost out the door when Zeb suddenly, sharply, yelled, "Jessica, wait!"

She turned, struck by the raw desperation in his voice.

But he merely lowered his head, shook it, turned his back and mumbled, "Just get on home, girl."

He waited till Jessica and Cowley were gone before rushing to reach through the bars and retrieve the hidden gun.

He had been right, he told his nagging conscience, not to give in to the impulse to tell her of his treachery. It was best she get on with her life without Derek Stanton in it.

She would probably be better off without her father around, too, he thought, because, finally, he knew what it was he had to do with whatever time he had left in this world.

Chapter Eighteen

The settlement was abuzz. Zeb Coulter had killed a man and escaped from jail. Everyone speculated he had headed north to fight with the Yankees. Deputy Cowley suspected, but couldn't prove, that Jessica was responsible for slipping him a gun. Folks shook their heads and said they weren't surprised at anything they heard about her, not after the scandal with the circuit rider. Reuben Walker told everyone who would listen how relieved he was to have found out in time how licentious she was, because he surely didn't want a woman like that for his wife. He then proceeded to formally court Leona Billingsley, much to Naomi's relief.

There was also gossip about Belinda Coulter being raped, and everyone wondered whether her rich beau from Raleigh would still want to marry her when he heard.

But no one really knew what was going on in the Coulter household, because Belinda refused to venture out at all, and Jessica went to the settlement store only when absolutely necessary. Then she left as quickly as possible, hurt and humiliated by the whispers and stares of contempt.

As January faded to February, however, attention turned from the Coulter family. Instead, focus was on the newly formed Confederate States of America. The just-elected president, Jefferson Davis of Mississippi, and his vice president, Alexander Stephens, were inaugurated at the capital of the Confederacy in Montgomery, Alabama. Many Federal military officers resigned their posts to take positions in the Southern army and navy.

March breezes were winds of impending war as Abraham Lincoln was sworn in as the sixteenth President of the United States in Washington. Thirty thousand people gathered to hear him explain his position on slavery in his inaugural address. He emphasized that states voting to secede were in error, for "the Union of these States is perpetual."

Belinda's visible bruises faded, but she was only the shadow of her former self. Most of the time she stayed in her room, composing love letters to Harmon, which Jessica dutifully mailed for her on her infrequent trips to the store. Jessica knew, without asking, that Belinda hadn't told him what had happened to her. She knew her sister was hoping that by some miracle he wouldn't hear of all the scandal, and that he'd come to take her away as soon as he could. The only news they heard about the threat of war was in his letters, which arrived about once a week. He was working with Colonel Daniel H. Hill, from the Military Institute in Charlotte, to organize the first state troops, though, he emphasized, their actions were as yet unofficial.

It was going to be hard, Jessica knew, for her and Belinda to survive with no money coming in. Ostracized and scorned by the people she'd known all her life, she had no one to turn to for help. She was forced to sell the livestock at a loss to buy food, and could only hope for spring to hurry and arrive so that she could plant a garden. She doubted she'd ever see her father again. How ironic and cruel it seemed that his selfish dream had led to the destruction of the entire Coulter family's hope for happiness.

A late snow in April kept the sisters housebound for nearly two weeks. On the first day the road was passable, Belinda, on one of her rare ventures out of the shell she'd built around herself, beseeched Jessica to go into town and see if there was a letter from Harmon. "It's been so long since I've heard from him, he's bound to have written by now.''

Jessica didn't want to go. The last time she went, before the snow, Amelia Hardin, Culver's wife, had been in Luther's store, and when she saw Jessica, her face had screwed up in anger and she'd lashed out, ''There's the hussy that set my son's killer free!'' She'd whirled on Luther, standing behind the counter, and cried, ''You must really be hard up for money to take hers!''

Jessica had fled without buying the dried beans she'd come for. It meant eating more potatoes dug from the root cellar, but she would not stay to be verbally abused. Worse, she had feared Amelia might even physically attack her.

So, when Belinda begged her to make the trip, Jessica balked. ''Everyone will be there today, needing things after the snow. I just don't want another scene. I'll go tomorrow or the next day.''

''No!'' Belinda cried, bursting into tears, which came so easily these days. ''No, Jessica, I can't wait till then. Please. You've got to go. If there isn't a letter from him after all this time, then I'll know he's heard about what happened to me.''

Jessica was not unsympathetic, nor had her compassion diminished for her sister's anguish, but she felt compelled to attempt to awaken her to the reality of the situation. ''If he hasn't heard, you're going to have to tell him the truth sooner or later. Better that he hear it from you.''

Eyes wide with horror, Belinda shook her head wildly. ''No. No, I can't. When we're married, I'll tell him then, but not before.''

''Then you're asking for heartache if you try to deceive him. He'll know. On your wedding night. And he'll hate you for not telling him. He'll wonder what else you've kept from him. Oh, Belinda,'' she pleaded, ''you can't keep hiding this, any more than you can keep hiding away in your room. I know what happened to you was terrible, but life goes on, and—''

"Listen to you!" Belinda cried then, and Jessica was stunned to see such a fiery display of spirit. "You wouldn't even buy food because Amelia Hardin said something ugly to you! You don't go to church. You don't go anywhere. I'd say you're hiding, too."

"I'm avoiding trouble. Besides, we're running out of money, so there won't be any reason to go to the store before long. We're probably going to lose this place, anyway, because we can't pay the taxes. What's the use?"

Belinda ran to where Jessica was sitting and dropped to her knees before her. Clutching her hands, she begged, "If there's a chance for me, then there's one for you, too. Don't you see? When I marry Harmon, you'll move to Raleigh with me, like I told you once before. It won't matter about this place or anything else. Time will lessen the scandal here, and you can get a job teaching there."

Jessica had given up hope for anything. "And what happens if you never hear from Harmon again? Have you given any thought to what will happen to us then?"

"We'll go to Richmond, like I'd planned to do before Harmon came along."

Jessica was suddenly ashamed of herself. *She* sadly considered her life over, all because a man had used her for his own pleasure, made a fool of her by making her think he loved her and wanted to marry her. Belinda had been brutally ravaged, yet she could look to tomorrow and dared envision a happy future. For the first time in her life, Jessica found herself looking to her younger sister for strength. "All right," she said finally, contritely. "I'll go into town and see if there's a letter."

Belinda gave her a hug, then further astonished her by bravely announcing, "And I'll go with you. We're going to show everybody we can still hold our heads up."

As they neared the crossroads, Jessica saw the crowd gathered ahead and instinctively pulled back on the reins to slow Rascal's pace. It was an even larger throng than on the day she'd been dismissed from her job and had the ugly scene with Culver Hardin.

Beside her, Belinda reached to grasp her arm in fear. "What do you suppose has happened now?" she cried.

Jessica murmured she had no idea but added, "Whatever it is, folks seem happy about what Luther's reading them from the loading dock."

"Do you think we should go on in?"

Jessica felt a strange lump in the pit of her stomach, an icy foreboding that, somehow, whatever was going on had to do with the final breakdown of the Union. "We'll draw in a little closer, but stay back from the crowd and see if we can hear."

Just then, she saw one of her former pupils, William Michaels, heading toward them. He waved cheerily, and she dared to wave back and motion him to stop. Her students, she was sure, did not despise her.

"Miss Jessica," he greeted, reining up beside the wagon and tipping his straw hat to both her and Belinda in turn. A shock of red hair tumbled onto his forehead, and his blue eyes shone brightly, excitedly, in the early April sun. "It's a great day, ain't it? At last, we ain't takin' nothing else off them Yankees."

She told him they hadn't heard, asked what on earth he was talking about. He was only too glad to convey what he felt was wonderful news. With the road finally open from Asheville, word had been received that Confederates in South Carolina had decided the flag of the United States flying over Fort Sumter at the mouth of Charleston Harbor was just more than they could bear. Since their state had seceded from the Union, they didn't want what they considered a foreign flag, flying in their harbor. They had asked the Union soldiers to evacuate the fort, and when they refused, the Confederates had fired on it. The Federal garrison, with no food remaining and too few men, had surrendered after some forty thousand shells had been fired during the battle.

"Now all hell has busted loose," he rushed on to inform them. "Lincoln has asked for 75,000 volunteers for the Union army and has ordered a blockade of all ports in the Confederate states. And there's been a big ruckus in Baltimore between Yankee troops and rioters carrying Confederate flags. They say nine civilians were killed and four soldiers.

"We've got ourselves a war, at last!" he finished with a triumphant cry. "And I'm gonna be the first one from these parts to join up." Taking off his hat to slap it against his horse's rump, William took off at a spirited gait, cheering as he went.

Jessica and Belinda exchanged nervous looks. "I know what you're thinking," Belinda said finally, "that we ought to get out of here and go home. But I've got to see if there's a letter. You wait here, and I'll slip in among the crowd, and no one will notice." She was scrambling down from the wagon before Jessica could protest.

Fortunately, there was no incident, and Belinda returned a few moments later happily waving a letter. They headed for home, and crying with joy, she read aloud Harmon's promise to come for her soon. The First North Carolina Regiment had been organized and was sure to be the first to march from North Carolina. No matter that the state had not yet seceded. It was just a matter of time. The general assembly would meet May 1, and it was expected to pass a convention bill, which ultimately would lead to a vote to officially become a part of the Confederate States of America. Harmon didn't know, he wrote, exactly when he'd come for Belinda, but it would be soon, very soon, and she should be ready to leave when he arrived.

"'When we march off to war,'" she read aloud to Jessica, "'the band is going to be playing "The Girl I Left Behind Me," but I'll be singing "The *Wife* I Left Behind Me."'" Her voice broke, and Jessica knew she was crying not with sadness, but joy.

Dear Lord, she prayed then, *Dear Lord, don't let her heart be broken. I know how much it hurts to lose the one you love.*

Belinda packed her belongings and spent every waking hour keeping vigil for Harmon's arrival. Jessica thought surely she'd wear a groove in the pine floor, pacing anxiously between side windows and front.

When Harmon did finally make his appearance, however, it was late one afternoon nearly two weeks after they had heard the news about the firing on Fort Sumter. Belinda's anxious pacing had got on her nerves so badly, Jessica had persuaded her to go to the root cellar and get them some turnips and potatoes for supper. She'd promised to fry up the last slab of ham from the smokehouse as a further inducement, so it happened she was alone when Harmon rode into the yard.

Jessica sought to quell her own excitement, but with difficulty, for his appearance meant her sister's future was secure, and perhaps her own, as well. More and more lately, she'd been thinking of Belinda's offer to take her with them to Raleigh to begin a new life. But as she stood on the porch and watched Harmon rein in his magnificent Arabian stallion, she took one look at his face and was washed with fearful apprehension.

He was wearing his new uniform of the Confederacy — gray coat with two rows of gold buttons, gray trousers with a crimson stripe up each side, spit-polished Jefferson boots and a saber hanging from a shiny black leather scabbard. His wide-brimmed gray felt hat even sported a bright red feather. Under normal circumstances, she might have thought him handsome. Now, however, his narrowed eyes and tight-set lips made him look virulent, arrogant.

He dismounted and stood before her with legs spread apart as he carefully removed his white gloves, plucking one finger at a time. Finally, with an exaggerated sigh, he said, "I wish someone had told me about this nightmare. I stopped at Gaither's store and heard all about it—your daddy killing a man, your shame and—'' he paused, shuddered to have to continue ''—the awful thing that happened to Belinda as a result of it all.''

Jessica stiffened with resentment. She didn't like his implication that her personal affairs had something to do with the violence inflicted on her sister. Yet, she opted not to say anything, for it was best his sympathy lie completely with Belinda.

''How is she?'' he asked suddenly. Jessica noted how cold his voice was, devoid of warmth or any trace of compassion.

''As well as any girl would be after what she went through,'' she told him.

''Well, as I said, I wish someone had told me sooner. Where is she?''

Jessica felt a stab of pain for her sister, because all at once she knew, by the look in his eyes, by the brusque, agitated way he was behaving, what he was about to do. Nodding toward the root cellar to the rear of the yard, she told him. He started in that direction, and she couldn't resist softly calling, ''Be gentle, Harmon. She was counting on you standing by her.''

He turned to give her an incredulous look, then laughed. ''Oh, really? Is that why she didn't write me one word about any of it? She thought I could just overlook something like this?'' He continued on his way.

Jessica stood right where she was, watched as he entered through the open wood doors and disappeared. He was inside not five minutes before reappearing. Then, without so much as a glance or nod in her direction, he went to his horse, mounted and rode away at a fast clip.

At last she came alive and lifted her skirt to run to the cellar and plunge inside. She found Belinda huddled on the floor, but she wasn't crying. She was very still, very quiet. Kneeling beside her, Jessica turned her sister's face with gentle trembling hands to meet her anxious gaze. But she didn't have to ask any questions. She knew by her dead, dull eyes that Belinda had just ceased to have any reason to live.

She helped her to bed, covered her with a blanket, then sat beside her should she want to talk. Belinda never said a word, merely lay with eyes closed, breathing evenly. Now and then, a shudder would go through her body, an echoing wave of her broken heart, and, finally, she fell asleep. Jessica tiptoed out, knowing there wasn't anything she could do except be close by if needed.

The next morning, Belinda was gone. And this time there was no note.

Allen Pinkerton burst into laughter when the suspected Confederate spy was brought before him. "Stanton, you must not look like a photographer."

With chagrin, Derek held out his wrists for the handcuffs to be unlocked. "I guess not. The last thing I expected, though, was that Federal troops would be the ones to charge me with spying."

In the guise of an itinerant artist, he'd started out for Alexandria, Virginia, but four miles out of the city he'd come to the Second Maine Regiment. A very irritable general had decided he was a Reb spy because of his Louisiana drawl, and had dispatched him to Washington.

"Just can't lose that accent, can you?" Pinkerton shook his head and sighed. "Well, there's only one thing to do with you, and that's send you into 'Rebeldom' among your own kind, where your loyalty won't be questioned. You wanted to be a chaplain, anyway, so we'll send you south to be just that for the Confederacy."

Derek accepted the assignment without question, because he knew he had to stand with the Union. No matter that he was born and raised in the South, had once called it home—he couldn't take up arms to defend slavery. "All right. Where do you want me to go?"

"Richmond," Pinkerton said easily. "Virginia has seceded and the convention offered the city as a capital for the Confederacy to replace Montgomery, Alabama. Go there and volunteer your services as a preacher.'' He gave Derek the name of the newspaper reporter who would be his contact, a man trained in codes who would inform the Secret Service of any information Derek thought pertinent.

"Just be careful," he tersely added. "You get caught by the Rebs, and you're on your own."

Chapter Nineteen

With Belinda gone, Jessica was unbearably lonely, finding herself completely ostracized in the Blue Ridge settlement where she had lived her whole life.

One beautiful morning in May, when she thought she would die if she didn't get out for a little while, she dared venture out to church in hopes that people in the business of forgiving would tolerate her presence. But no one spoke. Heads turned away if she offered a timorous smile to condemning stares. When she found herself sitting alone in the pew, because no one wanted to share it with her, she couldn't take any more. As the congregation stood to sing the opening hymn, she hurried out, humiliated to the core.

She was nearly out of money. She had planted a small garden that would feed her through the summer, but what then? She doubted her father would ever return. How could he with a murder charge hanging over his head?

In May, North Carolina seceded from the Union. No one shared any news with Jessica on her rare excursions to Luther's store, but she did buy a newspaper whenever possible to keep up with what was happening. She read that while the governor's call for troops had been answered by a great number, there was a problem with equipment. Even though the Federal arsenal at Fayetteville had been seized, providing thirty-seven thousand pieces of armament, these

were of little value. Many dated back to the war for inde
pendence—muskets of the old flintlock type.

Jessica just didn't know what to do with herself. With nc
job, and few chores because she had sold the livestock, she
felt useless. It would be futile to volunteer her services fo
rolling bandages at the church with the other ladies. They
would run her off if she dared appear.

Sometimes, in the still of the night, with no sound save for
the mournful plea of a whippoorwill, she would wonde
how different things might have been had she never got in
volved with Derek Stanton. They would all have been bet
ter off. No matter she would have been miserable a:
Reuben's wife—she would at least have had the consola
tion of her teaching. Her father would probably have con
tinued to get himself in trouble with his pro-Union, antiwar
views, but never would he have wound up being charged
with murder. Belinda would not have been raped, would
probably be married to Harmon now and contentedly liv
ing with his family in Raleigh.

When Jessica dared to think like that, she would wind up
angry with herself, for there was nothing to be gained by
looking back. It would not change anything. She had to
look forward—*but to what?* What was there left for her?
More and more, she was coming to realize that although she
did not want to leave, she had no reason to stay.

She was in Luther's store the morning everyone was so
excited over the news that in a place near Yorktown, Vir
ginia, called Big Bethel, Colonel John B. Magruder's smal
Confederate force had soundly defeated General Benjamir
F. Butler's much larger Federal army. The First North
Carolina Regiment had been proudly involved.

Jessica had scraped up a little bit of money to buy bear
seeds for late planting. She had not planned to tarry long a
the store. Yet with so much excitement around her she lin
gered, desperate for human contact, even if she were ig
nored.

She overheard Frank Temple exulting that the South was sure to win the war, and soon. "I wish I weren't too old to fight. I'd like to shoot me a few Yankees before they surrender. Maybe we don't have factories and supplies like the Yankees, but we got something better. We got guts!"

A round of cheers went up from the crowd of perhaps twenty people gathered on the dock, but the jubilation quickly died down as Deputy Cowley rode up, a grim expression on his face. He had just come in from Asheville with the latest war dispatch. Sadly, he announced, "Seems our celebration over victory is short-lived, folks. Our boys at Harper's Ferry, up in Virginia, have had to retreat. The Yankees are advancing."

Groans and moans echoed, and Jessica didn't miss the accusing glares she began to receive as people realized she was present. *It's not my fault,* she wanted to scream at them, moving to the counter to pay Luther for the seeds. *My only sin was loving a man I believed loved me! Do you want to crucify me for that for the rest of my life?* Her hands were shaking as she counted out the coins, and furiously she blinked back anguished tears.

"*Jessica Coulter!*"

She jumped, startled and not a little frightened by the accusing voice. Whipping around, she faced the indignant rage of Lucille Michaels, young William's mother.

"My boy was at Big Bethel," she said fiercely, proudly.

Jessica was puzzled as to the reason for the anger directed at her. William had been one of her best students, and she had always had a good relationship with his family. Nervously she asked, "Is he all right? He wasn't hurt, was he?"

The crowd at the front of the store had begun to gather around Mrs. Michaels. "No, he wasn't hurt," the woman went on, lips twitching as she struggled for control of the fury raging inside, "but it was no thanks to your traitorous daddy that he's still alive."

"I don't know what you mean." Jessica held her head high, while her knees shook violently. The woman's steady, angry gaze was unnerving.

"What I mean is that your daddy could've killed my boy. William wrote to me and said he saw Zeb Coulter wearin' a *Yankee* uniform. He was one of the damn Yankees shootin' at my boy, shootin' at all our boys." Tears spilled from her eyes, began to run down her flushed cheeks. "And if he'd killed my boy, it would've been your fault, 'cause everybody knows you helped him escape from jail. But he won't kill nobody else. William says he was taken prisoner, and I hope if they don't hang him for the traitor he is, he rots in prison!"

There was a furious rumbling of agreement from the others, and Jessica knew she had to get out of there and fast. There was no telling what they might do to her.

Amid jeers and taunts, she hurried out and got in her wagon and urged Rascal toward the farm as fast as his stubborn legs would carry him.

Now she knew. Her father was a prisoner of war, so his fighting was over. What would become of him, she had no idea; she knew only, through the haze of misery that engulfed her, that she had to stay out of the settlement as long as the war continued. She could be attacked in a fit of rage, maybe even killed, by some anguished, crazed mother taking out her grief the only way she knew how.

That evening, as Jessica paced up and down in the kitchen, wondering what to do with herself, with her life, the sound of a horse coming into the yard assailed her with even more despair.

When the visitor knocked on the back door, she didn't respond—until she recognized Reuben's voice, brusque and cold. "I know you're there, Jessica. I've got to talk to you."

She opened the door but had no intention of letting him in. It had been a blessing when she overheard the news he had married Leona Billingsley only a few weeks ago. "What do you want?" she demanded waspishly.

Expressionless, he suggested, "If you won't invite me in, can't you at least come out on the porch?"

She was in no mood to be sociable. "Just get to the point."

He gave a disgruntled sigh. "Very well. I heard what happened in town today, and I'm sorry things are like they are."

Her eyebrows shot up. "Really? Are you now? That's interesting, seeing as how *you* were the one who set out to make me an outcast."

Undaunted, he continued. "I came here to tell you that if you decide you want to leave these parts, which at this point seems like a good idea, I'll buy your house and land for the taxes owed on it. I checked at the courthouse the last time I was in Asheville and found out you're in arrears."

She knew the taxes were probably delinquent but hadn't got around to worrying about it just yet. "I'm going to pay them next week."

It was his turn to show surprise. Then, with a suspicious frown, he said, "I don't believe you. I don't believe you've got that kind of money."

She gave her head a haughty toss, and snickered. "I don't care what you believe. Now the farm isn't for sale, so we've got nothing further to discuss."

She started to close the door, but he pushed forward to cram his foot in the gap to prevent her. "Yes, we do," he harshly told her, "because we both know you can't stay here, and you've got to do something with this place. I want it."

"Well, you aren't going to have it."

"Listen." He was becoming desperate. "You have to be realistic about this. We both know your pa will never return to these parts. And neither will Belinda. No decent man would have you now, so what are you going to do? Stay here and starve? You can lie all you want to, but I figure you've got to be about broke."

She kept a tight rein on her temper and managed to pa
tiently repeat, "The farm isn't for sale, and I doubt I coul
sell it if I wanted to. The deed isn't in my name, you know."

"You could let me tenant-farm. I know you're lying
about being able to pay the taxes, but I'll pay them and kee
them paid, in exchange for you letting me move in and rui
the place while you're gone."

"That's crazy," she hooted.

Solemnly, he shook his head. "No, it isn't. It's a goo
deal for us both. I'll even sign papers saying I'll get out i
you or any of your family come back. If you don't agree
Jessica," he sharply pointed out, "you're going to lose th
place to the tax collector, anyway, and then you won't hav
anything.

"Now I don't have to go to war on account of my gam
leg," he pressed on, "and I'll be here to look after things
So you better think over my offer, because I don't see where
you've really got any options."

Reluctantly, she had to agree. There really was no othe
way out. "All right," she said finally, "but I will want
deposit."

"For what?"

"For good faith." She cocked her head to one side an
managed a saucy grin. "And also to give me some traveling
money."

He grumbled, but agreed, then asked where she planne
to go.

"That," she said with finality, as she pushed his foot ou
of the door and closed it, "is none of your business. Jus
have everything ready in two days."

Jessica had no intention of telling him or anybody else she
was going to Richmond to look for her sister.

She had come to terms with the sad reality there was n
reason to stay there any longer, and suddenly she was des
perate to find Belinda.

Derek was surprised at how easily and quickly he adapted
to being in the midst of a war. That was not, however, to say
he liked it.

Neither did he like being a spy!

As a preacher, he was called on to hold the hands of mortally wounded soldiers and comfort them as they lay dying. He listened to the confessions of men about to go into battle, who wanted to ease their conscience and, possibly, their souls, should it be their day to meet their Maker.

He soothed his own guilt by telling himself the end justified the means. If his sending information of Confederate troop movement back to the Union army would shorten the infernal war by even one day, then his feeling like a traitor to men who trusted him was justified.

Something else that surprised him was the ease with which he could minister to the men in his regiment. He talked to them every night by the fire, led prayers. He felt more like a preacher than any time since leaving seminary.

And alone in his tent at night, or asleep under the stars, the dreams came back to haunt him, dreams of the good life he and Jessica could have had, if only she had loved him enough to chance the future with him.

In the months since he had received the letter that cut him to the core, bitterness had slowly been replaced by smoldering hurt and disappointment, which would take a long time to heal, if it ever did. He hoped, despite all his doubts, that she would be happy. Maybe because of the way she had been raised, brought up to believe, it was only natural she would do the expected thing and obey her father's will.

Derek was not worrying about his own future. He had to get through a war first. Then he supposed he would stay in the North, for surely he would have earned a church of his own with his record as both chaplain and loyal spy.

He had spent a little time in Richmond after enlisting. There, he had learned to identify Confederate soldiers from different areas. Most wore gray, but the men from Alabama wore blue, and the ones from Georgia, brown, with full-skirted pants and green trim. Tennesseans wore coonskin caps, while it was easy to spot a Texas Rebel by his cowboy hat. The New Orleans Zouaves dressed in baggy scarlet trousers with white gaiters, low-cut blue shirts and heavily embroidered and braided jackets; they also carried bowie knives held in bright blue sashes.

It was in late June that Derek learned the Confederates planned to deflect what they feared would be a crippling blow to Richmond by McClellan's troops. Yet as the first of a series of engagements began, he could not get word out of any plans he overheard. General John Magruder was able to confuse the Yankees into thinking a much larger Rebel force had been assembled. General Lee was attacking McClellan east of Richmond, and for seven days, the fighting exploded.

When the sharp whistle of minie balls, the hideous screeching of shells and the thunderous roar of cannon finally ended, Derek joined the doctors and the medical corps to go into the battlefield, under a white flag for cease-fire to clear out the dead and wounded.

He stuffed a handkerchief in his mouth to keep from retching at the sight of faces torn away, stomachs and chests gaping open, guts hanging out, flies swarming. He knelt beside a boy of only fourteen or fifteen and heard his last prayer. There were others he ministered to who might live but would suffer the agonies of the damned while they were held down screaming to have a limb removed to prevent death by gangrene.

That night, after things had calmed down a bit, Derek was in his tent, wondering why he had not seen his contact, the newspaper reporter, in nearly two weeks. Had he been caught? Or killed in cross fire? If he did not appear soon, then Derek was stymied, for he knew of no other agent.

Suddenly, the flap was yanked open, and a soldier stuck his head in. "Parson, they need you over at the hospital. Seems there's some trouble, 'cause some Yankee prisoners being taken to Richmond got caught in all that mess, and one of 'em is hurt, and some of our boys are raisin' hell saying we shouldn't waste what little medicine we've got on a Yankee. One of the doctors said to get you, 'cause the colonel, he's gone to bed exhausted, and—''

Derek was already pulling on his boots. "I'm on my way." He grabbed his shirt and took off.

The field hospital was an eerie place of lanterns, and moans and screams of the sick and dying. He wondered how the doctors were able to stay on their feet for hours without sleep and supposed it was the inability to turn away from one suffering soul.

He saw the ruckus right away and charged in, not at all surprised to see the chief troublemaker was Sergeant Dooley Pope. He was a hotheaded bully who was always getting into scrapes. Now he was pointing his gun at a white-faced, terrified young surgeon, threatening to blow his head off if he lifted one finger to help the Yankee soldier lying on the ground at his feet. Pope fell silent as Derek pushed his way through to stand beside him and look down at the victim. Derek was no doctor but knew by the profuse bleeding, the man's arm needed to come off. Without warning, he jammed his elbow into Pope's big stomach, and spun about to knock the gun from his hand. Then he slammed his fists on the back of Pope's neck to send him crumpling to the ground beside the moaning, bleeding Yankee.

"Now listen to me, Sergeant," Derek hoarsely, furiously cried, standing over him after quickly kicking the gun beyond his reach. "If you want to let this war turn you into a savage, go do it somewhere else. Don't make others suffer with guilt over not being able to help their fellow man, regardless of which uniform he's wearing."

Sergeant Pope was not hurt, only dazed, and he got slowly to his feet, glaring menacingly at Derek as he did so.

Derek did not flinch. Even without the gun, he figured he could take the man, because he was fat and clumsy. "I'm making a full report of this to the colonel tomorrow morning. Any more trouble out of you tonight, and I'll wake him up myself to see you're arrested. You got that?"

He turned away without waiting for confirmation. The surgeon was already directing aides to lift the soldier onto a stretcher and take him into the operating tent. Derek asked him where the other prisoners were. "I'd like to make sure they're being treated humanely." Actually, he wanted to see whether one might be an agent. If so, he would find a way to make himself known to him.

The surgeon pointed to a small group of bedraggled-looking men lying on the ground at the edge of a steep ravine. They were being guarded by a weary soldier, but a sweeping glance confirmed they posed no threat of violence. It was obvious they were weak, probably from a combination of hunger and forced marching.

Derek moved about, stepping over and around them, meeting their eyes as they looked up at him, some with arrogance, others with hope. He did not spot a familiar face, but the strange, fixed stare of one man caught his attention. He was heavily bearded, sitting slouched against the tree a bit away from the others. There was something about him, something Derek could not put his finger on, so he went to him and dropped to his knees beside him. "Is there anything I can get for you?" he asked solicitously, thankful to note the guard was not paying any attention. If this prisoner was an agent, then he might know who Derek was and give some sign of recognition.

"No, I reckon you've done enough for me and mine, Preacher."

Derek froze, then, with narrowed eyes, took a closer look at the man and shook his head in disbelief. "Zeb Coulter. I don't believe it."

Zeb sneered. "Why not? I sure as hell wasn't gonna fight to defend slavery."

Derek was not interested in debating the politics of war. Instead he felt driven to ask, "Is Jessica all right?"

Zeb fought the impulse to smash his fist into the preacher's face. All of this was Stanton's fault, for turning his daughter's head, changing her from a moral, obedient girl to a rebellious jezebel. And Zeb was not going to give him the satisfaction of knowing the misery he had caused. Forcing a gloating smile, he exulted, "Oh, yes, she's fine, happy as a wet puppy behind a kitchen stove. Reuben don't have to go off to war, on account of his game leg, so she's one of the lucky Southern women who've still got a husband to look after her."

Derek winced, shuddered with pain at the image of Jessica as another man's wife, lying in his arms. He shook his head in an attempt to throw off the vision that tormented him. He said to Zeb, "I want you to know that I loved her. I still do. And neither one of us meant to hurt anybody. I was going to tell you how I felt about her, ask your permission to court her, but you were always drunk, Coulter, and I knew I'd never be able to reason with you and make you see how much I loved her, and..." His voice trailed off. He shook his head again. What was the use?

Zeb gloried in witnessing his pain. "Well, it all turned out for the best, Preacher. Jessica was just sowin' her wild oats before settlin' down. I guess girls got a right just like boys to do that, though folks frown on it. Anyway, she realized she couldn't never leave home. That land means as much to her as it does to me. So don't you fret no more about her. Just get on with your life.

"As for me—" he gave a shrug of futility "—I reckon I'll sit it out in that place in Richmond they call the Black Hole...unless I die there. Don't much matter to me no more." He leaned back his head, closed his eyes. He had nothing else to say.

Derek drew a sharp breath, let it out slowly, clenched and unclenched his fists. Damn it, he could not let it happen. Even though one part of him despised Jessica Coulter for what she had done to him, another part could not deny caring. And it was that other part that spoke to him now, making him realize he could not allow her father to be sent to Libby Prison, a converted tobacco warehouse in Richmond. He had heard it was, truly a black hole.

He placed his hand on Zeb's shoulder. Zeb's eyes shot open to glare menacingly. "Listen to me," Derek whispered in a rush. "I'm going to help you escape. I'll divert the guard's attention, and when you see him turn his back, you roll to the side, down the ravine. If you haven't broken your neck by the time you hit bottom, move fast to your right. You should reach Union lines by morning. Just be careful they don't mistake you for a Reb and shoot you," he finished, offered a lame smile meant to humor the man.

"Why?" Zeb asked, astonished. "Why are you doin' this for me?"

Derek told him, "I'm not doing it for you. I'm doing it for Jessica."

He stood, headed for the guard.

Zeb stared after him in wonder. For one flashing instant, he almost called after him to tell him the truth, but he knew that to do so would jeopardize the chance Stanton was giving him. And what good would it do now to reveal it all, anyway? For all he knew, Jessica *was* married to Reuben Walker by now. She might have come to her senses after he left. There was no way of knowing, and it just did not matter anymore, anyway. Best to forget the past ever happened.

Derek began an easy conversation with the guard, slowly, casually, led him away from the prisoners as he offered him a cheroot and asked his opinion on how the spirit and morale of his fellow soldiers could be raised.

Zeb watched intently, waited for just the right moment, then began to inch his way to the edge of the ravine. It was steep and rocky, and he very well *could* break his neck, but anything was better, he figured, than prison.

He made his break.

All might have gone well had another prisoner not been watching. Seeing Zeb make his bid for freedom, he lunged, also. His movement, however, was clumsy, and he tripped at the very top of the ravine to plunge downward screaming in terror at the top of his lungs. That caused the other prisoners to scramble, and the guard whipped around and started shooting.

Bedlam ensued, and when the excitement was over, two of the prisoners were dead and the others all rounded up—except for Zeb.

"One missing, sir," the guard said in chagrin to the colonel, who had been awakened by all the noise.

The colonel grumbled that one Yankee soldier, more or less, made no difference, and barked that he'd deal with the guard in the morning for being so negligent. He turned to go back to his tent, only to find Sergeant Pope blocking his way. "What is it, Sergeant?" he demanded irritably

Sergeant Pope was smirking. "I disagree with what you said about one Yankee, more or less, not making any difference, sir. I'd say it matters a whole lot...*when we've got one among us.*"

The colonel stiffened. "What are you talking about, man? Speak up! I've no time for riddles."

"I saw the whole thing. I saw the preacher whispering with the prisoner that's missing, saw him walk right over and get the guard's attention on something else. He set it up for that man to escape." Pope then whirled on Derek and bellowed, "You're a goddamn spy, Preacher!"

At that, the guard yelped, "He did maneuver me away, Colonel. I swear. Now that I think about it, he put his arm around my shoulder and walked me away, gave me a smoke, and I didn't think nothin' about it, him bein' a preacher and all, but I see now it was all set up."

Derek knew he was trapped but was not going to admit to anything. Instead, he denied the accusation, vehemently argued that he was being falsely accused because Sergeant Pope was angry over their earlier confrontation.

But the colonel believed otherwise. Ordering Derek to be tied up with the other prisoners, he taunted, ''You might've helped one bastard escape the Black Hole, Preacher, but you'll sure as hell take his place!''

Chapter Twenty

Richmond, Virginia, that summer of 1861, was a whole new world for Jessica. Everywhere, it seemed people were involved in the war in one way or another. Soldiers drilled on the streets. Units lined up to march off to combat. Women gathered in parlors and churches to make bandages. Taverns and saloons were filled with men drinking to forget—or to muster needed courage for the hell that surely lay ahead of them.

Jessica stepped off the train one steaming hot afternoon, every stitch of clothing she wore soaked with perspiration. She did not have a cent to her name. Reuben had paid for her ticket but refused anything extra, claiming he had no more money to give her.

She knew times were hard for the mountain folk, but in Richmond, there were huge amounts of money circulating. She had overheard some people talking on the train, saying it was all due to the army, and the war, and the trading in medicines, coffee, tea and sugar. But that did not help *her* situation on arriving. She could only pray to find Belinda right away and that she would have found work, a place to stay.

When Jessica left North Carolina, she had taken with her a small bag of food—boiled eggs, some dried fruit and what was left of a smoked ham, sliced and laid between biscuits made from the last of her flour and lard. But she had finished that the day before, and as she moved through the crowded depot, hunger, along with the stifling heat, made her feel nauseated and dizzy.

Forcing herself to keep moving, she went in every dance hall or bar she passed, to describe Belinda and ask if anyone had seen her. She even tried mentioning the name she remembered Belinda said she might use—Belva.

By dark, she had covered perhaps a quarter of the city's entertainment establishments, and no one knew anything. She doggedly returned to the depot to rest on a hard wood bench till morning.

A few times during the night, railway guards passed by and glanced at her curiously but to her relief did not prod her to move on. She knew, however, that she could not expect them to continue to do so night after night. She would have to find a place to stay. But where? And how could she pay, anyway, when she had no money? It all seemed hopeless, but she had no choice but to persevere.

The next morning, Jessica was about to start out on her quest once again when she saw an elegantly dressed, obviously well-to-do woman, attempting to force her son to eat a biscuit and fried drumstick that he apparently did not want. "Oh, all right!" she said finally, as the train they were waiting for was announced. "Bring it with you. You'll be begging for something within the hour." But the little boy tossed the food aside, and scrambled after his mother.

Jessica did not hesitate, did not even look about to see if anyone was watching. She lunged for the cast-aside food and was well on the way to devouring it when suddenly she glanced up to see the child staring at her in bewilderment.

"My mother told me to come back and get my food," he said accusingly.

Jessica blinked back humiliated tears, realizing how she must look, like a stray dog pouncing on garbage. "I—I'm sorry," she stammered, ashamed, lips quivering. "I…I was just so hungry."

Just then, the irate mother charged back into the depot, screeching, "James, if you don't hurry, the train is going to leave without us...." Her voice trailed off as she took in the scene—the young woman with tears streaming down her cheeks, a half-eaten chicken leg in one hand.

Jessica struggled once more to speak, apologizing.

The woman straightened, drew in her breath, motioned her son away, as though diseases could be caught from starving people. Then, in a flash of benevolence, she opened her purse, took out a few bills and flung them at Jessica's feet. "Here. Go get yourself something to eat." Grabbing her son by the hand, she hurried out, did not look back.

Jessica was aware others were watching then but did not care as she scooped up the money. Heart pounding, she realized there was nearly ten dollars—enough for room and board for a week! She whispered a prayer of thanksgiving for a very special blessing. But then she was stabbed with a painful reminder. Once before, she had praised God for a special gift, or so she had thought at the time—the love of Derek Stanton.

With a defiant lift of her chin as she left the depot, she told herself this was different—this was something she could actually *hold* and *touch*. Derek Stanton had been a fantasy, a myth, his love existing only in her mind because she had wanted so desperately to believe that it did. He had never meant a word he said, and she determined once more not to look back.

She remembered seeing a sign pointing toward the waterfront district, advertising clean rooms at cheap prices. She went directly there, where the owner, Mrs. Pearl Hubbard, looked at her suspiciously and said, "A body can't be too particular about who they take into their home these days. How come you're traveling alone? Where's your family?"

"That's why I'm here," Jessica attempted to explain. "I'm looking for my sister."

They were standing on the front porch, and Mrs. Hubbard, hands on her hips, circled her in scrutiny. Finally, with a resigned sigh, she said, "All right. I'll rent you a room, but you can't be entertaining men in it. I run a decent place here."

"I'm a decent woman," Jessica countered frostily.

"Good. We'll get along, then."

Jessica took a bath, ate a late breakfast, then set out to spend the rest of the day searching for Belinda, but without success.

At supper, she sat at Mrs. Hubbard's dining room table with five other boarders, all men. They asked her questions, curious why a lovely young woman like her was all alone in a city surrounded by war. She explained once more that she was searching for her sister, making up a tale that Belinda had aspired to be a singer and had run away from home to make her name, and fortune, in Richmond. The men laughed among themselves, saying the only women singers around were in taverns and saloons, and their voices weren't the reason they'd been hired. Mrs. Hubbard banged her spoon against her water glass and shot a condemning glance around the table that brought silence. She didn't put up with such sassy talk, she reminded them.

After they had eaten, Jessica wandered out to the front porch, washed with worry over what to do next. It had taken all the money the woman at the depot had given her to pay in advance for only one week at Mrs. Hubbard's. When that week was up, she knew she would have to leave or get a job. She was willing to do the latter, but where? Doing what? She supposed she could seek out a teaching position, but did she really want to stay in Richmond? Suddenly, she was terribly homesick then chided herself for being so silly. *She no longer had a home!* Not really. Not when everyone she had ever known hated her as they hated her father.

In her miserable reverie, Jessica was not even aware of staring at the distant building till one of the men she had met at supper, a Mr. Kearny, attempted to make conversation as he sat behind her in one of the rocking chairs. "That's Libby

Prison you're staring at. Otherwise known as the Black Hole."

Libby Prison. She blinked at the sight of the three-story brick building. In a flash, her mind whirled backward in time to that day in the settlement store when Lucille Michaels had hysterically screamed she hoped Jessica's father died in prison.

Turning slowly and choosing her words carefully, she asked of the pleasant-faced man, "What kind of prisoners do they keep there?"

"Why, Yankees, of course," he answered with an amused chuckle.

Someone else came out on the porch, and she was forgotten as another conversation began. But she continued to look at the prison, assailed with the thought that if indeed her father were a prisoner of war, captured at Big Bethel, then it was likely he was there. And oh, how much it would mean to see him, talk to him. Regardless of the sad reality that they had never been close, he was still her father, and she desperately needed to feel there was someone for her, somewhere. And maybe there was something she could do to make life a little easier for him.

She turned, waited for a lull in the conversation Mr. Kearny and another man were having, then asked, "Do they ever let people visit that prison?"

The men exchanged startled looks, raised their eyebrows. Mr. Kearny then regarded her skeptically and coolly asked, "Do you want to go there, Miss Coulter? I can't imagine why."

And she wasn't going to tell him, either. She made up a story quickly. "I'm in service to the Lord," she said. "I thought perhaps I could minister to those poor souls."

The men snickered, then Mr. Kearny told her he doubted the Confederates would allow visitors from outside, whatever their motives. He went on to tell a conversation he'd had recently with a sergeant in charge of feeding the prisoners. "He says conditions are so bad there that he pulls rank and won't go there, himself. He has to threaten the men under him with insubordination charges to make them deliver the slop buckets. You'd best offer your Christian love elsewhere, Miss Coulter. From all I've heard, the Black Hole isn't even fit for rats, much less a lady.''

They turned back to their previous discussion, dismissing her. She was glad they could not see her face, could not see the anguish surely mirrored there as she stifled the impulse to rage that her father did not belong in such a place, either.

She knew she had to see him, to find out if there were anything at all she could do to ease his misery, but how to go about it was another matter. She did not dare go to the prison authorities and request permission, not after realizing by Mr. Kearny's reaction how she would be regarded if it were known her father was a traitor to the Southern cause. Besides, the memories of how her own neighbors had treated her were still too vivid in her mind. She had to keep the shameful secret.

She continued her fruitless search for Belinda but toward the end of the week sadly acknowledged to herself she was probably not in Richmond. There was no way of knowing where she had gone, especially in her frame of mind. Jessica had other worries to face, also. Mrs. Hubbard asked for another week's board money, and she had to admit she was without funds.

Mrs. Hubbard listened to her tale of woe, then said, ''Well, I'm a Christian woman, and my heart goes out to you, dear, but the fact of the matter is, there are plenty of folks out there looking for a place to stay that have money, and I can't afford to give you charity. But,'' she added, to the sudden beating of Jessica's hopeful heart, ''Mr. Kearny was telling me how you'd said you'd like to do some missionary work to the poor souls in the Black Hole. Well, it just so happens that the ladies in my church feel it's their Christian duty to see that the poor devils in the prison hospital get decent food. They don't mind fixing soup and such, but there's not a one among them who dares go there. I took the liberty of telling them about you, and quite frankly, I told them I thought you were very near destitute. So they asked me to tell you if you want the job of serving the sick, you can sleep at the church at night, eat some of what's fixed for the prisoners. Maybe that'll tide you over for a while, anyway, if you're willing.''

Jessica was definitely willing and moved her few belongings into a tiny room in the Methodist Church just down the street. The next morning, she was up bright and early working with the women who were getting ready a big kettle of potato soup. They had been sending something to the prison hospital every day but had no way of knowing if the sick prisoners ever saw it. They feared the soldiers staffing the place just ate it themselves. Jessica assured they needn't fear that happening again.

Just before noon, Mrs. Hubbard did her part by sending her house Negro, Billy Bob, to the church with a cart to take Jessica and the soup to the prison. He regarded her with wide, frightened eyes as he loaded the kettle of soup in the back, and finally beseeched her, "You ain't gonna make me go in that place with you, are you, Miss Jessica? They is folks dyin' down there, and I don't want to be around no dyin' folks.''

Jessica attempted to shame him into assisting. "Why, Billy Bob!'' she cried. "You mean to tell me you're going to stand outside and let me, a helpless woman, go in there alone?''

He stared down at his bare feet, then shrugged and said he reckoned he'd go, but hoped it didn't take long.

The hospital, which was really a place where the mortally wounded or fatally sick were taken to await death, was located in what had once been a crude dirt cellar at the rear of the building, right on the waterfront. The guard posted outside looked bored, for he had nothing to fear from the wasted, wretched souls inside the thick, wood door. He filled his hours by throwing rocks at the huge wharf rats scurrying around. Regarding Jessica and her accompanying servant coolly, he motioned her inside without offering to help. "You'll need to turn up the lantern inside the door. We keep it turned down when nobody's inside. *They* don't need the light," he added with a sneer.

Billy Bob pulled the door open with one hand, while holding the kettle in the other.

The guard indifferently said, "Just pour the soup in the pans next to 'em on the floor. If they feel like eatin', they will. Make it fast, 'cause it don't smell too good in there."

Jessica was appalled by his callousness; she had already figured out the hospital was no more than a way station on the inevitable journey of the dying. "Aren't there any medical attendants here?" she asked, staring into the darkness as Billy Bob continued to hold the door open. A foul odor from within made her wrinkle her nose.

The guard smelled it, too, and irritably yelled, "Either go on in there or close the door, lady. And no, there ain't no medical folks around. The doc, he comes in the morning and makes his rounds and sends out the dead to make room for more, and that's about it. You want to just leave that soup out here?" he asked.

She shook her head. "No. We'll take it in." She stepped inside, found the lantern and turned it up as she fought to keep from gagging. The smell was horrible—blood, gangrene, vomit and human waste. It began to dawn on her that it was not the intent of the Confederate Army that these men ever get well. A patient's recovery would mean another prisoner to be watched over, or worse, if he escaped, another Yankee soldier to be reckoned with. Sadly, she thought it would be so much kinder and humane to just shoot these wretched beings and relieve them of their misery.

She saw that cots lined the wall on one side of the dungeonlike room, but most of the men lay on tattered rags and blankets on the floor. Not one of them seemed to be moving.

Billy Bob was holding his hand over his face. He whined through his fingers, "Missy, if you don't hurry up, I'm gonna be sick. Let's fill them bowls and get outta here, please."

Jessica didn't feel so well herself but was determined not to show it. She went to the first man, who was just lying on his back staring up at the ceiling. Gently, she asked, "Would you like some soup?" He didn't answer. She signaled to Billy Bob to fill his bowl, then said, "It's here if you feel like eating," and moved on.

How she wished she had time to spoon-feed each and every one but knew that was not possible. She was relieved, however, to see a few of the men start to sip from their bowls. She guessed it was the first decent food they'd had since being captured.

With horror, she discovered that two of the men on the left side of the room were dead. When she came upon the first, she had rushed to the door and called to the guard, but he'd quickly, curtly, snapped it wasn't his job to haul bodies out. There was a special detail for that, and they wouldn't be by till the next day. Jessica had covered the dead man with a sheet, and when she found the next one, did the same, that time without comment.

She made her way down the right side, finding two men near death, another already gone, but three seemed in good shape and gulped down the soup.

She was almost to the end of the row, nearing the door and glad **of** it. Not only was the odor terrible, but her heart was breaking to witness such suffering. Billy Bob was not even trying to hold back his gagging any longer. She began to hurry, filling each bowl and moving on to the next without attempting conversation.

"That's it," she said finally.

Billy Bob was already bolting out the door, the guard laughing at his haste. Jessica felt like running, too, but forced herself to move at a normal pace. No need, she felt, to let these men see how repelled she really was.

She hung up the lantern, turned down the flame. She was holding her breath, eager to step outside and breathe in clean, fresh air—and then she heard it.

Someone had whispered her name.

She froze, felt a wave of panic, told her suddenly pounding heart and shrieking mind that it was only her imagination, because she was nearly sick herself from the awful place, and—

It came again . . . like a whisper caught in a night breeze.

The guard cried, "Lady, will you hurry up? I'm not standin' here with this door open and lettin' the smell out much longer!"

When she didn't respond at once, he slammed the door, leaving her alone in the eerie gloom.

She did not want to remain there but it was as though her feet were frozen to the ground. She could not make her legs move.

"Jessica . . . here . . ." Slowly, sure the voice was only a cruel trick of her mind, she forced herself to turn in the direction of the sound. It had come from a shadowed alcove in a section she'd not noticed, and so had not left food there. One of the men was, no doubt, calling out to be fed, but how could he know her name? She had not introduced herself, had seen no need, for most of the prisoners were barely conscious, anyway.

She heard the call again.

"Jessica . . . here . . ."

She reached for the lantern, turned up the flame, held it high as she walked hesitantly toward the distant shadow, anxiously, nervously, wondering if it could be her father calling out to her. As she drew closer, she could see whoever it was had managed to raise himself to a sitting position.

"Oh, my God!" she breathed.

Derek Stanton, momentarily blinded by the sudden flare of light, instinctively threw his hands before his face to shield his eyes.

"Oh, my God!" she said again with more force, then stammered, "I—I don't believe it. It can't be."

He'd had time to overcome his own shock at recognizing her as she moved around the chamber, so he was composed as he urged, "The lantern, please. I'm not used to so much light."

She lowered it with trembling hands. "What . . . what are you doing here," she asked, "in a prison for Yankees?" She was starting to overcome the jolt, began to feel the first stabbing reminders of how he had broken her heart.

"It's a long story, too long to tell right now. But you . . ." He drank in the sight of her, familiar warmth spreading through him despite the painful memories of how she had lied when she swore to love him. "Why are you here? Why are you so far from home?"

"That's none of your concern," she snapped, angry with herself over the feelings he was able to evoke so easily. She was also furious to realize he had taken sides with the North. Her gaze flicked over him with contempt. "You don't look sick to me. You're faking, aren't you?"

He saw no reason to lie to her. All she had to do, anyway, was voice her suspicions, and he'd be thrown back in with the others. "Yes, I am, but for a reason. If I stayed with the other prisoners, I probably *would* get sick. I was lucky enough to fool one of the guards into thinking I was in a stupor, and I've escaped that much misery, at least. I stay over here in this corner, in the shadows, and nobody bothers me. I've been here for more than a week now, and frankly, I think they've forgot I'm even here."

"If they don't know you're here, what do you eat? How do you survive? I didn't see you over here."

He shrugged, for he was used to the despicable menu. "They bring in a big slop bucket once a day and set it down. Those who can, crawl over and eat. Those who can't, die. You're the first person to come in with decent food and fill the bowls. Bless you," he added, daring to offer a warm smile.

In horror, she asked, "If conditions are worse for the other prisoners than in here, dear God, what's it like out there?"

He decided not to spare her the ugly details, for she'd surely not minded his pain when she rejected his love. Bluntly, he told her, "They crowd two hundred men into a room large enough for fifty, and they lump them all together—deserters, murderers, idiots, lunatics, thieves. It makes no difference. Filth is everywhere. The floor is an inch deep in thick, greasy slime. Everyone uses one open privy that never gets cleaned. I was on the second floor, and the walls were smeared from the slop and excrement dripping down from the hundreds of men above me, just as the ones below got the same from us. Vermin are everywhere, crawling on everything and everybody. At night, the stench is terrible, but during the day, when the sun pours in through the windows to heat everything up, it's a thousand times worse.

"The 'death detail' is supposed to come once a day," he went on, "to pick up the bodies of those who've mercifully gone to meet their Maker and escape this hell on earth, but sometimes it doesn't come, so there's the added odor of rotting flesh to contend with. No blankets, nothing to lie on. Two meals a day of rancid beef and water.

"That's how it is up there," he finished matter-of-factly. "So now do you wonder why I fake being sick in order to stay here?"

"My father!" Jessica cried then, coming out of her horrified stupor. "Did you see him? He was fighting at a place called Big Bethel, a soldier in the Union army, and I heard he was captured."

Derek shook his head, grateful to be able to allay her fears. "He's not a prisoner, Jessica. The last time I saw him he was heading for the Union lines."

Her eyes grew wide, and she dropped to her knees to beg for confirmation. "Are you sure? You actually *saw* him?"

He wasn't going to tell her that her father's escape was the reason he, himself, was in this hellhole. She didn't care anything about him and might think he was making up the tale to gain favor in her eyes and look like a hero—and he didn't want that. No matter that just her nearness evoked pleasurable tremors of the love he still held for her. It was over. There was no going back. She belonged to another, and that was the way it was, and would be.

Yet in the back of his mind, a plan was already starting to form—a plan whereby she, unknowingly, would help him escape. But he had to move slowly, lest she become suspicious. Worse, she might even be so loyal to the Confederates, despite her father's being on the opposite side, that she'd actually turn Derek in again. He couldn't risk that.

"Yes," he said finally, "I saw him, and we talked."

"You *talked* to him?" she echoed incredulously. She started to move closer to him, then abruptly checked herself and stayed her distance. He was, after all, the enemy, and worse, he was still able to set her heart to pounding with love, which was *wrong, wrong, wrong!* All those hours they had spent together, the ecstasy and passion in his arms— those memories were cold ashes of a fire that had burned only in lust, never in love. How could those hours have meant anything to him when already he'd implanted his seed in another, had probably intended to marry that other woman all along? He had merely been taking his pleasure with Jessica to while away the loneliness of being separated from his real love.

But what on earth, she was desperate to know, had he talked to her father about? Her father despised Derek, blamed him for all the troubles that had come to their family. "I want to know everything he told you," she said tightly. "Tell me, please."

"Tomorrow," he hedged, realizing he had one weapon, one ace in the hole. "You've got to go now, before the guard decides to see what's keeping you. If they find out we know each other, they won't let you come back, figuring you'd help me escape," he added with an impudent wink, meant to goad her.

And it did.

Jessica stiffly got to her feet, glaring down at him. "That, you despicable Yankee," she informed him haughtily, "is out of the question, and frankly, if it weren't for wanting to hear news of my father, I'd tell them you're just faking and have you sent back where you belong."

She quaked within to think how she despised this man who had deserted her, made a mockery of everything they had shared together. And to make matters worse, her rage was fueled by the fact he was now the enemy—a Yankee soldier!

"Don't do that, please." He reached out to her in a gesture of pleading, for he was not too proud to beg. She moved farther away, and even in the dim light, he could see the hatred flashing in the cinnamon eyes that had haunted his sweetest dreams. He guessed that her guilt at her treatment of him combined with his representing the enemy of her homeland, evoked shameful memories in her. And there was no telling why she was in Richmond. Maybe Reuben had gone off to war, despite his game leg, and if Belinda had married the young man she had been so smitten with, then Jessica would have been all alone on the farm. Perhaps she had wanted to do her part in the war elsewhere—like here, in the middle of it all. So, if she were presenting the image of a dutiful, loyal wife, no doubt she did not want to be reminded of passion shared with another man. "I've no right to ask you for anything, Jessica, but I'm not hurting anybody here. I'm just trying to survive. And you won't gain anything by turning me in. Have some compassion, please."

Compassion. The word, coming from him, evoked even greater contempt in her mind. Did he have any compassion for her when he married another after stealing *her* heart, robbing her of her virtue, ruining her life and her family's by his cruel deception? The truth was, if he'd had any of the compassion of which he so easily spoke, he'd have found a way to return and stand up to her father and Reuben and the entire community and let them know they were wrong in what they were thinking, that their love had not been a shameful, sordid affair. Oh, how she longed to scream all of what she held inside! But she would not give him the satisfaction of knowing just how deeply she'd been crushed.

Solemnly, she told him, "Very well. I won't turn you in, but I warn you, if conditions get crowded, and space is needed for soldiers who are truly sick, I won't protect you."

His laugh was short, bitter. "I don't think there's any danger of that, Jessica. In just the week I've been here, the room out there has been emptied of occupants and refilled three times over. They don't last long here."

"Sooner or later, someone will notice your name hasn't come up on the list of the dead, and they'll start looking for you."

"Till that happens, I'll be grateful to you if you'll slide a bowl of soup my way."

"Out of Christian kindness only, Mr. Stanton," she coldly established. "Personally, I don't care what happens to you. But in exchange for a bowl of soup tomorrow, I will expect you to tell me everything you can about my father."

"Agreed."

She hurried away, glad of the darkness lest he read on her face that, amid her fury, there was also love she could not deny.

She determined she would just have to hate a little harder to overshadow that love.

Derek stared after her before finally melting back into the shadows of his personal abyss.

Try as he might, he could not despise Jessica. He could only hate himself for being so foolish as to love her so deeply.

Chapter Twenty-one

After the surprising encounter with Derek, Jessica was in a turmoil. One part of her commanded she turn him in for the goldbrick he was, while another part needled her to forget he was even there. After all, her job was to take soup to the sick prisoners. What else went on in the prison was none of her concern.

She had decided, based on her painful previous experience with Derek's lies, not to believe him when he said her father wasn't there. She had gone directly to the roster sergeant and asked to see the list of prisoners at Libby. He had regarded her coldly, almost with contempt, but she paid him no mind. What did she care what he thought, anyway?

So he scanned the seemingly endless pages of prisoners' names, finally, gruffly, told her with a scowl, "Naw! Ain't no Yankee here by the name of Zeb Coulter." He then swept her with curious, yet admiring, eyes and asked, "How come you want to waste your time workin' with those half-dead Yankees? I can get you a good job waitin' bar at Rudy's Tavern, just up the road. You'll make good money, and—"

"No, thank you," she curtly declined, turned to go.

"Hey you, wait a minute. Don't sashay outta here with your nose up at me, woman," he roared. When she kept on going, he reminded her, "I can deny you and them goody-goody church ladies permission to go to the hospital, you know."

She knew that, just as she knew it was necessary to placate the bullying officer. Pasting a smile on her lips, she faced him once more. "I wasn't trying to be rude, Sergeant. I just have a lot of work to do. I appreciate your wanting to find me a job that would pay more, but the fact is, I'm in service to the Lord, and—"

He silenced her with an impatient wave. No matter if she was a fine-looking woman, he knew she would never work in a tavern, much less be persuaded to warm his bed. "Yeah, yeah, I've heard all of that, how the church ladies want to give the enemy prisoners Christian love and care, in hopes the Northern church ladies will do the same. What I want to know is, why are you, a Southerner, looking for somebody in a prison for Yankees?"

Bluntly, she told him. "He's my father. Someone told me he'd been taken prisoner. I thought he might be here." She gave a careless shrug. "Obviously, he isn't, so I thank you for your time."

He hooted, "Your pappy is a Yankee?" With a raucous laugh he waved her away. "Hell, no wonder you don't mind that stinkin' hospital. Get on outta here! I don't want no part of a traitor's daughter, no how!"

She supposed she never should have gone to the registry office, anyway, but she'd felt she had to make sure her father wasn't in the prison. Even if she could believe Derek, he had no way of knowing who all the prisoners were.

Derek.

Oh, dear Lord, how she wished she had not stumbled upon him. She would rather never have met him again, for the painful reality was, she knew she still cared.

But no matter!

He belonged to another woman. He was a husband, maybe even a father by then, for all she knew—though she did not want to ask. It would hurt to hear him talk of his baby son or daughter, the infant *she* had hoped to bear.

The next day when she returned to the hospital, she purposely stayed away from the forgotten alcove where Derek was hiding. She hurried through the task of filling the bowls, then left the same time Billy Bob did. But all the while, she wondered whether it was her imagination that she felt Derek's eyes on her, watching, *willing* her to go to him.

The time when she was not working at the church kitchen or visiting the prison, she continued to walk the busy streets of Richmond in search of Belinda. Finally, after visiting every saloon, tavern and dance hall, and checking at every boardinghouse and hotel, she was forced to accept that her sister was obviously nowhere in the city. She could not venture to guess where else she might have gone, but knew only that she had to give up and admit defeat.

Finally, she was faced with having to make a decision as to her own future. The original reason for working with the church ladies had been twofold—to have access to the prison to try to find her father, and to have a place to stay. Now, however, Jessica knew she could not continue. Not only did she feel that she was merely wasting time, but she did not like knowing Derek was there, just waiting for her to— what? Did he even care that she came and went daily? Why should he? They meant nothing to each other anymore, had no ties. She told herself she was silly to regard him in any way.

She resolved to find another job, one that would pay her money so she could find a proper place to live. Yet she was burning with the desire to speak to Derek again, and tried to convince herself it was only to learn what he knew about her father. At their first encounter she had told him she would hear what he had to say about Zeb the next day, but she had not been able to bring herself to approach him again. Now, however, having decided to stop helping at the prison and move on, she knew she would have few chances left to talk to him.

She made her round that day, filling the bowls with hot, nourishing soup. Billy Bob always gave a terrified moan when they happened upon a prisoner who had died, and when the first two they saw were quite stiff and cold, Jessica seized the excuse to get rid of him, so she could make her way to Derek's hideaway. "Why don't you go on outside, Billy Bob?" she gently suggested. "I can manage by myself, and I know how upset you get."

"Yas'm!" He didn't need to be coaxed. He set down the kettle of soup and took off.

Once the door was closed behind him, Jessica quickly moved to minister to the remaining men. Sadly, she noted three others were dead, and several so near death that blowflies had already begun to settle on their half-closed eyelids. She kept the lantern turned very low, not wanting to see them. So useless, she thought, all of it. Why even feed them when they were brought there to die, anyway? Yet, despite her original motivation, she had to admit it gave her a warm feeling to at least try to give them some comfort.

"Bless you . . ." one of the men managed to whisper weakly as she filled his bowl. "Thanks to you, I think I might be well enough to get outta here soon."

She wondered why he even wanted to but didn't dare say so. Instead, she paused to prop his head with a folded blanket, in hopes of aiding him to eat.

Finally, she gathered her courage and went to the dark shadows of the alcove. "Are you still here?" she called into the stygian abyss.

"Right here."

She felt his touch on her ankle and was momentarily startled. "I—I brought you the rest of the soup," she said awkwardly.

He gave a soft chuckle. "You mean you aren't going to make me crawl out of here and get what's left in the pot? I've watched you every day for nearly a week, Jessica. You're avoiding me."

"Of course, I am," she snapped. "Why should I care what happens to you?"

He winced with pain at her words. All right, he could accept the fact she chose to marry Reuben Walker for whatever reasons she might have, but why did she have to act as

though she despised him? What had he done to make he
feel as she did? "Jessica," he began with a ragged sigh, "
think we need to talk."

"Yes, we do," she crisply agreed, setting down the kettl
in the darkness. He could feed himself when he was ready
then return the container to where she always left it, in cas
the guard got suspicious and went looking for it. "I wan
you to tell me everything you know about my father. I wan
to know his regiment, and—"

"I don't know any of that. All I know is, he was cap
tured, and he escaped and headed for Union lines."

"What did you talk to him about?"

Derek felt himself tense. He didn't want to think about hi
conversation with Coulter, how he'd gloated over Jessica'
happiness as Reuben Walker's wife. "Nothing in particu
lar," he hedged. "The war. That's all anybody talks abou
these days."

She persisted. "Well, how was he captured? And how dic
he escape?" She lowered herself to sit beside him.

He drew in his breath, let it out slowly, finally decided to
hell with it, he'd tell her the truth. Maybe it would make her
feel guilty over what she had done to him, instead of being
so arrogant, as though he was the villain in all of this. "
was serving as a chaplain with the Confederates, but ac
tually I was spying for the Union. Your father was cap
tured at Bull Run. I distracted the guard so he could escape.
Somebody saw me do it. He got away. I was sent here." Be
cause he could hardly see her in the dim light, he was un
able to discern her reaction. He waited anxiously for he
response.

Jessica wondered if he were telling the truth, then askec
herself why should he lie? "If what you say is true," she said
slowly, finally, "then I'm beholden to you." After a
thoughtful pause she went on. "But what I don't under
stand, is why you'd want to help him after what hap
pened."

Derek was jabbed by the sudden reminder of that night in the barn. He had wondered so many times what had taken place after he was forced to leave at gunpoint. Now with the chance to ask, however, he could not bring himself to do so. Instead, he offered, "He's your father. I guess I did it out of respect for what I thought you and I had for each other."

She grimaced, there in the eerie chamber. She did not want to dwell on broken dreams. "You don't owe me anything. Some things just aren't meant to be. I'd better be going now."

She started to move away, but his hand shot out to grasp her wrist. "Not yet. Stay a while longer, please."

"What for? We've nothing to talk about. The past is dead. Let it stay dead." All the while she was thinking of so much she wanted to ask him but did not dare, for fear he would see she still had feelings for him.

"I've got some questions, too—like what are you doing in Richmond?"

"Looking for my father, what else?" she lied. She wouldn't tell him about Belinda. No need to expose any more anguish. Nor did she want him to know her father had killed someone.

"How did he happen to join up with the North?"

"He never made a secret that's where his loyalties were."

"True," he conceded, "but I didn't figure he'd rush to answer the first bugle call. But enough about him. What I want to know is—do you have any news of the war? I used to hear a bit from new prisoners coming in, when I was in the other section, but here, I can't find out anything. Every time they bring in new people, I try to talk to them to find out whatever I can, but most of the time they're near dead and can't talk."

"If you want to hear news, why don't you go back out there?" she couldn't resist snapping. "I don't see how you stand it in here, anyway, with the smell, and . . ." Her voice trailed off. She gave a pitying shudder. "Why do you do it?"

"I told you. It's hell out there. Here I can at least escape some of the misery. I walk most of the day, when nobody is around, for exercise, to keep myself going."

"Well, what are you going to do? Stay here for as long as the war lasts?" She gave a mocking laugh. "Seems cowardly to me."

Tightly, he fired back. "I'll get out when the time is right. Now are you going to tell me the news, or not?" Again, he wondered why she harbored such animosity for him.

She saw no harm in sharing the latest information that had the South upset. Union forces had attacked Cape Hatteras, in North Carolina, and taken over Fort Clark and Fort Hatteras. The victory gave the Federals a strategic point on Hatteras Inlet, thus gaining for the Union an important advantage in its efforts to crush the blockade runners, since that area controlled an important route used by Confederate vessels.

Derek managed to conceal his joy over the information. The sooner the war was over, the better. Yet he knew he could not, as Jessica coolly accused, stay hidden in the bowels of Libby Prison for the duration, however long or short. He had to get out, and soon. The question was how.

"I do have to go now." Jessica stood.

This time he made no move to stop her, aware that the guard would soon become curious and check to see why she tarried so long. "Will you come back and talk to me tomorrow?"

She hesitated before agreeing. "I'm not sure how long I'll be coming back here." Later she wondered why she had felt the need to confide.

Inside, he was screaming, burning to know what she was planning to do. Was she going home to her husband? And where the hell *was* Reuben, anyway? Most of all, Derek yearned to know what had brought her to Richmond in the first place. Yet his pride kept him from asking. Loving her had led to the loss of his ministry and all the scorn and humiliation that accompanied that dismissal. And all for naught, for she had used him, then cast him aside. He had no intention of letting her know the anguish she had caused. Making his voice very casual, he feigned only mild curiosity to ask, "Really? Where are you heading?"

She wondered why he even cared. How she longed to ask him about his wife, where she was, whether she had given birth yet to their child? But of course, she had. She had to have. It was nearly eight months since she received that fateful letter, and—

"Jessica?" He was alarmed by her silence, slowly got to his feet. "What's wrong?"

Before she realized it, she blurted out, "Your letter nearly eight months..." She could say no more and fell silent. She backed away from him into the main chamber, where he could not follow. "Nothing," she finally said, attempting to cover. "Nothing is wrong. And I really do have to go."

He ached to follow her, for then he could see her face, the way her eyes glowed with both fury and pain all at once. "Then you did receive my letter," he said slowly, "and you knew—"

"Yes, I knew," she coldly cut him off.

He had been about to seek confirmation that she had, for in the back of his mind had always been the nagging thought that perhaps his letter had been intercepted. Maybe she hadn't known he wanted to meet her. Maybe... He shook his head to clear it. *Damn the torture! Damn the pain!* It was all in the past and none of it mattered anymore, because she was another man's wife!

She turned to go, then hesitated.

He saw and called out, unable to keep the misery from his voice as he dared to ask, "What's wrong?"

Slowly, she turned around again. She wished she could see his expression when she dared to ask, "The baby—"

"Hey, miss!"

Jessica whipped around, startled by the intruding voice of the guard as he shoved the door open and poked his head inside. By the time his eyes had adjusted to the dim light, she had quickly moved from the shadows of the alcove into the center of the main chamber.

"Is somethin' wrong?" he asked, an edge to his voice. Then he made a gagging sound before continuing, "How do you stand this stench? Jee-zus!"

She hurried to the door, murmuring she had stayed behind to hear a patient's prayers, but the guard was not listening, wanted only to get out of there.

Derek stared at the door from his hiding place for long moments after it closed. What had she been about to ask him? *The baby.* She had said something about a baby. What baby? Had she started to tell him she and Reuben had a baby? If so, where was it? Was someone keeping it for her while she dished up food at the hospital? What was the real reason she had left her home to come to Richmond, anyway, and...

Derek had been standing, but all of a sudden his legs wouldn't support him anymore as awareness crept into his mind. *A baby!* There was no way she could have had a baby by Reuben Walker. As best he could figure, even though he had lost track of time since hiding out, it was now September. She would have married Reuben around Christmas, not quite nine months ago. There was no way the baby could be Reuben's. Had she been about to tell him she had given birth to *his* baby? Maybe that was why she seemed to hate him so. She had been pregnant with his baby, married Reuben, and when Reuben found out, he had kicked her out. She had wound up in Richmond, with nowhere else to go. But, wait a minute! His heart leaped into his throat. That couldn't be it, either. He had seen Zeb, talked to him, and Zeb said she and Reuben were happy. But would Zeb have told the truth if he knew it?

Derek was too keyed up to sleep. All he wanted was for the hours to pass and Jessica to come back, so he could try to find out what she had been about to say. He knew he would have to go slowly, because something was terribly wrong, and it was going to take time to gain her confilence. He had to get her to talk to him and tell him what the hell was going on.

At daylight, he crouched farther back in the dark recess as a detail of soldiers arrived to clear out the dead and make room for more of the dying. He listened to the doctor as he brusquely made his rounds, heard him remark to the guard that two of the men were almost well enough to go back into the prison proper. "Yancy and Brenton," he snapped. "Move them out tomorrow. They'll be the first to go out the same door they came in," he added with a cruel laugh.

The guard joined in the humor, then speculated, "It must be the food them do-gooders are sendin' over."

"Well, soon enough they'll be eating the same as their friends." The doctor moved on.

When the chamber was once more clear of Confederates, Derek curiously ventured out to where the two men were lying. Indeed, they seemed much stronger and looked at him with eyes that were alert.

"What's the matter?" the one named Yancy quietly asked him, "did you think you were the only one smart enough to goldbrick?"

Derek pointed out, "At least I was smart enough to hide out. They know you two are here, and tomorrow you're going back."

The man shrugged, "Here, there, what damn difference does it make? As long as we're prisoners, we're gonna rot, anyway."

The other one, Brenton, asked, "What's your name, soldier?"

"Stanton. And I'm not a soldier. I'm a chaplain."

They exchanged incredulous looks in the muted light. Brenton asked, "What the hell did you do? I mean, they don't normally put chaplains...preachers in prison, do they?"

Derek saw no need to confide his story, just murmured that it made no difference now.

Brenton persisted. "But how long are you gonna hide out
back there? We wouldn't have even known you were there
if we hadn't seen that woman go back there, heard you two
talkin' just as she was leavin' yesterday. Who is she, anyway?"

"Just someone I used to know," Derek quietly said,
moving back toward the alcove, afraid someone would come
in and find him there and learn his secret. "As for how long
I'll hide out, I don't know yet. Till the time is right to escape, I suppose."

"Well, I wish to hell it had come while we were in here,"
Yancy grumbled as he settled back on his pallet.

The time dragged by. Derek slept little that night, willing
the hours to pass till Jessica returned. At last, the door
squeaked open, and she walked in. The Negro was right behind her, grumbling, as usual, over the smell and at being
near the dying and the dead.

Derek noticed Jessica did not glance in his direction, as
she made her way around the room serving up the soup. She
finished one side, and as she started on the other, Billy Bob
started pleading with her to hurry. Jessica seemed to be
taking longer than usual. Finally, she said the words Billy
Bob was waiting to hear. "Go on. I can finish. The kettle's
half-empty, and I can handle it myself."

He was out the door before she even finished the sentence.

When she was done, she walked over to the alcove and
cautiously peered in. Derek was waiting to pull her into the
darkness, and she gave a soft cry of surprise to realize he was
so close, and waiting.

As he grasped her shoulders, holding her in front of him,
she could feel his trembling and became frightened.
"What's wrong? Let me go, please—" She bit back the
tears. Oh, dear God, why had she even come today? All
night, she had lain awake, staring up at the ceiling and telling herself over and over not to return. Fiercely, she threat-
ened, "If you don't let me go, I'll scream. I swear I will!"

Derek released her then, ran anxious fingers through his hair. Damn it, he silently cursed, he had actually been about to kiss her, because he was so glad to see her, hold her. He had promised himself to have more control than that. It didn't make any sense, and all of a sudden, he felt like just giving up on life itself. How long could he keep hiding out in this spider-and-rat-infested corner of the dungeonlike hospital? What did he hope to accomplish? After seeing Jessica again, he had dared to hope there might be a way she would help him to escape, but not now, not when she seemed to hate him so.

"I shouldn't have come!" she suddenly cried.

Derek watched in stunned disbelief as she backed all the way out into the chamber, into the mellow glow of the lantern. "Jessica, wait," he cried then. "Don't go—"

"She ain't goin' nowhere!"

In a flash, Yancy and Brenton were on their feet. Yancy grabbed Jessica just as she let loose a startled scream. Brenton was at the door in a flash, ready when the guard, gun drawn, pushed it open. Brenton hit him on the back of his neck, and his knees buckled. He fell to the floor with a grunt and lay still.

"Grab the gun, and let's get out of here," Yancy roared.

Derek cried, "You aren't taking her with you!"

"The hell we ain't!" Brenton swung the rifle to point it at him. "We need a hostage. There's plenty more Rebs between us and freedom."

Yancy had clamped a hand over Jessica's mouth, lest she sound further alarm. "He's right," he said, nodding to Derek. "We got to have her. You can go with us, if you want, but get a move on."

Derek had no intention of being left behind.

Chapter Twenty-two

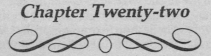

Using Jessica as a hostage, Yancy and Brenton forced Billy Bob to hide them in the back of his wagon. Derek had no choice but to go along. He had wanted to escape, Lord, yes, but not that way, not with someone holding a gun on Jessica. He couldn't let her out of his sight.

Billy Bob drove the four of them, hidden beneath piles of burlap bags, out of Richmond. At Yancy's instructions, he headed west, toward the Shenandoah Mountains.

Once they were safely out of the city, Yancy sent Brenton to take the reins.

"You gonna let me go now?" Billy Bob fearfully asked. "I done what you asked me to. And I won't say nothin' about helpin' you, or where I took you. I'm gonna be in big trouble jes' bein' gone this long. I sho' wish you'd let me go, suh," he continued to beg.

Brenton snickered. "Go where? Back to slavery? You can just keep on goin' with us, boy. To freedom."

Billy Bob thought about that. Mrs. Hubbard had never been mean to him, and he supposed he had it better than most slaves, but he was still a slave. He had no family, no reason to stay in Richmond, and things were getting mighty tense there, anyway, due to the war. He had even heard rumors that some slave owners were sending their Negroes off to fight for the South. Lordy, he knew he didn't want to do that. He'd fight for the North, to free his brothers, sure, but to defend slavery? He could not, would not do it.

Finally, having thought it over, he turned to give Brenton a big, toothy grin and heartily declared, "Well, suh, I reckon I will. I reckon I'll just declare myself a free man!" He settled back, folded his arms across his chest and took a deep breath of pleased resignation.

When they felt it was safe to shove away their covers and sit up, the first thing Derek noticed was the icy way that Jessica was ignoring him. "Listen," he began. "I know what you're thinking, but you're wrong. I had no idea they were planning anything. I admit that when I first saw you, I dared hope maybe you'd help me escape, but I wasn't in on what happened today. You've got to believe me."

She leaned back against the side of the wagon and closed her eyes. She hoped that if she tried very, very hard, she could pretend he was not there.

Yancy looked from one to the other and snickered. "Hey, I didn't mean to get a war goin' between you two." He addressed Jessica. "The truth is, lady, he didn't know nothin' about what we was plannin'. We was just goldbrickin' like he was, lookin' and waitin' for a chance to get outta that place. You were it. We heard you tell him you might not be comin' back, and we knew we had to make our move then, 'cause the doctor had already said we were bein' sent back to the other side in the mornin'. Stanton, here, he just came along for the ride."

He then turned his attention to Derek. "I guess you're wantin' to get back to your company, Preacher. You got any idea where they are?"

Derek shook his head. He was not going to confide he had been working as a spy, even though it no longer made any difference. He had lost all contact with Pinkerton and his men. All he could do was try to survive. The main thing he wanted for the immediate future, however, was to get Jessica away from the others as quickly as possible. Cautiously, because Yancy was still holding the gun, he began,

"We're far enough away now that you don't need a hostage any longer. I think we'll just go our own way."

Yancy's gaze flicked over him with mild disinterest. "Naw, I don't think you will. Not with her, anyway. We may need her later on. These hills are crawling with soldiers, and some of 'em just might be wearin' gray, instead o' blue. Believe me, we'll die before we let them capture us and send us back to Libby. Long as we got her, they'll let us pass, so either go your own way, or settle down, 'cause she stays with us."

Jessica looked frantically at Derek. Despite her fury over her belief he had planned all along to use her for escape, she desperately sought reassurance he would not abandon her now.

Derek threw caution to the wind. Eyes bulging, cords standing out on his neck, fists clenched, ready to spring, he furiously warned, "You'll have to kill me, before I'll let you touch her."

Yancy had no doubt he meant what he said, and he really did not want to kill Stanton. He hastened to assure him, "You don't have to worry about anything like that, preacher. She's your woman. We'll agree to that. It's just that we've got a ways to go, and we might need a hostage, like I said."

Sternly Derek said, "I want to know where you're going. It's not safe around here. And why aren't you heading for Washington? We need to go north, to find Union lines."

Yancy laid the gun across his knees. He doubted the preacher would try to wrest it away. With it still pointed in the direction of the girl, he could get off one shot in a hurry, and he figured Stanton knew that. "To tell you the truth, Preacher, me and Brenton are tired of this infernal war already. Back there in that goddamn Black Hole, we had lots of time to think about how we didn't really give a damn which side wins.

"So," he went on to explain, "we heard some of the other men talkin' about how the western counties of Virginia are against the war, and how when the state seceded, those counties started makin' plans to secede from Virginia. They just don't want no fightin' of any kind. Neither do me and Brenton. We figure on holin' up there for a while. Then we'll decide out what to do with ourselves while everybody else is either killin' or gettin' killed.''

Brenton turned to join the conversation. ''We heard somethin' else, too, Preacher. We heard how that big battle at Bull Run back in July woke up the North and made 'em see the South ain't gonna be beat as quick as they thought they were. We also heard President Lincoln called back General McClellan from the very mountains we're headed to, to put him in command of the army of the Potomac. He's to spend the winter building a real army. Sounds like somethin' big's gonna happen.''

''Right.'' Yancy spoke again. ''We also heard some of the Reb guards talkin' about their army trenchin' in around Manassas Junction, just twenty miles outside Washington. Patrols are real heavy, 'specially along the Potomac River, to keep watch for invasion that way. Seems with fall in the air, things are settlin' down a bit, but we'd have trouble gettin' through to our lines even if we wanted to.

''Yep.'' He exchanged a nod of agreement with Brenton. ''It's gearin' up to be a long war, and we ain't wantin' to be a part of it.''

''So why don't you just settle back and enjoy the ride, Preacher,'' Brenton suggested. ''The war is over for us, for a while, anyway.''

Jessica knew she was helpless, knew there was nothing she could do but bide her time and hope for a chance to escape. Although she was fairly confident Derek would let no harm come to her, it was agonizing to be in his company. She could not shut out from her mind the image of his wife and child, waiting somewhere for him to return. Neither could she cast aside all the golden cobwebs of a life that might have been . . . had he really loved her.

Late in the evening, Billy Bob guided the wagon deep into the woods alongside the road to make camp. By then, he had fallen into easy camaraderie with Yancy and Brenton. The trio laughed together, made plans for the future, while Derek and Jessica watched from the light of the campfire they built. Billy Bob took the rifle from Yancy, and in no time at all bagged two rabbits for their supper.

Jessica remained cold, aloof, silent. As everyone began to bed down for the night, she was given the back of the wagon to herself. She grudgingly accepted Derek's hand as she crawled up. "It would make things easier if we at least talked to each other," he suggested.

She hoped her contempt could be seen in the scant light of a quarter-moon as she blazed out at him. "I've nothing to say to you, Derek Stanton. Now or ever. Just leave me alone, please!"

"Fine!" he yelled right back at her. Damn it! he thought, whirling away, he had every right to be angry. After all, being fool enough to believe she returned his love had cost him his position, and the respect of his peers. And he could not understand why she seemed to hate him so. Then, suddenly remembering how he'd been burning to ask her what she meant the day before, just before she left the so-called hospital, he turned back to her and demanded furiously, "At least tell me one thing. Yesterday, you started to say something about a baby. What were you talking about?"

"I don't remember," she lied, turning away so he could not see her face. "And you must have misunderstood. I didn't say anything about a baby!"

He shook his head and walked away. Maybe he hadn't heard her right, he thought.

With Derek and Jessica most of the time ignoring each other, they all continued to move westward. On the third day, they came on an isolated cabin, where an old man, grateful for the company, obliged them with a hot, cooked meal. He gave Jessica some clothes that had belonged to his wife before she had died, and provided them with water and supplies to last several more days.

They were a week into their journey when they came on the remains of soldiers who had been killed in a skirmish. From the decomposed remains, it was obvious it had not been a recent fight. Jessica felt a wave of nausea to see the few strips of rotten flesh hanging from bones torn apart by wild animals. Derek saw her reaction and caught himself just as he was about to act on the impulse to comfort her. She had rejected him, he reminded himself. She wanted to be alone. So be it.

Billy Bob was the one to spot the horses, still grazing nearby. "These poor devils were Rebs," he affirmed. "That's gray rags you see, what's left of their uniforms. But even if there wasn't even that to go by, I'd know by the way their horses have hung around. Southern boys are takin' their horses with 'em, and horses are loyal. A horse'll hang around his master after death, just like a faithful old hound dog."

Yancy cracked a grin. "Well, let's be glad they didn't ride their hound dogs off to war, boy, 'cause we can't ride dogs up into them mountains, but we can damn sure ride them horses and move a hell of a lot faster than in that wagon. Now we can leave the trails and make our own."

Only four horses could be rounded up. "You got your choice of who you want to ride with," Brenton told Jessica with a hopeful smile. "Since you can't stand the preacher, how about straddlin' in front of me?"

Jessica shook her head. Derek was being as cold to her as she was to him. It was silently understood they could not stand each other. She figured he would not take advantage of her being so close. None of the others could be trusted. She had not missed the way even Billy Bob had started eyeing her lately, since becoming so chummy with Brenton and Yancy—especially the night the old man had shared a jug of popskull with them. "I'll ride with Stanton," she frostily replied.

"Notice how she don't never call him 'Preacher'?" Yancy said to Brenton with a laugh.

Brenton cackled. "Yeah, well, he said he used to know her. Maybe he knew her better'n either one of 'em is lettin' on, and she don't think of him as no preacher."

Even Billy Bob joined in the raucous laughter, and the three of them picked up their gait, moved out ahead of Derek and Jessica.

Derek had paused to adjust the stirrups to accommodate his long legs. Yancy yelled at him to hurry up and not to get any ideas about trying to run away with Jessica. Derek went on with what he was doing, but then noticed a bulge in the saddlebag. Looking inside, he found a clean, rolled-up Confederate uniform. Since the clothes he was wearing were filthy, he leaped at the chance to change. "Just turn your head," he excitedly told Jessica, who was looking on curiously.

She did so, chiding herself for the memories that suddenly surfaced—memories of that wondrous night when she had seen his body, marveled at its perfection . . . and reveled in the joys he had given her.

He felt better and said so when he mounted behind her, but she stubbornly continued to rebuke him with her silence.

"So be it!" He said it out loud that time, and with a grim set to his jaw, kicked the horse in his flanks and set him into a gallop to catch up with the others.

As the days passed, and they moved doggedly toward the west, the experience was grueling. Several times, they heard intermittent gunfire from the hills and ridges. They would dismount then and seek cover among the rocks and brush, knowing there was fighting all around them. They all hoped it would not come their way.

Derek wondered just how long they could go on, and what would happen when they reached their destination. And where the hell would they wind up, anyway?

Jessica was ever alert, despite soreness from constant riding, hunger from never enough to eat. She wanted to be ready for escape, when the time came.

The evening they came upon the dying Rebel soldier, Derek was the only one to hear the faint sound of his moans. He had dropped back from the others to allow Jessica time to tend to her personal needs. He was standing beside a ditch filled with slimy water that ran alongside a narrow path through tall pine trees. At first, he thought he'd only imagined the sound, then decided it was an animal. But then it came again, and he could make out what sounded like someone begging for help. Without hesitation, he waded through the water to the other side.

Behind him, he could hear Yancy screaming, "Preacher, you get your ass back here! I'll shoot you quicker'n hell if you don't."

He heard Jessica's hurried cry of explanation. "He's not running away. I think he heard something. I heard it, too."

The others turned back but stopped at the edge of the water to watch as Derek found the soldier lying near the opposite side of the ditch.

Derek figured the boy could be no more than fifteen or sixteen years old. Though he stared up at him, Derek knew he could not see him for the blood filling his eyes. His intestines protruded from the huge hole in his stomach. Blowflies had crusted in the wound, swarmed around his face.

"Help me...."

His cry was so feeble Derek wondered how he'd managed to hear him. He could not understand how, with such injuries, the wretched soul could still be alive. "I'm here, son. Just take it easy. You're not alone. I won't leave you."

Blood gurgled from the boy's mouth as he weakly asked, "Are you...the Yankee...what shot...me?"

"No, I didn't shoot you. I'm not a soldier. I'm a preacher." *And, oh, Lord,* Derek frantically prayed, *if I never was one before, help me to be one now. Help me to help this poor boy.* "Tell me what I can do for you," he said in an attempt to comfort.

"I'm . . . dyin' . . . Preacher." Every word spoken was an anguished effort. "Just . . . tell me . . . I'll see . . . Jesus . . . so I can . . . go easy. . . ."

"You will," Derek quickly assured him, knowing there was no time to ask him if he was ready to meet his Maker. "Trust in the Lord, and you'll see Him." He could only hope he was saying the right words. He'd been through seminary, he had studied and he had prayed, but most of all, he had made a promise to his mother; that was his only motivation in being what he was trying to be, and he could only hope it was enough.

"Preacher, I do. . . ." The boy suddenly smiled, and even with the blood clotted in his eyes, it was as though he actually saw something. "Thank you . . . for helpin' me . . . get home. . . ." His head lolled to one side, and he died.

Jessica watched, moved to tears by the hallowed scene she had just witnessed. No matter how she harbored anger and resentment for Derek Stanton, he had helped that poor boy die in peace. If only that one time, she had to admire him. "You did well . . . Preacher," she said.

Derek looked at her then, for he had forgotten what it sounded like to hear tenderness in her voice. He saw the compassion, the caring, in her lovely eyes. He got up and went to her, standing in the water as he caught her hands and held them. When she did not move away and continued to meet his piercing gaze, he dared say softly, "I don't know what I did to hurt you so, but I'm sorry. Truly sorry. You seem to hate me, and I never wanted it to be this way. All I did was love you. . . ."

She stiffened then, for his tender words stung like sand in the wind.

Yancy impatiently called, "You two quit lollygaggin' and get on up here. There's smoke ahead, maybe a skirmish. We might have to look for cover. He's dead. You can't do nothin' else. Now come on."

Jessica pulled her hands from Derek's.

He saw at once the coldness that had so quickly returned. All at once, he could stand it no longer. Voice breaking with emotion, he raggedly cried, "Damn it, woman, will you tell me what the hell I ever did to make you hate me so?"

She could only look at him in wonder that he even dared to ask. Perhaps, she suddenly decided, *she* should ask *him* some questions, and maybe finally she would learn how he could go on pretending to be ignorant of why she despised him. But not here, she thought sadly, staring beyond him to the pitiful body of the young boy. "Later," she said, then turned and started back to where the others waited.

Derek miserably watched her walk away, then suddenly remembered the weapon he had spotted lying next to the soldier. It was a smoothbore musket. If he had that, then maybe he could hold off Yancy long enough to get Jessica out of there. The miserable, tense situation could not continue.

He turned to reach down for it, and just as he did, Yancy fired, and it splintered just inches from his outstretched hand. With narrowed eyes he looked up, and Yancy laughed. "Now what does a preacher need with a gun?" he asked. But humor instantly faded as he commanded, "Get up here. Now. The woman rides with me, because you two are draggin' behind. That shootin' is gettin' closer all the time, and we gotta find us a place to hide."

"Why don't you fight?" Derek lashed out at him as he began to wade back through the muck, telling himself all the while to check his anger but unable to heed his own warning. "You damn coward! Why don't you just turn around and run all the way North? Why are you even heading into the thick of things if all you want to do is hide out?"

Brenton gave a sneer. "You're a good one to talk. How long was you hidin' out in that hospital?" He had reached out to grab Jessica and twist her arm behind her as she struggled. Shoving her along toward Yancy's horse, he angrily continued, "Besides, ain't nothin' worse than a preacher who'd turn on his own flock, like you did, even if he was on our side."

Yancy was quick to remind Brenton, "We don't have a side no more, goddamn it. Now stop that jawin' and let's get outta here." Then he addressed Derek. "Now move, Preacher, before I—"

Suddenly the world around them exploded in a volley of gunfire. Without realizing it, they had stepped right into the middle of a Union patrol lying in wait for a small group of Rebel soldiers heading their way. Too late to warn the innocent intruders, the officer in charge gave the signal to fire, for the Rebels were upon them.

Jessica was forgotten as Brenton lunged for his horse. He threw one leg over, then tumbled to the ground dead, as a minie ball slammed square in the back of his head. Jessica screamed, dropped to her knees just as Billy Bob found himself caught in cross fire. She watched in horror as his body was ripped to pieces by bullets.

Only Yancy had found cover behind a large tree, a few feet from where she crouched. Frantically, he held out his hand to her and beckoned, "Get over here, quick. Crawl. Don't stand up."

But instead of obeying, she turned instinctively to see whether Derek had been hit. He had stopped after stepping onto the bank and was staring down at his leg in disbelief. "Derek, come on!" she cried. "If you stay there, you'll be killed."

Just then, a soldier she'd not seen before, in a blue uniform, leaped out from hiding to scream and wave at others who appeared out of nowhere. "We got 'em on the run!" he screamed excitedly, "now let's go! Let's go!"

She was suddenly surrounded by men and horses, and even Yancy got caught up in the battle fever. He reached out to one of the charging mounted soldiers and was swung up behind him in the saddle. "You comin'?" he yelled to Jessica, and motioned to one of the others to reach for her.

Jessica jumped back. She did not have to think about it, because she knew she could not abandon Derek. Every nerve, every instinct, told her something was wrong. He was still staring at his leg, which was hidden from her by the dense reeds of the swampy ditch. The air hung heavy with the sickening smell of sulfur, and already the sound of the thundering horses was fading in the distance as the Union patrol took off after the Confederates. There was still time, she knew, to escape with them, for one soldier hung back in question. She waved him away. He yelled she was crazy and took off.

Maybe, she thought wildly, she was crazy, insane, but for whatever reason, she could not run away with them.

As she reached Derek, he snapped out of his absorbing stupor. He could utter only one word, but it filled her with instant, sick terror.

"Snake."

"Oh, God, no!" She dropped to her knees beside him. "Did you see it? Do you know what kind it was?"

"Moccasin. Copperhead. I felt him hit my ankle and looked down just in time to see him whip back into the slime."

"Lean on me." She was getting up, holding out her arm. "We've got to get you out so I can help you."

"No. I can make it. I guess I was just in shock for a minute there, but at least it took my mind off the battle." He managed a wry but feeble smile, then hopefully asked, "You ever tend a snakebite before?"

"I've seen it done. I know you have to cut into it and suck the poison out."

"Right. And I'm starting to hurt something fierce, and I can see it's already beginning to swell, so we've got to hurry. That dead soldier back there..." He paused, frowned. "Can you make your way back there and look around for a knife, anything to cut with?"

She was already on her way, and he stared after her, marveling at her courage even as the sickness descended. The

snake had been a big one, and he could die if Jessica didn'
know what she was doing. For the moment there was tim
to think of nothing but the sudden, raw, will to survive.

"He had a knife inside his boot." She waved the weapo
triumphantly, returning. "Now quick, let's get you out o
this ditch and up on dry land, behind those rocks over there
in case the shooting starts again. Now lean on me to keep the
weight off that ankle. We don't want any pressure on it, anc
we sure don't want your blood pumping fast, so don't try tc
talk."

She stifled a groan as he put his right arm around her, anc
she took his weight. Momentarily her knees buckled, anc
she thought for a terrified instant she could not get him u
and out of there, and they would both topple backward intc
the snake-infested ditch. But finally she staggered forwar
and, mustering every ounce of strength she had, manage
to get him behind the boulder.

She used the knife to slash open his trouser leg and sav
the pinhole fang marks. They oozed yellow serum anc
blood, and as Derek had said, the poisoned tissue was al
ready starting to swell.

Ripping off a strip from the bottom of her skirt, sh
wrapped it tightly several inches above the wound. "Al
right," she said, taking a deep breath. "I'm going to cu
now."

Using the tip of the knife, she stabbed first into one fan
mark, then into the other, laying open the flesh and cross
ing with another mark to make an X. She glanced at Derek,
saw how he was gritting his teeth to keep from screaming
fighting to hold back the moans that gurgled in his throat
Then, taking a deep breath, she began to suck out th
venom, promptly spitting it out of her mouth as she strug
gled to keep from vomiting.

After a few moments, she hoarsely declared, "That's al
I can do. Now we wait and see. You didn't move aroun
much, and the poison might not have spread, and you're

trong, and . . .'' Her voice trailed as she saw he had merci-
ully fainted.

She glanced fearfully about at the gathering shadows.
oon it would be dark, and the nights had started to get
hilly with the approach of fall. Placing a hand on Derek's
orehead, she could feel the beginning of a fever. If he made
t through the night, he would live, but he was going to be
erribly sick—and cold.

Moving quickly, she picked her way through the brush
arefully, lest she, too, be bitten by one of the slithering
reatures. A good thing that she was not scared of the dead,
he thought, as she prowled around gathering what she
ould from the scattered bodies—a canteen, a blanket, a
olled-up coat, a haversack with a pint of whiskey inside.
When she saw that, she ran back to Derek with it and knelt
o hold his head up and pour the liquid into his mouth. "It
ill help a little," she whispered as he coughed and gagged.
he slowed to make sure he did not choke. "It will make you
est easier, at least."

As the night passed, Jessica tried not to hear the omi-
ous sounds in the bushes and woods around her. Now and
hen she heard gunfire in the distance, knew soldiers were
ut there somewhere. What was she going to do when
norning came? She had no idea where she was. And what
f Derek died? Dear God, that fear gave her a jolt of pain.
He was not hers. He belonged to another.

But she did not want him to die.

And as she lay beside him, arms wrapped about him to
ive him benefit of her body heat, she knew that despite
verything, she had never stopped loving him. If nursing
im back to health only meant sending him home to his
vife, so be it.

She drank some whiskey from the bottle herself, relish-
ng the peace the burning liquid eventually gave her. At last
he slept, with a prayer on her lips that Derek would sur-
ive the night.

Chapter Twenty-three

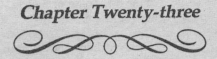

The soldier and the officer stared down at the couple on the ground. They were not moving. Their eyes were closed. The man, wearing the uniform of the Confederacy, was lying on his back. The woman was positioned across him, as though shielding him from the chilling mist that swirled about them.

The soldier excitedly whispered to his commander, "See Major? It's just like I told you. I came over here to take care of my mornin' business behind the rocks, and there they was. They ain't moved since I run to get you." He frowned dared lean closer. "They're dead, ain't they?"

The major shook his head. "I don't think so." He had drawn his saber and pointed with it to Derek's torn trousers and the swollen, protruding leg. "Snakebite. Looks like she cut it and tried to suck out the poison. Get the medical officer."

Jessica awoke then with a start and was terrified to see the strange man towering over her. As she groggily wondered who he was, the nightmare came flooding back. At once she turned to make sure Derek was still beside her. Quickly she laid her head against his chest to check that he was still alive. Then she stiffly, nervously, got to her feet and demanded, "Who are you?" The stranger was, she noted wearing the uniform of a Confederate officer.

Before he could answer, another officer came hurrying up to brusquely say, "I'll take over now."

Jessica felt the newcomer's air of authority and confidence, knew he had to be a doctor even before he confirmed that fact. He, also, wore a gray uniform with black piping and a green sash. His pants were black with a gold stripe down the side.

"I'm Dr. Martin of the First Virginia Infantry. Are you all right?" He quickly scrutinized the couple and guessed the man on the ground should be his immediate concern.

Quickly, Jessica assured him she was fine, then rushed to tell him about Derek's wound and what she had done to try to save his life. "Will he be all right?" she wanted to know, wringing her hands nervously as Dr. Martin knelt to examine Derek.

"Right away, I can tell he's burning with fever." His hand was on Derek's brow as he spoke. "As for that snakebite, I'll see to it as soon as we get him to the hospital wagon." He straightened as two men arrived with a stretcher.

Turning to Jessica, he placed a comforting hand on her shoulder and said, "Let's get you something to eat, and then I'll find a spot for you in one of the supply wagons. I'm afraid there's just no room in the hospital wagon, because we've got some mighty sick soldiers crowded in there. And we've got to keep moving.

"But don't worry," he finished, turning away, "we're going to take very good care of your husband."

Husband! Jessica's hand fluttered to her throat at the word. She couldn't let them think Derek was her husband—or could she?

Suddenly, she was struck by the possible consequences of revealing otherwise. These men were going to want to know who they were, what they were doing way out here. It would probably eventually come out that Derek was an escaped prisoner. He would be sent back to Libby. But what about her? Would she be suspected of aiding in the escape? Did they have prisons for women, too? She did not know and was taking no chances.

There would be no harm in the charade, she decided, just as the officer with the sword noticed her despair. "Your name," he said crisply, "and your husband's name, please."

"Stanton," she said then, firmly, clearly. "Reverend Derek Stanton. My name is Jessica...Stanton," she added, feeling a rush of pleasure at saying it, even if it was a lie.

"I'm Major Brooks," the officer said, and held out a gloved hand to her. She took it, falling in step beside him. They walked along beside the stretcher carrying Derek, and he continued his interrogation. "I see your husband is wearing a Confederate uniform. I'm wondering why the two of you were here in this part of Virginia, and particularly why you were with him."

The story rolled off her tongue easily, as though she had written and memorized it long ago. "My husband wanted to do his part, so he enlisted in service to the South but still in service to our Lord. I wanted to be with him. We were on our way to Richmond from the Blue Ridge, and we were taken hostage by some Yankee deserters heading for the western part of the state." She went on to tell him of their having been caught in a skirmish the evening before and how Derek had been bitten by the snake while listening to the dying prayers of a Confederate soldier. "Then the shooting started, and..." She fell silent as she looked up to see all the wagons and soldiers waiting.

Major Brooks explained, "We're also on our way to the western part of Virginia, Mrs. Stanton. We've been assigned to winter there to keep an eye on things. Due to the large number of Union sympathizers in that area, deserters from the Confederacy are taking refuge there, and we've reason to believe the Federals will be trying to recruit them to fight for the North. President Davis felt we should have men in the area as an intimidating deterrent.

"We'd be pleased," he went on, "to have you and your husband stay with us this winter. We could sure use a preacher."

"How about a good cook?"

Both Jessica and Major Brooks were surprised to hear the feeble voice coming from the stretcher. Jessica ran to Derek's side, stunned that he was awake and able to talk, however feebly. Major Brooks took position on the other side.

"She is a good cook...." Derek managed a weak smile. "Her specialty...is...chicken and dumplings...." His head rolled to the side and he lay very still.

Jessica turned apprehensive eyes to the doctor.

"He's all right," he was quick to assure her. "He just passed out again. No doubt, he's terribly weak. He lost some blood from that incision you had to make. But I think he's going to be fine, Mrs. Stanton," he continued. "I'm going to give him some quinine to lower his fever, and then I'll wash out that wound with turpentine and put a bandage on it. A few days of rest, and I think he'll be good as new.

"Maybe we'll even have a real prayer meeting come Sunday," he added with a merry, optimistic wink.

"Maybe so." She forced a smile, wondering exactly what she had got herself into by her lies.

Major Brooks arranged for Jessica to be made comfortable on a bed in the back of one of the covered wagons. After a meal of boiled eggs, crackers and warm tea, she curled up and fell into a deep slumber, and slept the clock around. The gentle sway of the wagon rocked her peacefully, and she was startled to awaken the next morning to the delicious smell of bacon frying and fresh, hot coffee.

Peering out the back of the covered wagon, she realized they had made camp sometime during the night beside a rushing mountain stream. The soldiers were moving about, preparing for another day of riding, and one of them saw her and called to Major Brooks. He hurried over.

She liked him, found him maturely attractive with nice, dark eyes, a friendly smile beneath a neat, trim mustache. He made her think of the image she had of her father when she was still a little girl, before he became a spiritless drunkard.

"Your husband is doing good," Major Brooks was happy to be able to tell her. With a laugh, he added, "He also said to tell you to start knitting high socks to cover the ugly scar you've left on his leg, but he'll forgive you, since you obviously saved his life.

"There's a private spot over there behind some plum bushes—" he pointed "—where you can freshen up in the stream, if you'd like."

She was quick to tell him, "I'd like very much." She hurried then to tend to her needs, take a welcomed bath and wash her hair. Hating to put her dirty clothes back on, she called out for a uniform, anything, and when at last she stepped back into the camp, she was greeting with a round of cheers and whistles.

"A female soldier!" Major Brooks cried. "In service to the Lord. What more can we ask for, men?"

There was another cheering round of approval, and she managed to smile at them, appear pleased at their acceptance. Inside, she was terrified. What if they found out the truth?

With mixed emotions of dread and anticipation she was led to the hospital wagon. Derek was sitting up, his still-swollen leg propped on a haversack. There were two other soldiers there, but they were sleeping—or unconscious. The air was fetid with the smell of turpentine, blood and death.

She did not want to meet Derek's probing gaze, didn't really know what to say to him, but finally offered, "You're going to be all right. I'm glad."

"I owe you my life, Jessica," he said quietly, almost reverently. "If you hadn't kept your head and done what had to be done, I would have died."

"You would have done the same for me."

"I'm glad you realize that." He managed a hesitant smile. "You know, I can't help thinking back to the first time I ever saw you. I remember how impressed I was, the way you stayed so calm about that snake, how you killed it without going all to pieces. Little did I know that one day that same calm about you would save my life."

She did not want to think about the past. Any of it. Focusing on the present situation, she confided the story she had told about how they happened to be there.

He nodded. "I suspected as much. The doctor kept saying how proud I had to be of my wife." He managed a wry grin.

"I had to let them think that, but now we've got to figure out how we're going to get out of this mess."

He hated to have to tell her. "I'm afraid we're stuck here till spring."

"No." She shook her head. "That's impossible. I'm not staying here, with you. Not with everyone thinking we're married, and—"

"You have no choice," he said fiercely. He didn't want to hurt her or make her angry, especially when he was indebted to her for his life, but he knew it was the only way he could avoid arousing suspicion and winding up back in prison. He attempted to make her understand that, but she just became more and more indignant and irate with each word he spoke.

"I told you," she said firmly, angrily, "I won't do it. I'll tell them the truth if I have to, but I'm going to ask to be sent back to Richmond so I can continue my search for Belinda."

"What does Belinda have to do with all of this?"

She bit her tongue. Oh, why had she got so upset and blurted it out, she fumed. Still not about to tell him the whole truth, she offered, "Harmon didn't ask her to marry him, and she went a little crazy and ran away from home. I've been looking for her."

He shook his head in sympathy but then became quite grim as he warned, "I can't let you go, Jessica. You're my only hope that I can pull off this little charade. And if you betray me, then you leave me no choice but to tell them that while we might not be married, we are lovers, and you helped me escape. You'll go to prison, then, too."

She stared at him aghast. "You would do that?"

"I have no choice."

"I wish—" She clenched her fists and bit back the torrent of fury bubbling in her throat, lest someone overhear. "I wish I'd just let you die!"

He grabbed her arms and gave her an almost rough shake. He suddenly had to know. "Just why do you hate me so? Can't you see I'm doing this to save your neck, too? How in the hell would you get home, anyway? You think they're going to send you back with an escort in the middle of a war? Be reasonable, Jessica. Stay here till spring, and then, I swear, I'll find a way to get you back."

"And till then you want me to pretend to be your wife? In every way? I can't! I won't!" She shook her head vehemently. There was no way she would allow him to touch her, no matter if desire still smoldered. He was another woman's husband!

"You think I'd force myself on you?" He gave a self-deprecating chuckle. "Don't worry, Jessica. I like to think I learned my lesson about fooling around with married women." He released her, laid his head back and closed his eyes. He still felt light-headed and a bit nauseated from the wound.

Jessica shook herself, sure she had heard wrong. She tremulously asked, "What are you talking about?"

"Reuben Walker gun-whipped me once upon a time for trying to take his fiancée away from him." He sneered, eyes still closed. "I guess a real brave man like that would probably shoot me in the back if I made love to his wife."

"His *wife?*" she echoed numbly. This time, she shook from head to toe, for deep within there was a tiny buzzing, but it was getting louder and louder, and she struggled to think against it. It was only with great effort she was able to keep from screaming as she tersely said, "Derek, I don't know what you're talking about."

He looked at her then, really looked at her, and he could see the perplexity written all over her face. She really didn't know. Past the constricting wave that was engulfing him, he sharply reminded her, "Your letter. You told me in your letter...."

He fell silent as the soldier lying next to him moaned. "Doctor..." he begged, "help me...." He began to cough, then started to heave and vomit blood.

Derek turned to him at the same time he barked at Jessica, "Get the doctor in here. Fast. He's hemorrhaging."

Jessica rushed to obey, leaping from the back of the wagon to shout at the nearest soldier that a man inside was bleeding to death. Before she could even turn back, Dr. Martin was there, pushing her aside as he leaped up into the wagon, muttering he had been afraid the poor soul wouldn't make it.

She stood rooted outside for what seemed like forever. From within, she could hear the anguished pleas of the dying soldier for Derek to pray for him. Derek reverently did so.

Despite the turmoil within, Jessica was awed as she listened once again to Derek helping ease a frightened man through the valley of the shadow of death. In that moment, she found herself wondering how he could ever have doubted his worth as a preacher. Maybe he had not been comfortable delivering a prepared sermon from the pulpit, but he had surely found his niche in this battlefield of souls.

But foremost in her mind was the question of why Derek had been talking about her as though she were married to Reuben Walker. Did he actually think she would have turned to Reuben after she got that heartbreaking letter saying Derek was marrying a woman who was carrying his child? And what letter from her was he talking about?

At last Dr. Martin came out. "He's gone," he said with that mingled sadness and acceptance physicians show when their skills lose out to death. He started to walk away, then turned back to say, "I'm sorry we can't move him out right now, Mrs. Stanton, but we're about to break camp, and there's no time for a burial detail. President Davis has asked that we do our best to send our boys who die home to their loved ones, anyway, so I'm going to do some embalming when we reach the winter camp site." He hesitated, suddenly embarrassed to be going on so. "I'm sorry. You don't want to hear all this. What I'm trying to say is that you should go back to the supply wagon instead of riding with your husband with a body in there. I was talking to the cook this morning, and he said he was looking forward to your helping him. We should be at our camp site by late tomorrow."

"That's right," Major Brooks interjected as he arrived on the scene. He touched Jessica's shoulder in a gesture of respect and said, "And I want you to know how happy I am we found you and your husband. We'd wanted a chaplain with us this winter, but there just wasn't one available. The two of you will be a real asset to our camp, and I want you to know I've already spoken to one of my sergeants about making sure the first hut built is for the two of you."

Jessica felt as though she were drowning in her own lies. "Th-thank you," she managed to stammer, then headed for the hospital wagon.

"Mrs. Stanton, we're about to pull out," Major Brooks called after her. "You'd best get to your own wagon."

She ignored him, hoisted herself up and inside. The body of the dead soldier was covered with a bloodied sheet, and she tried not to see it as she knelt once more beside Derek.

He was watching, waiting, for her to tell him why she'd been so stunned when he had mentioned her letter.

There was no time to do anything except quickly, almost harshly, tell him, "I don't know what letter you're talking about, Derek. I never wrote you a letter. The only one I know anything about is the one you sent to me, and—"

"Your letter!" He sat up then, eyes bulging with incredible fury and disbelief as he grabbed her again. This time, his fingers dug into the flesh of her shoulders as he commanded explanation. "Your letter telling me you were married to Reuben Walker! That's what I'm talking about, Jessica."

Her lips began to tremble, and within, she was suddenly nauseated, sick to the core of her being, for the pieces were starting to fit together. "I never wrote you a letter," she whispered, barely audible. "And I never married Reuben Walker. He wanted me to stand up in front of the church and declare my sin with you and ask forgiveness before he'd take me for his wife. I told him I would rather die. He married..." She choked on a sudden hysterical giggle. It was all so unreal she felt surely she had to be going insane, and she struggled past the maniacally bubbling laughter to tell him, "He married Leona Billingsley!"

He searched her face for some sign she was teasing, or lying, but all he saw was incredulity over the nightmare. "If you didn't marry Reuben," he reasoned aloud, "then the letter was a fake. And I think we know who's to blame."

"My father." She dropped her head, felt the tears stinging but did not even try to hold them back. "He and Reuben, no doubt, set it up to keep us apart.

"But..." she looked at him then, a sad little smile on her quivering lips, "they didn't have to go to the trouble, did they? It was already over for us. Fate took care of that."

He could only stare at her in muted wonder as she quickly made her way out of the wagon.

So, she had not married Reuben. The letter was a fake. He could rejoice in that blessed reality. But he was being needled by her parting statement . . . and also the burning question as to whether she had received his original letter.

Something was wrong.

Terribly wrong.

And he knew, somehow, when he found out what it was, he would finally discover why Jessica harbored so much hatred and resentment.

He settled back for the ride to their camp site. His wound was hurting, and so was his heart.

He closed his eyes and prayed that both would soon be healed.

Chapter Twenty-four

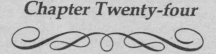

As soon as they reached the site that had been chosen for winter quarters, the soldiers rapidly began building shelters. For the officers, as well as Jessica and Derek, they constructed small huts of chinked and daubed logs. For themselves, they dug out holes in the ground, over which they placed logs, after first setting fires to dry and harden the bottoms of their cellars.

There was a pen for the horses, with log lean-tos for shelter against the wind, sleet and snow of the coming winter.

While the building was going on, Derek was recuperating from his leg wound. Unable to take part physically, he spent his time talking with the soldiers who sought his counsel. When a small cave was discovered in the side of a mountain, Major Brooks agreed it could be used as a church. Assigned a small group of soldiers to follow his directions, Derek then busied himself with seeing that wood benches were built, as well as a pulpit.

Jessica ignored him as much as possible. After all, just because he now knew she had never married Reuben, the fact remained *he* had a wife. No matter that her heart began to pound wildly whenever he was near, she kept tight rein on her emotions, tried not to see the yearning in his face when he looked at her.

Obligingly, he had not tried to sleep with her in the back of the supply tent, opting instead to berth in the hospital wagon. If any of the soldiers wondered about their separation, they did not let on.

Jessica devoted herself to her job as cook. Barley Davis the soldier who had been serving in that capacity, was only too glad to hand over his apron. He was tired of all the complaints. He was also happy to join the others in the enjoyment of the delicious meals she prepared.

There was a shortage of cooking utensils, and quickly Jessica learned to improvise with what she had. She made frying pans out of plates. Skillets, plates and corn graters were designed from halves of canteens. Hollow stumps and wood pestles were used to convert corn into grits for dodger pone.

She could never make enough drap dumplings, because they were so eagerly devoured. Her special stew of Irish potatoes, green apples and garlic was another favorite meal.

"You act like you really enjoy doing this," Major Brooks marveled one day, as he helped himself to a second helping of dumplings. "Frankly, I was afraid you might resent the way I sort of confiscated you and your husband."

Jessica thought about it and realized she actually enjoyed what she was doing. These men were, after all, her fellow countrymen. And no matter that she did not personally believe in slavery, she realized the war was being fought over more than that one issue. States' rights was an important consideration, because the South would not let the North dictate how it was to live. "Yes, Major," she said finally, "I do like my job, and I don't mind at all your keeping us here till spring."

"Your husband..." He hesitated. Like some of the others, he had a suspicion the Stantons were not a happy couple. "He's a special blessing for us, too. I've heard the soldiers talking about how they would've hated to try and make it through this time without a man of God to talk to, to listen to their problems. He's even been writing letters for those who can't write, and I'm going to try to send out a mail detail to the nearest post to see the letters get out before the snows come.

"He's a remarkable man," he said finally. "You can sure tell he had a real calling from God."

Jessica thought of the irony—it had taken a war to make Derek believe in himself. Once he had thought he needed her to help him do that. Now he could stand alone. She was not surprised to find that knowledge was uplifting. She had come to realize that despite everything that had happened, she did love Derek and wished for him to be happy—even if she could not be by his side to share that joy.

One day Major Brooks received word that there had been a skirmish between Union and Rebel soldiers near the South Branch Bridge, some twenty miles away. He sent out a patrol, which subsequently fought a battle at Romney, in the northern reaches of western Virginia. There were many casualties, and Jessica's time was divided between cooking for the soldiers and helping with nursing duties in the hospital hut.

War news filtered in. Weakened by combat losses, Major Brooks was unable to send in reinforcements to assist General John B. Floyd, who had attacked forces led by General Rosecrans near Gauly Bridge and Cotton Hill. After three days Floyd had to withdraw without success.

Then came the dispatch everyone groaned to hear. In Wheeling, Virginia, a convention had adopted a constitution calling for the formation of the new state of West Virginia, as that area seceded from the rest of the state. "Men," Major Brooks morosely announced to his regiment, "we now find ourselves encamped in Yankee territory!"

An air of tension descended. Major Brooks announced they would lie low till spring. Winter was in the air, and already the ominous hint of first snow.

Then came the day Derek had to tell Jessica their hut was complete. She was peeling potatoes for a stew, and for a few moments, continued what she was doing as she contem-

plated what it meant. At last, she said, without looking up
"I don't want to sleep with you, Derek."

"You've made that clear," he said tightly. "You've gon
out of your way to avoid me, and I think you work over
time trying to hate me. I just wish I knew why."

She started to ask him how in the world he could expec
her not to resent him, then pointed out instead, "We've go
to find a way to make the best of a bad situation. If we hav
to stay together this winter, then let's agree on a few rules."

"Agreed."

"You don't even know what they are."

"Does it matter? You're calling all the shots."

Ignoring his sarcasm, she recited, "I sleep in the bed
You'll have a pallet on the floor. You're only there at night
No other time. Understood?"

When he did not reply, she glanced up from her work t
see he had quietly walked away.

That night, he made his pallet in silence, coldly ignorin
her, and thus set the pattern for their existence.

Time passed slowly, as winter descended. But then cam
the first blizzard. Jessica lay in the bed of pine needles an
shivered from head to toe, teeth chattering. She had tw
blankets, all that were allotted, and knew that Derek, on th
drafty floor, had to be colder than she was. But she hear
no sound, for he did not complain.

Finally, she could stand it no longer and gingerly of
fered, "As long as you understand it's only for warmth, w
can share the covers."

He did not hesitate. Crawling in bed beside her, he turned
his back, lest temptation be too great to resist.

The winds picked up ferociously. The hastily built hut wa
hardly any protection against the frigid temperatures. Jes
sica would not have thought it possible, but she shivered
even harder, and suddenly Derek turned to jerk her angril
into his arms. He cried, "Damn it, woman, you're freez
ing, and so am I. At least, let me hold you, warm you
through this night."

Jessica felt herself becoming not only warm, but also roused, for his nearness was torment. He held her gently, possessively, their bodies pressed together. She could feel the swelling of his desire against her belly.

Tense moments passed. His hands, gripping her back so tightly, slowly became gentle, caressing. Her own, held frozen at her sides, moved ever so softly to clutch him in return.

Prisoners of the night, they could no longer deny the surging emotions. Derek's lips sought and found hers in the darkness, to claim her mouth for long, hungry moments. But then he withdrew, raggedly demanded, "Tell me to stop, Jessica. Make me stop, if this isn't what you want, too...."

No longer could she pretend. All resolve lay like cold ashes at her feet as the flames of passion ignited in her loins, her heart. "I do want you, Derek. I've always wanted you. I always will. Right or wrong, I love you."

It was said.

There was no turning back.

Derek felt as though summer sun had magically penetrated winter gloom, there in the tiny chinked log cabin. His hands moved down to pull up her gown, and she was exposed and vulnerable beneath him. He lowered his head beneath the quilt to kiss each breast in turn, and she reveled at the hot fire ignited in her belly.

Like a maestro in command performance, he played her body as if it were a fine, priceless instrument of music. Lovingly, he stroked her flesh till she wanted to scream out in ecstasy. He touched her all over with masterful hands that were bold, warm, leaving a trail of hungry fire in their wake.

She forgot he did not, could not, belong to her for always. She was determined only to seize the moment, to enjoy and savor for always.

Waves of frenzied, fevered longing washed over them, like the tide crashing along the shore. "I love you," Derek hoarsely avowed as he covered her body with hungry kisses, unbridled primal need taking over. "From the moment I first saw you, I think I loved you. You were God's special gift. You're all I ever wanted, and now that I've found you I'll never let you go.''

Jessica allowed herself to be carried away in passion, tossing aside all guilt and reservations. He could talk of always and forever, while she sadly knew this was all they would ever have.

At last, he entered her, then paused in his mighty thrust to smile down at her in the darkness and say in wonder, '' can feel you love me, too, Jessica, wrapped around me, like warm velvet....''

She moved with him, answering the call of passion he had so skillfully taught her to crave. She was filled with him, and despite the chill, kicked away the covers to wrap her leg about his strong back to afford yet deeper penetration of that which she had to have.

He took her to the highest pinnacle of pleasure, yet did not allow her to descend to earth again but held her there over and over. Her nails raked down his strong back as her teeth bit softly into his shoulder. Yet he continued to drive her deliriously insane with his love play. Only when he himself was nearly driven to madness by holding back his exultation, did he allow them both the ultimate release.

For long, spellbound moments, he held her without moving. Then, at last, he rolled to his side, taking her with him, remaining inside her, reluctant to give her up to reality once more.

Jessica did not know what to say. It was done. Like the original Eve, she had led a man to sin.

''Now we can revel in winter,'' he said happily, still holding her tight against him. ''Every night. All night. We're going to make up for all the time wasted with me thinking you were married, and you hating me for whatever reason—''

''Stop it!''

She tore from him then, whipping away and lunging from the bed. The frigid air attacked her, but she hardly noticed.

All she knew in that moment was that she had to get away from him, from the anguish of what she had done.

"Hear me, Derek!" she cried then. "I do love you. I can't, I won't, deny that. I thought you were a special gift from God, too, but I won't lie with another woman's husband. Maybe you do love me, but it's wrong, and we can't go on this way, and—"

"Wait a minute!" he roared, his turn to cut her off. In a flash, he was out of the bed to grab her and pull her back beneath the covers. She struggled angrily in his grasp, trying not to cry but feeling tears sting her eyes.

Pinning her arms behind her back, he pressed her down on the crude pine-needle mattress. "Will you tell me what this is all about, for God's sake?" he cried. "What do you mean—another woman's husband? Are you saying you think I'm married?"

"Are you going to try and deny it?" she said between clenched teeth, loathing herself for her weakness and taking out her wrath on him. "Are you also going to deny you're a father? I can deal with reality, Derek, but not a lie. Let's get it all out in the open and talk about it. You think I'm going to sleep with you all winter, keep you warm in bed, and then you'll go back to her? What happens to me then? Will I wind up scorned and ridiculed again? Will people turn their heads when I pass by, thinking I'm nothing but a . . . a whore?" Her voice cracked, and she struggled on to unleash the venom she'd been keeping inside all those weeks. "This time it will be worse. Last time I was just the harlot who brought about the preacher's downfall. This time they'll say I tried to take a man away from his wife and child!"

"Jessica, stop it!" he pleaded desperately. "Give me a chance to explain whatever it is you believe of me, because I do love you. I swear it. And I'm not married to anybody else. When I lost you, I knew I'd never want any woman, ever again. Now for God's sake, talk to me!"

She could barely make him out in the darkness but knew it didn't matter that she could not see his face. Something in his voice, and something inside of her, as well, told her he was not lying. Pushing the words past the lump in her throat, she said, "I received a letter from you saying you were marrying another woman, because she was going to have your baby. That's when I knew you weren't coming back for me."

She heard the ragged intake of his breath, knew he had been struck speechless. Then, finally, he was able to tell her, "Jessica, that's a lie. I wrote you asking you to meet me and marry me, but then I got your letter telling me you had married Reuben. That's when I left Asheville, heading north. I'd been relieved of my post as circuit rider, and I felt I had nothing left to live for. I think I was actually hoping I'd be the first to die when the war broke out."

"Why?" she tearfully asked him, as he released her from his rigid grasp and cradled her in his arms. "Why did they do it to us, Derek? Why did they try to destroy us?"

"They had their own reasons, and they didn't care who they destroyed to get what they wanted." He continued to hold her as he rolled to his back, and she lay close against him, head on his chest as he mused, "Now I know why you seemed to hate me. I started, so many times, to try and talk to you, find out why, but remember, I was bitter, too. I thought you had never really loved me, that the land had been more important to you, and when you found out I wouldn't stay and keep the farm going, you chose Reuben, instead.

"I guess I tried to hate you, too," he wearily finished, "but I just couldn't. I never stopped loving you."

"There's more," she said then. She told him everything—about Belinda's rape, and her father's killing one of the men responsible. "Harmon didn't want her for his wife then, and she couldn't face that and ran away. I helped Poppa escape from a lynch mob. He disappeared, and I didn't know what became of him till you said you saw him."

He gave a bitter snort. "Yeah. And he told me how happy you and Reuben were together." He shook away the painful memory, turned again to the subject of Belinda. "So that's why you ran away? To look for your sister?"

"Partly. The truth is, I had no reason to stay there. No friends. No family."

They talked on through the night in mingled anger and wonder. Cheated of so much happiness, they swore repeatedly to make up for lost time.

"So many dreams," Derek reminded her. "We had them then, and we can have them again, and when this war ends, they'll come true, Jessica. I know they will. I'll get a church, and you can teach, and it'll be as wonderful as we always thought it would be.

"And I'll tell you something else, too," he said, sweeping her into his arms again with newly igniting passion. "I don't doubt myself anymore, Jessica. Remember how I told you I didn't think I was meant to be a preacher? How I was feeling guilty for having made a promise I didn't think I'd be able to keep?"

"You don't have to say anything," she interrupted him then. "I saw you with that soldier in the ditch, how you helped him die in peace, and I heard you do the same with that soldier in the wagon. You have a comforting way about you, Derek. It's a very special gift from God. And you are needed now, terribly, in this awful time we're living in. These poor souls have to have someone like you. And when the war is over, it will truly have made a better man of you, because you won't have any more doubts. Not ever. Don't you see?"

"But you gave me that confidence, Jessica. You made me feel like I was worth something. If it hadn't been for you, I wouldn't have even tried, because I'd reached the point I just didn't care what happened to me anymore. But now I've got a reason for living—" he paused to kiss her fervently, deeply "—and I swear, I'll never let you go."

"We're going to make it through the winter, and through this war," she happily, blissfully told him, twining her arms about his neck, arching her body against his. "For now, just love me, my darling, and pretend I am your wife."

"You are, my sweet. In God's eyes. In my heart. For always..."

Chapter Twenty-Five

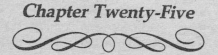

Jessica and Derek fell in love—again.

As winter settled in all around them, they were lost in each other.

Each night, as soon as darkness fell, they would crawl into bed to snuggle together, and in the afterglow of their passion they would talk for long hours, dreamily making plans for the future.

Derek said he would give serious consideration to returning to the Blue Ridge to take a church there.

"Maybe when the war is over, everyone will be willing to forgive and forget and just get on with their lives," he optimistically stated. "Forgiveness is what life is all about, anyway. If it takes getting up before the congregation and saying as much, so be it."

Jessica was enthralled. She had not known it was possible to be so much in love and so very, very happy. Yet, like Derek, she sometimes yielded to the depressing shadows that could not be avoided. After all, they were at war, and she was also haunted by worries over Belinda.

"If there is any way possible, we'll try to find her," Derek assured Jessica. Yet, he admitted, it would be a formidable task.

Everyone in the camp was delighted the two seemed to have resolved whatever problems they'd had earlier. No one had any idea Derek and Jessica were not really married, and

Derek said it did not matter, anyway. In their hearts, and i the eyes of God, they had to be, and that was all tha counted. Later, they would formally and legally take thei vows, perhaps in the spring.

As the winter wore on, supplies became scarce. Jessic learned to make coffee from parched peanuts, potatoe peas, dried apples and corn. She concocted a tea brewe from ginger and herbs. She mixed bread in turtle shells an pumpkin rinds. Dried beef and vegetables were the main stay of the soldiers' diet, and Jessica further won their heart by serving up delicious pies made from dried apples foun in an old orchard nearby.

During the day, Derek helped the soldiers with thei chores of gathering wood in the ice and snow. Horses woul drag back cut trees, and kindling and logs would be store in the church cave to dry out as much as possible. He als conducted a nightly prayer meeting, to try to keep the me from playing cards, gambling and drinking so much. Wit Jessica's help, he even wrote little plays and the men be came caught up in the fun and took part in acting out th various roles.

"I don't know what we would do without the two o you," Major Brooks said almost daily. "I'm sure we've go the best organized winter camp in the whole Confederat army!"

Just before Christmas, Jessica led a hunting expedition t shoot as many as seven wild turkeys. Pits were dug, and th birds were roasted over hickory nuts for a delicious holida meal that won the praise of everybody. Derek even toaste the occasion with a glass of scuppernong wine from a batcl secretly brewed by one of the soldiers.

Amid the struggle to survive the bitter cold, unfavorabl war news began to arrive as the new year, 1862, dawned.

The Confederates lost a battle at Mill Springs, Kentuck in mid-January.

Union forces captured Fort Henry on the Tennessee River in early February, followed by their victory two days later at Roanoke Island in North Carolina.

Another tragic loss for the South came when fifteen thousand Confederate soldiers were captured at Fort Donelson, Tennessee; the city of Nashville was abandoned on February 25.

Union forces marched on to victory at the battle of Pea Ridge on March 8, subsequently controlling the entire state of Missouri.

The worst word was the defeat of the great Confederate General, Stonewall Jackson at Kernstown, Virginia in the first battle of the Shenandoah Valley.

One day Major Brooks called the regiment together and announced he was awaiting word as to where they would be sent. Amid cheers from his restless soldiers, he said he was actually looking forward to getting back to the business of war. "It's time we came out of hibernation and started killing some Yankees."

Finally, the much-anticipated dispatch arrived.

"All hell is about to break loose in a place called Shiloh, in Tennessee," Major Brooks tersely announced to his men as they gathered before his hut on a frosty morning in mid-March, "but the Federals don't know it yet. We're to move out at once. We'll start breaking camp and set out at first light."

A cheer went up. The men were eager to be on the move after the long and boring winter.

Major Brooks summoned Jessica and Derek to his hut to tell them he was sending Jessica back to Richmond. "She'll be safer there. Granted, we could use a good cook to keep the men fit and nourished as we make our way into Tennessee, but I'll put Barley back at the post. A battle is no place for a woman, no matter how much we'll miss her," he added with a warm smile. Like his men, Major Brooks had become quite fond of Jessica.

Derek agreed, reluctant to be separated from her b[u]t knowing it was best.

Jessica looked from one to the other and promptly e[x]ploded. "Are you both out of your minds? Do you think fo[r] one minute you're getting rid of me now that we're going t[o] have some excitement? Why, I've twiddled my thumbs a[ll] winter like everyone else, and I'm ready to get out there an[d] do battle with the Yankees, too.

"And if either of you thinks for one minute—" sh[e] turned from one to the other, hands on her hips, defianc[e] and determination flashing in her eyes "—that you're goin[g] to send me back to Richmond to sit and make lint for ba[n]dages with a bunch of old ladies, you're crazy!"

Major Brooks and Derek exchanged bemused glance[s], not quite sure how to react to her outburst.

To Major Brooks, she said, "If that's all you wanted, si[r], I really need to go and start getting my wagon loaded to b[e] ready to move out tomorrow morning." She then turned o[n] her heel and briskly walked out.

Major Brooks stared after her, shook his head in adm[i]ration and respect as he told Derek, "In case you don't a[l]ready know it, Preacher, that's one hell of a woman you'v[e] got there."

"Oh, I know it, sir," Derek was quick to agree, a lovin[g] smile touching the corners of his lips, "why do you think [I] love her so much?"

It was Sunday, April 6, 1862.

Confederate forces under General Albert Sidney John[n]ston were attacking Union forces directed by General Ulys[s]ses S. Grant. The ground trembled with the distant sound o[f] cannons as they boomed like the drums of hell itself.

Major Brooks and his troops arrived to find the situa[tion] tion worse than anticipated. Derek found himself wishing h[e] had insisted Jessica had gone to Richmond. All around wer[e] the anguished moans of the injured and the dying. The a[ir] hung like a shroud, pungent with the odor of sulfur and thick with smoke.

Jessica was summoned to the hospital tents, to help the surgeons with an endless succession of amputations. She had to force herself not to be sickened by the metallic smell of blood, the screaming of the injured, the horrible crunching sound as a saw ground through human bone. She moved like a puppet, wooden, mute, doing as she was told.

Derek heard the prayers, held the hands of the dying. Always, before a wounded soldier was laid on the amputation table, he would go to him for a moment of prayer, an attempt to console. The amputations were necessary because of the terrible wounds on limbs hit by minie balls. They blasted tissue in a crippling smashing invasion, splitting bones like green twigs, so that there was little to be done except cut off the injured limb.

At the end of the first day of the battle, the sun sank in a blood-red sky. White flags of temporary truce were waved as both sides moved onto the battlefield to gather their dead and wounded. When Jessica realized Derek was preparing to accompany the stretcher teams, she was terrified.

He gathered her close for a reassuring kiss. "Don't worry. We're under truce now. And I've got to go out there, Jessica, and give those boys as much peace as possible. Some of them won't even live long enough to get back here, and I want to help as many as I can."

She knew she had to accept his new calling, and she could only whisper for him to be careful. Then it was time to return to her own duties, no matter how weary she was from endless hours on her feet.

The night wore on. The hospital tent became like a dim cavern of the catacombs. From the rafters flickering oil lamps swung mournfully, casting a ghostly light on the scene. Dim shadows loomed everywhere, and the screams of the suffering only personified the specter of death.

Jessica saw Derek several times during the night, moving in and out with stretcher teams. Then she realized through a haze of weariness that several hours had passed without a glimpse of him. This worried her, especially since the firs teasing fingers of dawn had begun to creep from the east ern horizon. It was understood by both sides that th shooting and shelling would commence again at dawn.

When she could break away from the amputation table she sought out the next stretcher team that arrived to as where Derek was.

One of the soldiers looked at her with bleary, bloodsho eyes and informed her, "He's out there in the field, Mi Stanton. I'm not sure just where, 'cause we came up on a pile of bodies from both sides, and he just started minis terin' right and left, wherever he heard a groan. Didn' matter what color uniform they was awearin', he was deter mined to give comfort where he could."

Terror ripped through her as she cried, "But he's got t get out of there. It's almost daybreak, and the shooting i going to start again."

"Yes ma'am, we know that," he said, exchanging a wor ried glance with his comrade. "We're only gonna make on more trip out there, and then we gotta take up arms again."

They started out of the tent, but Jessica was right behin them. "I'm going with you," she said, not hesitating, cast ing all fear aside. "Just show me where you saw him last."

They protested, but she refused to turn back. Stumblin along after them in the muck and mud and blood, sh strained to see in the light of the fires burning all around.

Finally, after what seemed forever, the soldiers pointed t a smoky field just ahead. "Over there. That's the last plac we saw him, Miz Stanton. But you need to get back and—"

But she was not listening, for she had already begun t run toward the haze and smoke, frantically calling Derek' name.

When she found him, he was kneeling beside a wounde soldier in a blue uniform. She could see the color, becaus brush fire burning nearby cast a bright glow. He was holding the man's hand.

She frantically cried, "Derek, you've got to get out of here. It's going to be sunrise any second now, and you'll be caught in cross fire, and..." Her voice trailed off as he looked up at her then. She could see the despair on his face, and knew in that instant something was terribly, terribly wrong.

His voice came to her then, through the icy fog that had descended. "It's your father, Jessica."

She screamed, then rushed to drop beside the injured man and take his cold, blue-white hand from Derek. "Poppa," she whispered through her tears. "Can you hear me?"

His eyelids fluttered open, and he looked in the direction of her voice but could not see past the pain. Feebly, he moaned, "I ain't got long, girl... I'm in a hurry to end this misery...."

She bit down on her lower lip, tasted blood, willed herself not to cry, to be coherent as she begged, "Don't talk like that, Poppa, please. You're going to be all right. We'll take you back and—"

"You'll take me home?" he cried with a sudden burst of strength, trying to lift his head and focus his eyes to look at her. "You'll take me home, girl? To the Blue Ridge?"

She looked at Derek, saw the pity in his eyes, the way he shook his head ever so slightly to let her know there was, sadly, no hope.

"Yes, Poppa," she lied then to comfort him, tears streaming down her face as anguish engulfed her. "I'll take you home."

"Home..." He smiled then, a sudden aura of peace descending over him. "Oh, girl, there ain't no home like the Blue Ridge, the mountains, the golden sunlight siftin' and quiverin' through the trees and flowers... and the gentle winds through the valleys at dawn... and the creep of early scarlet in the maples in the fall.

"There ain't no smell…" He struggled on to speak, blood flowing from the corners of his mouth as he managed a grotesque smile of happiness and peace. "No smell like that of the rich, wet dirt when it's tilled in the springtime. Oh Lordy, girl, that's where I'm goin' all right, back home to the Blue Ridge…."

"Yes, yes, Poppa," she cried, grateful for Derek's strong arm gathering her against him as she clung to her father' hand. "I'll take you there myself, and—"

"No." He shook his head suddenly, sharply. Almost vehemently he cried, "No, I ain't goin' home with you, girl I'm goin' to the *real* Blue Ridge, the Blue Ridge in the sky God gave me the sign I been waitin' for. He took the curse away. Now I'm really goin' home.

"But you," he went on, "you, girl, you're staying here to look after the land, and your sister. You keep the home together here, you promise me, girl?"

She nodded, too stricken to speak.

He closed his eyes. His chest heaved, rattled, and she cried aloud, thinking him gone. But then he miraculously fought to focus his glazed eyes once more to whisper, to beg, "Will you forgive me?"

"Forgive you?" she echoed, confused. "Oh, Poppa there's nothing to forgive you for."

"Oh, yes, oh, yes." He nodded, and then, with the last shreds of his strength, he told her what she already knew.

She looked at Derek. He seemed to be praying.

"Forgive me," Zeb begged once more.

"Poppa, I do," she managed to whisper.

"And promise to keep the family together, and the land…in the Blue Ridge…promise me, Jessica…my firstborn, my child…"

And then, with a gurgle of blood, his head slowly turned to one side, and he died.

Quickly, Derek scooped up the lifeless body and threw it over his shoulder. "Let's go," he yelled to Jessica, grabbing her hand and pulling her along. Together, they ran

cross the battlefield, as the war exploded around them in
he rising sunlight.

When they were safe, Derek laid down Zeb's body, then
d Jessica away to comfort her.

Gathering her in his arms, he said, "When this battle is
ver, Jessica, we're going to take your father home. He de-
erves to be buried on the land he loves.

"Then," he said and paused to draw a ragged breath,
I've no idea what the future holds, but I swear to God,
e'll try to keep your promise to your father and keep the
nd and find your sister. But no matter what destiny de-
rees, our love is never going to die."

"No matter what destiny decrees," she fervently echoed.

Then she welcomed his embrace, his kiss, as they faced
eir future, their destiny, together.

* * * * *

THIS JULY, HARLEQUIN OFFERS YOU THE PERFECT SUMMER READ!

Sunsational

EMMA DARCY
EMMA GOLDRICK
PENNY JORDAN
CAROLE MORTIMER

From top authors of Harlequin Presents comes HARLEQUIN SUNSATIONAL, a four-stories-in-one book with 768 pages of romantic reading.

Written by such prolific Harlequin authors as Emma Darcy, Emma Goldrick, Penny Jordan and Carole Mortimer, HARLEQUIN SUNSATIONAL is the perfect summer companion to take along to the beach, cottage, on your dream destination or just for reading at home in the warm sunshine!

Don't miss this unique reading opportunity.

Available wherever Harlequin books are sold.

This August, don't miss an exclusive
two-in-one collection of earlier love stories

MAN
WITH A PAST

TRUE COLORS

by one of today's hottest
romance authors,

Now, two of Jayne Ann Krentz's most loved books are
available together in this special edition that new and
longtime fans will want to add to their bookshelves.

Let Jayne Ann Krentz capture your hearts with the love
stories, MAN WITH A PAST and TRUE COLORS.

And in October, watch for the second two-in-one
collection by Barbara Delinsky!

Available wherever Harlequin books are sold.

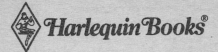

Harlequin Books®

GREAT NEWS...
HARLEQUIN UNVEILS NEW SHIPPING PLANS

For the convenience of customers, Harlequin has announced that Harlequin romances will now be available in stores at these convenient times each month*:

Harlequin Presents, American Romance, Historical, Intrigue:

> May titles: April 10
> June titles: May 8
> July titles: June 5
> August titles: July 10

Harlequin Romance, Superromance, Temptation, Regency Romance:

> May titles: April 24
> June titles: May 22
> July titles: June 19
> August titles: July 24

We hope this new schedule is convenient for you.

With only two trips each month to your local bookseller, you'll never miss any of your favorite authors!

*Please note: There may be slight variations in on-sale dates in your area due to differences in shipping and handling. HDATES-F

*Applicable to U.S. only.